T0196368

Apaches

in the

Santa Rita Mountains

Apaches

in the

Santa Rita Mountains

The Adventures of
Riley O'Rourke

DICK COLER

authorHOUSE®

AuthorHouse™ LLC
1663 Liberty Drive
Bloomington, IN 47403
www.authorhouse.com
Phone: 1-800-839-8640

© 2013 Dick Coler. All rights reserved.

No part of this book may be reproduced, stored in a retrieval system, or
transmitted by any means without the written permission of the author.

Published by AuthorHouse 10/04/2013

ISBN: 978-1-4918-2454-2 (sc)
ISBN: 978-1-4918-2444-3 (e)

Library of Congress Control Number: 2013918108

Any people depicted in stock imagery provided by Thinkstock are models,
and such images are being used for illustrative purposes only.
Certain stock imagery © Thinkstock.

This book is printed on acid-free paper.

Because of the dynamic nature of the Internet, any web addresses or
links contained in this book may have changed since publication and may
no longer be valid. The views expressed in this work are solely those
of the author and do not necessarily reflect the views of the publisher,
and the publisher hereby disclaims any responsibility for them.

. . . as sure as the sun sets and the world rides
on the wind—I'll be riding somewhere with the
Cowboys again.
—Gone with the Cowboys{

CHAPTER ONE

Riley'd spent a pretty rough night in spite of the provisions and bedding he'd packed. The snow started about two hours before dawn, and a bulky, wet blanket weighed heavy on the tarp that covered the bottom half of his bed roll, called soogans.

He had managed to spread his slicker over some lower branches of a small piñon pine tree and tied it so it covered a portion of where his head rested.

When he finally gathered both his legs under him and crawled out from his soogans, he carefully scraped snow from the top.

"What a mess," he sighed to himself. If I'd figured it to snow, I'd a-found a better spot to bed down. No tellin' just how long this'll keep up. Reckon I best try to get a fire a-goin' and start to coffee-up." He had to pee so bad, he didn't think he would make it to the bushes in time.

Both his horses were hobbled and they were busy gnawing bark from some trees at the edge of a clearing where they obviously spent most of the night. They nickered when the cowboy started to stir, hoping he would feed them their rations of grain.

Riley finished his nature chore and found an area that would serve him to build the morning fire. He started it in spite of the falling snow, and within minutes had a good fire going. He took his slicker down and covered himself with it, then cut some heavy, oak branches and arranged them as a wind break for is fire.

The coffee and bacon was tied up in an oilskin bag, along with the grain for the horses. His pot and pan and some other essentials were in there too, secured by a rope sling, high in a big, red oak tree.

On his way to fetch the coffee and the other supplies, he strapped on his gun belt and retrieved his M1839A carbine and placed it safely near the breakfast fire, just in case. Time now to strap on the morrall feed-bags for his horses.

According to the gold-covered pocket watch Riley treasured and always carried, a gift from his grandfather for his seventeenth birthday in 1857, it was time to depart.

It was three years later then, Seamus O'Rourke, Riley's dad, found his parents dead and their ranch burned and the livestock stolen by a band of Pinaléro Apaches. Riley had just turned twenty and was working on the ranch for his father and new step-mother, Maggie.

Riley closed the gold cover on his pocket watch and heard it snap before he placed it under his leather vest in his inside shirt pocket. He finished a portion of bacon and drained the last of the coffee pot before he packed up to continue on his journey.

Catching Dobé, his saddle horse, and Chapo, his pack horse, wasn't a problem. Saddling and retrofitting the pack onto Chapo was a chore, especially while the snow was heavy and the wind beginning its furious demands on the threesome.

Riley finally secured the oilskin tarp over the top of the panniers on the pack saddle, and climbed in Dobé's saddle.

As he carefully traversed the snow-covered, rock-strewn trail down the south side of the Santa Rita mountains, he was deep in thought of Bean, his faithful dog that was his constant companion for the last two years. "That was an act of mercy. It just had to be done," he sighed aloud.

Tears welled in his eyes and ran cold down his cheeks, as he brushed them away with the back of his gloved hand. "I don't know what made you chase that badger, you were no match for him by yourself," he openly scolded.

"Damn you, Bean, damn you!" He'd heard the snarling and growls and the whining yelps before he arrived on the pitiful scene. The badger's front leg was torn off, and ol' Bean lay dying, with a wide gash in his throat, pulsating with the great loss of blood. Riley mercifully shot Bean first, then stepped down to pull him off the trail and cover him with some rocks.

He knelt beside him and stroked the best old pal he felt he'd ever had. It was ten minutes past three o'clock that afternoon when he snapped shut his pocket watch case again and re-mounted his Dobé horse.

Riding at that altitude, the cold was penetrating very early in the morning. He kept an eye out constantly for any sign of the catamount, hoping he would cross its trail. He saw plenty of deer tracks, and he was certain they were apt to be white-tail, since there were only a few mule deer up this high.

This time he was looking for the old, crippled lion that was too slow to catch a deer, and had taken to killing some of his ranch beeves grazing the west side if these Santa Rita mountains.

Riley thought it would be easy for him to track the lion with the snow about a foot deep, but he hadn't even cut any sign.

Too bad he buried his dog, he thought aloud that ol' Beanie would've struck his trail by this time," he muttered to himself.

The farther down the mountain he rode, the less snow was apparent, and when he approached a small rise in the terrain he could see the ribbon of water flowing along the trail of cottonwood trees. The ground cover was less dense with trees and filled with the indigenous cholla cactus.

The closer Riley came to the river, the more prevalent were the beautiful Arizona sycamores and the huge, cottonwood trees lining the banks of the Santa Cruz river.

He felt the muscles of his horse start to bunch up slightly, and then he spied it. The small blue wisp of smoke was curling slowly through the nearly bare branches of a tall cottonwood and escaping into the gray-blue sky. The snow was descending with only an occasional flake, but the wind was starting to make its appearance felt.

Riley pulled rein on Dobé and jerked the lead rope attached to Chapo, causing him to check-up. He hoped they were all far enough back in the cover of brush so as not to be heard.

As he dismounted, Riley pulled his carbine from the saddle scabbard and wrapped the reins around his pony's left front knee. There were three of them. He thought they were some of the Western Apache that continued to hunt in the territory known as the San Cayetaño pass; but where were the horses? He crouched behind some cover of brush to try to get a better look at them.

They were Papago. Each had one blanket that covered most of their dark red bodies. They all wore high, leather moccasin-type boots with wrapping from about mid-calf to the knee.

Each wore a shirt, difficult to see, concealed under their blankets. Only one man wore trousers, and they were worn knicker style, bloused and tied at his knees. Although they were unarmed, he knew they had bows and arrows, for he saw bows on the ground nearby, as well as one hand-made axe.

By now, Riley determined they were a hunting party, and had stopped to consume several rabbits that were roasting on a spit at their fire.

The Indians were most likely about sixty yards from his concealment, and he felt it would be a wise choice to back up, retrieve his horses and try to slip away without being noticed.

Although the Papago did not have the reputation of the Apache, they were none-the-less a formidable foe, and save for a few "Mission Indians," sometimes very hostile.

As luck would have it, just as Riley was making good his getaway, he spotted a large party of Indians, moving down an old game trail single-file, toward the very area he just abandoned. There wasn't any mistaking these Indians as the Mimbrés Apache. Riley recognized the leader at once as "Chuchillo Negro," known as "Black Knife."

This Indian was a captive and in the jail at Agua Priéta when Riley and his dad, along with three other men, sold a remuda of horses to a government remount depot located in that border town. This very same Indian was displayed in the center of town and was to be tried when the circuit judge arrived, but managed to break-out and escape last year, and Riley vividly remembered him.

No sooner than Riley saw the Indians traversing the trail above him, he suddenly stumbled onto the three horses the Papagos had tethered near their encampment. His own horses were calm enough, but the Indian ponies were frightened, partly by the odor of a white man, and partly by the sudden emergence of two strange horses. They immediately nickered, and alerted the Papago, and hailed the attention of about fifteen Mimbrés Apaches.

Riley cut the tethers on the Indian ponies and chased them out of the brush toward the oncoming Apaches. This ploy diverted the attention to the Papagos' horses and away from him. When the Apaches saw the horses, they knew at once they were Papago ponies, and they were delighted with their new found treasures.

Approaching the Santa Cruz river, they immediately spotted the three hapless men who were attempting to make a stand there. It was probably all over in as long as it took for the arrows from fifteen Apaches to reach their marks on the three Papagos.

Riley took advantage of the coup and forded the river and headed due west into a very brushy and heavily treed area, and then turned directly north, hoping to circumvent the band of Apaches, and gain the high ground.

Riley wanted to go back up the side of the Santa Rita mountains, and head out and down the back side until he could make his way to the settlement of Tubac. He knew of a very large ranch nearby called El Reventon, and thought he could stay east of the river and stop over at the Reventon for the night.

CHAPTER TWO

Riley rode in past the front entrance to the Reventon hacienda, and was met by a brace of friendly guards who immediately took his animals and invited him inside.

It was very late in the afternoon, and since the snow had stopped, a sharp wind arrived. Riley was tired and so were his horses, and he welcomed the acceptance he received. He was told not to worry about his stock, they would be rubbed down and given a parcel of grain and sacaton grass.

"Bienvenido!" exclaimed Don Jorgé Luis Morales. "Entrada, por favor."

"I-I wasn't sure you'd remember me, Señor Moralés," Riley spoke, as he stood in the portål of the patio.

"My men saw you riding in and alerted me, Señor O'Rourke. It has been nearly two years since we've talked. I do hope your father and his new wife are very well."

"Yes, they are well. Thank you for inquiring, and they would send their greetings if they knew I would be so bold as to impose on your hospitality for the night, Don Jorgé."

"I assure, there is no imposition. What are you doing on this side of the Santa Ritas . . . checking on some of your 'perdida vacas'?"

"Actually, I've been hunting a cougar that has killed some of my "lost cows," and I tracked him a good ways before I lost his trail," Riley answered. "But, I ran into some unexpected trouble about a days ride south of here very early this morning."

Before Riley could expound on his days findings, the patron insisted he be shown a room in which to freshen, and asked another servant to draw a hot bath for him there.

Riley followed the man down the tile-laden salida with its massive ollas hung from the vigas that punctured the alabaster walls of the ramada. Inhaling the fragrance of freshly baked bread wafting throughout the confines, Riley suddenly remembered the hastily prepared meal he wolfed down at first light, and decided he could stand a well-prepared, ranch-style supper.

Don Jorgé escorted his guest along with his daughter, Anita Maria.

One of the servants brought Riley a karafe of aged, red wine, for him to taste while he relaxed in the giant, wooden tub. He also brought two more buckets of steaming hot water to add to the bath.

A box of cigars from the gulf port of Veracrüz lay open on the dressing table.

He found his trousers and shirt had been brushed and freshened and neatly hung, and his boots polished, when he stepped from the tub.

By the time Riley appeared in the main room of the hacienda, a roaring fire was establishing a delightful mood for all the inhabitants of the large household. "Ah, Señor," Don Jorgé spoke, as he arose to greet his guest. "Yo poder presentar miå esposa (may I present my wife) Maria Isabella." A gratified smile crossed the face of the patrøn, as he introduced Riley to his wife, when she entered the room.

"You have enhanced the family of the O'Rourkes', Señor," she said, as she nodded. I remember you well as a much younger fellow, a hard-working cowboy, and just a muchaco, who has crecer adulto (grown-up). Bienvenido, and I hope you will stay with us for a while."

She excused herself and left the men to their wine and cigars, and the serious approach of the tale that brought Riley to stop at the Rancho Reventon.

"Ya see, Señor," Riley said, with an answer to Don Jorgé's question of what the situation was he encountered this morning, "I stumbled onto three Papago's in their early morning camp near a bend in the Santa Cruz river. I decided not to disturb them and as I attempted to leave a large band of Mimbrés Apaches came into the picture. In my haste to get away, I ran into the tethered horses of the Papago and I choused them into the path of the Apaches."

"You are most fortunate, amigo miå," Don Jorgé replied. "How many of the Apache did you see?"

"I counted fifteen. They completely destroyed the three Papago, although I must admit I really didn't waste any time there by the river. I decided to backtrack and I crossed the river two times to get here."

One of the servants appeared at the doorway and announced that the evening meal was to begin. The men arose and continued their conversation as they proceeded to the ornately set dining room table.

"I forgot to tell you, Don Jorgé," Riley continued, "the leader of the Apaches was Chuchillo Negro, I recognized him from the time my dad and I saw him at the border a year or so ago. He's a Mimbrés, right?"

"He is; however, he has spent a great deal of time with the Chiricahua, to the east. Tiénente Whipple, an Army engineer with the Second California Dragoons, passed our haciénda several months ago, and said they had a skirmish with some Chiricahua. Apparently, Chuchillo Negro and Poncé were two of the Mimbrés that escaped the roundup of some of Mangus Colorado's Chiricahua Apaches. He's a very bad one, Riley."

The two reached the table in the grand dining room just as the ladies were about to enter to join them for supper.

"Ah," cried Don Jorgé. "Donña Isabella y hija miå. (my beautiful daughter) con mucho gustø (with pleasure) I present Anita Maria."

Donña Isabella was a striking woman, and her Andalusian heritage brought it out, but when Riley saw their daughter up close for the first time, he was nearly overcome with muteness. He guessed to himself she was probably the most beautiful girl he'd ever hoped to see . . . let alone, meet.

Home schooling was all Riley'd ever had, but he reacted as though he'd been coached in etiquette from his birth.

"I am very proud to make both your acquaintanceship," he said, as he stumbled over the correct wording. "My mother told me about you before she—before . . ."

"Yes, her accident was a very tragic occurrence," the Donña interjected. "But, it is wonderful to see the young people grow to their adulthood, as both you and our daughter have. Please be seated, Señor, we are to begin with asking a blessing from our Lord and a request that you travel on with safety."

Riley was so enamored with Anita that he nearly missed his chair when he went to sit down.

His reticence got the better of him and he said nothing.

13

The veal was served with a delicious sauce prepared by the cook from a recipe the Donña brought from Andalusia in 1836, when she arrived with her family and then met and married Don Jorgé in Fronteras.

The Moralés' were cousins of the Ortiz brothers who founded the la Canoå ranch in 1821 after a survey of the Baca Float land grant from Spain. The Moralés' inherited the Reventon ranch to the south when the family moved from Fronteras. They took over the rancho in 1841 when their daughter was almost two years old.

Now, nearing nineteen, she'd only been exposed to a very limited group of people. Twice she'd been to the Tucson Presîdio. Once when she was ten years old and again last year for her birthday.

The meal was nearly finished so Riley decided he'd better initiate a conversation with Anita; after all the answered questions from the Don and Donña. But Anita, true to her upbringing, did not speak unless she was addressed—and then, only a few words.

Anita was devastatingly beautiful and Riley just couldn't take his eyes off her.

"So, Señorita Anita," said Riley, who was more smitten by her each moment, "do you ride the caballo?" He knew the instant he asked that it was the dumbest thing he could possibly say.

"She rides like the wind, you should see her, Señor," her mother quickly answered his question. She does the Chariåda."

Anita blushed and averted her eyes, but managed a reply.

"I learn very queek-ly, señor, from my hermano, my brother, he ees el mejor. Best!"

Riley was silent—only to rephrase his previous question, and this time try to direct it to both.

"What I mean is, I know you are an excellent rider, and I meant do you ride out on your ranch for pleasure as well as to tend your grupa la vaca?" . . . (of course she does-you nitwit,) he thought to himself as he scooted his chair back in time to assist in moving the chair from the table for the Donña, who had risen.

"Thank you, Riley," she said to him less formally, hoping to put him more at ease . . . while suppressing a sly smile.

Don Jorgé escorted his guest along with his daughter and Donña Isabella to the sitting room, where a servant brought mugs of a strong herbal tea for everyone. Donña Isabella and Anita retarded their steps prior to their entrance into the room and were smiling at each other in girlish delight, especially aware as to not be seen by Don Jorgé or Riley.

"It now becomes time to furnish Anita with the background of this young man, our amigo, Riley O'Rourke," Don Jorgé said, as his daughter entered to be seated. "You see, in a way there is a closeness of our families. I shall try to tell."

"In the late 1500's, an Irishman by the name of Hugo O'Conner, was an explorer with the Conquîstadorés, and he beget many peoples from the Spanish putås that would follow the soldådos of wealthy families. In the next several hundred years the Spanish and Irish heritage became intermingled to a small degree, and Riley's biological mother was a descendant from that mix of family when Señor Seamus O'Rourke met her."

CHAPTER THREE

"So, you see, Señor Riley has some of the blood of the Espaniolés, although many decades removed. Also, you should be aware that this young man's father was extremely brave and resourceful about four years ago when two of my vaquéros and myself had gone hunting in the foothills of the beautiful Santa Rita mountains."

"Señor O'Rourke and about seven of his cowboys were nearby engaged in a rodeer or round-up, with some of his cattle, when we were set upon by a band of the Chiricahua Apaches numbering about twenty warriors."

"We were out-manned about two to one, which is about the only way Apaches will attack. They want to be sure they outnumber their enemy, or very seldom will they fight."

"O'Rourke's men came riding to our salvamento, our rescue, with their saddle rifles and the determination to out-fight Los Apaches. We suffered no casualties, except for one horse killed, and Seamus O'Rourke, himself killed five of the Apache. They lost eight men and two of their horses killed, before they fled south. It all lasted less than half an hour, but there is no question your father was responsible for saving my life and those of my men. For this, I shall always be grateful. So, now daughter, you will understand why the O'Rourkes' shall forever be welcome guests in our hacienda.

Riley sat, mouth agape, listening to the story unfurl from Don Jorgé and was duly impressed, for he had not been told of this deed his father performed. He only knew that his father told him of the rancho El Reventon, and of the good friends he knew there, and for him to never hesitate to visit when the opportunity arose.

Anita listened in like rapture, as her father related the tale; feeling even more close in friendship of the handsome, young cowboy. Riley was aware of Anita studying his demeanor, and he reddened, somewhat in his own way at this.

Don Jorgé suggested that the family retire for the evening and that tomorrow Anita would show Riley around the ranchero.

The morning greeted the rancheria with a dewy crispness that a February month often brought to this altitude of well over 3,000 feet.

After la desayüno, (breakfast),Anita showed Riley the way to the stables, escorted by an able vaquéro, true to the Don and Donña.

As soon as they reached los coråles, Riley knew his two horses were going to get an extra day of rest, for there stood two grand looking, very well conformed, saddle horses belonging to the ranch remuda.

"¿La yegua es muy bonita, si?" Anita asked Riley. "She ees my very fav-o-rite of thee entire horse remuda. What chu theenk?"

"Yes," Riley answered, "the mare is very beautiful, and I'm certain you make a good pair together. A beautiful horse and a beautiful girl" . . ."what's the matter with me," he thought. "I've got to keep my mouth shut." Riley 'rolled a cob' with his boot toe, as he blushed a bit and turned away.

Anita gently took hold of his arm and exclaimed, "I am very flattered, Ri-ley; how do you like the gelding we have chosen for chu?" He ees a four-year-old, and my brother broke heem las' year."

This was the second time Riley remembered hearing about Anita's brother, but he had yet to meet up with him.

"This is a very nice looking sorrel horse, Anita. It looks as if your brother did a good job of breaking him; he stands very quiet, yet cautiously observant. So, where is this brother of yours, I'd sure like to met him?"

"Oh, chu weel, Ri-ley, very soon he weel be back from Tuc-son. He and some of our vaquéros were delivering some horses that we sold las' month to the soldådos at the Presidîo, een fact, we expect heem to-day."

"Good," said Riley. "What is your brother's name; what is he called?"

"Hees name ees Esteban, Ramøn, Carlos, Jorgé Moralés. Es muy Calléro, an' he ees called Ramøn," Anita answered.

"I'm sure you're very fond of him, and I'm certain he watches over you. One thing, he has done very well by this sorrel, this one should be fun to ride. Should we mount up, I'm anxious to see your ranch?"

"Oh, Ri-ley, your horses' name ees Salvaje. Eet means 'the wild one'."

They rode away side by side from the stable area and down the long front lane leading to and from the rancheria. Quietly, in the distance, they were followed by one of Don Jorgé's vaquéros, on a small, clay-bank colored, Spanish-barb, dun horse.

Riley noticed the grounds that abutted the main buildings were cleared of most of the scrub brush and cactus growing profusely in this and the surrounding area. There was a large amount of tall, cottonwood trees closer to the river and a few mesquite and chaparral.

Anita explained that her father had the brush cut back to a low height, in order to better keep an eye out for Indian raids that often occurred.

This was done in a large circle surrounding the Rancho Reventon.

"How often have these raids taken place?" Riley quizzed her, as he began to furtively search the land in which they were riding.

"When the soldådos march from Tubac, these Indios watch and begin raiding. Often, even if the Presîdio is full, they try to steal our caballos, our horses," Anita sadly remarked.

It was mid-morning when they reached the foothills of the Santa Rita mountains. They stopped to water their horses at a small spring that came tumbling down the side of a large outcropping of boulders.

The sun decided to share its warm rays even though the air was still a bit crisp. Riley was more comfortable with this stunning young lady, and therefore was more at ease to make idle conversation. Anita was very easy to talk with, and very, very easy to look at.

As conversations continued, Anita found herself looking at the young cowboy with a great deal more of passion than she thought proper. It was almost as if she had no control over her thoughts, and since the two were young adults, with natural urges, she wondered if he too, shared some of the same feelings.

There was no question that they were both aware of the vaquéro who was discretely waiting nearby, and they knew he was certain they knew of his presence. Anita asked him to come in to water his horse and told him they would return to the Reventon.

The first three arrows struck the old vaquéro before he could ride to the spring. Riley was mounted in a flash and so was Anita. There was absolutely nothing they could do for their escort. He lay in a ghastly pool of blood next to his thirsty, coyote-dun horse.

Riley had a M1839A seven-shot carbine, and since it was on his saddle mounted on the young horse he rode, he drew it with confidence and began to fire in the direction the arrows came.

"Quick, to the west," he shouted to Anita, who was already riding ahead, "and stay to the high ground as much as you can. Ride hard for the ranch, I'm right behind you."

Riley was reloading as he rode, and as he came along side Anita on the mare, he reached out and handed her the five-shot Army pistol he carried in his belt holster.

"Take it!" he shouted, hoping she was as resourceful as he thought. "I've got my rifle." Their horses were young, fresh and strong. The smaller Indian ponies were no match, and they managed to not only stay ahead of the Indians, they were gaining distance on them.

CHAPTER FOUR

"Ri-ley," Anita shouted, "How many of the devils are after us? can you tell?"

"I counted nine or ten, but I know I hit one them, and I hit one of their horses, too. It should slow them up a little bit.

"They are Apache, no?" she questioned.

"I know they're 'Paches, but I don't know which tribe they are. It doesn't make any difference. We can't let them catch up to us. We can make it back in less than half an hour, so ride hard, little lady."

Riley and Anita were at least a mile ahead of the Indians by now, and still gaining distance. They were heading west and Riley said for them to turn more north and keep the ribbon of water in the Santa Cruz to their left. The warmth of the sun and the energy expounded from their horses caused their animals to labor.

"It's time to rest our horses," Riley exclaimed, as he pulled rein and nodded for Anita to do the same. We can rest them for 'bout ten minutes. You'd best get down and stay here with the horses, I'm going up on that small mesa there, to have a better look."

When Riley returned from his scout he noticed Anita sobbing, and begged her not to worry. "Everything will be fine," he said. "What seems to be the matter?"

"Oh, Ri-ley," Anita said, as she came closer to him and clutched his chest with her arms. "I am a leetle-bit frightened. Chu must hol' me close and become my røca."

Riley sensed her concern, and again tried to console her best he could.

"I am so sorry for el vaquéro viéjo. Poor Alejándro, eet did not look as if he had any chance. None of us saw los Indios."

"No one ever sees the Apache, Anita. They are treacherous and sneaky, and seldom will show themselves in a fight. As for your vaquéro, I know he died instantly and very bravely. Ironically, when we finally tell of this to your father, he will be disturbed that the man he sent along to offer us protection, lost his life in the process. These are hard times, but we are survivors."

Now it was Riley who returned her embrace, as the two stood locked together, searching each others eyes.

"It-it's time we should go," Riley spoke softly, as he gently started to release his wrapped-around hold on Anita.

"Ohh, Ri-ley, hol' me tight once more for I am secure in your strength and in your wisdom." She lifted her chin and tilted her head so that her lips met his lips, and she pressed them apart with a kiss that started softly, then pursued her emotions and stirred her desires.

Riley knew they had few precious moments to spare, but he was completely and totally absorbed with the same fervent and passionate thoughts as she, and he responded with a very firm but oh, so gentle kiss that completely enraptured her soul.

"Nita," he whispered softly, "I—I'm not sure what's happening, but we must get to the ranch. We have to get away from the Apaches. We must be able to share tomorrow."

She felt her heart beating stronger, not from fear any longer, but from the excitement of the moment. "I'm ready to go now Ri-ley, and I shall think of our future together."

They started to ride out from the side of the arroyo where they had rested their horses, when suddenly Riley raised his hand to signal a stop, and he quickly slid off his young sorrel and gave the rein to Anita to hold.

"What ees eet?" she questioned.

""Sh-h, up there, on that ridge going east, see them?" He pointed for Anita to look.

"I do see them, Ri-ley, but I count only seven, I tho . . ."

"They've split up," Riley answered, there are at least two more. Those Indians are going exactly the opposite direction of your ranch, maybe to make us think they've given up."

"But I don' see h . . ."

"The other two are probably lying in ambush waiting for us to show ourselves. They can't be far from here, 'Nita," he said, now addressing her with a more endearing term he preferred. "You stay here with the horses, I'm going to sneak back on foot to try to see where they are. Don't worry, I'll be fine, and I won't be that far away from you. I'll just be a minute."

"Be careful, Ri-ley," she gasped.

Sure enough, not two hundred yards from where the cowboy started out the back side of the arroyo, sat two Apaches with their backs to him, eying the trail leading out. The two Indians were concealed all right, from anything on the trail in the front of them, but unnaturally, their backs were exposed.

Riley crawled very slowly, so as not to make the slightest sound, until he was within about 120 yards behind them. It was too far for effective arrow power, but well within range of his carbine.

He took careful aim, after concealing himself against and behind a large boulder and drew a bead on the Apache farther away. Too bad he didn't have a bow and arrows to use, even though he was not versed in their use, they would be a silent kill for him and not likely to be heard, as the gunshot might. No sense in wasting time, he checked his load and took careful aim.

Riley's first shot struck the Apache square between his shoulders, in the small of his back, and he slumped forward-dead. Only an instant later, Riley's second shot hit the next Apache in his shoulder, and he came up running, but when he tried to nock his bow he was unable because of his shoulder wound. He kept running toward Riley with his long knife in hand and screaming an epithet.

Riley chambered another cartridge in the carbine and slowly squeezed the trigger. This time he sent the bullet into the man's knee, which toppled his legs from under him and he rolled forward so that he landed nearly in front of the stalwart cowboy.

Riley bashed the Apache's head open with the butt of the rifle. "No sense in wastin' good ammunition," he said out loud.

When he turned around, he was startled by the sudden appearance of Anita, standing behind one of the large Arizona sycamore trees, with both horses in rein, behind her.

They immediately ran toward each other and re-enacted the performance they did in the arroyo. This time, Riley threw his strong arms about her lithe body, and he lifted her off the ground, as their lips met again in an ardent moment of exctascy.

"I told you to stay put," he said, as he gently pushed back from her grasp.

"I just could not have you away from me, not knowing what was in store," she said, half grinning, half fearful for her disobedience. "Ohh, Ri-ley, hol' me tight, por favor."

He gave himself a moment, passionately before he backed away and held the mare for Anita to mount. "Hurry, 'Nita," he demanded. "I'm certain those shots were heard by the other Indians. They're far away, but they can double back, and come after us."

Like a cat, Anita vaulted to her mare and instantly was in the saddle.

"Hiaay, Jøya," she shouted, and off they started at a gallop. "Hur-ry, Ri-ley," she half-joked, la yegua weel outrun chu. My mare ees very queek." she said.

"Jøya, I heard you call her Jøya. Is that her name? What does it mean?"

"La Jøya Negra," she replied. "Eet mean, 'The Black Jewel'. I call her Jøya."

Riley figured the mare was six-or seven.

CHAPTER FIVE

Riley guessed they were about five or six miles from the Reventon, and the day was waning quickly. It would benefit them if they could head north long the Santa Cruz river, keeping it to their west, and thus presenting only one side as vulnerable to any surround by Apaches following them.

"Ri-ley!" Anita screamed, "look-out! Los Apaches are coming closer, hurry."

It was apparent now, to Riley, they had to make a stand. If they didn't take cover, the Indians could ride by and split them apart and capture or kill them both.

"Over here, quick," Riley shouted to Anita. "Take cover in that barånca, there."

They both dismounted in the thicket of dense cover in a complex of mesqüite trees. Some of the trunks were as large as some of the cottonwoods, because of their proximity to the abundant water of the Santa Cruz river.

It was almost impossible to move about in the thick underbrush, although this did afford the two some much needed cover. The Apaches that were after them had no guns and the brush was a great deterrent in warding the arrows that they expounded.

The place Riley chose to make a stand was at a cut-bank at the water's edge, and the embankment leading upward to the heavy brush was about four feet. They tied their two horses to some branches extending outward to the river, and fairly secure from a view the Indians had. Anita remained against the embankment with a tall mesqüite tree shielding her, while Riley took his stand on top, maybe ten feet away, behind some fallen trunks of the trees.

The Indians rode past them at first and then, cutting their tracks, returned. They were still mounted, but not for long.

❋　　❋　　❋

"Alma, miå," spoke the Donña softly, to Don Jorgé. "Eet grows late een esta tardes, and I worry for the youngsters. Chu theenk we should send some vaqüeros to locate them?"

31

"No, no. Eet would be extremely rude for us to do thees, beside, Alejåndro weel be nearby. They weel be back soon, alma; eet is almost time to prepare for the evening meal—and I don't theenk they will want to miss eet."

Thirty minutes later, Don Jorgé was at the stables, having rounded up a dozen of his vaquéros, ready to ride out through the front gate of the rancheria to look for his daughter and the young cowboy with her.

Even though he pretended his reasoning was all at his wife's insistence, he would not fool his segündo, his second-in-command, Joaquîn. The concern of the Don's face was apparent to any who would notice. After all, it was Indians that caused señor Riley to seek refuge, and the Apaches may well still be in the vicinity. When all were ready, he turned and said, "Ade las despedirse." (go.)

Within moments the vaquéros discovered the tracks made by the cowboy and Anita and also the tracks of their escort, Alejåndro. Joaquîn was convinced they headed to the spring and suggested a shortcut, and Don Jorgé agreed. He motioned three of his men to follow the original tracks, and the rest to take the short cut behind Joaquîn.

It was on this trail they first heard the distant gunshots, and as they neared a series of high-pitched yelling they knew emanated from an Indian attack.

While Don Jorgé and his men raced on toward the sounds, the three men who were following the other trail to the spring heard the distant gunfire and proceeded to converge at the sounds toward the river.

The saddle carbine and a pistol were the only arms available but Riley and Anita were making do the best they could against their Apache foes. While their ammunition was limited to belt cartridges Riley wore for his pistol, there were also several dozen extra cartridges for use in the carbine in his saddle bags.

The seven Apache warriors who engaged the duo of Anita and Riley were cautious in their attempt to strike their unseen enemy especially in the dense brush that afforded great cover.

Riley was equally cautious with his aim at the Indians. He wanted to be certain not to waste any of his ammunition but, at the same time, whenever a form appeared within his range and sight, he would fire a round in that direction. Riley told Anita to stay down against the embankment next to the horses, and to keep watch across the narrow river for any warrior who may try to sneak-up behind them.

The Apaches were a very superstitious lot and while they would yell and scream to try to frighten their adversaries, at the same time they relied on the power of their prophet, or medicine man, to perform some ceremony. The blood shed by them was supposed to be washed off only by the prophet's power, but the ceremony wasn't complete because they had no enemy scalp. It was needed so that each warrior could take a few hairs and burn them, in order that the fumes might purify the atmosphere of this battleground and prevent it from being pestilential to this band of Apaches.

It was this quest for a killing and a scalp that urged several Indians to rush the brave duo.

"Why do they scream so, Ri-ley?" Anita asked. "And why are they so excited?"

"They're scared, maybe drunk, and they scream at the top of their lungs for that reason. They feel it gives them courage."

While Riley was answering Anita, she turned in time to see one Apache crawling on his knees toward them from their right.

"Cuidado! look-out!" Anita gasped, as she yelled to Riley. "Derecho-on the right! Queek-ly."

The cowboy spun around in time to see the painted copper face, and the savage on one knee not forty yards away, notching his willow arrow in his oak-made bow. Apache bows were made by the men of the tribe, and usually they made their arrows. Sometimes the task was delegated to a man too old for the war path, yet versed in this craft. Strung with sinew taken from both sides of the backbone of a deer, it was their weapon of choice. The lance was next, and then a mace or club. Very few had any firearms or ammunition, nor were willing or able to practice so as to hit at what they aimed.

With the speed of a hawk, Riley fired his pistol at the Apache, and struck him in his hip. It was powerful enough to knock the man down, but it was not a killing shot and the Apache was ready to re-nock and disperse the arrow. When Riley hit him, the Indian fell an rolled, dropping the three other arrows he held in his bow hand.

Riley reached for his rifle which lay before him on the bank and tossed his hand gun to Anita for her to reload.

The shot from the carbine struck the Apache square in his throat, whereupon he immediately pitched forward dieing in the bushes he was using for concealment. The arrow released at less than full strength, yet embedded itself into the river bank.

Anita had reloaded and stood up and rested her arms in front of her on the bank and took careful aim at who she deemed to be the medicine man. He was chanting and directing others and preparing to fight.

Five Apaches remained, all afoot and still stalking their human prey, when Don Jorgé and his vaqüeros came riding on the scene. The Apaches abandoned their quarry and fled for their horses, tied together under some nearby sycamore trees. Too late!

The Reventon vaqüeros were upon them, and not giving the Indians any chance to loose their arrows, slaughtered the entire group within seconds. Each cowboy fired his pistøla many times into the hated Apaches.

Don Jorgé had spotted the two horses tied beside the river bed and knew Riley and his daughter were there. He called out their names as he rode up and dismounted into his daughter's arms.

"It is late and your madre ees worry," he spoke. "She thought eet would be forgiven eef we come to intercept chu both."

"Of certain, eet ees all right eef chu come to 'salvar' (rescue) us, mî padre. Chu must know I am in good keep weeth Ri-ley. He ees my héroe, and I . . ."

"Muchachamos Gracîas, Señor Riley," he interrupted. "Eet ees a short journåda to el rancho, so let us returno."

CHAPTER SIX

The pre-dawn was greeted by Riley as he awoke to a black, cloudless sky. He was quartered at the far end of the long, viga-studded vestibule lined with giant-sized ollås.

First light had not yet appeared from the eastern side of the Santa Rita range, to back-light the giant agave plants that grew behind the satîllo-tile covered patio.

The stillness was interrupted by an insistent flicker trying her best to start a nest in the very top of a nearby sagüaro.

Riley was seated on the edge of his bed in the process of stomping on his boots when he noticed the latch on his door to his room raise itself as if by magic.

He immediately stood up and behind the door as it slowly, softly opened. His gun was holstered on the peg on the opposite side of the door. He felt rather foolish in only his boots and his lindsey underwear.

Riley spoke not a word, intending instead to ambush whomever entered next.

"Nita!" he gasped, as he grabbed her form and spun her to meet him face-to-face.

"Ohh, Ri-ley, I know I am forbid to be here, but I-i have so much love for chu, I had to see you, hol' me in your a . . ."

"Don't say anything," he said, as he ardently kissed her moist, full, red-wine lips. His arms surrounded her warm body with the tightness of a slowly turning vise, and he gently caressed her soft breasts, under her robe-covered, french-silk nightgown.

"I dreamed of you the whole night long and i knew we'd find a way to . . ."

"Find one another?" She interrupted. "I, too," she continued, "dreamed only of chu, my heroé. I—I had to come to you now. I may have waited too long, for we have so leetle time, bot chu would never been able to attain my alcoba, my bedroom. There are vaquéro aficionados of mia padre, and they freely roam our premises."

"Here," Riley spoke, as he placed the top of the square-backed chair under the door-latch to seal the downward thrust of the iron peg to open. "Sit here, on the bed while I light this candle. We're safe, for at least a while, and don't be frightened. there's so many things I want to ask you and I guess I really don't know exactly how to begin."

"We begin weeth a kiss," Anita replied, "Hol' me tight and besar mia, Ri-ley, Oh, kiss me."

Riley thought how he'd change his mind and then he thought back to what he had decided last night. There was just not any way that he could allow himself to become involved with this lovely, magnificent creature.

"You are an incredibly beautiful girl, 'Nita, and I am totally captured by your wonderful sense of being, your courage and grit, and the common sense of someone far beyond your years. But . . . . I feel that it will never work out for the two of us . . . our social positions are different in both our worlds and I fear we would not be permitted to be seen together openly and alone. It will . . . ." "Ri—ley, don't talk for now I want for chu to make love weeth me, an hol' me tight some more, an' tell me how very much chu do love me."

Riley kissed her gently as they both quickly and skillfully undressed.

A half hour passed and the morning was almost ready to make its appearance. As difficult as it was for Riley to abandon their bed, he knew there could be serious trouble if he and Anita were found together under the existing circumstances.

He walked to the bed and softly kissed Anita to waken her from her dreams. "You stay here for the moment, I'll check around to see if there is a way for you to safely return back to your room."

Anita sat up to respond to his kiss, exposing her breasts as the top bed cover slid to her waist. "Yo tî amo, Ri-ley," she whispered, as she returned her lips to his.

Riley backed away and placed a finger to his lips while he carefully opened his door. Outside the entry, covered with a serape, was a square, cloth-wrapped package almost hidden from view, but noticed by the keen eye of Riley, cautious as he was when he exited. "Oh, ho!, what's this?" he said to himself, stooping to retrieve the parcel. He quickly stepped back inside, to open it.

"What ed eet?" Anita questioned him when she saw the package. What chu have?"

"Open it," he said.

When Anita opened the package, covered by the colorful serape, it revealed her entire riding habit, including her boots, a crop, a split-riding skirt, a blouse, a hat, her gloves and a bra and underwear.

"Dolores! . . . eet was Dolores," she cried, when she unwrapped it all.

"Dolores? Who's Dolores?" Riley quizzed. "Oh, oh," sobbed Anita.:

"She ees my sirvienta, my maid. She ees my hope and my guardian. She loves me very much. Yo no sé. She must have seen me leave my habitaciøn, my room, and followed me to know what eet ees I attempt. She must have seen me enter here and returned to bring my clothes so I am able to hide from madre mia."

Anita quickly dressed in her riding outfit and bravely accompanied Riley down the passage way leading to the kitchen. Her maid would gather her night clothes at a later time. Meanwhile, she and Riley held each other and embraced once more, dangerously close to the entrance to the cocina, or the ranch kitchen.

Both Anita and Riley made their entry trough the portål at the far end of the kitchen, where the cooks had been laboring for several hours, baking bread and preparing a traditional ranch breakfast. As they skittered across the cool, Satîllo tile floor in hopes of reaching the dining area, they were met with a sharp exclamation.

"¡Anita, por aqui! . . . come here!"

Riley stopped and Anita, startled, turned. "¡Ramøn!, she cried in joy. Oh, Ramøn." They embraced and her brother questioned . . .

"Anita Maria, where have you been? I returned too late last night, so I came to see you early this morning, but chu were not een your habitation. Thee only person I encountered was Delores, and she say you were going to the corallés. I am so glad to see you; and who's thees chu are weeth?"

"Mucho gusto, señor." Ramon said to Riley. "What story do you have to tell us?"

41

"Well," said Riley, "I sure am glad to meet you, Ramon. Your sister speaks of you with a mighty fervent gush of words. She claims you've taught her everything that you know."

"Oh, no, señor, I've taught her everything she knows . . . but, not everything that I know!"

Ramon chuckled a his own wit as he shook the hand of the shy cowboy. "And now let us enter to thee comedor, the dining room, señor. Chu must tell of thees adventure you both have survived."

Breakfast was always a happy meal that was enjoyed by everyone who partook of the wonderful breads and fruit served, along with the traditional huévos ranchéros. Don Jorgé and Doña Isabella entered the room for the seating and a blessing was offered.

Ramøn was told of the encounter that his sister and the cowboy were exposed to the day before, and the explanation of the rescue by Don Jorgé and his vaquéros, who slaughtered the Indians believed to be Chirachuca Apaches.

Ramøn listened intently and concluded that his new friend, Riley, was indeed a hero . . . and that was not all he concluded. He knew his sister very well, and he was certain the admiring looks in her dark eyes came from some inner-glow that emanated from her heart.

The way she kept referring to Riley in every sentence she spoke. The way she would cast her eyes deep into his when he spoke, and the admiration she felt for him shone clear to Ramøn with every action she waxed.

Ramøn surreptitiously leaned aside to his sister and whispered from the corner of his mouth to her, saying;?Anita, por . . . en poco tiempo? . . . how long have chu been een love weeth thees cowboy?"

"Ra-mon," she answered, red-faced, under her breath. "Chu must be discreet, no?"

He laughed and sat back up to finish sipping the strong coffee, and stared over at Riley, who had over-heard some of the whispered conversation between the two.

Riley stood, abruptly, and addressed Don Jorgé and Doña Isabella. "Con permission mi favorito amigos, I wish to excuse myself so I can prepare my journey home."

"But of course, my son," the Don answered. "First, join me en la salon, una momento."

CHAPTER SEVEN

Anita's eyes followed every move that Riley made as he strode into the salon to speak with Don Jorgé. She intently watched as her father also disappeared into that same room. Too upset to finish the rest of her breakfast, she too, excused herself and fled the table, un-certain what Riley and her father were going to discuss.

Ramøn excused himself when Anita rose and followed her to the vestibule where he confronted her.

"Anita Maria, una momento, por favor." Ramøn reached out and gathered Anita by her arms, spun her around and smiled as he said: "You are both much een love with each other, but I theenk that your young cowboy has made his decision to get along with his life without you at his side. ¿Am I correcto, miå hermana?"

Anita looked into the dark eyes of her brother with her eyes that were moist from hidden tears, gasping when she answered.

✳︎   ✳︎   ✳︎

"I am truly sorry, señor," Riley said, "to leave such wonderful hospitality, but I feel I must start for the other side of the Santa Ritas, and back to my home ranch. I wish to express my appreciation to you and your vaquéros for saving the life of your beautiful daughter and me, against those Apaches. I regret the loss of the old man, but thankful there were no other losses."

"Señor Riley O'Rourke, you are indeed a brave young man, and a respected friend. I would like you to know that I am totally aware of your—uh—thoughts for my Anita. She wears her heart on her sleeve, amigo, and she has openly bleed a heart full of love and admiration for you, ever since you rode into El Reventon rancheria."

"You no doubt share the same—shall we say— admiration . . . no, love . . . she has for you, but you have shown a potent resourcefulness with a tactful approach to remain a gentleman in the Moralés casa."

"Don Jorgé . . ."

45

"No, Riley, I know what you wish to say, and I beg you not to speak. I will say your farewells to the Doñna and—your love."

As Riley turned to leave he saw Ramøn in the vestibule and cautiously approached him to speak.

"Sorry, Ramøn, that it must end this way, but you must tell 'Nita how very much I care for her and that . . ."

"Amigo miø," Ramøn answered, "You know my seester weel be hurt from your decision, but you are doing the right theeng. For, you see, eet ees very obvious you both have the great love for one another, and I realize you are of a different breed, señor. You are just like me, you are not yet ready to hitch-up double to the wagon. So, you flee to your own ranchero, only someday to find the true love of your life, no?"

"No," said Riley, emphatically. "I'm probably not doing the right thing, but I do love and respect your sister so very much that I only want what is right for her and I feel this is the right decision or her sake. Some day she will meet a titled man, a man befitting her station, and she will marry and have a family. But, Ramøn my amigo . . . I shall never forget her, and perhaps I shall never stop loving her."

As long as it took for Riley to gather his possibles and saddle his horse and make ready his pack horse, was all the time he needed to ride out the front entrance of the Reventon and head toward the east. He was so forlorn he dared not look back at anyone who may be watching him depart.

"Why wouldn't he just tell me what was on his mind? If only he'd allow me to speak to him."

"Please do not cry, my seester," Ramøn interrupted her, while he comforted her by the large, hand-carved, oak double-doors that graced the entry to the hacienda.

"I have a feeling that chu weel see heem again, very soon. Eet ees possible he ees more distraught than you are. He is a brave hombré, to do what he has done, loving you as much as he does."

"What ever shall I do, Ramøn? I dread to speak weeth father, for fear I weel say something he may not wish to understand."

"Fear not, he'll understand," he said. And then, Ramøn said, "Tü te quedarås, pero yo me iré mañana." (You'll remain but I am going away tomorrow).

"Oh, Ramøn," Anita said, as she started to sob, "Chu are going away again, so soon?"

"Only for a short while thees time," he replied. "I must go to Frontéras to see the military comandånté who's arriving from Hermesillo, about a contract to purchase some of our potros, our colts, to train for the Army. He ees meeting weeth seis other rancheros de los cabållos.

"Six other horse ranchers? Are you to furnish thees Army only een Mexîco?"

47

"Perhaps I have tol' you too much, mî hermaña. Do not say anything to father just yet . . . do you promise me?"

Anita was still too distressed about losing her cowboy to pay close attention to her brother, and she answered him with a shrug and a wave of her hand.

"Of certain," she answered. "I trust you, Ramøn. What ees the difference anyway, now that I am to become a spinster and live my miserable life een thees remoteness?"

They both watched Riley disappear with his horses beyond the bend of the river, and fade into the dense brush that led from its banks to the Santa Rita mountains.

Riley reached the pass that led behind the mountain proturbance known today as "Elephant Head" and followed the rocky trail toward a cool spring that was tumbling down the side of the deep barrånca in the Santa Rita mountains.

He tethered his horses and stripped the saddle from Dobé, and loosened the pack on Chapo, figuring he'd rest them and himself. He took a portion of the pre-cooked deer haunch from his oil-skin packet, and started a coffee fire.

He had anther twenty to twenty-five miles to travel before he'd reach the land claimed by his father as the 'home ranch,' and he figured if he didn't reach it yet tonight, he'd sure get in by noon tomorrow.

❋ ❋ ❋

Riley awoke with a start, rubbing sleep from his eyes. he was somewhat disoriented, not pleased that he had fallen completely asleep, and now the daylight was waning.

The warm sunlight coaxed away clouds from the northeastern pinnacles of the Santa Ritas, as he arose to catch-up his Dobé horse and retro-fit the pack on Chapo before he would continue his journey home.

In less than ten minutes he abandoned his camp and was heading for 'Black Mountain' pass and over a seldom used trail. At first he paid little attention to Dobé when the horse bunched his muscles and lifted his head in a more upright position, eyes wide and ears pointing forward.

Riley guessed the horse was spooking at some wildlife critters they may be passing . . . but then . . . he figured he'd better trust his horse's instincts; this was something other than a critter in the brush, something told him the horse smelled another horse—or—a human.

Riley pulled rein and stepped down from his horse, sliding his carbine from the saddle scabbard at the same time. He took the lead rope of Chapos' and wrapped it around the saddle horn on Dobé, and left the trail a few steps to climb a short rise on the side, affording him a better view.

He looked back at his horses and they were seemingly more quiet now, not paying attention to anything except how to extract some of the flora along the trail where they were standing.

Maybe he was too hasty.

Riley's thoughts vacillated between the memory of that early morning tryst he shared with 'Nita, the reasons he gave himself for leaving her the way he did, and the sudden realization that there may be some imminent danger lurking up ahead.

He was furious with himself for his lack of concentration on the moment. This could be a serious situation, he thought, and it calls for a clear mind. "What's the matter with me?"

He caught a glimpse of the second arrow shaft passing his shoulder and embedding itself in the side of a gnarled Arizona sycamore.

Riley instantly crouched behind a large boulder and strained his eyes to see where he thought the arrows were dispersed. He recognized the fletching as Western Apache, and his suspicions were confirmed.

"How many? One, a dozen? is it a war party or a hunting party, or a single brave on a medicine quest? Or, what?" Riley spoke aloud, as if to quell his concerns.

He would soon discover the answers.

CHAPTER EIGHT

Riley saw him. He was about fifty feet from the side of a rock outcropping and he was about to nock another arrow in his yew bow.

The Apache apparently didn't see where Riley had moved, and thought he was nearer the horses. A quick move by the cowboy was made by placing the wooden stock of his .40 ca. carbine to his cheek and squeezing off a cartridge. No sooner than this occurred, than a second warrior appeared from behind a small mountain fir tree.

The Apache that Riley put a bullet in pitched forward, coughed blood and died at the spot where he fell.

The second Apache was running up the steep slope of the nearly hidden trail, to access Riley from the side, who whirled and immediately fired a round at the warrior. The shot ricocheted off a rock next to the Indian and spent itself down the trail.

The Apache kept coming, oblivious to the fact the cowboy had a firearm and he did not. He drew his long knife he kept in his moccasin top, and proceeded to lunge at Riley with tremendous strength.

By turning at the last moment, Riley was able to move his body just enough that he averted the slash of the knife. In his haste he dropped the carbine, and it was kicked off to the side in the confusion.

Riley quickly picked up a handful of dirt and small stones and tossed them underhand into the eyes of the brave. This move enabled Riley the time to retrieve his carbine. He managed to snap off a shot just as the warrior came after him again. This final shot did the job.

The bullet opened a hole in the middle of the Indians chest, and spilled his blood mixed with intestines that finished the life of the enemy.

The Indian was as tough as a pine knot and died hard at Riley's feet. Was that the last of them? Riley was breathing hard as he searched the surrounding area for more.

After a moment that seemed an hour, the cowboy decided the faint sound he heard below was the two ponies belonging to the Apaches pulling at their tethers in the brush.

He had to make up his mind what to do next. Riley decided there was about two hours of daylight still remaining and since he didn't plan on reaching home until later tomorrow, he'd look for a better and safer place to camp . . . likely on the eastern slope of this tall mountain range.

He decided he may as well take the two captured horses along with him, he could sell them if his father had no use for them.

The fight with the two Apache warriors made Riley a lot more cautious, and he reflected on the physical condition of them both Physically, the Apaches had become a specialized type. Not tall—the typical Apache warrior was maybe five foot seven. They were lean and muscular, broad in the shoulder, deep of chest, with legs that seemed fitted with spring steel. The women aged fast but were exceedingly tough.

The Apaches were consummate marauders. Plunder was their normal way of life. They took most everything they owned from their victims, including clothing, and food. The Apache was a hunter and a gatherer; to some degree, nomads, not good farmers, and they ate most anything, especially dog and horse meat.

Riley rode off about ten minutes down the trail, when he suddenly realized that he'd better dispose of the bodies of those two Apaches. Sooner or later someone would look for them and if they found the bodies they would be able to track him, especially with the entourage of animals he had with him.

He turned around and when he reached the spot where they'd been slain—there—was—no—trace—of—them— . . .—anywhere!.

"What th' hell!" he spoke aloud. "I don't believe this. Where are the bodies?"

Could he have miscalculated the spot on the trail? Had he gone far enough? "Just what's goin' on, here?"

"No, this is it, all right. There's the ground all messed up, and . . . and there's blood right there." Cautiously, he pulled his .44-.40 side arm and stepped down from ol' Dobé. He let the loose ropes go that he used to lead the horses, and knelt to re-inspect the earth.

"It couldn't be an animal," he thought aloud. "I've only been gone less than half an hour, but something . . . or somebody, has moved them."

He saw where the ground had been disturbed and where the brush was bent and broken, and the lines in the dirt that may have been caused by dragging a body. Riley started to follow these signs, and then he suddenly thought better of it. "It could be a trap," he remarked, as he backed off.

Returning, he passed some pony tracks and some fresh manure, and now he was sure the bodies were dragged away and most likely placed on the back of a single horse.

It had to be that. There were no other horse tracks leading off in that direction. There must have been foot tracks, but if it was Apaches, they knew how to cover them.

It was almost getting too dark for him to see, and while Riley's nerves were full of snake blood, it was the better part of valor for him to pull back, gather all his horses and get away from this part of the mountain, even if he had to trail farther to set-up his night camp.

He was certain he remembered the trail to the next spring, and soon he came onto a path he knew would lead to this particular water hole. He would stop there.

Maneuvering along the trail toward the spring, Riley's curiosity was churning in his mind. He just constantly questioned the disappearance of the two warrior's bodies. The only logical conclusion he came to was that there had to be more than the two Apaches.

But, with the signs he made out, only one more person. And, "why wouldn't the one remaining join his brothers in the fight?" Riley was talking aloud again, and this time he directed the question to his horses.

"Come to think of it, that first brave I killed wasn't a young man . . . in fact, he was an old Indian, Dobé—and the other one was young . . . and strong."

Riley began to think this may have been a family, or a father and son, or maybe a shaman and a neophyte, with the other person a helper or a relative;—"aha—a woman! That's who it was—a woman! Either a wife or a daughter, or a mother or sister . . . or a sweetheart, or . . ."

"Ah, hell, Dobé, I don't know, for certain, but it sure is spooky."

The one thing he knew was whoever it was would eventually find help at a camp or a spot predetermined as to where they would meet at a later time, and this meant that the Apaches would send a scouting party out to trail him and try to kill him.

Riley didn't think they would be able to track him since darkness was coming fast, but he guessed they knew where the spring was; for which he was headed.

Riley decided to swing north, toward Helvita Springs. It was out of his way, but he knew there was water there, so he made up his mind to go. Darkness now surrounded him quickly, inhibiting his movements to travel with any haste. It was increasingly more difficult with less light, to handle his horses with ease.

He reached his destination at Helvita Springs about three hours later, and found an abandoned mining shack next to an old corral.

The sight was an excellent place to fort-up. The cabin was built into the edge of a cave, exposing only two sides, and it sat atop a steep rise in the foothills. the spring was at the base of the cliff, and a corral twenty yards away.

CHAPTER NINE

The girl reached her destination about an hour after she placed the two, dead Apaches bodies on her horse and walked the two miles in darkness to reach seven, mud and stick-made hogans comprising the Indian encampment.

She was met by the night sentries, who gathered the rest of the twelve men and the sixteen women and children. Nah-kah-yen, also known as 'Keen-Sighted,' a reputation of which he rightly earned, took the horse from Pah-ah-sen, or 'Green-Leaf,' and then removed the dead men from the horses back.

Her story unfolded, among wailing of the women, to reveal the events causing the deaths of Gian-nah-tah, the

'Wise One,' and his son, Gian—as-sah-yah-te, 'One Who Will Follow His Horses.'

Green Leaf was the daughter of Gian-as-sah—yah-te, and she told of how they were all ready to return to camp after a purification ceremony, when they saw the Pinda-Lickoyee, or 'White-Eyes,' approaching. They did not dare reveal the sacred place they used for their ceremony, so while Green Leaf was safe from sight, her father and brother set out to slay the white-man.

"Unfortunately," cried the sister, "the thunder-sticks spoke death for my family. I became frightened, and when the white-eye left, I gathered the bodies of my father and brother to bring to camp for a burial to 'Ussen.'"

The Apaches are extremely reserved about letting anyone approach their dead, and they invariably bury them under cover of night. Sometimes the corpses are left untouched for several days, in order to escape duty of a dreaded burial service.

Nah-kah-yen instructed two braves to remove the bodies from camp and dispose of them where no one would find them, place them so they could not be upturned by any predator, and no longer speak their names.

Green Leaf's mother was dead, and her younger brother was south with a band from the Chiricahuas, so she would be alone.

The one room shack that Riley reached was at one time a miners hut. Scattered all over Arizona are mines of ponderous wealth that are totally useless to mankind so long as the Apache Indian remains unconquered.

This was obviously one of the lodes that was promising, but no doubt there was never anyone who mined it that remained alive long enough to stake permanent claims.

Riley felt that someone would eventually track him to this spot, but he was positive he could garner four or five hours of sleep and rest for his horses, until morning.

He made a coffee fire at the side of the cave, and increased its size when he took out the last of the deer haunch he kept in his oil-skin supply bag, finishing a needed meal.

He unrolled his 'soogans', and checked his cartridge supply for his M1839A carbine and his .44-.40 Walker Colt pistol. All the horses would have to share the balance of grain he had in supply, and tomorrow they could graze on some of the meadow grass at the foothills of the eastern slope of the Santa Rita mountains. He finished watering them, and crawled in bed inside the shack.

First light found Riley up and almost finished packing Chapo. Dobé stood saddled beside the corral gate, and inside, the two Indian ponies waited, wide-eyed and unsure of their new owner. Riley fashioned stout rope halters for the two ponies, and tied their lead ropes so they'd follow Chapo.

The last of the coffee was added to the grounds he saved from when he made it last night; somewhat bitter, but it was an eye-opener, never-the-less.

He finished his morning toilet, and while he was among the bushes he saw the remains of a human skeleton, and a few torn rags that once were clothes. What the wolf or coyote hadn't dragged away, the vultures finished, and because of a few bones and a skull, Riley guessed it was once a hard-rock miner.

The sun was flirting with the gray of the dawn and it was past time for him to be on his way. Now he had to go an extra ten or more miles to get back to the trails that would lead him to his dad's ranch, and it would take more time than he'd like. One thing was certain; he'd be extra cautious, and on the lookout for any more Apache Indians.

As the morning progressed, Riley began to relax his overly cautious alertness and settle down to finding a reasonably smooth trail over which to travel.

The terrain was becoming a bit tougher the farther he rode down the back side of the mountain pass he chose. He was below the growth of the pine and only a few scrub oak were spaced now and then. Most of the cover was iron wood and mesquite, and barrel cactus along with ocotillo and rabbit brush.

As Riley approached the base of a small mesa, where it turned into a rolling hillside of gramma grass and sacaton, he suddenly pulled rein and saw a whole herd of white-tailed deer.

There could have been fifteen or more, he didn't actually count, but he quickly removed his carbine, and dropping the lead rope to the pack string of Chapo and the two Indian ponies, steadied himself in the saddle, and squeezed off an easy shot at the nearest buck.

It was a clean kill, and he could have killed a second deer, before they bolted and ran, but he chose not to.

It would delay him for a while, to stop and skin-out the deer, but obtaining the fresh meat was worth the risk of time.

Working fast, Riley had the deer hung on a tree branch, gutted and the hide peeled and skinned, scraped and folded, and set aside. He honed his knife with the small whet-stone he carried in his saddle bag, to put a keener edge on the blade, and began the sectioning and carving of the torso.

Wrapping the butchered parts of the deer in some extra clothing, and using the oil-skin as a cover, he put the hide and the meat on the back of Chapo.

"Sorry, old boy," I know you think you're already packin' too much, but I can't take a chance with those Injun ponies by strapping this on their backs. First off, there isn't anymore pack saddles, and I'm not sure they're broke to pack, and I ain't got time to start a training program today."

Actually, the extra weight of the dressed out carcass remains of the deer, most likely didn't weigh sixty-five pounds. In less than an hour, they rode off again.

Riley was approaching the path to what is called Box Canyon today, and starting his ascent, gave a good look over his back trail. What he saw not only surprised him but caused him concerns as to how much of a head-start he really had.

There must have been nine or ten of the Indians following each other, horses nose to tail, seemingly not in a hurry, but in a dogged pursuit. Riley figured they must have started last night, and found his trail toward Helvetia Springs.

Now he decided he'd make his way over the next long rise of a small mountain, to a ranch he remembered from when he and his dad, Seamus, and his uncle Patrick, stopped once when they were all in the area searching for a herd of their strayed cattle.

The ranch belonged to the Henthorn brothers, but Walter was the only one left, since Myron was killed ten years ago when his horse fell with him in Coati Canyon. He left his wife, Bessie, and a daughter, and a son, Lyle. Riley remembered Walter was an old bachelor, and he remembered very well that Lyle's sister, Diana, was a beautiful gal.

CHAPTER TEN

Riley was trying to make faster time as he hurried to reach that next rise without Chapo and the Indian ponies breaking loose from his rope leads. It was a rough trail to follow, and he wanted to be sure he stayed far enough ahead and out of sight from the Apaches.

He urged Dobé ahead at as fast a pace as he dare while he clamored up the side of a short mesa. "Stay off the horizon," he spoke to himself, they're probably a good hour behind me, and "I can't let'm see me or they'll come runnin' after me."

The sun was out in full force and it was bearing down on the cowboy, who was sweating now about as much as his horses.

At one point on the side of the rise, he thought he spied the barn roof of the Henthorn ranch, and then he saw a happy sight; spinning blades of a metal and wooden wind-mill. He couldn't be more than a mile away from the ranch.

He felt his horse's muscles bunch-up, and watched in disbelief as he was being surrounded by ten Chiracauha Apaches.

There was only a split-second to react, and Riley made the best of it. He let go the lead ropes to his pack horse and the two captured Indian ponies, and yelled a loud "Hi-yah," as he spurred Dobé. The horse lunged ahead knocking into a flea-bit gray horse mounted by a young brave.

The surprise element was just not what the Indian expected, and as Riley passed him he shoved the warrior from his horse. This caused immediate confusion, as Riley broke through the circle of Apaches, and fled through the brush toward the Henthorn ranch.

A hail of arrows followed Riley, one striking his horse in the hip, and one landing into his own left leg, below his knee and into the fleshy, back part of his calf. He desperately tried to jerk it out with his left hand, while racing as fast as the horse could under the circumstances.

He couldn't extract the arrow from his leg, nor could he remove the one sticking into the meaty part of Dobé's upper leg. At this point he knew the horse was hurt, but the sheer power of the animal kept him running and it didn't seem to be embedded into any functional muscle or tendon.

He was not so sure with his leg. He kept on feeling the stinging, hot sensation of pressure, and his boot was beginning to fill with some blood. "If only I could get this arrow out, I know it would help," he said to himself. And then, he said to Dobé, "Hang-in-there, old pal, we've got to make it to the Henthorn ranch."

The Apaches were after him immediately and they were shouting as they rode. It was becoming more difficult for the warriors to fire their arrows with great accuracy, with the amount of high brush and stands of mesquite surrounding the riders.

Riley reached the small canyon and he plunged into it and held to its boulder-strewn floor for about a quarter of a mile. When he came to a place where the down-tapering walls had broken in a slide of rubble, he urged his horse up the rim. It was a rough climb, but he stayed ahead of the Apaches and kept increasing his lead.

Riley was feeling somewhat light-headed but he needed to keep his wits about him, and gather his bearings. His horse was starting to tire rapidly and he knew it couldn't go very far.

One Apache, on a small, coyote-colored dun horse, was far ahead of the other nine and Riley could see him back down in the canyon. When he reached the rubble-strewn side and started up, Riley leveled a shot from his saddle carbine, and was amazed but pleased when he saw the Indian throw up his hands and topple backwards off his horse. Riley thought he may have slowed the Indians a little with this death-shot to one of their kinsmen, so he attempted to dismount. He noticed that the arrow in the horse's flank had broken, and only a small part of the shaft remained.

With a deftness of experience, he got out his bone-handled, pocket-knife and dug into Dobé's hip to release the flint point. The horse flinched, as to be expected, but the gentle reassurance of Riley's voice to Dobe seemed to quiet him, and he noticed there was very little loss of blood. Horse blood usually clots much faster and with greater efficiency than does human blood, and now that he was at rest, his heart was not pumping nearly as hard.

It was time for Riley to attempt to take the arrow from his own leg. Oddly, he noticed the arrow had buried itself only in the flesh, and not into any bone. He simply could not pull it loose, and he had to lean against a tree to keep from passing out; the pain was almost too much to bear.

Finally, he cut the shaft of the arrow very close to his leg, and with the open palm of his hand, hit the shaft a sharp, quick blow, and drove the point all the way through the flesh, and at once it was out.

It hurt so much he nearly fainted, but he steeled himself long enough to wrap his neckerchief tightly around the wound. Dobé was experiencing some trauma, in that he was not putting any weight on his right rear leg, and carried his head very low.

Riley had no choice, he barricaded himself against a large layer of rocks after tying off his horse, and waited.

The Indians had dismounted and were now pursuing him on foot, attempting to scale the short rise to the top where he was concealed.

There were numerous arrows dispersed but most fell short, some were wide, and none were accurate. One of the Apaches had a firearm. Riley decided it was a rifle, and the warrior was trying to get in a better position to fire it. There was only one with a gun, and he waited until now to use it. He was likely short on ammo.

Riley couldn't see the Apache that was shooting, but with each report he saw the tiny puff of blue smoke, and then heard the shot. Riley had plenty of cartridges . . . he just now realized that there was a box of fifty rounds in the pack equipment on Chapo's pack equipment.

"Whoa,' he thought aloud, "I could be in a real jam if they've found them. Damn, I sure hated to give up ol' Chapo, I've had him for almost two years. Chances are they tied out those horses, and plan to come back for them later; won't bring 'em while they're after me."

Riley noticed the arrows sent his way weren't having much effect, either they couldn't see him, or were cautious and remaining hidden from his rifle power.

He was certain the Indian with the gun did not have a lot of cartridges left, and obviously hadn't found the box in Chapo's pack. However, every so often, that rifle was being fired. Interestingly, from a different spot each time. Riley was sure they were trading off, trying to make him think they had more rifles. With each shot fired at him, he'd fire one back.

His leg was beginning to throb more the longer he stayed in one position. He found he could handle it better if he kept his leg straight and stiff, and kept it elevated. It placed him in a very awkward position.

Strangely enough, the rifle shots that were exchanged could be heard clearly from the Henthorn ranch, and Lyle Henthorn and his uncle, Walter, decided to saddle-up and have a better look.

CHAPTER ELEVEN

Lyle Henthorn was riding his big, blue roan horse, and he was ahead on the trail with Walter, who was following on his sorrel mare.

The shots were sporadic, but were definitely coming from west of the hilltop near the canyon that ran below the south border of their ranch.

As Lyle peeled off the embankment and slid his blue roan onto the canyon floor, he had to pull rein and strain his eyes ahead.

"What's a-goin' on?" Walter hollered.

Lyle immediately raised his hand in the air as a signal for Walter to rein-up.

"Wal, lookie here," said Walt, as three horses were making their way up the canyon; one, a horse with a pack lashed on, and the other two, pintos, both with halters and lead shanks dragging. "I b'leev' them is Injun ponies," Walter finished saying.

"Might be," Lyle answered, "but they weren't the ones doin' the shootin'.

"Look, this one's got a cowboy bedroll lashed on top of them panniers. That ain't no Injun's horse. Don't know 'bout them two other ones, though," Walter mused.

"Lissen, Walt, those shots are comin' from just around that draw up yonder, and the others are comin from off'n that short bank to the north. We best find us some cover."

The next instant, while Walter was off his horse attempting to catch the animal with the pack, an Apache appeared running up the wash.

He quickly dropped behind a boulder when he was surprised by Lyle, who was still mounted.

"Apaches, Walt!!" Lyle shouted the warning, "Take cover, quick!" Lyle Henthorn fired his pistol in the direction he felt the Indian was hiding, but of course, it was an Apache, and he wasted his cartridge.

Walter had the pack horse by its lead rope, and as gentle as it was he had no trouble securing him by looping his rope on the saddle horn.

Lyle spun his blue roan around and headed him up the side of the canyon floor in the direction of the other shots.

The rifle fire from the Apaches had stopped, and even the occasional arrow also ceased its flight. Riley heard the shots that Lyle fired, and knew it was from a hand gun; now he wondered if the Apaches had more guns than the one rifle he heard.

Curious, Riley attempted to move his body to a nearby tree and rock formation, and to do this he had to partially expose his body for at least several yards. He thought he would have a much better view to spot the Indians who were below him.

His leg was turning progressively worse, and the loss of blood caused him a momentary lapse into a black-out.

He jerked himself awake and wondered just how long he'd been unconscious. The spot where he moved did afford him a much clearer view of the canyon floor and the area beneath him. At least ten minutes passed without his seeing any enemy Apaches.

Suddenly, to his left he could make out a rider heading toward him. Riley had his gun cheeked and ready to shoot, when his head filled with blackness . . . and . . . everything started to whirl and spin.

It was a clear, crisp morning that greeted Riley, as he sat up in the bed from where he lay, and tried to figure out just exactly what had occurred. The dull ache in his leg jolted him into reality, while he tried to figure where he was.

"I must be at the Henthorn ranch," he thought, "but-who. . . how did . . ."

"Well, good morning, Riley O'Rourke," Bess Henthorn called from her kitchen. She set aside her utensils, wiped her hands on her apron and made her way to the bedroom. "You've had a rough day and a half."

"Missus Henthorn, that you? I wasn't sartin you'd of remembered me," Riley answered her. "And what d'ya mean. . . a day and a half? How did . . . I mean, what happened? How did I get here? What day is it, anyway?"

"Take it easy," she laughed, "you're going to be just fine. We had to drain the poison out of that leg of yours. A mighty nasty wound, and outside of some soreness for several days, you're going to live."

For several minutes, Bessie Henthorn sat beside Riley's bed and explained all the events that took place since Lyle and Walter showed up with him and four horses.

"Are you hungry, Riley?" Bess asked him. "You probably ate last when you had some of that deer haunch Walter found on your pack horse. "I've fixed you some broth to start, and after you get that down, there's more vittles ready for you to eat."

But, I've had a bath and a shave and these clothes . . . they're . . . uh, I-I don't remem . . ." "You were drifting in and out of consciousness, Riley, we did what we thought was best. Your own clothes are washed and they should be dry, if you think you want them right now, but why not eat first?"

"I'm mighty beholdin' to you all for takin' care of me, and I'm pleased that my Dobé horse is doin' okay. I'm proud, too, that they found my little pack horse."

"Here's your broth," Bessie said, "now finish that and I'll get you some stew."

"Who found me?" Riley questioned, "and what happened to the Apaches?"

"I think I can answer that," a voice rang out from the doorway, as Lyle stepped inside and greeted Riley with a smile.

"It's been a few moons since we've seen one another," Lyle said, as he approached Riley. "Uncle Walt and I heard all the shootin' t'other day and set out to find out what was causin' it."

"So, it was you two who found me. I-I musta passed out— er sumpthin', my ol' leg was a-hurtin' somethin' fierce. How'd you get my pack horse?" Riley kept up with the questioning.

"Damn Chiricahua Apaches," Lyle said. "I think they're a little west of their home range, in the Dragoons."

Soon, Walter Henthorn appeared, and explained the balance of the story to Riley. A moment or two passed, and finally, Riley could stand it no longer. Abashed, he meekly asked, "Who, uh, who gave me a bath and a shave? That'us you, right, Lyle?"

"That'd be Diana," he answered, "and Ma, too, I reckon. Walt and I were busy goin' after the rest of them redbellies."

Oh!" . . . uh, where is, uh, Diana?"

"She's in the milk barn, Riley," Bess answered. "She should be here in a minute."

"Oh!," responded the red-faced cowboy.

The state of lost consciousness Riley endured just after he'd been brought to the Henthorn ranch, enabled him to lose himself in a constant dream. He kept dreaming he was some where on a vast prairie, with the yellow grass waving in the sunlight, and a flowing stream of clear, sky-blue water, tumbling through the center of the vastness.

He was running, hand-in-hand, with Anita. Lovely, sweet, Anita, and they were heading toward a large, alabaster-white, walled rancheria, where inside was a team of matched Andalusian horses, one for him and one for Anita . . . Lovely, sweet, Anita.

The ranch was filled with servants and there were no other family members around; none from his family and none from hers.

The dream kept recurring, always the same identical dream, and each time they'd leave the ranch, they would start all over again on the yellow-grass prairie, and head for the alabaster—white, walled rancheria.

Riley was sitting among the Henthorn family when Diana entered from the barn.

He grabbed the bedside for support.

"I can't believe my eyes—that really you?"

CHAPTER TWELVE

With the sunlight pouring in through the kitchen window and open door, a black, silhouetted, fantastically beautiful figure entered and started toward Riley's bed.

Since the light shone from behind her, and was directly in Riley's face, her countenance set forth a spitting image of the girl he'd forsaken and who remained boldly stained in his memory.

"Well . . . yes, it is me," her husky voice spoke softly. "We're surely pleased you're awake and that you seem to be doing much better, Mister O'Rou . . . uh, Riley."

"D-Di-Diana," he stuttered, "you're a vision of . . . I-I remembered you from several years ago . . . y-you've—uh, ulp!"

Riley was almost speechless, the first instant he saw Diana, he was befuddled and almost mistook her for Anita.

The lighting caused him to think she looked exactly like the dark-haired beauty at the Reventon. His mind was playing tricks on him, so he thought.

Diana Henthorn was indeed a gorgeous young lady, ranch-reared, extremely self-sufficient, and as handy with a weapon as her brother, Lyle. An expert horsewoman, exceedingly helpful to her mother, a great cook . . . although a selection of foodstuffs was not always available, and she really was devastatingly beautiful.

"I-uh, for a minute there, you uh, reminded me of someone else, uh, someone I met uh, a long time ago," Riley lied. "I do want to thank you for the shave, I'm sartin I needed it—and uh, the ba-bath—oh . . ."

"Quite welcome," she purred, not mentioning that it was her mother that really gave him his 'bath'. "I must say, Mister—uh, Riley, your face is a little flushed, are you running a fever?"

"Oh, no, I'm fine, in fact I feel well enough to take my leave if you all w-will pardon me," he stammered.

"Not on your tin-type," said Bessie, you're in no shape to sit a horse yet."

"I figured you'd want to stay a spell, Riley," Lyle said, "anyway that big horse of yours could use a few more days of healin'."

The morning of the fifth day arrived and Riley was maneuvering with much more assurance that his leg was healing well.

He'd been able to use the crutch that Lyle made for him and it was helpful when he went to the outhouse each time.

Everyone took their evening meals together, and this gave Riley time to recall earlier times when his dad, Seamus, spoke of cattle gathers he had with the Henthorns'.

Diana was completely smitten with the blond cowboy. She asked him many questions about his past young life, and listened intently as he recited the many times he'd been involved with the marauding Apache Indians.

Most of the various Apache tribes were scattered throughout the southwest from south and central Arizona territory, well into Mexico and throughout the whole of the New Mexico territory. They ranged eastward to the edge of the Antelope mountains where the fierce Comanche and Kiowa tribes roamed in Texas.

The Apache fought the Navahos, Utes, Piautes, the Yumas, and Opata, as well as the Comanche and the Kiowa. Their fiercest fighting usually was with the Yaqui Indians in Sonora, Mexico.

Seamus had told Riley, who delighted in retelling it while Diana was an eager, interested listener, that in many cases the taking of a scalp wasn't always especially creditable.

"Anyone could scalp a dead man, but if it was done under danger it was considered worthy. It became a sort of trophy."

"With the Plains Indians, especially, the bravest act performed was to count coup on a live enemy. When they were hunting, if a dangerous animal was wounded or killed, boys and young men would race to see who could be first to touch it. Stealing tethered horses probably ranked second in bravery, as well as drawing blood from any enemy in hand-to-hand combat," Riley said.

Some of the fiercest of the Apaches tribes included the Chiricahuas, Pinaléros, Tonto and Mescaléros. The White Mountain and the Mimbrés, were also to be feared The Jicarîlla Apache, roaming mostly in New Mexico, were formidable foes, and they were responsible for slaughtering many Mexicans, especially on raids into remote villages. Still, the Chiricahuas, to which tribe Geronimo joined, were the worst.

Geronimo, was born a Bedonkøhe Apache. Diana was listening intently to Riley expound on the background of these Apache tribes that frequented the entire Santa Cruz valley, and especially the Santa Rita mountains where the Henthorn ranch was founded.

Lyle spoke up and informed Riley the answer to his earlier question concerning the Apaches that followed and attacked him.

"Walter and I weren't certain just how many total Injuns there were in the gunfight with you, but the shots were slacking off when we arrived. We think there was only one of them with a rifle, and he was most likely out of ammunition."

"When we came on the scene most all the 'Paches had scattered, and after we found you and brought you home, we went back to try to pick up their tracks. We found where there had been two bodies and lots of blood lost, but whether they were dead or not, it was too hard to tell. We were just too late . . . they were long gone," Walter sadly related.

"As far as the horses are concerned, it warn't no trouble a-ketchin' yore packer; them other two Injun ponies is broke well, and I reckon we kin use 'em."

With the evening supper finished, Lyle and Riley retired to the front porch of the ranch house while Walter set out to check on all the corralled livestock, and feed the six dogs they used for hunting lions.

There were several mixtures; two Walker and two Plott hounds, a red-bone hound and an Oørang-Airedale, which is most likely the toughest of all the breeds. (source AKC).

Riley limped to the porch and settled in the wooden swing mounted at the edge. He gingerly lifted his sore leg and spread it on the balance of the seat beside him.

Lyle sat on the top of the two front steps and fingered the papers he used to roll a cigarette. He opened a small, cloth sack to tap out the prescribed amount of tobacco it took to fill the paper he held.

The sweet-smelling, blue smoke wafting from the lit cigarette, curled straight up toward a windless but cloudy sky, and this triggered an urge that Riley had himself.

"I b'leve I'll just roll one, too, if'n you'll toss me the makins?"

Just about then, Diana, who finished her inside chores, opened the screen door and made her appearance on the porch.

"Lyle," Diana said softly, "Momma can use a little help with the well-buckets, or would you mind?"

"Not a bit, Sis," he replied. "I was fixin' to head-off in a minute, anyways,"

Diana didn't let a second slip by before she sidled over to the swing where Riley was sitting and reached down and cradled his leg onto her lap, as she made herself some room beside where Riley sat, swinging.

"You don't mind, do you, Riley?" She grinned at the cowboy and watched as he flinched somewhat, more at her frankness than at her forceful movements.

"Uh, oh, a—not at all," he answered." Walter was at the corrals, Lyle was helping his mother in the kitchen, and no one could see the two young people on the front porch.

Diana let go his leg and encircled her arms around Riley's shoulders and neck, and immediately placed her warm, moist lips against his, and pulled his head forcefully against her open mouth.

Her breathing increased in short gasps and Riley, who was astounded, readily and eagerly complied with her ardent approach.

CHAPTER THIRTEEN

The two passionately fondled each other, and Riley, regaining his aplomb, suggested they find a more secure spot in order to continue this pursuit of adventure.

"Oh, Riley, I can't help myself," Diana demurely spoke. "I must have your strong body next to me. You're strong and handsome and someone I can't get out of my mind. It's been this way ever since we first met, those several years ago. I-I need you, Riley."

"You-you're fantastically beautiful and I'm willing to uh, to—to, you know . . . but I really think we have to go someplace where we won't, you know . . . become stumbled on!"

"Just come with me," she purred, "I'd already told Mother that I thought you and I may go for a long walk if your leg was any better—and I can see now that it is."

"So, you're saying we won't be missed, is that correct?" Riley questioned her.

"Darlin' boy, just trust me. I know a beautiful, quiet spot beyond that mesa."

It wasn't easy. Riley had to adjust his gait to fit the terrain, but he managed to follow Diana's lead as she guided him past the last corral, and into the desert foothills.

Diana, now unclad and perspiring, was helping the cowboy divest himself of the last of his clothing. The evening was mild and moonlit, but the clouds were heavy and the moisture that they held emitted a higher than average percentage of humidity.

"I'll swear," remarked Riley, "I never met anyone quite like you, Diana. What did I say to make you feel the way you do?"

"I-I guess I'm just naturally an excitable little girl," she coyly answered. "I've never been around any real men; of course, Lyle doesn't count. In most of the books I've read, they tell about the daring cowboys that ride the rim-rocks, and herd all the cattle, and marry the ladies they love, and I've always wanted to meet one of these men. Oh, Riley, I-I guess you're the hero of my many dreams, and you showed up just especially for my dreams to come true."

"My, God," he thought. "Th-hell have I got myself into. What in-hell, am I gonna do now?"

Their two, warm bodies kept them both free of any chill that may have accompanied the night air as they continued with their passionate performance for a while longer.

"Y' know, Diana, I was all set to say goodbye to everyone and head out for my daddy's ranch, but you've made me re-think some plans. I'm not sure if I'm really ready to . . . you know . . . settle down, or get hitched-up, double-to-the wagon . . . but you'd make a feller think more'n twice about it. "Cept I ain't really got 'nuff money yet to be the rancher I've always dreamed of—at least, not just yet." Riley was rambling, and she was still smothering him with kisses.

"Don't talk," she whispered, "just do this, what I'm doing . . . now."

An inordinate amount of lovemaking was emerging from her heart, and she was urging the cowboy to be her partner in a way she felt was highly exotic.

Riley's leg was beginning to ache, and he was experiencing some pain with it. He knew he had to get up, get dressed, and get back to the ranch, regardless of how ardent Diana may feel.

There had to be a better solution than just submit to all her whims.

※　　※　　※

"Nymphomania was an excessive sexual desire in any female species." that was what Walter told Riley the next morning when he saw him at the corrals. Riley had never heard of the word or the explanation.

"I seen you both when you passed the barn last evenin', and I knew what was a-goin' on," Walter continued. "This happened twice before, when some cowboys showed up a couple months ago to help us with the brandin'."

"Her ma cain't help her, and Lyle won't get involved, but I've knowed about it fer some time. She jes' cain't let any man git past her, 'thou't her jumpin' on him."

"What're you drivin' at, Walter? Are you sayin' Diana can't exactly help herself when it comes to . . . uh, you know?"

"'Zactly right," he replied. "Ol' Doc Brant called it a sickness that ain't got no cure fer it. Told my sister-in-law that, but she says Diana'll grow tired of it. 'Sides, she don't take to ol' Doc Brant . . . claims he tried to squire her at my brother's funeral, 'fore his body even got cold."

Riley was a little stunned, to say the least. Still, his memory of last night was haunting, and he wondered if a recurrence was imminent.

Riley was walking much better this morning as he circled back from the barn and headed toward the main ranch house. He was still pondering what Walter'd said to him when he heard Lyle's voice behind him.

"Hold on there, amigo," Lyle said to Riley. "You know our families have been friends for a long number of years, but I think I'm gonna have to ask you to pack your gear and leave us, now."

"Sure," Riley responded, "I was fixin' to pull out as early as t'morra, but I'll sure oblige you and go now . . . what's wrong?"

"Riley, Diana told me this morning that you made a play for her last night, after I left you two on the porch, and she said you frightened her. She said nothing really came of it, but she thought I ought to know, and so, I think you'd better ride out."

"She said that? She told you that I'd made a move on her?" Riley was carefully watching Lyle's eyes when he answered him.

"I'm surprised she sa . . . yeah—yeah, I guess she's right. She's a powerful beauty, and mighty easy to look at, Lyle, I-I guess I just got carried away . . . I sure didn't mean her no harm, though. It its been quite a while since I've been in that position, and I guess I just messed up. I'm mighty sorry, Lyle," he lied. "I'll pack up all my possibles and be gone in a few minutes."

"Wel-I-I," Lyle drawled, "since you've 'apologized to me I reckon you'd do the same for Diana, and I don't think we want Mom to know anything 'bout this, maybe, if you'd talk to Diana this morning . . . uh, maybe she could make a decision 'bout you a-leavin'."

"I don't think so, Lyle. It's probably just as well I pack ol' Chapo, saddle Dobé, and make for the mountain this morning."

About the time the two men reached the house, Diana came bounding out the door to greet Riley as if not a thing in the world went on between the two of them.

"Oh, Lyle, there you are. Momma was asking me if I'd seen you this morning, I think she needs your help with something."

"Well, you bet, sis, I'll find her."

"I'll help you, Lyle," Riley spoke up. "I've been meaning to tell your mom what a great cook and nurse, that she's been to me."

Riley limped past Diana without even glancing her way, disturbing her ego immensely, and attempted to follow Lyle inside.

"Oh, I don't think Mother will need the help of someone in your condition . . . I mean, you having such a sore leg and all . . . perhaps you could let me take a look at it—just to see if its mending properly.

Diana's remark halted Lyle at the steps, where upon he turned and said to Riley:

"That's right, amigo, you stay there. Maybe you'd like to ask Diana something?"

Lyle was gone before Riley spoke back. He looked at Diana directly and she was coyly grinning, looking like the proverbial canary-swallowing cat.

"Look, lady-bug, I don't know what your game is, but I had a pretty good idea after last night. Just what are y . . . .?"

Diana interrupted him by lunging at him and throwing her arms around him. She kissed him recklessly and fervently. Her breathing became shallow and hurriedly.

"Pay no attention to what my brother may have told you, you can't leave here, or leave without making love with me again." Diana was tugging at Riley's arm and leading him away from the house.

"C'mon," she whispered, "follow me, you know where we can go, hurry. I need you ever so much. Oh, Riley, please, please, let's make love, and I promise if you have to leave I'll not stand in your way."

"Well, why'd you tell Lyle that I went after you last night, and that you were a-scairt of me? You know that wasn't true."

"Riley, don't talk about that now. I don't remember exactly what I said to Lyle. He's my big brother and he likes to watch over me. I pretend to let him think he can protect me. Oh,— here we are. See how quiet and away from everything this place is? Even in the daylight. Oh, Riley, hold me tight. It'll be so wonderful—just you and me—here, alone."

It was no use. She was so beautiful, and Riley was an Adam in the garden of Eden. He was no match for her tempting ways. He was human, after all, and he really didn't want an explanation of her gossip.

"Right after this," he swore to himself, "Im on my way out of this place."

CHAPTER FOURTEEN

"Quick," Riley said, in an extremely soft yet urgent tone. "For God's sake, get your clothes on . . . do it now!"

"Riley,—lover, what's the matter with you? Why are you suddenly speaking so low?"

"Here, quick, get your britches on and try to stay as low as you can."

"What is it?" Diana insisted, as she interrupted him. "What is the matter?"

"Look," he said. "Right past that tree over there . . . Apaches! And they're headed right this way . . . stay down, Diana, down."

"Oh, my God! What will we do now?"

"They haven't seen us," Riley answered her, "maybe they'll pass us by."

The Indians weren't fifty yards away. Riley counted eleven mounted, red warriors making their way ever so slowly, through the rock out-croppings that surrounded the south side of the partially forested mesa.

As soon as the first warrior rode up and around the side, his horse suddenly lifted its head and flared its nostrils, and then stopped in fear of some predator.

The brave slid from his horse and indicated with an arm movement for the others to dismount. It was apparent to Riley that these scoundrels were reconnoitering the Henthorn ranch, and intending to some way raid, and kill.

This was a dangerous time. The ranch was less than a quarter-mile away, and not much heavy cover between, so it would be disastrous to try to run for the corral. The only weapon Riley had was the knife he kept in his boot, and the crutch that he used to help him walk.

Anyway, it was just too late.

"Ho!" cried the Apache. "Pindah-Lickolee." This was their name for 'white-eyes'. In Apache, he shouted to the others that he, 'Klo-Sen', or 'Hair-Rope', has discovered "nah-kee Pindah-Lickolee," or two of the white-eyes.

Riley and Diana had absolutely no way to defend themselves, as several of the men surrounded them and began to tie their arms together. Riley wondered when they intended to kill them; now . . . or later.

One of the young Apaches approached the pair and shoved Riley backward, so that he lost his balance and fell. Diana, with her wrists bound tried to reach her cowboy but the Indian grabbed her and started to take her to a grassy spot near a cut-bank.

Klo-Sen interfered with his movement and told him to stay away from her.

"She is my prisoner, and I alone will be the only one to have my way with her." Klo-Sen reached over and helped Riley to his feet. "This one is also my prisoner, and I shall decide what is to be done with him. Now, place a cloth in their mouth."

All the braves were Chiricahua Apaches, and they were indeed on a raiding mission to steal horses and anything else of value from the various ranches located sparsely throughout the Santa Rita mountains where a main camp was located.

It was great medicine to capture these Pindah-Lickolee, especially a white woman, whom they would make a slave in their camp.

Their decision was to get closer to the ranch and study it before they raided.

For all their cunning, this band of eleven failed to notice the concealed knife Riley had in his boot. They were more interested in feasting on the white woman and also hoping to obtain great status with the rest of their tribe by taking spoils from the ranch nearby.

Diana was unable to openly communicate with Riley, but she continually made total eye contact. Riley was deeply concerned as to their future, but continued to be stalwart.

Ponce, a respected brave, and one of th best trackers, called to Klo-Sen and to Amarillo to come look at what he'd found.

Most Apaches are so well versed in tracking that they can tell, by appearance of the grass, how many days have passed since it was trod on. They can tell if they were Indian or white, how many there were, and usually, to which tribe they belonged.

Ponce determined there had been a mounted party that had passed on this trail not more than twenty-four hours before. They were Indians, maybe Cibucue, but then he thought either Maricopa or perhaps, Pima.

Their mode was very similar. He also said there were more than thirty-five; closer to forty. He said with a little time he could determine the precise sex and species of their mounts.

He could open the dung he found and with its moisture and other properties, he could tell the date of travel. It depended on whether the dung was made up of gramma grass, barley and grass, bunch grass or sacaton, or even alfalfa or timothy. If he found barley he would determine the group was usually whites. if it was maize, it was probably Mexicans. sacaton or bunch grass meant they're usually Indians.

The difference in sexes of the animal was easy to tell when he found where they urinated. The male stretches and ejects his urine forward, while the mare ejects to the rear of her hoof prints. Most always, if the horses were shod, it meant Americans.

Ponce was trying to decide if these were Maricopa, or Pinaléros, both war tribes, or made by a hunting party of Pima Indians. The Pima villages remained in their same locality for many years, mostly near the mission San Xavier del Bac. Also, from there, north to the Gila river.

Perhaps a century earlier the Maricopa and Yuma and Cocopahs composed one tribe, known as the Coco-Maricopa. A dispute arose and the Cocopahs split off, forming with the Yuma tribe. The Maricopa went up the Colorado river to the Gila and points east until they counseled with the Pimas. There was an alliance but the Maricopas continued their war-like ways, while the Pimas farmed and most made peace with the whites.

Klo-Sen felt sure the thirty-five or forty Indians were a war party of Maricopa braves, likely camped nearby. Rather than risk a raid on the ranch now, he'd take his prisoners and return to where Delgadito was his leader, who remained ill in their camp.

Unknown to the eleven Chiricahua men, and unknown to the band of about forty of the other Indians only twelve miles from the Henthorn ranch, were United States and Mexican soldiers.

The Mexicans, were led by Joaquîn de Lopez, a Tienénte of the Fifth Provincial Army of Federales de Mexico, and the U.S. troops were commanded by Captain W. S. Carter from the 2nd California Division of the Third Cavalry, three hours away.

Permission was granted by the Commandant at the Presidio of Tubac for a platoon of twenty-two men, including a sergeant and a Lieutenant of the Mexican Army, to cross the border and join two, fifty-man companies of U.S. Army troops with two lieutenants and a captain to pursue this huge band of Apaches who'd just fled from a Mexican border raid.

Forty-seven Mexican men, women and children were beaten, raped and massacred and some livestock stolen. The trail led north past Calabasas, Tumacaccori, and Tubac and into the foothills of the Santa Rita mountains along the banks of the Santa Cruz river.

Since the terrain and the routes north of the border were unfamiliar to both Captain Carter and Lieutenant Lopez, their units were guided by Lopez' long-time friend, Señor Esteubio, (Ramon), Carlos Moralés, from the Reventon ranchero, whom

Lopez met again in Fronteras when the Commandanté sent his own troops to intercept the warriors.

The morning that Diana and Riley were captured was gaining intensity.

CHAPTER FIFTEEN

"We weel leave the reever at chor ranchero, Ramøn, amigo mia," the lieutenant said to his compadré, "and turn este, into los montañas del la Santa Ritas."

"We weel no doubt find los Apaches there, Joaquin," Ramøn said to the Tienénte.

"Do thees Apaches all live en thees mountain range, Ramøn?"

"Oh, no," he replied, "only a few make eet their permanent campamento. There are many lodges in the Dragoon mountains to the este, where the Chiricahua band dominates.

No one can approach without much peril. Eet eed known as "Cochise stronghold," and is im-pregnable. Most of the

Apache that raid een thees mountains are called the "Western Apache." There are a few Mescaleros, and El Pinal, some White Mountain and Tonto roam here, but they are mostly Mimbrés and Chiricahuas."

"I understand, Ramøn," Captain Carter interjected, "These Apaches are raiding in smaller bands, so they become harder to find."

Klo-Sen directed his ten braves to get mounted, and instructed the swarthy one who had grappled the white girl to give up his horse.

"They can both ride your grey horse and you will ride double with 'Arbol Rojas.'" Red Tree was not happy with Klo-Sen's words but 'Runs-With-Knife', the swarthy one, was even more upset with the command.

Two of the Apaches immediately lifted the girl on the grey, while two more put Riley behind her on the horse. There was a blanket on its back and a hair rope encircling its girth. No stirrups, but a hand-loop woven in its mane.

Runs-With-Knife was arguing with Klo-Sen about his woman-ways of avoiding the raid on the ranch that was so close by, and berating him for not finishing what he had set out to do.

"You have a heart of a weak rabbit," he bellowed, "and when I tell of it to Delgadito, he will no longer entrust you to lead any ranks."

"You will see who is the wise one," Klo-Sen replied, when we all arrive safely back and are able to raid another time."

❋   ❋   ❋

The trail was steep as the eleven rode down into the back side of the canyon. It was imperative they leave no trail for the large band of Indians, surely hostile, to be able to follow. They would continue out of their way for several miles before they would cut back, out of the canyon, and turn south toward their camp.

Captain Carter and Lieutenant Lopez had turned off east and started up into the foothills of the Santa Ritas, leading their troops who only shortly before, watered and rested their mounts for the next leg of the journey.

The armies left Tubac that morning and would bivouac in the cooler heights of the first mountain pass later in the day. So far, they'd covered about ten miles, and it would be another ten climbing miles before they reached a spot to set their camp.

"Ramøn," Lopez addressed his friend, "can you tell me how soon chu have thee cabållos gathered for our Comandånté?"

"I have arranged for trecinco-ciento about thirty-five hundred to arrive for you in Fronterås weeth in thee next seex months."

"As for our cabållos del Reventon, by thee time we all returno from thees mission, most all of our potros (colts) will be weaned from their yegas (mares) and thee stallions weel have their minds changed from ass to grass."

"If we catch our enemigos, our adversaries, before thee end of thees month, I would say from that time on eet weel be approximately trés anøs (three years). ¿Not long, no?"

"Do not bother weeth the cas'tration of your stallions, señor, el soldådos valiénte (brave soldiers) weel ride stallions and weel relish eet con mucho gusto (with pleasure).

Sometimes women accompanied a Mexican soldier expedition, brought along by some of the higher ranking officers. Since there were no wagons to accommodate them they'd have to ride extra mules if they came along.

They started with the group but turned back at the border for fear of being too uncomfortable, although they would've been treated quite well. It was not uncommon for putas (whores) to follow professional soldiers of the Army, but in this case they decided against it, disappointing a few.

It was still early evening when the two Otopah Indian scouts rode back down the trail to seek-out Ramøn Moralés, who had hired them. The Otopah were fierce enemies of the Apache, who'd always been subjected to raids on their villages. It was easy for Ramøn to recruit these revengeful Indians.

Wa-ka-say-golathin-te, or "Tigré," as the Mexicans named him, and his companion, they called "Serpiénte Negro," or the Black Snake, were very excited as they dismounted and reported to their "jefe", (boss) Ramøn.

Ramøn immediately translated their conversation from their Otopah tongue into Spanish for Lieutenant Lopez's benefit.

In their scout for the thirty Apaches they sought, they inadvertently discovered a different trail that led from north to west, and turned back south, and crossed in front of them. They counted eleven horses.

The excitement was that these were Apaches and they were only about two miles from where the column was about to camp.

Captain Carter and Lieutenant Lopez sent three squads comprised of forty-two men to follow with the scouts to capture these eleven.

It as important for Ramøn to go along with the scouts, since he was familiar with this area of the Santa Rita mountains, and especially the canyons and cut-backs that were prevalent throughout the terrain.

Tigré spotted the column of Apaches first, and waved the rear guard to halt. Ramøn made his way up to the scout and he dismounted to have a better look. The squads were positioned on higher ground amid some larger scrub oak and many piñion trees. The two men made their way to the edge of the mesa for a better view of the Indian column below.

Now it was apparent to Ramøn there were eleven horses, but to were carrying four people. In front rode the Apache, Klo-Sen, followed by Ponce and Amarillo. Then came a grey horse with two riders whose hands seemed to be tied. A woman in front and a white man behind her! The horse behind them carried two Indians, followed by six more riders.

The trail led slowly up the incline and would eventually pass where Ramøn was standing. He instantly recognized Riley.

Ramøn signaled for Carter, Lopez and the first sergeant. Plans were made when Ramøn explained the situation.

"There are dos presos, (two prisoners)" he said, "and I know thee caballéro who ees one. He was at our Reventon ranchero not a fortnight ago. Hees family and mine are bienes amigos, (very good friends) and the other ees a woman, whom I do not recognize."

"We must recapture thees presos, with no harm to them. We can ambush the column with our soldados hidden in the trees along the trail. Sergeant, dispatch your men up there, higher, among the roblés." (oak trees).

Lieutenant Lopez was certain these weren't the Apaches he and the Captain were after, and was concerned that the group they were seeking may be nearby, and this fight may warn them of the soldiers.

Ramøn was dissuading him, and that it was in his best interest to arrest these Apaches.

It would take the better part of half an hour for the eleven to reach the ambush spot, and it must be in concealment that would not warn the alert marauders. The trap was set.

CHAPTER SIXTEEN

The Apaches were careless. The trail was steep leading to the top and the Indian ponies were allowed to take their time in climbing this rocky trail. The first horse and the second one up the trail were thirty to forty yards from the third horse, ridden by Amarillo, who was at least that far ahead of the grey that carried Diana and Riley.

Red Tree and also Runs-With-Knife had dismounted and were walking up the incline while leading their horses. The six men who followed them were strung out, rappelling for at least another hundred yards.

Klo-Sen and Ponce were allowed to pass by and then the trap was sprung. Two soldiers jumped in front of the grey horse and took its chin rope, and pulled him off the path.

The two Indians leading their horses leaped off the trail into the brush, and were killed immediately by the soldiers. Klo-Sen and Ponce somehow managed to ride their horses ahead fast enough to be quickly out of the range of the soldiers rifle fire. Amarillo was struck with a ball in his arm and unseated to be taken prisoner by several soldiers.

The last two Apaches, farther down the mountain, managed to turn their ponies around and race down the back trail. It proved fruitless, as a detachment of the soldiers were deployed in that area and they made quick work of those two hostile Apaches.

The four braves who were riding behind the two who were walking, had their bows nocked and were sending a hail of arrows at any target they could see. One was struck with a bullet to his neck and he toppled backward and fell into the canyon.

Lieutenant Lopez, who was an excellent shot, fired at another in the group of four and slew an Indian with his only shot to the heart.

The two Otopah scouts were at the side of the trail where it turned back at a sharp angle. From this spot they were able to leap from above onto the backs of the two Apaches who remained, and each of the scouts avenged the many atrocities by slitting the throats of the two warriors.

It was over in less than five minutes Diana and Riley were being assisted off the grey horse when Ramøn rode up. "Hola, amigo mia, eet ees I Esteubio, Ramøn, Carlos, Jorgé Moralés . . . Anita Maria's hermana . . . her brother! What has hoppen?"

"R-Ramøn, wh—is it really you?" Riley answered, as he removed his gag. Thank God, you found us. But what are Mexican and U.S. Army troops doing in the Santa Ritas?"

"Una momento, Señor, paciencia favor. Be patient, please, and tell me who ees this lovely señorita." Diana clung to Riley like moss on a tree, and followed him with each step he took.

Riley explained as best he could, the presence of Diana, without disclosing just exactly how the Apaches found them, and he told Ramøn of the Henthorn ranch where he asked for them both to be taken.

"But of course, amigo," replied Ramøn. "May I present Teniénté Joaquîn Lopez. He has been ordered by the Federalés de Mexico for the purpose of capturing los Apaches who raided and plundered a town in Mexico.

"The soldados were allowed to join with your Army to chase these murderers. We thought at first, you were part of the raiders. Now we know the original prey is still to be discovered."

Captain Carter assured Diana and Riley they would be escorted to their ranch with all due haste. He wanted his surgeon to see them first.

Diana was feeling much better and no longer clung to Riley. Instead, she began to question Ramøn as to his presence with the soldiers; more about his ranch in the valley, and just how long did he feel he would accompany these soldiers?

Riley saw the two walk away together after they all had eaten an early supper. He figured there was no way they would be escorted back to the Henthorn ranch this late in the day.

Riley guessed correctly. He heard the sergeant major tell his other noncommissioned officers to make ready for a bivouac at this place, and they would start after the other Apaches in the morning.

Lieutenant Lopez came over to where Riley was resting against a large boulder, and wanted to know a little more about Señorita Henthorn. He assured Riley that his intentions were honorable, and he meant nothing by his questions, but he needed information for his report to the Alcadé, the mayor of the province at their fort.

"I suggest you question Ramøn," Riley answered, "I think he may have all the latest information you are seeking."

"But of course, Señor," Lopez said, grinning. "Perhaps we should both greet them on their return. I have noticed the young señorita may have turned his thoughts from our task of killing los Apaches to her thoughts of—perhaps—killing time!"

"It just so happens," Riley went on, "that Ramøn's sister, Anita, is really the girl I guess I miss very much, and . . ."

"I know who Anita ees, she was a müy bonîta muchacha (a very pretty girl) last I saw her and I'm certain she ees even more beautiful now that she's grown up."

"You have no idea, Lieutenant. That is not to say this one, Diana, is hard to look at, it . . . it's just that Diana has a certain way of expressing herself, in a very forceful manner—believe me,—I know."

It was after midnight when Ramøn and Diana returned to camp. Ramøn was not concerned with the Indian situation, for he knew there were two sentries within about fifty yards from where he and Diana had stopped to "talk."

For a short time Diana's questions to Ramøn were about his sister and what part she played with the handsome cowboy, Riley.

She really had no deep seated interest in what Ramøn told her other than she still felt all men to her liking were fair game, and there was no question as to her intent to seduce Señor Ramøn Moralés.

Riley was awake when the couple crept into the camp sight, and Ramøn escorted Diana to a tent set up for her, He watched as they shared a long kiss before Ramøn departed for the tent he shared with Lopez.

Riley counted out what he felt was about five minutes, and then as he expected he heard the slightest rustling as his tent flap was carefully drawn back and a figure slipped inside.

Just about then, the night sky over this cloudy, Arizona mountain, set forth with a crack of lightning, a rumble of thunder, and a deluge of rain that came quick as a cannon shot, soaking everything.

"I've been expecting you, Diana," he said, as she approached his blankets. "Are you frightened after all we've been through together, or did you just get tired of your new conquest?"

"Riley,—it—it's storming out and I-I need you to protect me. It-it's true we've been through an awful time together, and I know now that you are really meant for me."

"What about Ramøn,?" he asked, wh . . ." Diana had already divested herself of her clothing and was burying her body along side of Riley in his bedroll.

"Never mind about Ramøn, you are the one, Riley," she interrupted, as she took hold of him with an iron grip around his waist. "Kiss me, hold me, take me . . . now!"

Riley was reacting ardently, but with some reservations. He recalled what Walter had said to him that night at the corral. Then his thoughts quickly changed to recall the one he truly felt he loved, "'Nita," he whispered aloud, almost subconsciously, as Diana smothered his lips with hers.

The lovemaking continued almost endlessly, and let up on occasion, even as the rain fell.

CHAPTER SEVENTEEN

The ground was deluged at first light. It had rained steadily throughout the rest of the black night, and only slacked some by the time the Mexican Army troops were being assembled. The temporary horse corrals were ankle deep in mud and slick as wet glass.

Ramøn was curiously disturbed when he checked Diana's tent and found no evidence she had used it. He was even more so when he saw Diana emerging from Riley's sleeping tent on the way to the cook tents for some breakfast. It was nearly five a.m.

The sergeant major appeared with the two Otopah scouts at the cook fires to see Captain Carter, and to inform him that any delay in their departure could result in losing the original trail of the Apaches they were trying to locate.

Even now, the two scouts said it would be difficult to pick up any trail. The captain was angry. They may not find the trail, and they had only one prisoner to show for yesterdays ambush.

Ramøn was eating when Riley and Diana came up to sit down at the officers table. He instantly rose and offered Diana his stool, and greeted Riley with a wave.

"Thees miserable weather weel cause us more delays. It may be difficult to find a good trail back to the Henthorn hacienda until thees lluvia (rain) stops," Ramøn said.

"Yeah," replied Riley, "this is as much rain as we usually get over three months."

"I theenk, amigo, we weel not be able to leave for Diana's hacienda 'til mañana."

"No one needs to escort us, pal, just give me a rifle and some ammunition, and I can take Diana home. You forget that I know my way around these Santa Ritas, too."

"No, no, I eensist that chu let me go weeth chu both, I weel look forward to renewing a friendship I had weeth Diana's hermano, her brother, Lyle."

Ramøn denied himself the thought that he had an ulterior motive, but Riley was an astute young man, and saw the reason Ramøn wanted to go along, easy enough.

"Besides thees," Ramøn continued, "we are promise to protect chu from los Apaches. Eet weel be fine weeth El Capîtan Carter, I ahm most certain."

✳   ✳   ✳

Klo-Sen and Ponce had completed a large circle of about fifty miles, by riding all night during the storm. They were camped at a small cave entrance on the west side of one of the canyons that tumbled out of the south end of the Santa Ritas.

Even though Ponce wanted to ride back directly to where they were taking their two captives before they were all ambushed, Klo-Sen would not listen.

"Delgadito will listen to reason," Ponce replied, "we were not responsible."

"I will not give Delgadito the satisfaction of berating us for not bringing in the two captives. He will say my medicine is not strong, and he will say that you are a cow for not staying to fight for Amarillo when he was captured. You were the nearest to him."

"It remains of no importance when we measure that against the deaths of all our brothers. I say we go, Klo-Sen."

"You are a cow, Poncé. I say we return and recapture the nah-kay Pindah-Lickoyee, and Amarillo. I will prove to

Delgadito my medicine is strong, and I can outsmart the soldier dogs."

Amarillo, the only Apache the soldiers were able to capture, was tied-up with both hands bound by rawhide to two, six-foot oak poles crossed behind his back. His guard, a sloven Mexican soldier, was not careful when it came to guarding an Indian as sharp as this one.

The rain was not diminishing when the slothful soldier reluctantly brought his ward a bowl of food, untied him, and sat in watch until it was consumed by Amarillo.

Amarillo spoke the Spanish language most Apaches learned from many contacts on raids into Mexico, and from the prisoners they kept as slaves, and sometimes, from intermarriage. He'd carefully studied his guard since the moment of capture, and he finally, quietly spoke to the soldier.

"O yez, un moménto, soldado. Bien aqüî." (come here). He summoned the guard to him.

¿Por qué, Indio?" he answered, (Why)

"Yo indicar pesh-klitso mucho." When roughly translated by the greedy guard, was to mean, "I can show you much yellow-iron. or gold." Of course, the underpaid, overworked, niggardly soldier was most interested.

"¿Dondé, Cuåndo?" (Where, when)? The soldier's eyes widened, as he questioned his captive. "¿Es pequeño, o mucho?

"Pesh-klitso muchisimo," (much yellow iron) the Apache insisted, holding his arms as to indicate the poles be removed so he could escape with the soldier and show him where the "gold" was located. There was no immediate response, but fifteen minutes later the soldier was back with an oil-skin sack with some food, and one horse—his.

He cut the rope that held the poles but he didn't untie the Indian's wrists, and indicated the Apache walk while he would ride, and for the Indian to watch for his word as to when he thought they could make their getaway. The rain was making their escape much easier, as the sentries were not nearly as alert, trying to stay as dry as possible.

It was time. The soldier guard made out he was taking his prisoner into the bushes for him to answer natures call, and led him farther to where he'd tied his own horse, earlier.

The plan was complete; they were on their way to escape when Amarillo passed a willow tree he spotted and sprung the branch with one of his tied hands, so as to pull it with him as he passed beside it in the rainy darkness.

The soldier was riding his horse immediately behind the walking Indian, and his horse forcibly shied when Amarillo let the branch whip-saw backward into the steed.

The horse reared and the soldier was thrown and caught a rear hoof from the frightened horse, which dazed him just long enough for Amarillo to place a well-aimed kick into the face and nose of the fallen soldier. The Apache quickly sought the knife the soldier carried at his belt and placed it between two boulders, and used it to sever his hand bindings.

Freed, Amarillo slit the throat of the soldier and immediately caught his horse to make his escape good. It was never in the mind of the crafty Apache, that his capture was final. He would have to hurry, before he was missed by the Mexican encampment, so he hastily made hi way to the south.

There was pesh-klitso, all right, but it was farther to the south, and he would not reveal it to any Pindah-Lickoyee, or Mejo.

Amarillo rode the soldiers horse into the same wet night that covered Klo-Sen and Ponces' tracks, and headed the same south direction, toward the Chiricahua camp of Delgadito and the rest of the renegades. He was not sure that Klo-Sen or Ponce or any other Apache escaped the soldiers ambush.

Dawn of the next morning brought the torrential rains to a standstill, and now a gentle breeze cooled down all the shady areas along the trail.

At the same time these Indians were traveling toward their southern destination, Riley and Ramøn and a squad of United states Cavalry were escorting Diana over the back side of the canyon, toward the Henthorn ranch.

Lyle and Walter had been searching for any sign of Diana and Riley for the past day and a half, but the rain-washed trails offered them little or no clues.

Walter was trying to convince Lyle that Diana had "run off with that O'Rourke cowboy, and we're a-wastin' our time a-lookin'."

Lyle wasn't believing any of it. He figured if that was the case, she would've taken her own possibles, including her dresses and also her own horse. "Keep lookin'," he insisted.

CHAPTER EIGHTEEN

It was late in the day when Riley pointed to the landmark windmill blades that shown above the mountain-side brush.

"There," he said, "your windmill is up ahead, Diana, we've only a couple miles to ride. Ramøn, you can tell the soldiers they are excused. I'm not sure why you insisted on them coming; I told you that I would have no trouble finding the ranch."

"Ri-ley, chu know thees mountains as well as any of the Indios," Ramøn said.

"Y'right," Riley answered. "I know the back side of this range a whole lot better, though I haven't been here for a spell."

"Señorita Diana, con permissîon," Ramon asked. "Weeth chor permission, I should be honored to meet weeth your hermano, Lyle."

"Eet has been also a long period since we hov talked weeth one and another."

Diana was as pleased as she could be. Not only was she safe—she had two men now.

They smelled it before they saw it. It was the unmistakable odor of stale smoke. Then they saw the corrals, burned to the ground, then the tool and wagon shed, only partially standing next to the barn, which had collapsed under the strain of fire.

The terrible downpour of rain evidentially quelled the fire that ravished the main house without completely razing it.

"Madré de Dîos," shouted Ramøn. Diana screamed, as she reached for the support of Ramøn, riding beside her.

Riley dismounted immediately, and with an issued U.S. Army carbine, headed for the dredges of the house. The squad was halted and the corporal placed his men in a line of skirmish, preparing for a fire-fight.

Ramøn had difficulty restraining Diana from entering the yard to the front porch.

"Chu must not go, chu must not look." cried Ramøn, as he desperately held tight a struggling and near-hysterical Diana.

"Corporal," Riley shouted from inside a half-burned room, "get in here, pronto."

The corporal bolted to the sound and found Riley kneeling beside the charred remains of Bessie Henthorn, four arrows still embedded n her chest. Her dress had been ripped from her lower body which was bloody and ravaged.

The corporal directed two men to search the grounds for any survivors. Diana was nearly beside herself. Ramøn was doing his best to comfort her, but she was sobbing almost uncontrollably. He persuaded her to rest underneath one of the largest sycamore trees, in the shade, and proceeded to offer her water and comfort, when Riley appeared with the grim news of her mother.

Diana seemed now to stoically accept the inevitable and questioned him bout Lyle and her uncle Walter, and was told that no one has found them yet.

Within minutes, word reached them that two soldiers found a body described as to be Walter, not scalped, but mutilated, amid fallen timbers of the tool shed. No sigh of anyone else. One cow and a mule were found full of arrows, with their throats cut.

Riley was certain the Indians absconded with the rest of the horse herd, including his own saddle horse, Dobé, and Chapo, his stout little pack horse.

Over an hour passed before Riley and Ramøn were able to console Diana, after a continuing amount of purposeful direction of reassurance that somehow Lyle would be found and together she and Lyle would survive and rebuild.

It was Riley who determined exactly who the perpetrators were and decided it was caused by a band of Tonto Apaches.

Ramøn was convinced, after a discussion with Riley, they were who he said. The arrow fletching was unique, as were the symbols painted on the spent shafts.

The Tonto's were the only Indians that used the feathers of the Pygmy Owl for their fletching. All the other clans and tribes would not go near the owl. Their beliefs forbade any reference to any kind of owl, which they considered to be bad medicine, except for the Tonto tribe, who worshiped them.

This same band of Apaches were the ones responsible for many attacks on the hardy settlers in the lower Santa Cruz valley, and they ranged from the Tonto basin well into northern Mexico. Their home base was the Tonto Rim area, hence their name.

There was still plenty of the main house at the Henthorn ranch in good enough condition that with only minimal effort, by Riley and Ramøn and the soldier squad, it was soon cleared of rubble and cleaned well enough for habitation. The weather cleared during the long night and the dawn awakened Riley who proceeded to discuss the events of the day with the platoon leader.

The soldiers rations were enough to share with all for a breakfast, and the cook fire was started for this purpose.

Corporal Albany McFadden was the non-commissioned officer in charge of the squad sent to escort Riley and Diana. He was a capable soldier who was serving his second hitch.

He informed Riley that he'd sent two of his men on a hunting scout and they had left very early; actually, before first light.

By noon the corrals had been rebuilt and the work shed was being shored-up with timber cut nearby, It was expanded to act as a temporary small barn. Within the hour the hunters returned with a good supply of deer meat and it was supplemented with a salvaged portion of the milk cow the Indians killed.

Later in the afternoon, Diana's mother and her Uncle Walter were buried with small service extended. Preparations were made for the squad of soldiers to return to its main body in their quest to conquer Apaches for whom they were dispatched.

Plans were discussed concerning Diana and the search for her brother. There never was any sign of Lyle, or a body found.

Finally, Ramøn insisted that Diana accompany him and the squad back to their bivouac, with the intent he then take her with him to El Reventon on the Santa Cruz.

Riley was agreeable, and he promised Diana he would spend another day searching for any sign of Lyle, and when found, send him to the Reventon to fetch her.

"Oh, Riley, I'm not sure how I shall fare without both of you watching out for lil' ol' me," Diana said, forcing a pout.

"You'll take special care of her, won't you, Ramøn?" Riley asked, tongue in cheek.

"Absoluto," replied Ramøn, as he grabbed her waist. "You can trust on eet."

"Diana, as soon as I find Lyle, I may just decide to come along to the Reventon."

CHAPTER NINETEEN

The Army horse that Captain Carter issued to Riley was a capable mount, but his own horse, Dobé, was the one he really missed.

It was almost dusk of the second day since the Army squad rode away from the Henthorn ranch. Riley'd spent one full day scouting the immediate vicinity for any sign of the Apache band that set the ranch on fire and slaughtered the Henthorns.

He was about to put his saddle horse in the remade barn and start some supper for himself, when he heard something odd as he started past the new corrals.

It sounded almost like several animals stepping through brush surrounding the area, when Riley went to investigate. It turned out to be one of the biggest of any surprise that Riley'd ever had.

There stood before him, grazing on all the scrub grass available, and heading in the direction of the corrals for water, both Dobé and little Chapo.

"Well, well," Riley gulped, as he spoke to them, both. "How t'hell did ya' get away from the Injuns? Or did they ever have you?" He carefully examined both animals looking for any signs of marks or wounds on them.

I don't believe those Apaches ever found you two. Where th' . . . .?

Suddenly, it came to him. Why hadn't he thought to look there before? He'd forgotten completely, the rock corral that Walter and Lyle built about five miles from their main ranch, that they used when they branded their stock that was running on the spread known as "South mountain."

"Maybe Lyle had taken these horses down there to use before the attack came," he said aloud to himself. "He probably knew nothing about it; but he must've seen the smoke."

It wasn't dark yet, and Riley decided he would ride down to the rock corral and have a good look around. He put Chapo in the corral with his Army horse he called "Doc," and saddled Dobé for the journey.

He had an Army issue Walker Colt 1841 pistol as well as his issued carbine, and took both along as he climbed aboard Dobé.

He was certain Lyle was dead when he found him in a heap behind the west wall of the corral. Riley counted two Tonto Apache warriors, both shot through their head and bodies, about ten yards in front of Lyle.

As Riley approached Lyle's body, he heard a faint groan, and then saw that his eyes were open; glazed, but open.

"W-water," Lyle weakly cried. "Water." Riley knew Lyle's wounds were bad, but he still felt this was his lucky day. First, he found Lyle, hurt but safe, and then he'd found both his horses.

He felt confident he could save him if he could get him back to the main ranch. He knelt down beside him with his water bag, and carefully gave him a drink of cool, mountain spring water.

"W-where . . . h-ho did . . . .?" Lyle passed out before he could finish with his question, and Riley guessed that was the time to lift him up and across the withers of his reliable cow horse. It was then he noticed the two large wounds in Lyle's body. One large hole in his rib cage, below his chest, and another torn one in his left leg, above the knee. Terrible wounds, still seeping some blood.

After he reached the Henthorn ranch and the main house with Lyle still cradled across Dobé's withers, Riley gently lifted

Lyle's body down and placed him in the front bedroom. He left his horse tied while he drew a large bucket of well water and began to heat it on the kitchen stove.

About an hour passed before Riley had finished the task of trying to tend to the wounds Lyle suffered. The knee wound needed cauterizing, and Riley used a large butcher knife he'd heated to white hot in the stove fire.

He found a needle and thread from a box in Bessie's sewing materials and did a good job of stitching up the rib cage and the leg.

Lyle was placed on his back and Riley strapped both arms to the bed side before he tied his feet tight to the bed. He found some cut-heal medicine Walter used on the horses, that was in a medicine bag in the kitchen, to pour on the wounds.

The pain was too much for Lyle most of the time and he passed out on occasion. It was at these times Riley would perform his back-woods surgery. What worried him the most was the loss of blood that occurred.

The morning of the third day found Riley, as usual, checking on the makeshift bandages on Lyle's wounds. Everything looked so much better as the healing process had begun.

"Looks as though you're gettin' better each hour," Riley said, as he neared Lyle.

"With thanks to you, Riley. Sure glad you found me when you did," he answered. Lyle hesitated when he talked of the raid made by the Apaches, but he had to speak of it to ease the ache in his heart.

"I guess my mother and Walter never had a chance; where I was, there wasn't any indication of what went on here, and I had no idea there was any trouble."

"I was fixing a corner on the rock corral when I saw the two Indians. I had time to fetch my rifle before they saw me. My first shot was high, and that startled the Apaches. They had their bows nocked and arrows flying before I could fire any more rounds.

I was hit in the leg first, and the Indian that shot me showed himself long enough for me to get a clear shot at him. The second warrior threw his axe at me as he came running forward. I guess I pulled the trigger as I was passing out, I really don't remember. From what you told me, the shot must have hit him square on. The next thing I remember was seeing a strange form trying to get me a drink of water."

The talk drifted to Diana, and Lyle seemed a little more comfortable discussing her situation with Riley. He admitted that he was aware of his sister's "condition," but was so concerned for her welfare he didn't want to allow anyone to take advantage of her situation.

Riley told Lyle about Ramøn Moralés taking Diana with him to the Reventon ranch ostensibly to wait for an outcome of the whereabouts of her brother.

"It's entirely possible," Riley said, "for you and Diana to run this ranch, even better than before. The base of cattle are here, and the land is yours. About all you need do is arrange to hire a capable crew to help."

"It does sound plausible," Lyle agreed, and as soon as I'm able to ride, I'll go to the Reventon to talk with my sister."

"You can buy horses there, meanwhile you can ride Doc or Chapo," said Riley, smiling.

Two more days passed before Lyle was ready to travel. Lyle was well enough to stand the ride and insisted they leave at once. They had to travel a little over twenty miles over some rough mountain trails, and they stopped often to rest—their horses and themselves.

Mid morning of the second day Lyle and Riley rode toward the new presidio wall and main gate of El Reventon rancheria. The last two hundred yards they found they were escorted by a dozen vaqüeros from the ranch.

"Bienveîdo, Señores, en El Reventon," spoke Don Jorgé Moralés. They were greeted inside the portal at the face of the courtyard by the Don, and accompanying him was Diana, standing next to Ramøn Moralés.

Diana broke from the arms of Ramón and raced to te side of her brother, who was being helped off his horse by Riley.

"Oh, L-Lyle, Lyle, it's so wonderful, oh, honey, I was so worried, I . . . we're so thankful you're safe. Are you all right?"

"H'lo, Diana," Riley spoke softly, "Your brother had a rough scrape with some Injuns and he's packin' a few hurts, but he's a survivor now . . . uh, . . . Hola, Ramøn."

Joaquîn, Don Jorgé's segundo, was at the side of the pair and assisted Riley with Lyle Henthorn. He greeted his good friend, Riley, and handled his horse, also.

"Bienvenîdo, compadré . . . ¿Como está usted? Joaquin said. (How are you, my friend?)

"Bien, Gracîas," (Good, thank-you)Riley replied. "¿Dondé está ella?" he whispered (where is she)?

"En la casa, señor, con la madre."

"Oh, with her mother, I wonder if she knows I'm here?" he asked.

"Si, she knows. She weel greet chu en la hacienda. She ees preparing a bata, a gown, especially for you, señor." Joaquin smiled when he saw Riley's eyes light up.

"She has done nothing but speak of you since you departed that sad day, Señor."

"Tell you the truth, Joaquîn, she's been on my mind a lot, too. How does Don Jorgé feel about me, amigo?" Riley awaited his answer and was surprised when Joaquîn said; "No hoy problemå." (No problem today).

"Diana," Riley addressed her. "I guess you're mighty happy to be safe and under a watchful eye of a man like Ramøn."

CHAPTER TWENTY

The second day at the Reventon ranch was greeted with unusually cold weather. None of the horses had shed all of their winter coats, and there was a good reason; Mother Nature wasn't ready to allow the warm, spring weather to settle in, as yet.

Breakfast was served in the large dining room where a roaring, mesquite-wood fire served to abate the morning chill.

Lyle Henthorn was nearly recovered from his injures and he was explaining to Don Jorgé that he and his sister would most likely start for their own ranch early the next morning.

Ramøn was seated directly across the table from Diana, and watched as she reacted to her brothers statement.

Seated next to Diana was Riley, and to his left was Anita. Her mother was at the far end of the table, and next to her sat Joaquîn—he, to the right of Ramøn.

From the head of the table and next to Ramøn, Don Jorgé spoke to Lyle.

"My son, Ramøn, and two of my vaquéros shall go to your ranch with you, and assist you in getting organized. They can oversee your cow herd, help rebuild some important buildings and see that your ranch is in good operation until you return from Tucson city and the abogados."

"Oh, my," said Diana, intensely gazing into Ramøn's eyes, "that's very generous."

"I don't think that will be necessary, Don Jorgé," Lyle seriously replied.

Riley acknowledged that it was a very generous undertaking and said thet he, too, would ride along on his way to his ranch.

"O-o-oh," Diana gleefully replied.

Anita, resplendent in her starched white shirt and her cobalt-colored, flared-bottom riding breeches, embroidered with gold and white braiding, spoke next.

"¿Ri-ley, may I speak to you een the sala, por favor, would you excuse us from the table, father, we are both finished?"

Riley nodded. "Please excuse me Donnã Isabella?" Riley replaced his chair as he stood to leave, and perplexed, followed a serious Anita into the living room.

133

"Ri-ley," Anita spoke, as they both entered the room,"I know you have made the decision regarding our future, yours and mine, and I must tell you now, I do not agree. However, that ees another story. ¿Do you not see how my brother cannot take hees eyes off that Hen-der-sohn chiqüita?"

"Well," Riley began, "I s'pose he does cotton to her quite a bit, but I b'leeve Diana has a lot to do with that."

"¿Oh, ho, Señor O'Rourke, you do not see she also has the favors for you? She, how you say, "switches like thee tail of a fly-bit cow. If you ride weeth them both, I want you to keep an eye on Ramøn, and do not let heem get involved weeth thees girl."

"Well, now 'Nita, if that's what you called me in here to discuss, I don't think you'll have anything to worry about. I've got to get back to my own ranch, and she and her brother have a lot of work to do to get their ranch back in shape, and there's going to be two of your father's vaquéros to help, and . . ."

"Those pistoleros take orders from my brother, too, remember. I don't like eet."

Breakfast was over for everyone and as folks were leaving, Ramøn spoke to Diana.

"It will be a pleasant journey for us back to your ranch, Diana, and you will be pleased to know that I have a surprise for you."

"Dear me," she cried, "I'm not certain I can stand it. O-oo, what's the surprise?"

"My vaquéros will bring along seis, fine potros, which I give to you and your brother to bolster your ranch horse cavy."

"Oh, Ramøn,' she carefully answered,"I suspect you mean you are giving us six of your colts that you recently broke. That is most generous, and I shall be forever grateful."

"One more reason," Ramøn said, "for me to accompany you to your home. I know each of those young horses well, and I want to continue to train and work with them."

"Lyle," Diana called after him, "did you hear what Ramøn just said?"

It was too late, Lyle had already left the room, as if she really cared what her brother thought about the horse gift. She suddenly felt obligated to Ramøn for his generosity, and was planning her next move.

CHAPTER TWENTY ONE

There was quite a bit more work to be done on the Henthorn ranch than at first was thought. When Diana and Lyle arrived with Riley and Ramøn and his two vaquéros, this became even more apparent.

The temporary corrals needed more work and more mindfulness was needed on some of the outbuildings and the horse herd needed more careful attention, especially shoeing.

What remained of the cattle herd was scattered, and this was probably a good thing since perhaps the Indian raiders did not make off with as many as first thought. It didn't take long for the vaquéros to gather and herd them into the corrals for an inspection and a correct tally.

Four of the five wells were working with precision and Riley set out to repair the broken one before he'd have to leave.

All the men were kept busy with their many chores, so Diana thought she'd better get busy with some chore work of her own.

At supper that evening, Lyle brought up the discussion of the ranch deed and the idea that he should ride to Tucson to see an attorney about the legality of he and sister taking over the home ranch.

"Ees an excellent plan, amigo miå," said Ramøn, perhaps I should join you in your journey." "Oh, Lyle," questioned Diana, "are you sure you are up to it? It hasn't been very long since your injuries have healed."

"Maybe I should join you instead, my friend," Riley addressed Lyle, "I'm on my way home and at least I can ride part way with you, whatta' you say?"

"Lyle, can't you take one of Ramøn's vaquéros, instead?"

"It'll be fine, sis, don't worry. You have your hands full managing our ranch, and Riley's headin' for his home anyway; I'd be proud if he would join me part way, and Ramøn and his men can keep the place up 'til I get back . . . Diana, what was the name of that man that handled our folks legal affairs?"

"It's most likely written in the bible I found when I was rearranging goods left in Mother's bedroom."

"'McAllister,'" she stated, returning with the bible, "Abel McAllister, esquire, attorney at law.

102 Bonita street, Tucson, Arizona Territory." She handed the big book to Lyle.

"That settles it," Lyle spoke, "If you are of a mind, Riley, we can leave tomorrow at first light. You figure I should take a pack horse, same as you?"

"I doubt it. It won't take but a day to reach Tucson, and you can ride home 'thout havin' to camp overnight."

"Lyle, amigo miå," Ramøn interjected, "Eet ees admirable of chu to allow me to care take your rancho een your absence, I shall honor all your weeshes, and protect your worldly goods as if they were mine."

"Not too difficult, my friend, since I haven't much of anything left to be stolen. One thing you must promise, however; you must watch over my sister, help her make the right decisions running the ranch."

Riley moved toward the door and said, "G'night everyone, I'll see you mañana."

Food was not abundant at the Henthorn ranch when Lyle and Riley earlier departed. the garden was only recently planted from seeds Diana found in her mothers cabinet.

There was, however, sufficient meat to eat since the two vaquéros had slain two mule deer.

Riley and Lyle packed a haunch along and split meat at their first stop.

The trail they took ambled along the north rim of the Santa Rita mountains. From where they were camped they could see the outline of the Catalina mountains nearing Tucson.

Riley told Lyle he was turning off the trail ahead, and pointed the direction Lyle should follow to reach the Mission of San Xavier del Bac From there it was only an hours ride to the "Old Pueblo" presidio.

Both men had rested and they finished watering their horses at a small spring by their camp. They resaddled their riding horses and retro-fitted the pack on Riley's pack horse. They split the rest of the meat, and each put some in their saddle bags, as they turned and bade a farewell.

The trail that Riley chose to follow was almost entirely overgrown, indicating it had been some time since it had been in use. In order for him to maneuver Dobé and Chapo, Riley had to snap off a lot of scrub branches from trees whose limbs covered a portion of the trail. These were higher off the ground and the game that followed he trail passed under without contacting them.

The two men had been separated about twenty minutes when Riley and both horses faintly heard distant shots and the yelling of hostiles likely engaging in some kind of a battle nearby.

Riley heard many rifle shots and he thought there may be soldiers involved in a skirmish, but due to the heavy cover of brush he had to manipulate he not only couldn't see well, but he couldn't get to the area in any great haste.

Finally, Riley broke out of the heavy cover and into a much more open space on a flat top mesa overlooking a large wash. It was then he was able to focus in on what had happened, and where the shots he heard came from, He rode off down the mesa.

Three of the four horses hitched to a wagon were dead where they lay, still in there traces in front of the partly upset wagon. Riley could see four men, one close by the side of the wagon, and three others about forty yards beyond.

They were all dead when he pulled up, and their clothing was stripped from them; horribly mutilated, it was all Riley could do to dismount and inspect everything.

The Indians had apparently finished their raid and had just pulled away. It was probably as Riley was making his way toward the mesa above the wash. There was no one in the wagon, but behind the wagon, almost a hundred yards, he found the bodies of two women and another man. They most likely were trying to make it to cover of some trees beside the wash.

He found one man behind a large rock, with a large amount of brass shell casings scattered around him. Not the copper casing used by the soldiers, and he guessed this man put up quite a fight before the end came.

The Indians couldn't have been gone more than thirty minutes. The bodies were still warm, though quite dead, and one of the wheel horses, badly wounded, had not died. He was struggling in his traces, but couldn't rise, and Riley put a shot in his brain to relieve his terrible misery.

There were no weapons to be found, and no dead Indians that Riley could find. He was certain the raiders had taken both.

There were several boxes of dry goods in the wagon, that had been plundered of clothing, and ten or twelve books scattered.

Reflecting on this terrible tragedy, Riley determined these must have been folks on their way to a settlement, perhaps lost or unsure of their destination, and caught in a raid by the renegade Indians that were wreaking havoc on the settlers in the Santa Cruz river valley . . . all the way to Tubac.

It took Riley several hours to bury the bodies, and since he couldn't move them all, he merely dug a large trench next to them and rolled them into it. Piling rocks on top of the graves to discourage animals from exhuming the bodies. Riley made a sketch of the sites and some description of each one to give to the marshal when he saw him.

He guessed that by now he would be wise to change his course and ride north west toward Tucson. He'd abandoned the idea of riding to his home, especially since he found the remains of the wagon travelers.

It might just be he could meet up with Lyle Henthorn, although he was a long half-day behind him and ten miles southeast.

The carnage he had witnessed was now beginning to prey on his mind, and he knew he had to reach the marshal's office or someone at the presidio in Tucson to inform them of this tragic event.

He turned toward Tucson looking for a trail to follow. Crossing a small stream he saw where the main body of warriors stopped to water their horses then continue south in a direction away from where he was now.

Riley figured he had about an hour of daylight left, so he trailed down the mountain side and headed toward the Santa Cruz river.

CHAPTER TWENTY TWO

By the time Riley reached the Santa Cruz river from off the mountain, and then turned north along its banks, he decided he would be better off to make a small camp and start for Tucson in early morning.

His horses were tired and he was still worked up over the unhappy events he found earlier. He hadn't determined exactly how many Indians were involved in the massacre, but he was quite sure it was a massive number.

"Who could have done it?" he said to himself. "Apaches, I know, but just who, I really ain't sartin'; 'Cheery-cows', I'll bet."

Tethering his ponies, he made a small fire, drank some coffee, and settled in to sleep.

※   ※   ※

It was dawn in the Santa Ritas. Purple darkness in the twisting canyons. Ripples of faint daylight breaking against the tall peaks. A great silence breathed over the mountains, and finally, an incandescent splash of the morning star appeared.

Riley walked naked back to the bank line of the river, dripping from a quick morning bath and surprising his horses, who stared in amazement at an unrecognizable form emerging from the brush. He poured the remaining coffee in his cup before he put the fire out and dressed, then slowly sipped the balance before he saddled up again.

He thought it would be close to twenty-some miles for him to ride in order to reach the presidio at Tucson. He would follow the river all the way or until he crossed one of the main road ways coming from Fronteras or Calabasas.

"I think that bath in the river made me feel a whole lot better, boys," he said aloud to his horses, as he rode along. "I guess I was gettin' a might whiffy. Come to think of it, it wouldn't hurt you two to do the same," he laughingly spoke.

In unadulterated fields of river-based sand and silt, the land grew richer as the nutrients leached into the soil, and Riley thought the grass that grew between the river and the foothills was of some of the best quality, especially for the horses.

Riley arrived in the predominately Spanish speaking town, easily growing, yet still backward in any form of local government. The streets led a traveler past some adobe walls, through wide portåls to several main business streets.

He guided Dobé past the general store at the south west end of the town, and led his pack horse, Chapo, along behind. Riley passed the blacksmith shop and feed and grain store, before he neared the first of two hotels. Next to this was a small café.

Across the street there was a large cantîna and inside he figured were gambling tables. Another saloon was next door, a clothing store abutted this. The other hotel and a restaurant were near the northeast end of town, and the marshal's office was next to the livery stables at the far end.

It was dusk in the active and dusty streets, and the lamp lighter was busy with his lantern-lighting job along a boarded walk on two of the several streets. Three cowboys were pushing a small gather of beeves toward the livery, and several of the soldiers were grouped at a gate.

Riley pulled rein in front of the marshal's office and tied his ponies to a convenient hitch rail in front. The deputy leaned his tilted-back chair forward as he howdied the stranger who had just ridden up.

"Evenin', mister," he spoke. "What is it you're a-lookin' for?"

"Need to talk with the marshal, I reckon, or maybe the soldier chief at the presidio," Riley answered. "Also, I'd like to find out where I could find a lawyer named McAllister."

"Marshal Wilson's in Tombstone, likely be back t'morra, whut you need with the soldiers?

"Don't know whose jurisdiction it is, but about twenty-five miles southwest of here, in the Santa Rita mountains, is a group of pilgrims that was butchered just yesterday, late morning. I come on 'em as the Injuns was pullin' away." Riley was on the porch area in front of the office now, as he directed his talk to the deputy.

"How many was they?" Deputy Pierce asked Riley.

"Don't know. I told you when I got there the Injuns had all left."

"Not the Injuns," Pierce replied. "I mean how many people was massa-creed?"

"I dug eight graves, friend, but I couldn't drag the hitched teams, so they'll be in an ugly condition by the time anyone gets there. Here's some drawings I made and a few possibles I collected that the Apaches missed. I reckon they stole their guns and any other livestock they had, but I figured that you and the Army ought to know about it."

"Wal-ll," drawled the deputy, "that's a mighty big task you undertook. I know the Marshall wants to know all about it, but

I think them Army boys is the ones to handle the outcome. Hit's their respon-si-bility to pertect the travelers and ranchers in this here territ'ry and I'll tell 'em 'bout it this evenin' er fust thang in the mornin'. Now, whut about this Lawyer McAllister?"

"I'm expecting my friend Lyle Henthorn to be in town and meetin' up with this lawyer. My friend and I had just parted-up when I came upon that massacre. He was headin' here to Tucson, and I was headin' east to my home ranch, afore this happened. We couldn't of been more than ten'r twenty minutes apart. I'm surprised he didn't run into any of 'em."

"You say his name is Henthorn?" the deputy asked, "I saw him earlier today when he inquired about the lawyer's office, too."

"That's him," Riley offered, "he had to see the attorney to straighten out some legal business that's come up since his own home ranch was burned and his mother and uncle were killed by the Apaches, couple weeks ago. He and his sister aim to inherit their family ranch, and he needs the help of this lawyer."

"Wal-ll, his office is closed, but he lives out of town about a mile on the east side of the presidio. It's a white frame house with two windmills standin' next to each other in the front yard. Hard to miss it if'n you was to ride out there yet this evenin," the deputy remarked. "Maybe he took that there Henthorn feller to home with him fer some supper."

"I'm obliged to you, Deputy, b'leeve I will ride on out there. How 'bout my packer?"

"Jes tell ol' Jubal at the livery, he'll put 'em both up, ef'n ya want a fresh one, too."

Riley made arrangements at the livery to feed his horses and rent one to ride out to the lawyers house, but first he thought of eating.

"Where would I get some bait?" Riley asked the stable keeper, "B'leeve I'll eat a dab a-fore I ride out to the McAllister place."

"Victors' cafe is as good as any," he answered, "'bout a block upon yer left."

"The cafe'll suit me fine. Got to get to the McAllister place after I grab a bite of chow."

"I know whar he lives," said Jubal, "it's . . ." "Yeah, I know, two windmills in the front," interrupted Riley. "How much do I owe you for my two ponies and to rent one?"

"It all comes to two dollars," Jubal said, countin' the grain . . . good luck, pard."

CHAPTER TWENTY THREE

Riley changed his mind about Victor's cafe, so he took his rental horse and rode back a ways into town to look for a different spot. He decided on the cantîna he remembered seeing across the street from the Congress Hotel. He tied the paint horse to the crowded hitch-rail and walked inside the leaded, glass-top door to find a table.

The gas lights were lit upon the side walls since darkness had begun in this dusty, sentinel town in the southwest.

"Hello," said the waitress, "what are you fixin' to have?"

"'Evenin', ma'am, reckon I'll have some beef steak and white bread, and a beer to wash it down." Riley was busy looking all around the cantîna when he answered her.

He noticed the long, wooden bar that ran the length of the establishment. It was almost filled with vagabond customers, some in a state of inebriation, and others just starting their evening libation.

The gal that brought Riley his steak and pitcher of beer wasn't the same one who took his order, a beauty, and she wasn't unnoticed.

"Buy me a drink, cowboy," she whispered, as she placed his order in front of him and pulled the other chair out to sit.

"I 'spect I can afford you one," he answered, "what's your name?"

"Priscilla," she smiled, "but you can call me 'Prissy', everyone else does."

"Fair enough, mine's Riley. Now go get your drink and be sure you drink it here."

"Oh, I will, Ri-ley, you're cute, and I'm thirsty . . . among other things."

Riley noted two nefarious looking men at the end of the mahogany bar trying to gain the attention of Prissy as she made her way to to the bar to gather her drink.

"Hey, sis!," the ugliest one shouted, "you're s'pos'd to sarve us'ns drinks, not cow-tow to some ign'nerent stranger."

"This happens to be my drink, Curly," Priscilla answered him, "b'sides, I'm off'n my duty fer a while, and you better leave my friend alone, i ain't seen him fer a spell, an I 'spect to spend some time just with him."

Riley couldn't help overhear this bit of conversation and started to speak when she returned with her drink and sat down.

"Please, mister," Prissy, eyes wide with obvious fear, said to Riley, "just go along with this for a few minutes, please! Act like you've not seen me since . . . Abilene! H-he thinks he owns me 'cause he lent me some money once. I know it was stolen money, and he threatened me if I was to tell the marshal. I-I'm scairt of him, mister Riley."

"Texas? Abilene, Texas? I've never been to Texas in my whole lifetime, I don't know anything about Texas. Why not Utah?"

"I've never been to Utah," she giggled.

"Aw-right," he grinned, and stood up and gave her a salty hug and kiss, just as the two hombrés walked over to the table.

"Who is this pilgrim, Prissy? You've never said nuthin' 'bout a Texas boyfriend."

Riley was no gunfighter by any means, but he was ready to go along with this girl in view of the fact he really didn't like the looks of the slovenly drunkard with the big mouth. Anyway, he thought she might be in need of some protection for the moment.

Curly got to the table as the kiss broke up, and he reached out and grabbed Prissy by her hair and spun her around to face him. She slapped him without thinking, and then cowered behind Riley as the punch thrown missed her and struck Riley's ear.

"Outta my way, you Texas calf, I'll teach you to mess with my woman," he hollered.

Curly's partner, who was almost as whisky soaked as Curly, kept egging him on and shouting for Riley to "fight or git".

Riley was caught in a dilemma. His reaction was involuntary, while his mind was racing as to what the outcome of this mess would eventually lead.

SPLAT! Riley's left hook was placed perfectly on the unshaven jaw of the drunk, and he fell as if pole-axed. Riley's right hand was a level punch to the nose of Curly's partner, and the blood was mixed with the snap of gristle.

It was over almost as soon as it had begun. Two wooly characters lay next to one another on the floor of the split-oak planks in the cantîna, all before eight o'clock.

There was a roar of approval from the men standing near enough to witness the entire event, and finally, the barkeep and his helper came over and pulled the two drunks away by their feet and left them to sober-up in the alley.

When the bartender returned he told Riley that everything was okay for now, but that he should watch himself for those two men after they became sober. He told Prissy it was time for her to get back to work and to excuse herself from the 'Texas Cowboy'.

"I'm not from Texas," Riley stated to the barkeep, "that was Prissy's idea."

"Anyway," said the 'tender, "don't worry none about a-payin' fer the beer and the steak, it's on the house. So's Prissy's drink. Anyone that can knock-out two beefs like you did deserves a free meal. Just be sure to watch yourself fer them two later."

"So, Riley, where do you hail from? I know you're a stranger to these parts, and what brings you to the Old Pueblo?" she asked, as she cleared the dishes.

"I'm from south of here about thirty miles, and I'm here lookin' for a friend, who's meeting an attorney in town."

Riley finished the last of his beer and was ready to take his leave when Prissy came back to the table with a proposition.

"Listen," she softly spoke, "I'm off in another hour, and I would really like to see you. Where are you staying tonight?"

"Don't know," he replied, "I haven't made any arrangements to bunk down. I've got two horses boarded at the livery, and the paint horse tied outside is a rental from ol' Jubal, 'til tomorrow. Maybe I'll ride around a bit and check-out the rest of the town. It's been a while since I . . ."

"My place," she interrupted, "I can put you up at my place for the night and feed you a good breakfast in the morning, before you have to do whatever you have to do."

"No, I don't . . ."

"Nonsense, I insist, it's the least I can do for what you did for me tonight." She carefully cradled her arm around his side and placed her head up close to his ear, as she whispered her thoughts to him.

"You make it sound exciting, Prissy," he candidly said, as he squeezed her hand.

"It's 206, Second street," she stated.

Riley carefully mounted the spotted horse and mused to himself the outcome of events leading up to this.

"Now what am I gettin' myself into?" he muttered to himself, "Oh, well, I reckon I can look for Lyle and that attorney in the mornin'. I must admit, Prissy sure is a mighty fine lookin' woman, maybe we can find something in common to talk about."

The hour passed slowly as Riley rode by the house several times, just to make sure he had the right address. It was a long, four-room, box house, typical of all the territorial architecture, with a broad remuda-type, wooden roof extending over the front side of the building. A fence around the yard separated it from the next house built the same way; number 208.

Riley was putting his horse inside the yard and unsaddling him, allowing him the freedom of space for the night. There was a good supply of grass hay and a large tub of water.

Two horses shared the yard two houses from hers, so it was common for the people to keep livestock at their home.

Ten minutes later, Prissy walked up.

"Oh, it's O'Rourke," he answered, when she told him she didn't even know his last name, "and what's yours, pray tell?" he asked.

"Well, . . . it's Sullivan. I am sorry I didn't tell you at the cantîna. There, it's Priscilla Petersen. I was married to an Army man for two years. H-he was killed in the Fetterman massacre two years ago. This was his house and I've kept it since. I did get some settlement money from the Army, and I do get his small pension, Fifteen dollars and fifty cents a month. Unfortunately, due to some circumstances, I do have to work."

"The cantîna pays me twenty one a week and all the money I can hustle for drinks pays me two cents each. Oh, on a good night I can earn a couple dollars extra."

Riley was listening to her as she poured a glass of wine for each of them and he was carefully looking over the trim, well-kept house, when he heard a door in one of the rooms close, and saw a thin light seep through the cracks.

Riley didn't un-holster his .44-.40 pistol.

CHAPTER TWENTY FOUR

Riley deftly and carefully opened the door to the room, while Prissy hurriedly followed him and started to speak.

"I-I was intending to tell you . . . I-I just didn't get the chance," she said.

As Riley urged the door to open wider, he saw a sleeping child in a trundle bed next to a large, tester with a wrought-iron headboard, and covered with a quilt.

"Well, for cryin' . . ."

"I was trying to tell you about . . . my son. His name is Andrew, he's almost two. That noise was Maria Dolores Ontivos, she was leaving through this back door. She watches him and gets his supper, and stays until I get home every night. She knew I was home, so she left until tomorrow." He holstered his pistol and turned to Prissy with a grin as wide as his face.

"What were you a-goin' to tell me," he chuckled, as they both quietly backed out of the room and returned to the parlor.

"Oh, Riley, it's a long story, but I met my husband when he was a recruit at Fort Lowell. We married on his next leave and when he returned to the Fort the Army sent his company to Montana to Fort Phil Kearney, to help fight the Sioux Indians."

"I never saw him after that first month, and I received word from the War Department that he had been killed with the eighty man force of a Captain William James Fetterman that December, from the terrible Sioux massacre near the Powder river."

"But, the baby," Riley asked.

"Andy, Jr,. was born on Christmas day." "Well, I'm mighty sorry, Prissy, but I 'spect you'll raise the boy right. These are some tough times," he replied, "reckon I'd best get on out of here, now."

With her eyes fighting back the tears, she took hold of both his hands and looked up in his face . . ."You promised," she sighed, "just stay the night, Riley. I-I'm so lonely, I need you to help me and talk to me. Just talk to me and hold me. You're warm and caring, and I desperately need to be with you tonight."

❋　　❋　　❋

The 'Old Pueblo' had never produced a better night. The southwestern skies were filled with a plethora of shining stars.

The cool breezes that flowed through the dusty streets seemed to settle with a gentle wafting of melodious tunes that came to ear from the nearby cantîna music.

Riley felt the passion of an emotional state in which intense joy possessed his mind with total satisfaction. They held each other with a gentle caress and softly confessed their pleasures together.

"Riley," she spoke, "you're the reason I put so much trust in men . . . I know I probably shouldn't, but I keep searching for an answer to the void I've felt since . . . since . . ."

"Since you lost your husband," he said.

"Well, I guess so, except that I never seem to find that answer after all—except now . . . tonight, with you, Riley."

"Hold on, sweet gal, I'm not your real answer, I'm just a lonesome cowboy, like you're a lonesome prairie flower. We seem to have both found a temporary haven in which to satisfy our forlorn thoughts, but tomorrow we must both part."

Morning arrived quickly, and with it came the gurgling and semi-squalling sounds from the next room, from where they'd moved the trundle bed last night. It was this strange sound to Riley's ears that caused him to awake and discover Prissy had already arisen. "Mother's instinct," he mused.

Riley played with the happily fed baby while, as promised, Priscilla prepared some eggs and corn-meal mush for their breakfast.

It was nearing seven o'clock when Riley finished saddling the livery horse and stepped to the doorway to bid goodbye to a delightfully accommodating, lonely, most beautiful and temporarily satisfied lady.

"When will I see you again, Riley?" she asked with another tear in her eye. "You've meant a great deal to me in a very short time—I hope you'll find a way . . ."

"Take care of yourself, Prissy, and take good care of little Andy. Maybe, if I can get my business taken care of today, I can stop and see you at the cantîna later."

She was holding a smiling baby in her arms as she waved goodbye to a friend and lover. He turned while mounted and waved back.

It was a short ride over to the livery stable and Riley pulled rein in front and stepped down to check in. He was greeted by Jubal Whitlow and the deputy from Marshal Wilson's office.

"This here's Deputy Pierce," Jubal said to Riley, when he handed him the reins. "We've met," exclaimed Riley'

"Sorry, mister," the deputy stated, "but you're under arrest."

"Under arrest, th-hell for?"

"It seems there was a shootin' last night in the alley behind the Cantîna la Roca. Feller by the name of Wendell Hart was shot in the back and witnesses say you had a fight with him earlier last night."

"Wendell Hart, I don't know any . . ."

"That would be the real name of the feller we all know as 'Curly'." Jubal interrupted Riley's statement.

"I have to hold you at the jail," the deputy said," and the marshal's due back today. I reckon he'll want to look into it."

"There was no way I shot that drunk," Riley snapped. "Who was the witness?"

"His partner. He described the paint horse you're a ridin', so I came to see ol' Jubal here, and he said you'd be a-bringin' him back this mornin' to git both yore other hosses. Got yer name off'n the register he keeps here at the livery. So, Mister Riley O'Rourke, come with me, you're under arrest."

The marshal's office and the jail was only a short walk from the livery, and so Riley was escorted over and put in one of the cells inside. The deputy took the pistol Riley carried and placed it with his cartridge belt in the locked cabinet behind the big desk inside the office.

Riley hadn't counted on this turn of events. He questioned now whether he should have just gone to Victors' cafe, as Jubal said, or for that matter, why did he even pursue the task of riding to Tucson to report the ugly killings by the renegade Indians. Someone else would eventually find them. "No . . ." he thought, "that's not what it's all about. That could've been some of my family or friends in that massacre, it had to be resolved as quickly as possible . . . but now this mess about a killing that I never done . . . looks like I'm in another tight fix."

CHAPTER TWENTY FIVE

It was late afternoon when the marshal arrived from Tombstone, and it was almost time for Prissy to start her job at the Cantîna la Roca.

Marshal Wilson was consulting with his deputy concerning the business that had occurred while he was away, and he inquired of the 'cowboy in cell three, back there'.

"Witness said he shot ol' Curly last night in the alley by the Roca. The two had a fight earlier and I reckon the cowboy did him in—later, in the alley," he replied.

"Who is this witness?" the marshal asked, "did you get a statement, Clyde?"

"Wal-ll, no . . . he-uh, the cowboy was seen earlier inside, and they say he and Curly got in a fight over Prissy, and the cowboy knocked Curly out with one punch."

"Who's they, you're talkin 'bout, boy?"

"Wal-ll, about a half a dozen boys at the bar, and everybo. . . "

"And you never got one statement?"

The marshal questioned his deputy. Did you see any of the shooting, Clyde?"

"No, but the witness did—I guess—anyway, his name's 'Snake' Harcourt, and he said the cowboy came into the alley a while later and just shot ol' Curly in the back. Snake said he had gone to get a horse for Curly and as he was a-comin' in the alley he saw the cowboy shoot Curly, and then run out the back side and lit out. Snake said he knew it was the cowboy, all right, he remembered him from the fight inside."

"So, no one else saw our prisoner do the shooting? They just saw the fight!" The marshal pondered the situation, but according to law, he could lock him up on a legal complaint of murder, for forty-eight hours.

"Where is this Harcourt, Clyde? I'd like to talk to him myself," said Marshal Wilson.

"He said he was going to take care of everything with the undertaker," the deputy replied, "but, I'll bet he's done by now and over to the cantîna fer the night. I'll go see if I can fetch him right now, Marshal."

"Tell him we need to talk, Clyde,"

Inside the Cantîna la Roca, the drinks were beginning to flow and the music was starting to become festive. The usual body of souls were in attendance, swilling their glasses full of libation watered down more as the hour grew late,

Among the group of soldiers, miners, cowboys and ne'er-do-wells stood 'Snake', a drink in hand and confiding to a less than sober listener, the shooting he witnessed in the alley last night.

"Yesser, me an ol' Curly had a snoot full las' night, an some cowboy socked us whilst we was too drunk to fight. Well, sir, they tossed us in the alley fer awhile and when I come to, I tells ol' Curly to stay there and I'd go git his horse."

"Jes as I was bringin' the horse fer him, I seen that same cowboy whut fit us, jes shoot poor ol' Curly in the back and run off."

"At's a wooly story, Snake. Hey, you still buyin' the drinks?" the toper asked, "you seem to have plen—urp—a plent . . . a lots o' money."

"Yeah, well, see that's mah business, how I come by it . . . I jes never spent it." "Hokay . . . sphend it now, ol' fren."

The two men, by now, far "into their cups," continued to drink the cheap alcohol, and Snake continued to buy the drinks for him and his cohort. Finally, Snake said they should both set in on the poker game at the table near the back.

"Don't worry, ol' fren, I'll stake ya to a pot er two, we still gots plenty money. Siddoun here."

It was during this time that Prissy was bringing drinks to the poker players and the patrons who were watching what started to become a high stakes game. One where Snake and his obtuse, new-found pal, had no business playing.

Prissy immediately noticed the the man as one of the two that were insulting to her and that Riley'd knocked down last night, she, too, remembered they called him 'Snake'. Each time she came to the table she would observe his obnoxious actions.

Moments later, Deputy Pierce came into the cantîna and asked Prissy if anyone had seen Snake Harcourt; he said the marshal wanted to question him about the shooting that he witnessed last night in the alley.

"Shooting?" questioned Prissy.

"Yeah, some cowboy shot Snakes' partner last night. Snake claims to have witnessed it and the marshal jes got back and wants to talk with him about it," the deputy replied.

"Cowboy,?" Prissy cautiously asked.

"Yep. He and Snake and a feller named Curly got into it here in the bar, and the cowboy s'posed'ly knocked the both of 'em down and out. 'Cordin' to Snake they was both drug to the alley to sleep it off and when Snake finally came to, he went to git Curly's horse, and when he was a-comin' back he saw the cowboy shoot Curly in the back. We got the boy in jail rat now and we . . ."

In a flash, Prissy was out of the saloon and heading to the marshal's office not knowing in her mind just what happened.

Her foremost thought was that it must be Riley they're holding in jail, given the right description, but it was impossible that he would have shot anyone . . . after all, he was with (me) since right after the fight.

Prissy stepped through the door to the marshal's office and confronted him at his desk with an excited air of concern.

"Marshal, I'm Patricia Sullivan . . . uh, Prissy Petersen, from the Roca Cantîna. The deputy's at the saloon asking for a Snake Harcourt for you to question. he claims you have a man locked up charged with shooting Snake's partner, Curly."

"That's right, Prissy, what is it that brings you over here,?" the marshal asked her.

"Well, if you've arrested who I think you have, you've obviously made a bad mistake."

"The prisoner's name is Riley O'Rourke and he's in cell number three, in the back."

Prissy slumped in a heap in the chair next to the desk, dismayed and ashen-faced.

"It-it just can't be, Marshal Wilson. I-I'd like to see him, if I may, please."

"S'pose there's no problem, come on."

Riley's eyes lit up when the marshal opened the cell door and he saw Prissy standing along side of him.

"Got a visitor, cowboy . . . and a mighty pretty one, too. Claims you're innocent."

"Prissy!" Riley announced, "what a good surprise. How did you know I was . . ."

"It's a long story, but do you know what they're saying—that you shot Curly in the back last night, it—it's just . . . oh, Marshal Wilson, there has been a terrible mistake. You see . . . well, Riley was at my house last night. He needed a place to stay and after he helped me from being beat around by those two drunken bums last night, I just . . ."

"Look, Prissy, I know who you are. I've seen you at the cantîna many times, and I've no reason not to believe you, but Deputy Pierce says he has a witness to the killing and he's bringing that witness here, so you just set tight 'til I get some answers to a few questions."

Prissy went to the cell bars and put her hand through to grasp Riley's hand, and with a stronger reassuring smile she said, "Don't worry, Riley, I'll explain to the marshal just exactly where you were, and how those two men threatened us both."

"Prissy, maybe you could try to locate my friend Lyle Henthorn, or the attorney he came to see. His name's McAllister, and he has an office here in Tucson, somewhere. It just might help if I could tell McAllister about this mess, he may be able to help me."

"Of course, I'll leave right away."

The marshal, however, had a thought and he asked her to wait in the adjoining room with the door ajar. He would have his deputy stay with her to listen to all the questions to be asked Snake Harcourt, and define his answers.

Marshal Wilson asked Snake once again to describe exactly what happened from when he and Curly were in the bar and what they said to Miss Prissy and to the cowboy named O'Rourke. This time Snake changed it around somewhat.

"We wus mindin' our own bidness, Marshal, when this cowboy came over to the bar and said we wus causin' trouble."

When Snake had finished his deposition, Marshal Wilson asked him to sign it and Snake answered with a half-witted, half-grin, and a quizzical look before his final admission that he could not read nor write.

"Make your mark, then, and I'll ask my deputy to witness that,"

When Prissy finally talked to the marshal she told him about the card game earlier where Snake was betting money with the same coins that she had loaned Curly some hours before when he threatened her if she failed to give him some money. "I considered it a loan of the sixty dollars," Prissy stated, "but Curly must have felt that I just gave it to him, with no strings."

The marshal returned to the room where Snake was seated and asked him where he got all the money he was betting with in the poker game, and wrote down what he said. The marshal then instructed Deputy Pierce to get a statement from the undertaker as to the polk that Curly carried, and any contents—without disclosing what he knew about any red marks on some of the coins.

"You're lying, aren't you, Snake?"

CHAPTER TWENTY SIX

Lyle Henthorn rode along in the buggy when lawyer Abel McAllister started to his office that morning. His bay horse was tied to the back and retied again to a hitch rail in front of the downtown office of the barrister.

Prissy was waiting in front when the two men rode in. She recognized lawyer McAllister. whom she'd met before, and he greeted her and introduced Lyle Henthorn to her.

McAllister bade them enter and proceed to his office, but Prissy was too excited and insisted they hear about Riley O'Rourke.

"It would be prudent, Ma'am, if you and Mister Henthorn would come on inside."

"At the mention of Riley's name, Lyle was extremely eager to hear Prissy's story.

It wasn't long before both men heard Prissy's version of the mess in which Riley became involved, his reason why he'd come to Tucson, and also, that she promised him she would ask the lawyer if he or someone he'd recommend would represent Riley.

Thirty minutes later, Prissy, Lyle and the attorney were at the jail to see Riley.

Marshal Wilson was very accommodating and suggested that the lawyer spend some time with his proposed client first, and then Riley could visit with his friend, Lyle.

In a short while the attorney appeared at the marshal's desk and requested Riley be released in his custody. This was all completed in accordance with procedure.

After the attorney and the marshal had their discussion pertaining to the shooting of Curly, the marshal disclosed that he felt the only, so called, witness to the shooting was not creditable, and he probably was lying. In fact, the marshal was convinced after many facts came out, that the "witness," Snake, was likely the one who had shot Curly and then robbed him.

In the meantime, Prissy related to the marshal that Riley spent the night at her house, and Maria Ontovîs saw him there and would confirm it. She felt Snake shot Curly to rob him of the coins he'd taken from her.

She told the attorney and he said that she had a very good case for Riley's innocence.

The marshal had his deputy immediately arrest Snake Harcourt and bring him to the jail.

"You're under arrest for the murder and robbery of your cohort, Wendell Hart," the marshal stated to him.

"Who-th-hell's Wendell Hart?" Snake asked, perplexed, "Never heerd o'him."

"That's the man you shot and robbed."

"You mean 'ats Curly's real name?" the self-incriminator asked.

"You said it," answered a grinning marshal, "just get in that cell, Harcourt."

※ ※ ※

One day later, A.P.K.Safford, who was appointed the territorial governor in 1865, rode into Tucson and performed the various legal procedures the town needed to solve— among which included the trial of two horse thieves and the sentencing of a murderer.

The investigative detail the Army sent to cover the massacre in the Santa Rita mountains returned the afternoon of the trial and the scouts reported the raid was carried out by a large band of Pinaléro Apaches.

Many of the townspeople were beholden to Riley O'Rourke for his information about the column of people who lost their lives in that raid, and a dance in his honor was planned for the evening at the la Roca bar.

Since Lyle and Riley had spent last night at the McAllister home, outside of town, they weren't aware of the dance until they came into the cantîna when they rode back into town.

Riley, of course, was looking around for Prissy, and Lyle just wanted a drink before they were to both ride back to the Henthorn ranch.

It was only a moment, under the gas lights in the smoke filled cantîna, until Prissy spotted her newly found friend and paramour, who hurried to greet her.

"Riley, I've missed you, I . . ."

"I've only been gone a day. Lyle and I were staying at the McAllister place," he interrupted, "besides, I intended to see you before we leave and how's little Andy?"

"He's fine, Riley, but I did miss you and I was hoping we could spend some more time togeth—Leave? . . . I didn't know you planned to leave-uh, I-I mean, uh, leave so soon." She had Riley at a disadvantage.

She was talking to him in a corner recess and they were standing near a doorway that separated a cubicle used for a special game of cards . . . or, whatever, but not now in use. A large drapery covered the unlocked entrance.

Prissy was a vision of beauty dressed in a low-cut, peasant blouse with a colored skirt of deep blue and green. Her auburn hair was glistening from the shaft of light that filtered through the room and her ruby-red, full lips, pouted as she spoke.

"Prissy," Riley repeated, "I surely wasn't going to leave until I could see you again and tell you how much I do care for you. You're truly beautiful and I know I'll miss you, too, but my mind's made up. Lyle and I are heading back after the dance.

With misty eyes and a very compelling embrace, she maneuvered him behind the long, burgundy drape hiding the cubicle. Here, they both succumbed to the passions they felt and fervently and recklessly kissed with any abandonment of proper behavior.

"It just isn't in my cards," he said, responding to her plea that he remain in Tucson. "Not that I haven't given it some strong thought, Prissy, but for now Lyle and I should be riding southeast."

"I-I know, Riley," she replied, breathing heavily, "it was wishful thinking on my part and very selfish. You've given me pleasures that I've missed for a long, long time, and for that I'm grateful. I'm glad I met you, Riley O'Ro . . ."

Riley interrupted her with a gentle force by laying her warm body on the long bench against the soft, woolen, red and tan Indian blanket that covered it. She ardently gave herself unto his advances, and she passionately returned his aggressive kisses.

It was a spur of the moment reaction for them both, and after about a fifteen minute interlude they sheepishly emerged from behind the draped door that covered their sanctuary of romantic pleasures.

"I'm always gettin' myself into these situations," Riley thought to himself, "how am I gonna' slip out of this one without it causin' deep hurt for us both?"

※　　　※　　　※

"There you are!" Lyle exclaimed, "I've been looking all over this place for you."

"I've been here all the time, you just don't know the right places to look (thank God!)," he answered with a grin. "C'm on, I'll buy the drinks, and we'll talk about how far we want to ride after the dance is over."

"Are you certain you want to ride out tonight?" Prissy joined them at the bar and posed the question for them to answer.

"That's a good question," Lyle stated, "'cept we'd have to make arrangements for us and our horses to actually stay over."

"That'll be no problem," Riley quickly interjected, "Ol' Jubal, at the livery will surely put us up for just one night."

Lyle gave his partner a perplexed look and spoke a word of doubt.

"Really?"

Riley nodded, as he squeezed Prissy's hand, winked, and then said to Lyle, "Why don't you go make arrangements, pard?"

"Maybe it does make sense to start out early tomorrow, rather than on this dark ol' starless night."

They carried their drinks to a table and talked a spell before Lyle said he'd ride to the livery and talk to Jubal.

Prissy then asked Riley to dance.

CHAPTER TWENTY SEVEN

A cooling and light breeze set the leaves of the tall cottonwoods in motion as Riley and Lyle followed the concourse of the Santa Cruz river south and east when they departed the Old Pueblo.

"It cost a hundred dollars," Lyle remarked, when Riley asked him if all the paperwork was in order so that he and his sister, Diana, could have a clear title and deed to the almost four sections of land that once belonged to their parents.

"But the homestead act of 1849 returns us almost five hundred dollars from our federal government, figured at about twenty cents per acre. That can help pay for two or three good bulls that Ramøn says we can purchase from their ranch," Lyle stated.

"Near as I figure," Riley opined, "I'll most likely turn due east when we get about a mile farther up the river. I 'spect you are going to start your climb at Red pass."

They couldn't have been more than half a mile from the river when they saw a band of Apaches they felt certain was a raiding party. Lyle counted twenty-two warriors; he and Riley considered whether their presence had been discovered by the hostiles.

The Indians were moving very slowly, taking their time descending the rocky slopes in the foothills of the Santa Rita mountains. Riley noted that eight of the riders seemed wounded and very badly hurt. These eight carried no weapons or shields and they were slumped against the withers close toward their pony's necks.

Momentarily, two youthful warriors came into view following the main band and leading seven rider-less horses. the entire caballåda (horse band) was heading south.

"I believe these scoundrels have been in a fight and are heading for a camp or a village past the Siérrita mountains," said Riley, "and they're far enough in front of us that I don't think we've been spotted."

"You don't suppose that's the band the soldiers and Ramøn have been looking for?" said Lyle, "or have they already fought them?"

"It looks as though those Indians have been in a scrape, all right," Riley replied.

"Yeah, and they look like they've been whipped. I don't see any prisoners nor many weapons, and they're going slow so the crippled ones can keep up," said Lyle.

"Well, you know what they say about a wounded bear . . . don't mess with 'em, 'cause they're even more dangerous when they're hurt." Riley almost whispered this remark to Lyle, as he cautiously maneuvered his horse away from any opening so he wouldn't be seen. Just as quickly, Lyle followed him.

"You know, Lyle, I just may trail along with you to your ranch, afore I head on home, at any rate we'd best ride out of here fast if we don't want to be caught."

"Yup, that's a good decision. I was hoping you'd come on to our ranch with me. I know you'll want to see Diana . . . at least she'll want to see you—you can also check with Ramøn as to what's going on with the Mexican troop and our own soldier boys."

Riley was smiling at Lyle when he said that Diana would want to see him.

It was nearly dusk when the two men pulled rein at the Henthorn ranch and stepped down at the newly finished, large barn next to the new corrals. They were unsaddling their horses and bedding them down for the night when Ramøn appeared.

"¿Qué tal? amigo miå," (What's up, my friend)? Lyle said as he saw Ramøn coming into the barn. "How are you—it's good to be home again. Everything went we . . ."

"Mucho tristeza,(much sadness) amigo miå, a very bad thing has hoppen," Ramon said, as he quietly interrupted Lyle.

Riley walked over to where the two were standing and posed the same question.

"Oh, señores, I am having to tell you about chor seester, señor Lyle."

"Diana? What happened? Is she . . . is she all right? Tell me, Ramøn . . . what?"

The morning of yesterday, she fell from her yega (mare) and struck her head. One of my vaquéros saw the whole event, He brought her inside and called to me—but eet was of no use. her neck was broken, and we could not help her.

'Madre dé Dios' paz en descansar, ellé." (Mother of God, may she rest in peace).

Ramøn was nearly beside himself with grief as he related the bitter events to Lyle and Riley. The three men gathered at the end of the barn beside the tack room.

"Riley," Lyle spoke, "this is almost too much to bear, I can't imagine my life without Diana in it—her presence is going to be missed—terribly," he sobbed.

Riley, himself in near shock at the awful turn, was almost at a loss for words.

"It-it's terrifying for you to have to deal with this, especially after what happened to your ma and your uncle. These are mighty tough times, Lyle, mighty tough."

In a sense, Ramøn most likely felt the loss as much as Lyle, if not more, for he had fallen hopelessly in love with Diana.

"We've done nothing with—with her body, amigo, eet ees importante, now that chu are here, to have la voz ultimo. (The final say). I am! lo siento mucho! (So very sorry)"

The two vaquéros who'd been preparing supper, suddenly appeared at the barn and expressed their condolences to Lyle and to Riley, and asked if they could be of any help.

It was a dreadful evening. Riley and Lyle, who'd been in the saddle all day, were tired and hungry, but appetites were not of concern under the circumstances.

There had to be a decision made as to what they would do with Diana's body, and this was the reason Ramøn wanted Lyle to make the decision.

Lyle excused himself momentarily and they went to the house. Lyle went to the far corner of the corral area where he could watch the western-setting sun settle itself beyond the Tumacacori mountains to the southwest, and think by himself.

The lamps were burning inside the main house when Lyle entered and sat in the big chair by the fireplace in the front room.

"I've made up my mind," he softly spoke, "I'd like to bury my sister here, on the ranch where she grew up, and where we shared our young lives together. We should place her next to my mother and my uncle and let her spirit watch over me while I attempt to make this ranch into something very special." Lyle breathed a deep sigh.

"The right thing to do," Riley agreed.

The next day, after a brief service for Diana, Lyle told Riley and Ramøn his plans. "I'd like to take you up on that promise you made Diana, Ramøn, about some extra horses we can purchase to bring here, and also, I'd like to buy two bulls from your herd to carry on the fine breeding stock you and your father started."

"Si, si, muy buéno (Yes, very good) decision, bot chu weel have to come to our ranchero to pick out thee ones chu want, and also, they need to be driven back to your ranch."

"Whatta ya' lookin' at me for?" said Riley. positive what Lyle had in his mind.

"Aw, hell, partner, you're such a good cowboy, I don't think I could handle all this without your help," Lyle pleaded.

Ramøn was encouraging Riley and said he'd have one of his vaquéros remain at the ranch while the other would accompany the three of them to the El Reventon and help herd the animal entourage back up here.

"That would be a wonderful gesture," Lyle told Ramøn. "How 'bout it, Riley? You think we can all leave in the morning.?"

First light saw four of the men finish their breakfast of beans, coffee, and pån vaqureo (cowboy bread), saddle their horses and strike out down the west side of the Santa Rita mountains for the El Reventon.

It was cold when they left the ranch on the mountain, but they expected warmer weather as they left the foothills toward the Santa Cruz river valley.

Ramøn was pleased they were dealing with his ranch for the livestock and he would also be glad to see his parents, but he was concerned for Lieutenant Lopez and Captain Carter, too.

The three wondered whether the soldiers had any encounter with the renegade Apaches.

It would take several more hours into the afternoon before they would reach the base of the foothills and head southwest to the "Rancho Grandé El Reventon," hard by the banks of the agua püra (pure water) of the north flowing, Santa Cruz river.

CHAPTER TWENTY EIGHT

Rifle shots were heard long before the Indians were spotted. An occasional tremelo sounded from a distance amid some shouting.

Ramøn was leading their party and he was guiding them toward his ranch when he pulled rein and threw up his hand.

"There they are," he shouted, pulling his horse away from an open clearing.

Riley had already seen them and Lyle and their vaquero companion, Hernando, rode up beside the front two, for a better look.

It was hard to tell just how many hostiles were laying siege outside the front walls of the Reventon ranch. The men determined the Indians had surprised some of the men who were outside the ranch gates cutting firewood, of whom Hernando said were six.

Apparently, this event had just begun for the rest of the vaqueros, still inside, were only now starting their own rifle fire.

Riley told his friends that he thought there were at least seventy-five Apaches.

One of the two mules hitched to the wagon partly filled with cut-wood had been slain. The other was fighting his traces and trying to get away and run back inside.

Since the wood-cutters were only a few hundred yards from the ranch gates they had no horses with them and they were only armed with pistols. Paco was trying to cut the traces from the standing mule when he suddenly cried, "mi tirador!" (I'm shot). He fell forward, shot through his stomach.

Riley positioned himself on his horse so that he was behind some of the Indians, trying to catch them in a cross-fire. Lyle immediately rode wide to the south attempting to flank the raiders. Hernando rode out to the front trying to reach his compådres at the ditch by the wood wagon, and Ramøn began firing his rifle from where he sat.

The Apaches were astonished and partly confounded at the sudden emergence of the four men throwing rifle fire at them from the side and behind them. Two more Apaches were shot as they were running away.

Suddenly, the front gates flew open and about twelve vaqueros from inside charged into the fray and scattered a dozen or so of the warriors closest to the wood cutters.

As several of the Apaches ran to where their horses were held. They unknowingly ran directly where Lyle was concealed behind some heavy brush hosting two large saguaros and a multitude of cholla cactus.

Lyle had a Sharps-Cooper, rear-loading carbine, capable of firing seven shots in rapid succession. The first two shots he fired at one renegade found their mark and toppled him to his bloody death. The next shot hit an Indian in his foot and upset his running stride. While he tried hard to regain his footing, Lyle shot him.

Riley had dismounted from Dobé and was in a position to fire his carbine from some concealment in a heavy stand of mesquites.

Most of the Apaches were armed with Winchester and Springfield rifles likely stolen from ranches or wagon trains. A few Apaches had abandoned their rifles for the bow, and could keep several arrows in the air at one time. One reason for using the bow and arrow was their adeptness for it, but they also lacked much rifle ammunition.

Ramøn had just killed another Apache when he took an arrow in his left shoulder. He struggled to dismount and tie off his horse and regain his position from where he could cross-fire into the savages.

He knew he couldn't extract the shaft from his shoulder by himself and decided to wait for help, although he was feeling some dizziness from a loss of blood.

The extra vaqueros from the ranch were the catalyst that caused the rest of the Apaches to flee as fast as they could reach their horses, with no time for them to retrieve their dead or wounded. Outnumbered, the ranch cowboys pursued the Indians only a short way, but certain they had completely deterred them, they returned.

Hernando saw Ramøn who was only a short distance away, and rushed to give him the help he needed. When Don Jorgé arrived he welcomed his son and urged him to retire to his quarters and there be attended for his wound.

Riley rode in with Lyle and they counted eleven dead Chiricahua Apaches, and one badly wounded warrior lying beside six, blanket-saddled, Indian ponies.

Don Jorgé instructed several of his men to retrieve the wounded Apache and take him and the horses back to the ranch.

The men were grumbling about having to handle any member of the hated Apache, and some thought this savage should be left to die; better yet, a vaquero valiénte (brave cowboy) should just cut his throat instead.

It was then Joaquîn, Don Jorgé's segundo (second in command), and two others bound the Indian's arms and brought him inside to the main sala (living room.)

His wounds were treated and bound and Joaquîn, who was well versed in the Apache language, began to question the Indian.

The stoic Apache, at first, was not going to answer any questions until Joaquîn explained that he had been able to contact "the spirit god that awaited dead Apaches", and he told him the six grandfathers of the other world wanted him to tell the Mexican and the Pindah-Lickoyee what they wished.

"He said his name is Quîjos Césped." (in Apache this meant grass basket). "He's a Bedonkohe Apache; same clan as Geronimo."

So, Joaquîn's next question was apparent. "Hieronymo," said the Apache, "is in Mejîco, somewhere in the Sierra Mådres, near Bavispe. Your soldier chief (Crook) is looking for him. His Jefé, (Captain John Bourke) has joined forces with Blue coats and Mejican soldådos who are chasing us in the Santa Rita and San Cayentano mountains."

"What band are you with today?" was Joaquîn's following question.

"Chato's," (flat nose) came the reply.

All the chiefs of the Chirichaua Apaches, 'Chato', 'Hieronymo', Kantenné', 'Loco', 'Zele',

'Bonito', and 'Chihuahua', were plenty wise and noticeably always in good physical condition, and offered up no reason to surrender to the U.S.Army and be transported to the San Carlos reservation.

As with most of the hostiles, they were reluctant to give out their correct names when confronted by an enemy, and often offered a ficticious name instead.

This was the case of Quîjos Césped.

Delores, the maid servant of Don Jorgé's daughter, Anita, was assisting with the bandaging of the Indian's wounds, and recognized him as "Néne," a sub-chief of the Chiricahuas, and she told Joaquîn about it.

It was this information that put Joaquîn in a position to be able to exchange prisoners with any Apache bands that held any Mexican men, women or children in captivity.

Joaquîn summoned Ramøn, whose shoulder wound was dressed, to join him questioning the Apache, 'Néne'. Ramøn was interested in finding out about Lieutenant Lopez and the men sent to roust, most likely, this same band.

The questioning continued as Lyle and Riley appeared in the room. Immediately upon seeing the Apache warrior Ramøn and Joaquîn were talking to, Lyle became very incensed and rushed the prisoner with intent to slay him.

Riley caught Lyle just as he was about to plunge his long knife into the red man. He was incoherently shouting epithets as to all the "red devils" that slaughtered his mother, and especially this one whom he mistakenly felt was surely the perpetrator.

"No, Lyle," Riley calmly said to his friend, "I know exactly how you must feel, but this is one Apache that they want to keep alive."

CHAPTER TWENTY NINE

A large baile (dance) was arranged for the evening after the victorious defeat of the attacking Apaches, and a bar-be-que was started with the roasting of a fat steer.

While there was mourning for the death of Påco, most prepared to celebrate.

"¿La musica es bonito, sî," came a voice behind Anita.

"Sî, esta maravilloso, es muy bien," replied Anita, before spinning around to see who spoke. "Ho-la—uh, hello, Ri-ley, I-uh, I . . ."

"You've been avoiding me, you know. We arrived 'en las tardes,' but I suppose with all the excitement of the raid and all, your pr . . ."

"Mi Madré—my mother forbade me to appear during the fighting. I could not see you. '

"There's been a tragic accident, 'Nita, at the Henthorn ranch, and that's one of the reasons I'm—er, we're here. You see, Diana was thrown from her horse and killed."

"Of course, Lyle is extremely upset, but I must say Ramøn is also having a hard time dealing with it. He'd fallen in love with her, as you're probably very aware, like it—or not—they were both planning to marry."

"One of the last things I asked you to do was to try to keep them apart, but I don't suppose that matters now," replied Anita, "and I'm very sorry—for Lyle."

"Don't be too hard on Ramøn, 'Nita, it's all over now and he needs a few kind words from you . . . anyway, now that I'm here, I'm really glad to see you, and the truth is, I've missed you, terribly."

Anita was gazing deeply into the steel-gray eyes of the handsome cowboy, and she hesitated before responding to his say.

"Oh, Ri-ley, you know how I feel about chu. I-I care very much for you—but your mind was made up when we parted before, 'y mi padré es nerviso, ademüs (besides, my father is nervous) seeing us together."

"I think your father is over those bad thoughts by now, 'Nita, anyway, your mother still likes me, and it . . ."

I never said that father did not like you. I only said he gets nervous when he sees us together—in—in a 'serious mood'.

"I know," replied Riley, "anyway, I've acted a little foolishly, I s'pose, an' you should know that I really have missed your beautiful smile, and your beautiful b . . ."

Riley stopped short, before he embarrassed himself any further.

"Go on, Riley," Anita spoke, while she moved closer to him, "say what chu theenk. Chu mos know I have those same thoughts for you and I guess I always have. You are right about mî madré, she ees very much care for chu . . . and she has tol' me so. Eet has been deef-o-cult for me when chu left our rancheria.

By now, Anita had artfully escorted Riley from the room to the terrace next to the patio, where she enfolded herself into his arms and offered her scarlet lips to his chiseled face that extolled a perplexed look, but which eagerly and ardently responded.

Kisses, exchanged on the patio, under an Arizona sky filled with glistening stars in the darkness, while the moon darted amid few clouds, were meant to convey desires.

The melodious voices of the musicians rising above their instruments in the background, offered a desirable setting for a very purposeful evening.

Riley started to speak. "'Nita, we . . ."

"No," she interrupted, placing two of her slender fingers to his lips, "we must return, before we are missed, and we must not be close inside; if you wish Ri-ley, I shall find you later, as before."

"That's a pleasant thought," Riley answered, "and this time it won't be unexpected. I'll just leave the latch undone."

Riley thought to himself, she was taking no small chance, but Anita was so sure of herself, he dismissed the thought.

Anita walked back inside through a large portál and mingled in with several people standing beside the floor near the musicians.

Riley left the patio and walked in through a side door near the front.

The baile was extraordinarily welcomed by all the inhabitants at the famed ranch in the Santa Cruz valley. A rare chance for all the workers as well as the family to get together in a joyous celebration. The Reventon ranch was noted for the fine herd of ganado (cattle) raised on the ranch, as well as the caballeriza (stable) of pure-bred, Spanish-Barb and Andalusian horses.

These horses were in demand, not only by the ranches in the valley, but also by the Apaches who coveted them. The horses were used by the vaqueros continually to perform their everyday chores working the cattle.

The Barb horse is second only to the Arabian as one of the foundation breeds of the world. It's a desert horse, but unrelated in appearance and character to the Arabian horse. Don Jorgé insisted his string would be perpetuated by keeping two famed stallions, descendants of the Morocco stallions.

Ramøn told Riley the Barb horse was renowned for it speed over short distances and stands between fourteen-two and fifteen two hands tall. (a hand equals four inches).

"How's your shoulder feeling?" asked Riley, when he came in and saw Ramøn.

"Eet's sore, my fren', bot I am very lucky, and een several days eet weel be as good as new. We are fortunate we were able to send los Apaches on their way."

"This was a good thing your parents did, have this fiesta for everyone, it will take their minds off some of the hard work that it takes to operate this ranch. I see Anita over there, next to your mother, and I guess I should go over and talk to her."

"Riley, I know your feelings for her, and they are reciprocal I am positive, and you have my approval, my fren', but take caution . . . she ees very vulnerable and very fragile, you comprende?" "You're right, amigo, I do have strong feelings for Anita, and I'm aware she has feelings for me, too. I'm also aware that your father has some thoughts concerning my attentions to Anita, and I intend to make certain he does not misunderstand any of my intentions," Riley answered, as he shook hands with his compañero (pal).

It would have caused some suspicious thoughts, especially from members of the Moralés family, if Riley did not ask for a dance with Anita Maria, although Riley felt the opposite may be true. However, he did dance with Donna Isabella and with Delores.

"You had best ask my seester for a dance, amigo miå," Ramøn kidded Riley, as the music started to play a 'fandango'.

Riley, somewhat perplexed, agreed, and he casually sauntered to where Anita was.

"May I have the pleasure of your hand for this dance, Miss Moralés?" and looking toward he mother, said, "con permission?"

"Of course, you have my permission, Señor O'Rourke," she answered with a smile.

"You might have to ej'icate me, 'Nita, I'm not sure I ever tried a 'fandango'."

"Eet's easy," she said, laughing, "just watch my brother—an' he's only using one arm. here, place your hand on my waist like thees, and just step out weeth chor left foots first—and then, swing me—like so!"

Lyle was dancing with Delores and he nearly broke up laughing watching Riley.

"Way to go, pard! Way to go!" he said.

It was almost midnight when the baile finally ended but Señor Moralés had retired an hour earlier. Riley made certain he was seen leaving alone, as he bade the remaining revelers a buenas noches. (good night).

Twenty minutes passed by, then another five, according to the watch his grandfather had given him many years earlier.

Riley was trying to curb his anxiety for the anticipated event soon to take place and was concerned for her safety.

There was no knock, just the lifting of the iron latch, as she quietly slipped into his room, this time dressed with her riding habit-and quickly bolting the door.

No words were spoken as they fell into each others arms and embraced momentarily.

"I knew you'd come," Riley said, as he removed her capa y camiseta (her cape and vest) and placed them over a chair back.

"Oh, Ri-ley, yo enamorase de amor." (I am falling in love with you.).

"It's no use for me to deny my love for you, I've known for some time how much I care for you, and I want you to share your life with me—I-I do love you, Anita Maria."

CHAPTER THIRTY

The short night at the El Reventon was interrupted at the very first light of dawn with the sound of musket and pistol fire.

A loud tremolo of sound was emanating from outside the ranch compound. Vaqueros were heard scrambling from within their quarters and commands from Joaquîn to his men to form up and gather arms was given.

The obvious early morning Indian raid was unexpected, to say the least, even the sentries were caught unaware.

At the corrals, vaqueros were catching and saddling their horses who were, by nature, alert to changes in their routines, especially if they were hurried.

"Roberto!" one of the men called to the horse wrangler who stayed at the pens where the herd was kept confined at night, "¿Dondé esta los Indios, Roberto?" (where are the Indians, Robert?) "Por aquî,!dése prisal!," (over here, hurry) cried the hung-over vaquero.

There were at least a dozen Apaches attempting to scale the enclosure to reach the horse herd and stampede them outside.

Joaquîn, was one of the first to reach the corral and saw two of the Apaches jump Roberto, slit his throat, and leap to the ground by the pole gates to the corral.

While his men were shooting at the savages outside the escarpment, Joaquîn was able to duck behind one of the horses who ran in front of him at the last second, and it took the arrow in its flank.

This gave Joaquîn a clear shot at the warrior, and he dispatched him easily to his death with two shots to his chest.

At this moment, several more of the Apaches managed to reach the corrals and were trying to loosen the pole gates to run the animals outside. Again, the fire power from the ranch hands kept the Indians pinned down and unable to advance.

Riley and Anita were simultaneously awakened from deep slumber attributed to an interlude filled with pleasure and romance.

They both reacted immediately after an instant exclamation and explanation from Riley, that the ranch was most likely under siege from the same band of renegades who attacked yesterday, likely now with many more braves and more firepower.

"Ri-ley, whatever shall we do? Anita asked, while holding her lover tightly in her arms.

"You'd best stay right here, sweet gal. I think I'd better hurry to join in the fight . . . and don't worry, I'll be all right."

Strapping on his pistol, Riley grabbed his carbine and a box of cartridges and in a split second was outside his room.

"Riley, what's happening? Is it the Apaches again?' asked Lyle, who saw Riley emerge from his room with his weapons.

"No doubt. I'm headin' for the front of the ranch buildings, they may try to rush the front gates. Bring your rifle and hurry, it sounds like there's a million of 'em."

"Damn!" hollered Lyle, as he ran to catch up with Riley.

"'S-matter with you?" asked Riley. "I've only got about six cartridges."

Before he thought, Riley shouted to Lyle. "Right there in my room—there's an extra box of cartridges on the dresser."

Lyle turned and made his way the few steps to the room and started to enter.

"Wait!" shouted Riley, "I-I'll get them for you." It was too late, Lyle was as surprised as she was when he flung the door wide and saw an abashed Anita covering her semi-nude body with the seråpe used for a bed spread.

"Oh-my-God! Oh-my God," he stammered. "Yeah, well . . . just get the damn shells and let's go," Riley barked. "I'll try to explain later—and fer God's sake, Lyle . . ."

"I know, I know. Don't say anything."

As the two men hurried along the tiled ramada, they met Delorés, and Riley stopped and told her where she could find Anita.

"Yo no hablar, señor, an' I know where she will be. No probléma., yo preocupaciøn." (do not worry, I will take care of her and I will not speak of it).

The fighting was furious; there must have been close to two hundred warriors in the surrounding area of the ranch buildings.

Riley and Lyle ran toward one of the parapets affixed to the front wall placed in each corner. Don Jorgé was mounted on his gray Andalusian stallion, "Ganzo de Griz," (gray goose) who was only three years old.

As Riley passed by Don Jorgé on his way to climb the parapet, he thought the greeting from the patrøn was mixed with a touch of concern, not for him, but rather for Anita. Riley answered the Don's "buenos dias." with a loud response that 'Anita's safe'.

"Now why did I say that?" he thought to himself, "what a fool he must think me."

"All the women are safe, Don Jorgé," Lyle immediately shouted, as he gazed back at Riley, with a quizzical look.

Don Jorgé had amassed a mounted force of about a dozen of his men, well armed with rifles and ammunition bandoliers crossing their chests and awaiting orders.

Ramøn suddenly appeared on the scene and managed to persuade his father not to open the gates to pursue the Apache forces.

There still were about ten men afoot, and shooting at the Indians from inside. Six or seven more vaqueros were at the side and rear of the haciendas, plus Ramøn and Riley and Lyle. Altogether, the Reventon defenders numbered about thirty-three men.

As most were married and had families, the total population may have included near eighty-five people in the compound.

At times the air would be filled with a flag of arrows, aimed to fall inside the wall, but the steady flump, flump of rifle fire came from the hostiles indicating many more rifles than previously figured.

It was well into mid-morning, with neither side relinquishing their shooting.

Suddenly the Apache rifles were silent and only the arrows flew sparsely. Ramøn said the Indians were gathering to perform a medicine dance, and to expect another attack in only a short while.

Don Jorgé was certain that this break in the shooting from the hostiles was the right time to reassemble his 'cavalry' and ride out to confront the Apaches. He felt they were not expecting an assault from his vaquéros valientés, (brave cowboys) and this would give him an advantage to kill more.

"Abierto la puerta, muy pronto, tengo prisa!" (open the gate at once, I'm in a hurry), commanded Don Jorgé. "Ade lan támos" (let us go forward, he said to his men.

Twelve brave men, loyal to Don Jorgé, well mounted and well armed, dispersed out the front gate into the oft-cut mesquites and underbrush of the desert surroundings.

The Apaches did have sentinels out and saw the charge of the Reventon horsemen.

While the main body of warriors were nearly a mile beyond, about six of the well hidden lookouts began to fire on the horsemen, which alerted the rest who were in their medicine-making camp, concentrating on conjuring up enough medicine to attack.

Unfortunately, for the horsemen, the Apache lookouts were hidden and shot at the men as they passed by their concealments.

The first two men and their horses were struck down by Apache bullets, fired from their Springfield rifles. So well concealed were the Apaches, that Don Jorgé's men had great difficulty seeing where they were; only by the discharged smoke from the weapons, could they tell.

Ten were left, and as they turned to ride back, Don Jorgé's horse was hit and he threw his rider to the earth. The vaquero closest to his Jefé, dismounted and offered his horse to the Don, who was hit in his back while mounting. his vaquero leapt up behind him and immediately raced for the front gate while supporting his injured patrøn.

The rifle fire alerted the Apaches who were finishing their ceremonies, and they started back to continue the fight at the ranch, now rejuvenated spiritually. Alas, one more brave vaquero was killed before the rest made it safely back inside.

CHAPTER THIRTY ONE

Three men killed and Don Jorgé's injury caused Ramøn to become intensely upset. He ordered his father be taken to one of the rooms off the kitchen where a nurse station was set up. This, of course, was already being done. There was no time now to mourn the loss of the vaqueros; the Indians, being dominate in their tactics, were advancing.

There was some heavy fighting that broke out again near the corrals. Several more Apaches managed to scale the corral wall in their attempt to get to the horses.

Most of the swarthy warriors were clad in breech clouts with a long-sleeved shirt of muslin or calico covering them and fastened around their waist with a riåta or a concho-belt.

Their feet and legs were bound to their knees with with leather moccasins whose toes were curled back aiding them in avoiding cactus.

Their long, black hair was encircled with a colorful band and their faces painted with a white stripe.

Foreboding in their appearance and stealthy in their approach, The Apache man was a difficult enemy to engage in combat.

In addition to a bandolier of rifle ammunition, which not all carried, the typical warrior either had a short bow and a quiver of long arrows, or a rifle. Each holstered a metal knife, fashioned from discarded iron pieces or wagon wheels and heated, pounded and shaped to their liking.

The Apache's ability to live off the desert's natural resources, a faculty to go for long, long periods of time without any water, and the endurance and body strength nurtured from early childhood provided them with an exceptional and methodical resolve.

One of several Apaches who was able to scale the corral wall managed to hide himself from sight of the defenders, and then proceeded to search for his cohort, known well to him as 'Néne', and set him free.

Just as the renegade crawled out from behind the cover of stacked hay, he was seen by Joaquîn, who immediately knocked him down from behind and took his rifle. It was a surprise to Joaquîn to find this man was none other than 'Chato', the hereditary chief of this band.

Joaquîn and one other man bound the Apache and took him to the back side of the stable where Néne was kept tied inside a stall.

The other two Apaches who managed to scale the corral wall were both caught in a crossfire from the defenders and were slain.

Some of the warriors were sniping from the front side of the ranch, and were concealed in a few of the tall Arizona sycamore trees that lined a pathway to the north side of the ranch. They had an advantage of a higher trajectory for their rifle fire, but were too far away for effective arrow use.

With the large number of Indians it was not likely they were informed of the plight of Chato, at least none in the main group at the south side. Ramøn had seen Lyle temporarily abandon his position at one parapet and climb up to fire against movements of the enemy at the front gate.

Lyle had killed four of the renegades when he left to get more ammunition, and now Ramøn had open shots at several of the red men.

After Lyle abandoned his spot on the corner parapet in his search to locate more cartridges, he came upon Francisco Valdéz. He was one of Joaquîn's men in charge of a small armory the ranch kept exactly for any confrontations such as prevailed this day.

The armory was in a small, adobe-brick structure located across from the stables where two Apache sub-chiefs were being held prisoners, and used to mete out arms and ammunition to the vaquéros.

He was present in the room when Lyle made an attempt to kill the Apache, Néne, so he was careful not to allow Lyle to see where the prisoners were tied, fearing the wrath of Joaquîn, let alone, Ramøn.

Unknown to Lyle and Francisco, Chato had managed to loosen his tied hands and he began to untie Néne and himself from the bonds that held them in the stall.

Francisco started in the room to get more cartridges for Lyle, who was outside in the breezeway observing the area.

Ramøn and Joaquîn were headed for the armory when they turned the corner and saw what was about to happen.

Chato was loose, so was Néne and both Indians reacted with lightning speed. They grabbed Lyle, whose back was to them, and disarmed him then pushed him through the doorway into the armory room with Francisco.

While Néne thrust a stick through the door hasp, trapping Francisco and Lyle inside, Chato whirled around and dropped to one knee, and took level aim at Joaquîn and Ramøn.

No one, save Lyle, knew the rifle that Chato took from him, was empty of any bullets.

Joaquîn and Ramøn stopped at once and Joaquîn spoke to both Indians in Spanish, a language both chiefs understood.

"Momento, hombrés, no tirar; nos hablås" (don't shoot, wait a minute, we talk).

"Los Apache matar Mexicanos, en todos y ustedes primeros auxilîos," said Chato, assuredly. (the Apaches will kill all the Mexicans and you are to be first).

No sooner than Chato spoke, but Riley came around the corner and saw the two Apaches confronting Joaquîn and Ramøn. He instantly fired his carbine into Chato knocking him down and then shot Néne. The bullet that struck Néne passed through his arm and struck his rib cage, only wounding him, again. However, the shot which felled Chato ended his life at once.

"What's happened here?" Riley asked. "How'd that Injun get loose? Who is this other one?—looks like he's a goner, boys."

While Ramøn explained the situation to Riley, Joaquîn quickly unlatched the armory door and freed Lyle and Francisco.

They were unaware of the outcome and while Francisco and Joaquîn checked on both Apaches—Lyle merely grinned and thanked Riley, saying the rifle they took from him had no cartridges in it—"that's why I was looking for more ammunition."

"Whatta ya plan to do with that one that's hurt?" asked Riley, "fix him up?"

"I say we kill him dead and hoist his head up high on a pole with the other one, so them 'Paches can see what happened to their big medicine-chiefs," Lyle answered.

While the men were discussing the plight of these wretches, they were told by others that the Apaches were running away.

Four men rushed to the front of the ranch, while Francisco took Néne back to the stable and retied him before tending his wounds. When Ramøn reached the front gate with Joaquîn, Lyle and Riley, they were greeted with cheers from other vaqueros, saying the fighting stopped.

Riley climbed the parapet again and shouted down that he could see a column of Army soldiers approaching. The Apaches had seen them, too, prompting their departure.

Ramøn joined Riley on the parapet and declared, "Eet ees Tenienté Lopez, and also Capîtan Car-tîer weeth hees soldados."

Carter deployed his men systematically according to their training, thus they were able to cut off most of the fleeing Apaches.

Lieutenant Lopez brought one company straight ahead toward the front gate of the Reventon, which by now was opened, and had them form up inside for defense purposes.

Captain Carter sent one company to flank the Apaches and one to pursue, which proved prudent and resourceful, resulting, after a final count, of killing forty-six Apaches—the rest of them finally escaped.

It was late afternoon when the fight ended. Ramøn was sensitive to take over until he felt Don Jorgé was well enough to preside.

Four vaqueros were slain and three more wounded, one badly. All the women and children gathered around the troops who bivouaqued outside the gates for the night.

Lieutenant Lopez sent a detail to dispose of all the bodies they could find, and drag away the dead horses. The soldiers found two horses that had wounds severe enough so they needed attention. As luck would have it, one of the horses was Don Jorgé's big grey.

When Joaquîn examined him he felt he could treat his wounds so that he would survive any problems.

Ramøn couldn't wait to tell his father.

CHAPTER THIRTY TWO

While all the people were pleased the Apache was defeated again, the mood was somber and preparations were made to hold the burial services.

Don Jorgé requested there be no more celebrations, at least for a while. There was much work to do, repairing the grounds of the ranch, and rebuilding better corrals.

Purple shadows started to fall when Riley and Anita finally found one another. This time there was little formality. The two greeted each other openly, exchanging a lingering kiss before they sought out the presence of Donna Isabella, for supper.

There was plenty of food in the larder of the huge ranch kitchens, and the tables were set to feed not only the family, but the rest of the people in the compound.

Captain Carter and Lieutenant Lopez were invited to eat inside with Ramøn and were grateful for a hearty meal; their men being relegated to their own bivouac food.

Two men brought Don Jorgé to the table at his insistence, where he could dine with other members of his family. He was placed at the head of the table and made a little more comfortable by being propped up with large pillows.

A Portuguese wine was opened in which to toast the health of all the survivors.

Wild turkey was served with squash and black-eyed peas the ranch had harvested and stored. Sweet melons and flan was offered for desert, enough for everyone.

Conversation turned from discussions of the days fighting, to more personal questions as to everyone's future plans.

"I know that I've decided to return to our—my ranch, and prepare to work to make it an enterprising development," Lyle said, in answer to Ramøn's question to him. "With the help you've already offered me and a few of your registered herd bulls, plus some of the horses we've talked about, it should not take along time to bring to fruition."

"Eet ees well to hear your decision, amigo miå," stated Ramøn, "and I shall make haste to honor my part of thees bargain."

213

"Tell us your plans, Riley O'Rourke," Donna Isabella inquired. "or have you decided as yet?" she finished, giving him an out in which to respond.

Before Riley answered he carefully searched the eyes of both the Donna and Don Jorgé, whose steely glance seemed to easily penetrate into Riley's mind.

"Fact is, amigos bienes, (good friends) I have not yet made a decision as to just when I should leave. It may be, Don Jorgé, that I might be of some assistance to you."

"Tell me, friend Riley.'

"Well, sir . . . I figured with Ramøn going with Lyle, as he promised, to accompany the livestock to the Henthorn ranch, that I might be able to help here . . . 'til his—uh, return. Besides, I'm beholden to you for so many things, this may be one way to repay." Riley looked quickly at Donna Isabella, who was not at all taken in by his statement, and then glanced at the blushing Anita.

As if in defense of Riley, Joaquîn arose and stated, "Jefé, it would be of great help if he remained. We lost Renåldo, our horse breaker, to the Apache devils."

"I commend you, señor," Don Jorgé said to Riley, "Eet will be our pleasure to have you weeth us, at least until Ramøn returns."

The conversation was absorbed by everyone at the table, and none were pleased as much as Anita, who averted her eyes when her mother looked over to her.

"Well, that settles it," spoke Lyle. "I figure I can be ready to leave tomorrow, how say you?" "Dos dios," Ramøn answered. "I theenk I weel need two days, amigo, to round up and collect the proper stock for us to take."

"No problem, meanwhile, let's have a look at those colts, Ramøn."

"If you will excuse me," Riley said, "I see Joaquîn is finished, and I may as well go with him now and start to get lined-out on what's expected of me. Con permissîon, Donna y Don Jorgé."

"Of course, my son," answered Donna Isabella, while Don Jorgé issued forth a loud clearing of his throat.

Anita couldn't keep her eyes off Riley when he stood to leave, and excused herself that she may immediately follow.

The day arrived that Lyle and Ramøn were to leave for the Henthorn ranch high in the Santa Ritas with two good, young bulls and four heifers (the cows made it easier to drive the bulls), plus six, young ranch horses.

Five were recent geldings who had not yet reached their third birthday. They all comprised the livestock to be moved.

Armando and Miguel were the vaqueros who volunteered as the stock men this time.

It had been two and a half days since the assault on El Reventon, and no one felt the Apaches would gather enough warriors to start up again . . . especially since the Third Cavalry of U.S. soldiers soundly defeated the main force they'd been pursuing since they formed some time ago.

Two days of work on the new corrals presented much larger spaces and much more convenience to work penned cattle and the horses. This morning, Riley was to begin his job of breaking and riding some of the "rough stock" horses that were needed soon, as the replacement for the ranch's "caballåda".

The early morning brought several of the ranch people to watch Riley perform.

The first horse Riley was to ride was brought into a round corral, already under saddle but snubbed up close to an older horse ridden by Joaquîn. This big, dark bay horse had the saddle on his back only once before.

Renåldo, the horse breaker who'd been slain in the fight with the Apaches, worked this colt only one time, putting the saddle on and off his back enough times that he became a little bit more used to it. He climbed on his back only once, however.

Riley was aware that he would be riding "second-saddle." Often, the second or third time a bronc rider attempts to ride an unbroken horse it's more likely to try to get the rider off his back. The first time, the horse is more frightened, the next time it's more determined.

Joaquîn placed a blindfold over the horses' eyes, and over the halter it wore, and Riley started to mount. When the rider was ready Joaquîn jerked the blindfold off and unloosened the snub-rope.

The round corral where the ride began was about fifty feet in circumference and heavy, hand-hewn oak poles surrounded it.

With the blindfold removed, the bay suddenly realized he was under saddle with a strange object on his back. His first move was to stretch out with his front legs and place his belly close to the ground; so close, in fact, Riley's stirrups were nearly touching the soft, dirt ground.

Riley could feel the muscles in the horse bunch-up and prepared himself for the mighty leap up and forward the beast took.

The horse was squealing and snorting and trying his best to get his head between his front legs, which he accomplished with relative ease, given his size and strength.

As he surged ahead he literally had all his feet in the air at one time, and landed with such power he actually jarred the stirrup loose on one side. Riley was still in the middle of the saddle but he was going higher and higher off it with each jump.

This performance lasted at least two minutes which is exhausting not only for the rider, but also the animal. Next, he started to spin and then spin and jump, a most difficult movement in which to adjust. The cowboy lined him out after a few more jumps and let the horse run around the inside of the corral.

After Riley regained his stirrup, he was more comfortable with his ride. The horse was tiring some and it was slowing down with each pass around.

When finally the horse came to a full standstill, Riley reached forward, grabbed one ear of the horse, near the top of the halter, slid his hand lower on the saddle and then slipped off the horse's back.

Joaquîn rode alongside the bronc and grabbed the dangling halter rope and dallied it around his own saddle horn. He led the semi-exhausted horse around for a very short time, while speaking softly to him as he did so.

Two men, afoot, slowly went to the horse, and while one gently stroked his neck, the other removed the big saddle, then they turned him loose in the adjoining corral with other horses.

Riley was ready for the next horse and another ride, as soon as his saddle was put on the new horse, a smaller, grulla with a black mane and tail, and a kinder eye than the bay . . . at least, Riley thought so.

As soon as the blindfold was off and the dally rope loosened, Riley knew he had a handful of one tough, little horse. This one leapt straight up in the air and while doing, lunged forward a full twenty feet. He dropped his head and snaked around with his tail almost covering his nose, and then reversed himself with a whip-saw move that nearly lost Riley from the saddle.

Amid some whoops and howls from the attending vaqueros, appreciating a good balanced ride, Riley managed a smile as he passed by the heavy rails on his way around the corral again.

He glanced up once, quick enough, to see Anita and Delores among several others watching from outside the corral. When Riley looked again he made the fatal mistake of losing his concentration, and as quick as an instant the wiry beast had unseated him.

He totally lost his balance and was flipped as easily as a pancake through the air, landing against the side rails of the oak corral. Not only did the horse throw him, Riley caught a hind foot to the side of his head before he landed.

CHAPTER THIRTY THREE

Anita and Delores were both at Riley's bedside when he awoke from the trauma of the kick to his head, suffered earlier that morning at the bronc corral. No bones were broken, they'd earlier determined, but the side of his face and jaw was very swollen and discolored.

The moment Riley opened his eyes and recognized Anita, Delores discretely slid past the door from his room and slipped away.

"Oh, Ri-ley, no dado usted, alma miå." (you did not die, my darling.) Müy valiénte usted, (you are so brave.) Anita exclaimed.

"Well, well," he meekly replied, "the last thing I remember is you watching me as I passed by you on that horse the devil made, back at the corral." Riley tried smiling when he said this but his jaw hurt when he did so. It hurt to talk.

"Don't say anything now, Ri-ley, just stay quiet and I weel help chu get comfortable."

While he wanted to speak, he didn't, he just kept thinking how he got into this mess.

A day passed bringing great improvement not only in Riley's slight concussion, but in the reduction of all the swelling in his jaw and also improvement in his appetite, for now he was certain it wouldn't hurt him to chew.

Early evening brought Anita to Riley's room, instead of Delores, with his supper.

"Looks like I'm becoming quite a care for you and your family," Riley said, when she entered his spacious room with his meal.

"La concinera (cook) ees thee wan who prepare thees for chu, Ri-ley, not me, Anita answered, "and she ees cooking for no matter who eats eet . . . it's her chob. She say I must bring eet to you, then eet weel taste much better . . . I hope so!"

"Everyone's been so great to me, and especially your family, it's no wonder I've fallen in love with . . . with . . ."

"Yes, Ri-ley?" Anita interrupted.

"Well,—with everyone here," he said, teasing her, while he watched her beautiful dark eyes narrow and then widen again.

Before Anita could respond, Riley rose from his bed and captured her, holding her waist for support, and ardently kissed her moist lips with his. Startled, and concerned for him, she started to back away.

"It's all right, darlin', my jaw doesn't hurt, and even if it did—which it doesn't, your soft lips would ease any pain there might be, I really do feel much better."

It was early evening and darkness had not found this beautiful ranch beside the Santa Cruz river, and would not for a while so Riley closed the inside shutter to the only window in the room, bolted the door, and returned to enfold Anita in his arms.

"Ri-ley," she whispered softly, "are you certain you know what you're getting into?"

"Of course . . . I do now."

"I mean, what thees weel lead to een the long term—how I feel about chu—and how chu say you feel about me . . . do you?"

"I'm positive, 'Nita. I've been thinking about you and our situation for a long time, but especially since I've been here, by myself, in this room . . . and I've got to say something to you . . . now."

She held her breath, as he held her.

"Anita Maria, will you do me the honor of being my wife?"

She threw her arms around him, as he ever-so-gently eased her on to the bed beside him, and answered with tears in both eyes, an emphatic and dramatic—"Oh, yes—yes."

"You know, meester cow-boy, chu weel have to ask my father for my hand in marry-age . . . and he weel say . . . no!" she teased.

"I think I'll just ask your mother," Riley said to her, as he carefully untied the ribbon in her hair, and unloosened the belt she wore to her corriénte trousers.

"Yo creer loco, usted," she giggled.

"You think I'm crazy?" Riley said with a straight face.

"Oh, no—no—well, maybe a leetle."

"For wanting to marry you, or for only wanting to ask your mother if I could?"

She didn't respond to his questions. Instead, she very seriously divested herself from the rest of her clothing and laid back down beside her handsome cowboy in the warm, dusky confines of his chambers.

"Kiss me, again," she whispered, alma miå, an' hol' me close that I may never be apart from you. I love you so very much . . . you make me so very hoppy."

Joaquîn was at the horse corral when Riley walked up to the swinging gate;

"¿Buenos dias, qe tal, amigo miå,?" (good morning, how you doing, my friend?) Riley signaled Joaquîn,

"Dias, señor, eet ees good to see you.

It was very early. The stabled horses were only now being fed their morning hay. Obviously, there were two souls who, most likely, did not sleep the night away.

Several hours earlier, during the blackness of the early morning, Anita was able to discretely slip away to her own habitatiøn (bedroom), and nervously await the early dawn.

Anita would join everyone at the large ranch dining salon for breakfast later.

Riley was explaining to Joaquîn how he was feeling so much better, and imploring him to allow him to continue with his horse breaking chore as soon as possible.

"Of course, señor, as you wish, I theenk we can continue de la mañana." (early in the morning, tomorrow.)

"Muchas gracias, (many thanks) Joaquin," Riley answered, as he made his way up to the dining room.

Everyone was surprised and pleased to see Riley arrive for breakfast, especially Donna Isabella, and they welcomed him with questions pertaining to his well-being.

He answered by announcing he'd spoken to Joaquîn earlier arranging to continue his job of horse breaking tomorrow morning.

As he finished saying this, his eyes lit up with brightness as Anita casually walked into the room and after greeting her parents, took a chair right next to Riley.

He immediately rose, assisted in seating her, and duly impressed Donna Isabella.

The talk progressed with Riley telling Don Jorgé how well he was healing, and also what his feeling was of the Indian exigency.

"With Chato (Flat Nose) dead, and Néne captured," the Don responded, "I do not theenk we shall see much hostile action. Een fact, I spoke weeth Ramøn before he left and hees thoughts were thee very same."

"Two of my vaqueros weel take Néne to the Indian agent een Tucson next week, and they weel deal weeth heem. I have heard that a General Crook, weeth the Army is starting a campaign against the Chiricahuas soon."

The Fifth Cavalry and Twenty-third Infantry, both veteran Indian-fighting outfits, had arrived in Arizona and settled in at the few, scattered military posts.

General Crook had his pack trains, his wagon units, animals, and his communication networks at top efficiency. His scout units were compromised of mostly Indians, such as reservation Apaches, Walapais, and a few Piautes. His orders were that all roving bands of Indians would have to go on reservations, or be classified hostile and be severely punished.

The Fifth cavalry was dispatched, at first, farther north toward the Salt river canyon, where they mainly sought the large band of Tonto-Apaches who were making life miserable for settlers near the Gila. Soon they would start south after the might of the renegade Chiricahuas and Geronimo.

Captain Carter had been reassigned to the Fifth cavalry from the Third, which was the force that drove the Apache from the Reventon ranch, and was united with the Fifth on their way south from the Gila river to the confines of the lush Santa Cruz valley.

The discussions concerning the outcome of the serious Indian situation continued as small talk until breakfast was over.

Since Ramøn, the only other member of the Moralés family was not present, the table consisted of Don Jorgé, Donna Isabella and Anita Maria, plus Riley O'Rourke.

It was he, then, who suddenly arose, placed one hand on Anita's shoulder, and with the other gesticulated a movement.

"If it would please you, Don Jorgé, and Donna Isabella, I would most humbly request you hear my thoughts regarding your hija (daughter) Anita Maria. You see, I have fallen totally in love with her, as she has with me, and I wish to ask you both for her hand in marriage, and your blessings for our lifetime of a wedded unison."

"Absol . . ." the Donna started to say.

"Riley," the Don interrupted his wife, and started to interject his thoughts, I wish to . . ."

"Yo té amo los dos," (I love you both) Anita stood to say, "and I shall respect your decision, but I wish to tell you both how much in love I am weeth Ri-ley, an' I weesh very much to be marry—ed to heem and become his wife . . . please geeve to us chor blessings."

Don Jorgé summoned all his strength, and pushed his chair away from the table so he could rise. "Señor Riley O'Rourke, as I started to say, you shall be a most welcome member of this family, and I most heartily extend my blessing for you and Anita Maria to become casado (married)."

Donna Isabella breathed an extended sigh, and smiling, with tears in the corner of her eye, greeted them with sincere words for their perpetual happiness.

In the moment that it took Anita to rush to the outstretched arms of her mother, Riley walked to Don Jorgé and grasped his hand in eternal gratitude and with words reassuring the Don of his intentions to care for his daughter.

Anita and Riley exchanged places with each other and were welcomed accordingly in the same manner, Riley, with the Donna and Anita, joyfully, in their father's loving arms.

Preparations were started for a "Baile Grande," and a wedding ceremony to be held in the beautiful gardens of the Reventon ranch.

A rider was dispatched to the Henthorn ranch so Ramøn and Lyle would have time to prepare to attend the festivities planned for the end of the following month.

The everyday chores continued. Vaqueros tended the cattle and Riley performed his role as horse breaker, certain Ramøn would be proud of him on his return.

Riley and Anita were very much in love and carefully contained their amorous plans until the wedding, although they rode together often.

Joaquîn was so pleased for his friend that he offered Riley and Anita the gift of a young pup from the litter his dog whelped.

Riley grinned and said, aloud, "This pup should do just fine, when he and I ride over the Santa Ritas. I reckon I might surprise my folks when I show up at the ranch with a new dog—oh, yeah . . . and also with a brand new, beautiful wife."

THE END

dislocation, but it's also our very strangeness as a lost and dis-
pecies that accounts for our being funny, and being funny is
ates us from the basic lies of the Success Propaganda, all that's
m and blah, blah, blah. It's being funny that's liberating, that
saves us.

t's that we are almost always just *so incredibly lost* that serves
ompass, my ballast, whatever dark, molecularly dense material
laced in the hold of my soul that gives me stability in heavy seas,
s is why failure is so *valuable* to me and why I keep it stuffed in
st secret pocket of my jacket like a little thingy of Kryptonite.

is wrongness I come by genetically, in that it derives from why
like mine even ended up in the West, where the sun's blaze has
ly turned against me and my skin has become bizarrely allergic.

he name of this condition is photosensitivity, which is a height-
response to ultraviolet radiation, but what I really think is that I've
oversaturated by the sunniness of the place and its relentless opti-
, that my skin—and I have always somehow reasoned with either
elly or my skin—has now just basically *had it*.

I've always done an adequate job of masquerading as an ordinary
on, having learned this by living with my aunt and uncle. I've learned
omport myself and think of this as *passing*. I have somehow even
ked this man I love into loving me, and this man isn't even some-
flawed and broken and wrecked, like the usual guys who'd come
und, all hangdog and slobbery, but someone I actually adore, about
om I was and am still ardent.

What's wrong with me is that I have so many conflicting things go-
g on, and *all at once*, that I feel crowded, also lonely, also buffered and
alled off and numb. This pertains to something I've read somewhere:
at the dead surround the living, that our work in being alive is to
rve as the beating heart of them, that the living and the dead are all

things as proof of evil in the world, he told me once: my mother and
the Republican Party.

But he believed the best about almost everyone else and still thought
the errant wife was probably, one day, coming back to him. He wasn't
cynical. He had no idea at all of his effect on women. And despite his
mother, or maybe even because of her, he actually *liked* women and had as
many women friends as he did men. He seemed to listen to everyone with
an air of respectful attentiveness, as if this person might have something
interesting to say and he, Jack, was maybe going to learn something.

And there was no doubt that it was because I was already so sicken-
ingly married and he was completely unattainable that made it easy for
me to love him. It helped, too, that he did nothing to act seductive, in
that acting seductive is so often fake.

In those days he'd walk me back to my SUV and open the door, and
in his mannerly way that was in no way reserved for me, he'd close the
door, then lean in through the open window to kiss me on the lips—but
then, he kissed everyone on the lips, I'd noticed. I'd seen him kiss his
own grown sons on the lips.

He'd kiss me, then say in parting, So, call me next week and we'll
have lunch? and I'd say okay, but I'd be thinking, *But we just* had
lunch. I didn't think this was *exactly* how the writer/editor relationship
was supposed to go, but what did I know, since I'd never before been
in one?

So we'd have lunch, then another lunch, and when I was back out
on the road again a little while later, promoting my book—this may
have been the paperback—it happened that, by sheer coincidence, Jack
and I were going to be in New York over the same few days. It was
purely lucky in that this happened through neither his guile nor mine.

Neither of us had any control over any of these events: that someone else had arranged that I'd be staying at the Westbury on the Upper

East Side, this being paid for by some media entity that can afford this sort of travel—and it was here, I'd discover, that a bowl of berries with cream and a pot of room-service coffee cost $28, *and this was in the 1990s!*—and Jack was going to be staying at the Algonquin, which was where he always stayed, where he had a sales conference.

As he walked me to the car, he asked me to call him when I got to New York, so that we could go out for coffee or maybe go to a museum together. Call me, he said, looking at me over the tops of his sunglasses, and maybe we can get into a little trouble.

loss and
located
what ele
humdru
actually
So
as my
that's p
and th
the mo

The Lea

Th
peopl
sudde

T
ened
been
misn
my

IT IS MY PROFOUND belief that there is something
that it's this wrongness that keeps me loyal to my

I believe in failure. This means *failure* isn't anyth
with. My parents were just *so good* at being *such spe*
better than almost anyone. And I'm *proud* of this a
these are *my people*, my own mother and my own f
born to, and I have no real wish to ever let them go.

So *failure* profoundly appeals to me, as it feels bot
and I believe in failure in the way I don't basically be
Propaganda that people put out in their Christmas lette
seem to stink of the ink of faint Republicanism, and eve
verifiably, fact-checkably true, it still just doesn't much i

Failure just seems like the more intimate and import
you're born, that then you die, and that life between ust
as one long grim trudge westward into the hinterlands, a
there are these bright moments of almost unaccountable jo
ly? mostly? it just is not that. Mostly, it's this story of rest

pers
to
tric
on
ar
w

in
w
t
s

in this together, that we form, in fact, one elaborated body, and for the moment we're the ones who are representative of what it is to *be alive*, which was once the job of our dead, and they are stationed only slightly off and out from us, but in close proximity, only occupying another intimate plane in time.

I feel them, the physical spirit of my parents, who are as fellow travelers on my journey, and I'm like Whitman, I believe, and self-contradictory—I contain *multitudes*. Though I often feel almost starving in my loneliness, I also am pressed by how everyone is always crowding me and how they're all loud, fractious, bossy, everyone pushing and jostling like we're all trying to simultaneously board this once-a-week train in some remote part of India. I am honestly *never* alone, and all I want—I believe—is to be left alone for one goddamn minute so I can maybe concentrate. I think if I'm alone for a moment, I can maybe hear the song someone might be out there trying to sing, and that this someone might be me.

The dead cluster around us, they depend upon us to keep them alive in our thoughts, and as we are the beating heart of them, they inform us of who we are. But we now have the human body upon which experience may still be written and that still may do useful work, and this is the holy function of our physicality.

We are the body and they depend upon our bodies to carry on enacting them, so it is with their will and urging that we go on into life to do these things we are destined for—they want us to because they know our bodies, too, will so soon be gone, and with them these physical pleasures. Then we go to join them, clustered as they are off in the vast forever, which is Timelessness.

So it could be that what's wrong with me is that my own family's time in the West is too brief, too thin, that our dead are so outnumbered by those who've walked here throughout millennia, and that people like my father and me—those of us who suffer from sensitivities, photo-istically or otherwise—cannot help but intuit this.

Our dead are simply outnumbered, which is why we're so lonely here. We stole this place from others, and others are better at witnessing the transparency of all existence. Ishi saw it. He was standing on a cliff overlooking bathers on the beach when he turned to Kroeber and gestured, saying wistfully, So many ghosts.

〰

So I am living with Jack and my kids in this big gray house on Virginia Street in the flats of Berkeley, and everything ought to be perfect. We live only a couple of blocks from Chez Panisse and it's the boom in the middle of the '90s, tech driven, the Clinton years. With a Democrat in the White House, we can even *afford* to eat at Chez Panisse—if not downstairs, we can at least get a salad and a calzone in the upstairs café every once in a while.

Everything's fine, in theory—has never been more fine, in fact—in that I'm a novelist who's actually published a novel, a mother who has these two great kids, and never mind that the name of my book contains the word *Failure*. This is the kind of thing I keep magnetized next to the iron keel as a secret counterweight. I need weight and counterweight so I don't go get so ecstatic and joyous—and I have inherited from my parents a great talent for unadulterated joy—that I go flying off a roof somewhere.

I'm a *failure* because I am being *careful*.

And it ought to be easy to write another book, but it actually isn't. If anything, writing a second book is even harder than writing the first, in that I was supposed to have somehow learned how to write a novel through the act of doing it, but I obviously haven't. I'm shocked to find

I haven't learned the first thing about how to write a novel, nor am I a better writer.

I am not better—as a matter of fact, I am way, way worse.

What I'm trying to write about does happen to be something I actually know something about, which is having your entire life go stupendously to hell when you least suspect it, having shored your poor, frail, damaged, secretly waifish, really pretty adolescent self up in the fortress of a marriage to this really crabby old guy, who's like something out of a fairy tale and has this ogreish streak that you no doubt have actually exacerbated in him with your usual tricks and antics. And it was never really fair when all he really was was this rather old-fashioned person who wanted an old-fashioned marriage and who didn't go by the tricks of a person like you, with your newfangled sort of New Age-ish rules of being a Californian of your own specific generation—and it's true and you can't help it that you're one of the dread 77 Million Baby Boomers who are *always* changing the rules, and it isn't really because we've meant to, it's only actually that there are *so many of us* that when we decide something, more often than not, what we say goes.

This is the name of the rule we mainly go by: Majority Rules.

And the rules will be the same, the same, the same, then abruptly change, might remind you of is idling out beyond the breakline on the longboard you used to use, in that it was never exactly your own board, as it was junky and you had to sometimes share it with your cousin Jordy, but then at least you weren't always responsible for carrying it, as it was dinged and waterlogged. But you'd be out there face-first, belly down, just paddling around and basically waiting on the smooth, glassy, almost entirely placid sea, and everyone you'd be with, who were much better, more determined surfers, would be all pissed and impatient, but you weren't; you were happy enough to be doing nothing so much as *waiting*, as you had this great and confident talent for waiting, and what you were waiting for wasn't even the next big wave or the rogue one that would smash whatever's peaceful and Pacific, it was simply to be in this state of keen, buoyant, watchful, even extraordinarily alert *anticipation.*

And out of this watchfulness and sense of anticipation, you're writing about these two troubled Berkeley marriages, comedies of bad behavior among articulate, well-intentioned people, people who are smart, even basically kind, and who aren't exemplars of anything except folks who live in one or two very specific Zip Codes.

Which is basically just *so* not true. The book, very basically, is about sex, and you're writing it because it's occurred to you that most women don't write about sex at all, or if they do they don't do it very well, or they write from received notions that are basically lies, or from this uninvolved sort of philosophical Situation in the Sky, whose secret subtext is I'm Actually a Lofty Virgin Like Whoever the Greek Goddess Is Whose Name I'm Not Just Now Remembering, or they write from the *real down-low*, which is equally dishonest, as the secret subtext of this perspective is I'm Really a Whore, Which Should Make You Totally Want Me.

Or women write all purplish or silly and blushing or get gothic or medieval or do it with Space Aliens or become all mannered, elaborate, and Victorian, and all of this is just about equally irksome to me, and some of it makes me almost physically ill. Most writing about sex is so bad and soft core–ish and tame, which is to say conflicted, that I actually prefer the most hardcore of hardcore pornography because even if it is perverted in the eyes of some, what it *isn't* is dishonest; what it *isn't* is ulterior and creepy.

And you still suffer from the same old Word Magic, wherein Words and Deeds don't seem to have a really strong border that's particularly well maintained, so it seems like women who are writers and take all this seriously have some important work to do here, yet Your People, and by this you mean girls and women who are members of the 77 Million, are suddenly putting all these weird, really gacky words into their writing about sex, such as typing the letters that bump around, then clump together to form the clusters that spell out, really loudly, I HAVE MY PERIOD, when what you're wondering is, first, why is this something I really need to know? and second, why is this supposedly sexy?

And you suddenly realize that it isn't usually even *about sex* at all, that it's usually about shame, and that the creepy subtext almost always derives from shame, and that *everyone* is ashamed, and that we are all really so heartily sorry, and what we're sorry about is that we show up in these poor, flawed, sad, fundamentally mortal bodies, and this shame is actually something basic to us as Americans—that is, were we Pacific Islanders, we'd no doubt have our own special problems, but it wouldn't be this one.

And you realize you're ashamed as well, and that this shame is part of the secret thing that is bequeathed to you and you don't even know how you got it. Your own parents did do so many parenting things *wrong*, but teaching you to be ashamed of your human body wasn't one of them. And it occurs to you that it is because of their example that you've been able to fall in love, and that falling in love with a man who's in love with you and staying in love with this man are practically revolutionary acts, and that maybe you can write about sex from the delirious-falling-in-love-with-someone perspective, and that, having finally learned something about sex, you can maybe write something that helps to exorcise your own shame, as writing is the only thing that you've ever done that honestly feels completely helpful.

⦿⦿⦿

This is during the Time Period, as my daughter says, and it is probably as a corollary to the economic boom, when every other marriage in Berkeley, or at least in these two or three little Zip Codes with which I have an acquaintance, has foundered or struggled and either does or doesn't come apart but rattles on down the road, and it is very often true that Somebody Else *is* involved, despite all these protestations to the contrary.

Somebody Else is usually involved. What people around here prefer to say is that it's a mutual parting of the ways, and My People, by which I mean the 77 Million—who honestly believed this kind of thing was basically beneath us—feel it's just so sickly retro, so sort of fifties, sixties, seventies, and clichéd to have Somebody Else Being Involved as a reason to wreck your marriage, which ruins not only your own life but also the lives of all your various loved ones.

It's almost *always* Someone Else, at least in my experience, and what this person's name is, frankly, honey? *Anyone* But You.

I believed it was beneath my basic dignity to have fallen in love with one man while I was married to my children's father, and I was so ashamed at the Glamour-Trashy nature of this not particularly original plotline, how it made me feel *exactly* like a friend of mine, a woman I really liked whose kids went to school with my kids. This woman who one week was laughing affectionately at how her truly diminutive husband, a man who in truth was as preternaturally small as he was almost astonishingly wealthy, needed to buy his suits in the boys' department, and wasn't that sweet?

That was one week. The next she was there in the carpool lane in her new sports car in a badass color, top down, and her car was being driven by her black, unbelievably beautiful, and almost embarrassingly studly personal trainer whose name is Marcus, and she was waving, waving, like she was on a float and was *ecstatic*, having just been crowned queen of the Rose Parade.

So I'm evolving this theory that this has something to do with the stats on my side of the 77 Million, all these women who have just turned forty or are turning forty in a little while, and how forty is the new thirty, or maybe it's more descriptively the new twenty-six, so we're all now acting *exactly* like we did when we were way, way younger, having basically missed this important step in growing up, and we're all back up to our same old tricks and acts of mischief.

So I've created these characters who enact these half-patched-together, semi-sociological theories of mine, my characters being composites or sometimes flat-out caricatures of the French I've met through my children's school, which is Ecole Bilingue, and the eventual publication of this book will result in some of these people's never again speaking to me.

I'm coming to realize that we are collectively—by which I mean both My People and the 77 Million—one of history's worst nightmares. We are *exactly* what everyone was afraid of. We are what happens when the woman side of the 77 Million takes control of Our Own Reproductive Destiny, then sets out to teach this simple truth not only to our daughters, but also to our sons.

The new rules are simple: Henceforth, we say, we refuse to bleed to death on the trail west, nor will we stay married to the man who walks into the house and automatically shouts at us, Hang up the goddamned phone.

So it's now actually the wives in almost every case I've personally encountered who have simply one day—and probably while shopping in the produce aisles of Andronico's—decided they've just *had it* with these poor, long-suffering, sad-sackish schlubs who walk around the streets of Berkeley with their advanced degrees from excellent universities, cringing, self-pityingly counting out their vitamins in their seven-day plastic compacts from the health-food store, as they daintily sip their decafs outside Café Romano on Shattuck, looking basically poleaxed or at least fundamentally and even existentially startled, as if they've been jolted with a psychic stun gun.

What My People, because of the rigors of biology, have caught sight of is something it was never possible to see before, and this is that the journey westward goes on and on, maybe infinitely, and there is amazing hope in this. We also know we basically don't need them, and they know we know that now, so what underlies the tattered souls of the solitary castoffs is this dark and growing desperation, as they measure out their herbal vitamins and count them one by one.

〇〇〇

And it is the wives in each of the two marriages I'm writing about who one day, while gazing away into the middle distance, realize they must *get out!*, that they are at least profoundly and fundamentally bored, if not turned off, repulsed, and this is a deep secret in the straw poll of marriage in these, the last waning days of the twentieth century: Women who aren't happy in their marriages are no longer forced to stay!

But it's the husband in the one marriage who's fallen in love with the wife in the other one, though this husband is such a *man*, which is to say, dutiful and rule bound and Eastern, so blown down by the changes in the manners and mores of such an echt Californian place as Berkeley is turning out to be, which is kind of like it's California Squared or like California multiplied by California a hundred million times, all this California-ness pushed down into this one specific Zip Code made so tiny and dense, it'd fit into the size of the dot at the end of this sentence.

But I'm not getting anywhere with this book, in that my friend Ross Feld, who's a writer and an editor, reads a draft of what I've written and phones me to say, That, Jane, is perhaps the most angry book I have ever read, which somewhat mystifies me because—on account of childhood trauma, early loss of a parent, blah, blah, so forth—I lack what's clinically known as signal affect, in which a person may say and do these *really angry things*, such as indict one's former husband on the grounds that he's basically a total asshole, but the synapses or other neural connections are missing or at least blunted, so that while you *are* secretly really angry, you don't actually *experience* being angry, so you believe you are being fairly courteous.

And Time is ticking and we are riding this gigantic financial boom, the likes of which has never been seen, that becomes this huge rogue wave of economic prosperity, and the whole American century is winding down and everyone knows this century is the only one America will ever get and that basically we've probably blown it.

So I write and write and write and am still not getting anything done, so I regularly burn the whole fucking thing in the fireplace, which reminds me of my own parents and the nihilistic way they'd often almost *ritualistically* act.

And I'm always talking on the phone to my writer friends, as this is in advance of email and Facebook, and I'm being pointedly amusing to my own detriment as a writer and I'm driving to and from the French school where my kids are learning, as Jack says, to misspell in a couple of languages and I'm driving my daughter to soccer and my son to row crew, and there are days I drive so many miles that I get the mommy cramp in the calf of my right leg, from alternatingly braking and accelerating, and at times this is so painful and debilitating I have to get out of the car at a stoplight and hobble up and down on the asphalt to try to walk it off.

I'm trying to be a good mom and—in spite of leaving their father for another man—to not set a bad example, and I'm trying to not instill in my children shame in their human bodies and their humanly desires, so I will sometimes hear myself, at the crack of dawn, issuing these random, almost ad hoc instructions, as my own mother might have done, and I will say to the boys in the back of my SUV who are on their way to the Oakland Estuary to row crew, You guys all know about condoms, right? and they say nothing, so I say, And you do know what I mean when I say *safe sex*? and they say nothing, and so I go on, And you do know that when a girl says No, this actually does mean No? but there's no answer to even this, except the soft sound of their snoring, but I continue to tell them these things in those dark mornings as I drive, hoping that these things get through to them, as posthypnotic suggestions.

000

And it's right about here that Jack starts getting calls at home at night, proposing something that he might find interesting, but he says, Nope, he just does not find this interesting. He thinks, in fact, that it's a stockbroker making cold calls to try to drum up business, and Jack politely, because he's always polite, simply hangs up on him.

This isn't, in fact, a stockbroker and is, in fact, a headhunter from a really very famous executive placement firm that we've naturally never heard of, and Jack's hanging up on the headhunter only makes the rich man who has hired this firm want Jack all the more.

The headhunter finally has to call Jack at his office to have his assistant relay a message that *someone important* wants to speak to Jack about *something important*, but this is all so hush-hush and secret, he can give no other details. Jack is finally pestered into giving the important man two days in Washington, D.C., a single visit, for which Jack will be really very well compensated and that is actually only a consultation. So Jack agrees to be flown first-class across the country to stay at the

Hay-Adams, where you put your shoes outside your door at night and they reappear in the morning fairly *glinting*, they're so perfectly shined, and the shoe transaction happens by stealth and entirely wordlessly.

And so it evolves over one winter and spring that Jack is somehow inveigled into entering into negotiations with the important man, not a circumstance in which Jack ever wanted to find himself.

The man wants Jack to move east, but Jack doesn't want to go. This is because Jack—as he almost always is—is already in *exactly* the place he wants to be, which is living on Virginia Street in Berkeley, California, a couple of blocks below Shattuck, with me and my two kids, and his sons, who are now just about grown and are anyway out on their own, are right in our vicinity.

And we've just planted seven native species of grasses in the back-yard of the house and he has plans for renovating the falling-down garage out back as my writing studio and he's trying to quit smoking with his friend Bob, so they go on yoga weekend retreats to places in Marin where they talk the whole time the yoga lady's trying to get them to practice mindfulness, and they talk but do not smoke all weekend, then get in the car to drive home, talking, and without even discussing it, one or the other gets the pack of Marlboros out of the glove compartment and they each automatically light up, and, still talking, they drive home.

Jack is different from me in that he never exhibits the rash need to sneak out a window and race off to another climate. In the rooms of Alcoholics Anonymous, the name given this urge is Pulling a Geographic, and you can trace it genetically all the way back on my father's side to the two drunken brothers who, in the 1640s, got thrown out of Holland.

The psychology goes like this: What's really wrong with you is all *external*—another way of saying it is, Everybody Else's Fault—so all you basically have to do is change your situation, then you can show up in this New World to discover what you've always secretly hoped: that deep down, you are basically fine, that you're even *more than fine*; in fact, there's nothing at all really wrong with you.

What's wrong with me, I think, is that I'm a *Californian* who lives in *California*.

〇〇〇

The *someone important* is the man who wants Jack to come to Washington, D.C., to start a publishing company, to which Jack says absolutely not. Jack's already fully and happily working as he has always worked, doing what he loves to do and at which he's actually good, which is publishing books that are actually worth publishing, in that you can actually read them and sometimes even learn something.

And Jack has recently hung new birdfeeders in the trees in our backyard—some of these feeders hold thistle, some suet, some a mix of seeds—and he now has a new little stack of bird books, so he can sit in the shade and smoke and drink his iced tea utterly peacefully while glancing at the illustrations, then read the descriptions, then stare through binoculars at birds who are only about six or eight feet away.

Look at him, Mom, my daughter Eva whispers as we watch him from an upstairs window. He says he's memorizing the differences in three different kinds of *finches*, and her tone carries equal parts awe and accusation.

And my son, Noah, and I have recently discovered that our hands already know masonry, in that we've learned without learning how to set bricks expertly by making a ballast of coarse gravel for drainage, then loosely mortaring it with layers of sand. We're laying a path in the backyard leading from the kitchen door out to where the birder sits with his iced tea and his *Sibley's Guide to Birds*, and there's a lemon tree in the backyard that blossoms year-round, so when you fling open the windows at the back of the house, the rooms explode with the scent of citrus.

But the important man has people, who keep calling. Because he's an important man, he isn't actually used to this kind of resistance. So we begin this sideways discussion of what moving there might mean, and we're trying to think of anyone we know in Washington, D.C., which is almost literally no one aside from Mark, who works on the Hill for Representative George Miller. Mark's from Jack's old softball team, whose name is The Minds. The name of the team is actually *I saw the best minds of my generation destroyed by madness, starving hysterical naked, dragging themselves through the negro streets at dawn looking for an angry fix . . .*

The name of their softball team is actually *the entire poem.*

But Jack doesn't want to go and neither does Eva, and Noah has started Berkeley High, where he is rowing crew and has his buddies, so he says, very definitively, that he actually *will not be going,* so it's basically me. I am, after all, the haunted one, the one who feels oppressed by my personal history, who can hardly even imagine a problem that might not be readily solved by building a body in my bed and going out to change husbands.

Because I just want, for once, to live somewhere that isn't *California,* all right? Because I'm like everyone else in my family, and all of us have something basically wrong with us, and whatever it is is the genetic glitch that says, *All right, let's pack up and GO.*

And the house on Virginia Street is located literally one and three-quarters blocks from the house on McGee Avenue to which my mother and father brought me from the hospital after I was born, and with the windows open and behind the rustles of trees and the rise and fall of birdsong—the flight call of the coastal finches is described as a soft and

husky *jeeef, jeeef*—I can hear the Campanile on the campus at Cal toll-
ing the hour, and the songs pealing from the bell tower, a carillon still
being played by human hands. It feels like subtle harm is being done to
me, as if I live in a room equipped with dozens of speakers but whose
only soundtrack is the one that's called *My Loss*.

My mother has died and my parents, as ever, are crowding very
close to me. And my older brother has moved east and my younger one
has now vanished so successfully, it's as if he has been vaporized. Geo
is now one of those individuals who no longer exist on paper in any
kind of manner, and so is no longer counted in any census that isn't the
head count of homeless on a night so cold that the bureaucrats debate
whether or not to open the Armory. George Charles Vandenburgh,
born August 28, 1952, is the last direct male descendent of the last
direct male descendant, all down through the generations, and therefore on the roster of the Holland Society, last of our tribe, and—like
Ishi—gone.

And I have told myself that I will somehow be able to write of all
this from Exile, because I can't shop in the produce aisles of the Park
and Rob without being reminded that Berkeley, my Berkeley, the last
place where my mother and father were truly happy, has begun to reek
to me of generational doom.

෮

This person wooing Jack is wealthy in a way neither of us is used to—
new wealth, but this in no way shows. That his taste is impeccable is
illustrated in his single-minded pursuit of Jack, and he has Dürer's *Small
Horse* sitting newly framed on the floor of his living room in town, sitting there even casually, as it's being placed here and there in anticipation of being hung, and he has his better-than-the-Met's *St. Jerome* in

the den, and the couches in the study are the exact shade of the silvery-gray coat of his twin Weimaraners so the dog hair doesn't show.

And when Jack asks him which book he'd most like to have published, this man says, *The Meditations of Marcus Aurelius*, and Jack thinks—or so he tells me—*This is surely the least frivolous person I have ever met.*

And the man has already searched out the world's most accomplished harpsichord builder and has had this man come to the United States to live for however long it takes to build his wife a harpsichord, and though the wife doesn't actually know how to play the harpsichord, the instrument is built and they both commence their lessons, but she once whispers to me when we're off in the ladies' room of a restaurant, But I have so little musical talent . . .

And theirs is their original marriage, which I think counts for something in this day and age. I find this out as I'm wanding them for what is secretly wrong with them, whatever it is that doesn't go in the Christmas letter and that they don't want anyone to know.

They aren't drunks, I can tell, since it takes one to know one, and they may actually be almost entirely viceless, which is its own kind of problem in that it makes you so basically unlikable. He once smoked cigarettes and now only occasionally, when tense, uses the most infinitesimal speck of Nicorette that he chews with the flat edges of his front teeth.

They are formal people but not pretentious. The wife, particularly, is gracious, which I attribute to her being a Westerner and coming from Oregon. She has the same things in her various houses—in the one in the District, and in the dressing room of the poolhouse at the farm in Rappahannock County, Virginia, where the hands, a married couple who have gone to college, raise organic fruits and vegetables for the rich man's various households.

The wife keeps this serviceable and modest clutch of really good makeup—one nice lipliner, a lipstick, moisturizer, and mascara, say—all neatly organized and on the same side of the sink so she'll know where to reach for it, and her robe is hung just so, and the people who work for them and travel back and forth from town to country, who are named, no kidding, Carlos and Maria, have worked for them for a long, long time, and it occurs to me that wealth of this kind enables these people to access what is honestly excellent, to lay hands on what they need, and to surround themselves with what's worthwhile, so they don't have to waste all the time the rest of us waste trying to find what we've just mislaid.

And there's no striving in the way these people are wealthy, I notice, and being really, really rich doesn't seem to make them nervous. Nor do they act belligerently cheap, as was the style in one kind of upper crust–ish part of my own family, who'd buy off-brand liquor to serve at a party and have it conspicuously poured from the cheap bottles, just to make sure the guests knew a conscious choice had been made to *in no way* seek to impress them.

We're at the farm in Virginia, having been swimming, and are sitting in the shade by the pool when the rich man asks me, Have you ever imagined living in Zürich? Then, without actually waiting for an answer, he turns to Eva to say, Would you like to own a horse?

11
My Intended

WASHINGTON, D.C., IS A Southern town, so Jack, whose dad was from North Carolina, immediately gets it in a way I simply don't. But then, he always feels comfortable no matter where he is, which I do, too, for maybe the better part of a longish weekend before the inevitable gut-wrench thing begins in me, the tiny thought balloon that rises and presses upward on the underside of my heart, insisting, *You are* nothing *like these people.*

He quickly establishes his habits, his routines and rituals, and does this bodily by putting his boots on the ground, finding a barber, walking to and from our apartment in Dupont Circle to his offices in the Army and Navy Club on Farragut Square, his going out to the gym with Mark and LeRue. This is the same one where George Stephanopoulos trains, and Mark and LeRue—who goes by Doc—go through the roster of all the sweatily famous, all huffing along on their treadmills, pointing out who among them either is or isn't gay, and who either is or isn't gay might actually surprise you.

But then, there are *many things* about this town that are truly startling, such as seeing someone working out at the gym while wearing an FBI T-shirt, and realizing that this person is *in no way kidding.*

It also startles me to understand that we've moved directly across the country to a place where The Young are so different from the way we were when we were that age, in that they're only twenty or thirty years old but already Mean Business. They're up really early in the morning, for one thing, and they're all very nattily turned out, as if out of Another Era.

It was back in the 1950s when kids were still expected to dress and act and think like they were nothing so much as miniature adults, and it was at this juncture that my own dear parents got off *that* merry-go-round and went to pursue their more personal preferences.

Now it's the '90s, but it's a little throwbackish. It's the Clinton White House and Brooks Brothers for all, the pantsuit thing, for instance? The girls getting those odd, stretchy, slackish trousers that are just like a guy's but tighter, and everyone's striding downtown with this great seriousness of purpose, briefcases swinging along in one hand, Starbucks in the other, and there is indeed this geographical slope to the city, so it is as I sit drinking my own coffee in my sloe-eyed writerly way that makes me look like a layabout who's floating facedown out beyond the breakline believing she has *all the time in the world.*

And they do seem to flow like water toward the mighty epicenters of power, being the White House, the World Bank, the Capitol, and the various August Institutions, such as Brookings, that—because I very early on identified power as one of the truly toxic elements—I know as one of those elements I've always needed to avoid.

And in Washington, it's also important to remember this isn't even *make-believe* power, like being the *maître d'* in some hard-to-get-into restaurant. This is real might, the kind that will unelect a lawful president and appoint a different one—a person who, in his emptiness, is *positively dangerous*, who will go on to really fuck up the world by bombing countries, for instance, for transparently specious reasons, and, as we'll then live to see, by playing golf in his bland way as the money men ruin the world economy, remembering the man has ruined every institution he has ever touched, from the Texas Rangers to the Republican Party!

Which is why it's clear to me that we need to remember we really *do not* want another alcoholic in the White House, because, as the saying goes, you take the alcohol away from the alcoholic, but you still have the drunk, with his riddled alcoholic soul that he stuffs with any imaginable substance—all those pretzels and O'Doul's—trying to fill the nothingness, but there will never be *enough* of anything for a man like this, so he begins to abuse other substances, such as money or military might.

◌◌◌

So I sit on my perch, putting pen to paper, writing postcards home to California at a small table in the sunshine outside Kramer's Books and Records, a couple of blocks from where we live in the flat made from the first floor of William Jennings Bryan's mansion. Our living room is the ballroom in which he declared himself, in 1896, to be a candidate for president, running as a Democrat against the gold standard and what he called "the money men of the East."

And I am looking all larky and confident, which is one of my several disguises, and I am happy because I know almost exactly no one, and being in a foreign city knowing no one and barely speaking the language is one of my favorite states, as this is the way I *almost always* feel, and having it be externally true at least accounts for the strangeness I feel in the produce aisles, where I don't actually recognize the fruits and vegetables. I shop at the one called the Soviet Safeway—long lines, no food—and am told I need to drive into Maryland to find a Whole Foods.

You cannot imagine the strangeness of this concept, that in order to buy good fruits and vegetables, you must *cross state lines?*

I watch all these young people being drawn forth toward Power, with their bright faces raised upward as the sun shines down on this very touching and beautiful city, which represents My America, which is actually a very moving idea, and I know that some very large percentage of these kids will be taken down by what they are moving toward, that they will simply be psychologically deformed by their proximity to it.

Nor should they even be *asking* themselves to handle that kind of intoxicant at such a young age—that's exactly the same as putting a weapon into the hand of a young man in the desert or a young man on the streets, then asking him not to fire it. So I'm always vibing them, going, *No! No! Slow Down! GO HOME! You're going the wrong way! This is your* childhood! *You don't need to act like this just yet. Go and despoil your youth.*

〽

I'm a little shocked to discover it's hard to make friends in Washington. It seems like folks don't really rush to make friends in Washington, as everyone's on his way from somewhere and in a hurry getting somewhere else, and this is because of the waves of changes in personnel brought about by two-year terms in the House and six in the Senate, and the various political administrations that come shuffling through, and the comings and goings of diplomatic postings—three years here, then four off in the United Arab Emirates—entire households of human beings who are right there before your eyes three-dimensionally one day, then magically teleported the next to the realm where they exist only on the front pages of the world's most important papers, or fourteen inches tall on the TV screen.

We live next door to Joseph Stiglitz, and I'm guessing I wouldn't *even mind* knowing him, as he's an economic genius and he'd maybe drop off a couple of helpful tips, but then these enormous moving vans pull up and overnight, this important person with his entire family of kids, cats, dogs, and canaries is simply—poof—gone, like Kevin Spacey playing Keyser Söze in *The Usual Suspects*.

And I'm often thinking about these things because I am often really unclear about what's even being discussed. For instance, what is an NGO, or what do they mean by an Inside the Beltway Mentality? I've only recently found out—and only accidentally—what a Beltway is.

And here Jack and I are, with our laid-back California openness that isn't fake, and we're suddenly trying to earnestly answer these really impossible, prey-driven Eastern questions, always asked so people can *place you*, get you, know where you *come from* and what you can do for them, and this tells them where to seat you—that is, Above or Below the Salt?

Because even the seating chart in a town like this is very deeply encoded, and this code is almost impossible to crack, since knowledge *is* power, and power in Washington honestly *is* the Drop the Bomb, I intend to totally *FUCK YOU UP*, Dick Cheney sort of *really scary* power that can tap your phone and kick your door in, like it's paying a whole country back for some imagined slight to some twit drunk's equally twittish father.

I once said to a woman I was only getting to know, Know what I really like about you, Jenny? You're one of the few people in Washington who'll actually say what's really on her mind, to which she said, Know what, Jane? This isn't what's *really* on my mind.

Washington is this class/caste–conscious kind of place that asks questions that are seemingly innocuous, but aren't. The first question asked is usually the hardest one, though it looks pretty easy on paper. It's this: *Where did you go to school?*

Jack, as usual, has an easier time of it, since he is way more left-brained and linear than I am. Jack's answer is Westmont College in Santa Barbara for two months, which is when he got thrown out for having a gallon of Dago Red in his room, left there by his roommate. Dago Red is what we then called Daddy Cribari. Jack got thrown out, though he did not yet drink alcohol of any kind, since he was a doper who looked down upon drinkers, who reminded him of his parents, just as I looked down upon drinkers, too, until I very seriously became one.

And Jack by rights *should* have been thrown out by those Christers, but for very different reasons—not for the wine that he didn't drink, but for the whole huge baggy of pot, which we then called dope, that was lying in plain view on top of his dresser, but Westmont didn't *know that* because the Baby Jesus Thought Police, or whoever was doing this dorm-room door-to-door patrolling, were *so out of it* they'd never *even heard* of marijuana, and this was this truly insidious place where they used Westmont kids to go up and down the aisles with flashlights at the movie houses in town to make sure other Westmont kids weren't in there kissing, which is just *so* not Jack, in that he is and was just *so too good* for that bunch of Baptist losers.

Jack's answer—his being at Westmont College for two months—is something he's been advised by his business partner in their prestigious literary publishing house to *never reveal to anyone.* You're to say nothing about your past because doing so is *self-revelatory,* which means people who know this would then have some kind of magical leveraged power over you, like they might then do what? *Tell . . . ?*

It's as if Washington has these fairy-tale aspects that have to do with belief, and this fairy tale's spell isn't easily broken, and this is why Jack is asked to sign a confidentiality agreement as part of his employment package, but it's *Jack* who is asked to sign the confidentiality clause, as I like to say—not me.

⁂

In Washington you're never supposed to mention anything to anyone that is the least bit interesting or self-revelatory, those things that make you, well, unusual, such as the kinds of things I am always saying, which include: My father *committed suicide* and my mother was in a *mental institution*, one brother is *homeless*, the other one a PhD in Sociology whose specialty is *deviance*, and . . .

But you're not supposed to *say* these things, as they're embarrassing. You also don't, in this town, mention the entire realm of human behavior that has to do with secondary sex characteristics, which is why many people here seem to have slept through the pocket history of sex I used to pepper my son and his crew with as I drove them to predawn practice.

You wand folks for their sexuality in Washington and get this odd, bland no-reading-whatsoever; it'd be like *nnnnnnnnnnnnnn* on the Interesting Meter—no spike, no blip, no nothing.

There are whole huge realms of material, I guess, to which I am not supposed to allude, so allude I inevitably do, in that I start chirping this random stuff and sound to myself like birdsong, like a whole chorus of coastal finches, *jeef, jeef, jeeeefff.*

What are you working on, Jane? I'll be asked, and I'll say, Well, *awwwwctuallly*, I'm working on a book called *The Etiquette of Suicide*, and it's about how this subject is still so taboo that it's rude to even *mention* it, yet suicide is so pervasive in our society that almost everyone knows someone whose life has been irrevocably altered by the act of suicide, in that the violent and unexpected death of a person—particularly one who's young—changes, it's estimated, the lives of at least thirty people forever, and *my father* killed himself, and . . . .

And I'm not supposed to mention that my husband spent a year or so supporting his bride (first wife, not me) and infant son by traveling in central California as a professional bowler, though this seems *vastly* more interesting to me than does the neutered-seeming guy, the satellite male (who gives off an Interesting reading of *nnnnnnnnnnnnnnn*) whom I am invariably seated next to at some Table for Twelve, which is the way Washington does these things, and a Table for Twelve in a room full of Tables for Twelve is a really terrible idea, since its physics preclude your talking to anyone aside from the two other Below-the-Salt types you've been seated next to, and everyone will have impeccable credentials, and that always makes me feel the intense need to excuse myself, saying, Pardon me, I'm have to go find the *ladies'* room so I can . . . (smile at them, they smile back at you) . . . *go kill myself.* Then I wander off to look in closets, pat walls and curtains, looking for the Secret Exit, and do eventually find a bathroom, where I dig through the lint at the bottom of my bag looking for *anything*—the merest crumb of Xanax? a Benadryl?—with which to somehow alter my consciousness.

Which is one of the more terrible things about being a not-drinking drunk: how you're still so *hypervigilant* about everything in your immediate surroundings.

〇〇〇

I came to Washington as a TS, a Trailing Spouse, as I am laughingly informed by one of the VBs—or Valium Blondes—I meet. These women are always gorgeously preserved, if somewhat later-in-life divorcees, who've been summarily replaced. They might be anywhere from forty to seventy or even eighty or ninety—you can't ever really tell. What I can tell is they are *bitter! bitter!* about what I cannot imagine, since if they wanted a new guy they could just so easily go find one in the produce aisle.

This VB is a realtor who's trying to sell us a row house in Georgetown that's three stories tall but is only twelve feet wide, and is—sure, sure, I'll admit—completely tricked out and luxe (she calls this *aaaawwwlllll the bells and whistles*), but it's on the market for three-quarters of a million dollars, and I mean it is literally *twelve feet wide* and this is the reason: It was built to accommodate human beings, long ago, who were *being kept as slaves*, and when I say something about this to the VB, she looks at me as if to ask, *What's the* matter *with you?*

Washington is just plain nuts about the TLAs, or Two- or Three-Letter Acronyms, because they're confusing and often actually inscrutable. An expression like *trailing spouse* is always said in this droll, Sally Quinn–ish, insiderlike accent that shows it's intended to be funny. It's like saying the Clintons have spent *their entire lives*, my dear, in government housing, or that so-and-so-forth—Adrian Fenty—lives on the *other side of the Moat.*

The Moat is Rock Creek Park. It's generally true that the more Sally Quinn–type people—by which I mean the white, affluent, connected—live on the left of the park as you study it on the map, while on the right side you will find *your teeming masses*, oh ah ha ha, hee hee hee . . .

Because I'm a TS, I basically do not count, which is basically okay with me because I have always enjoyed this Flaubert-type remove and invisibility whereby I can observe the bourgeoisie and make my caustic comments. As a Trailing Spouse you're supposed to be like a dark shape at the bottom of the important person you're lucky enough to be married to, in that your job is essentially *grounding*. You're like the shadow that Peter Pan lost and had to get Wendy to reattach to him.

There are many other world-weary and droll sayings regarding spouseness here, such as this one: *Washington is full of powerful men and the women they married when they were young.*

My being a TS means that Jack and I aren't necessarily even seated at the same table at a dinner party, where he is off there, Far Above the Salt, with the other interesting and important types. Because my husband actually *is* interesting to talk to, I always longingly track where he's seated at any banquet or social gathering by watching the butler carrying a silver tray on which is perched a single glass of shimmering iced tea.

Jack doesn't drink alcohol for reasons different from my own. He was maybe nineteen years old and bowling professionally—this was after the getting-thrown-out-of-Westmont incident—when he suffered the crisis of faith that resulted in his becoming a practicing Buddhist. Now, by my lights, there are *plenty of people* out there who are married to people with PhDs from really distinguished schools—I, in fact, used to be one of these—but *how many people* can go to an important cocktail party of really influential people in Washington, D.C., and brag about being married to someone—and a Buddhist yet!—who, while bowling for money, once scored a 297, which is just three points shy of a perfect game?

So, this being Washington and I being nothing if not adaptive, I've begun to develop my own verbal defenses, one of the best being to bury whatever small truth I might be willing to reveal in *reams and reams* of distracting paper.

So the answer to the question And where did *you* go to school, dear? has begun to provoke in me this long Faulknerian disquisition on any number of ranging topics, starting off very naturally with suicide,

suicide, suicide; then, normally enough, veering off to include how Ronald Reagan closed the mental hospitals in the state of California as a cost-cutting measure, sending the mentally ill back to their *quote* communities *unquote*, meaning the mentally ill now get to sleep under freeway underpasses and eat out of Dumpsters and panhandle; then moving without pause to the state of public schooling in California versus that of the District of Columbia, where our daughter is in middle school; then ranging outward to include the education of our various sons—my one, Jack's two—and where they went or are currently going to school, as Where Your Kids Go to School is just another way the Anonymous They of the District of Columbia have of Placing You. And I eventually get to the part about my own kids' French/English bilingualism and why we couldn't use public elementary schools and how this had to do with Gann-Rudman of 1977 and the ruination of one of the best systems of public education ever devised in the history of man, ruined—as everything else has been ruined—by the crazed, bloodsucking, starfucking right wing of the Republican Party, which is evil incarnate. And I sometimes even go off on how my great-uncle, who was in the State Department in oil-producing countries and *very obviously* CIA, came to rescue me from one of the more unlikely situations in which I found myself, as a young person living alone in an incense-scented beachside cottage, writing pretty excruciatingly bad poetry, going barefoot, usually wearing only a silken sarong over my bathing suit, and being constantly stoned, and how this CIA great-uncle, who found me with his spy connections, hauled me back to college, where I was enrolled over one weekend because he was, as my mother liked to say, Rather High Up in Administration, and this was somewhat like what would these days be called An Intervention.

So I was sometimes more or less enrolled *almost against my will* and attended first one state college and then another and then yet another one, and by now even I myself have *no idea* how I came to be speaking of these things, since I too have completely lost my place.

Point being, I have *no idea* why I picked *any* school I have ever gone to, aside from when I was a little kid and it was the one I walked to with my brothers because it was right down the street from our house. I once very literally went to a certain college and got an advanced degree because—as I was in the basement of the library, researching law schools—this catalog fell off the shelf and sprang open to the pages that read: Creative Writing, San Francisco State University.

My college education was complicated by the fact that I'd been kicked out of my family—the legal term is *emancipated*—for one or another infraction and, let's face it, I was like most seventeen- and eighteen-year-olds in that I had *no idea* what I was doing and had no long-term goals and was completely incompetent at making any kind of Life Choice and had absolutely no guidance, so I chose what was actually a very terrible school for me. And though I had that Inevitable English Major thing written all over me, as if in Sanskrit in amber Indian henna, I'd still impulsively Change Majors in trying to escape what was so very obviously my destiny, and I'd change to Pre-Med or Pre-Law or American Studies or Pre- or Post-anything that wasn't Art or English so I wouldn't turn out *exactly* like my parents.

The first school I went to turned out to be only good at things that started with the letter *A*, such as Animal Husbandry, Aeronautical Engineering, Agra Business, Architecture . . .

HA! I think, as I'm thinking about it. *Maybe* that's *it*. Maybe I was thinking, *If I go to a school that is mostly guys*—and the ratio at this school was about nine boys to every girl—*and some of these guys are architects, maybe I'll meet someone who is exactly like my father, and I can marry him and we can have three beautiful children, as he and my mother did, but this time, we won't fuck it up . . .*

But instead of meeting anyone attractive in architecture at Cal Poly, San Luis Obispo, I seem to have zoomed outside the ART, ARCHITECTURE, ENGLISH lines—which were probably all way too long for me to have the patience to stand in—and I seem to have gone on down and gotten in a much shorter one at the other end of the alphabet that enrolled me in ZOOLOGY, which was lucky for me, because this school was good at zoology because it had *actual animals.*

Which is maybe where I met the animal husbandry guy with whom I was suddenly raising nineteen pigs and two steer, this being another of these boyfriends who had something tragically wrong with him; in this case, it was that he didn't read, and while he was smart enough, his intellect was not *elastic*, so he'd go on stolidly to become a Large-Animal Vet, just not with me.

And I'd invariably get thrown out of my dorm if not school or this or that portion of my family for some minor infraction—if not for the jug of Daddy Cribari or the building the body in the bed, then for some analogous and equally stupid thing, for Hours or Demerits or other sexist crap that was just then finally being extinguished.

I'd get tossed out of wherever for me being me and for doing the kinds of things I *always* do, which is whatever impulsively occurs to me.

000

So in Washington, when asked the where-did-you-go-to-school question, I just meander along anecdotally in this almost impossible-to-follow manner, trying in my open, honest California way to point out some of the interesting detours here and there, with side trips and excursions.

And how about when I went to school for one small piece of one semester in San Diego County while living on an avocado ranch? This was during the era of the two Simultaneous Davids, these being boyfriends I had who were named the same, so when I got a dozen roses with a card at Christmas I didn't know which to thank?

And how the time I quit college *entirely* for a whole summer and my school—this was Long Beach, where my CIA great-uncle was dean of international studies—didn't even realize I wasn't coming back, because I'd gotten this great job at the phone company at Ninth and Hope in downtown Los Angeles? This was no mere *summer* job, this was a *real* one that might lead to a really promising career, the kind of thing some women simply did. If you were one of My People and wanted a good job, it was just widely accepted that you could go work for the phone company.

It was even a traditional thing to do if you were trying to start behaving like a grown-up. You got a job at the phone company, which was considered a *women's company* because there were about seven women for every man, and you'd live modestly and buy dresses and shoes that went together at the May Company, and carry a neat little virginal handbag to hold your lipstick and your compact, and there you'd stay for the rest of your life.

The phone company—since Jack and I are roughly the same age—is what I was doing just as Jack was getting thrown out of Westmont College, getting his girlfriend pregnant, getting married, then going out to bowl for money.

And it's true that my path and Jack's often did seem—in retrospect—to have crossed and recrossed, then run parallel for a time, as if we were on the same trek. It's as if we were California Indians of roughly the same language grouping who might have glimpsed each other far off there, in our mutual future, and—while never actually speaking—would have known, if our eyes met across a room, to give each other that little chin lift of recognition.

The phone company—and there was only one then, remember? as this was before the Great Age of Deregulation—was the way some people, you know? *lived* in those days, which really interested me, if only in a touristy, shallow sort of way, like you could time-travel to the 1950s.

It must be the way gay people feel when they try to act straight: If they just *practice* hard enough, it'll begin to one day get a little easier, except that something invariably comes along to completely fuck you up by revealing the More Real You.

Because certain parts of what we might call My Surroundings would always then begin to intensely bother me, like that the elevator in the phone company building was, to my mind, unsafe in that it had no interior doors. It was an old-fashioned apparatus in which the doors slid closed on each floor, but inside the cage of the elevator itself there was just this folding grate at the front controlled by a Colored Gentleman, which is exactly how this man would have thought of himself, as he was elderly and though this was a good long while after Civil Rights had supposedly extinguished Jim Crow in the workplace, this hadn't actually even begun to happen. Also, it's true that people can't just readily completely *change* the things they call themselves in certain circumstances, and the phone company, when I was working there, was one of those circumstances.

For instance, no *Negro* or *colored* women worked there, I'd noticed, except at night on the cleaning crew or maybe doing data entry, and there were no Hispanics, who would have been called Mexicans, because they, of course, could not be expected to speak English, and all the regular or *white* women I worked with got off by the seventh floor, while the men went on up in the elevator and worked on the higher and more important floors.

So this elevator grate was supposed to keep you from sticking your fingers or hand through and potentially doing grievous harm to yourself or others, so I decided—as the daughter of a suicide and of a woman

locked up in a mental institution for almost a decade for what was probably no more than the kind of grief you encounter in Greek tragedies,
which is *epic*, also universal and therefore, like it or not, almost perfectly understandable—I didn't want to ride on said elevator, and began
walking up and down the seven flights of stairs to and from my desk,
minding my own damned business, which was doing a job at which I
truly excelled.

This was manually alphabetizing some or another item; it may have
been data entry cards done by the women who came in invisibly in the
night and who probably thought of themselves as *gals*. My job was
something completely rote and normal, which I really enjoyed, as it was
the exact opposite of being creative, which had always seemed like a
pernicious illness or malady that might eventually get to me.

I did this job and had a really wonderful boyfriend who was perfect
in all ways, smart and funny and well read and good looking and tall
and curly haired, and he looked to me like Paul Newman, aside from the
fact that Paul Newman was actually short, which didn't read because he
had such presence.[+]

[+]Paul Leonard Newman, born on January 26, 1925, in Shaker Heights, Ohio, and who
died in his home in Westport, Connecticut, on September 27, 2008, was, in fact, rather
short, a fact I have firsthand from the time Jack and I met him and Joanne Woodward in
a receiving line at the Hollywood premiere of *Mr. and Mrs. Bridge*, the movie made from
the Evan S. Connell novels Jack published. Jack wore a tux to this premiere, and I had
on a black dress spangled with about a million tiny rhinestones that might have *cost the
earth*, as my fancy grandmother would have said, had I not got it cheap at Loehmann's,
but the panty hose I bought that day on Rodeo Drive cost, no shit, *fifty dollars!* and this
was all the way back in oh, say, 1990? Joanne Woodward was wearing a plaid pantsuit,
and Paul Newman had on blue jeans and a soft, washed-many-times light blue work shirt
open at the collar to show his white T-shirt underneath, so Jack, in black tie, leaned over
and whispered to Paul Newman, *I feel like I should be parking cars*, and Paul Newman
put his arm on Jack's shoulder, man to man, and whispered back, *I never know what to
wear to these things, either . . .*

So I had this perfectly ordinary life constructed, wherein I was working at the phone company—and no one, including my CIA great-uncle, could *make me* go back to school and be an English major—and living simply in a nice normal working girl's apartment, with a normal workaday job alphabetizing shit, the kind of job other people would actively *not* want to have because it wasn't *creative*, when I had no wish to be creative, seeing what being creative did to my parents, who were honest to God killed by it, which is why Allen Ginsberg spelt this place Amerika, and my parents were too *creative* to live somewhere spelt Amerika . . .

So I'd be trudging up and down seven flights of stairs to the lunch-room, bringing my lunch in a paper bag, its top neatly sealed over with a folded paper napkin tucked inside, the kind of well balanced and healthy Californian lunch I'd have made for my own three children had I married one of the regular, nonsuicidal, and less sexually conflicted architects I might have met at Cal Poly but didn't.

⚭

So Long Beach came *after* Cal Poly and *before* San Francisco State, okay? as I'd be trying to explain to whoever'd been stupid enough to ask me this question at a cocktail party in Washington, D.C., and by this time this person's eyes would be glazing over and they'd be scanning the room for someone else who could in some way *help them* with their Career Advancement, which I very obviously cannot, because the real question or subtext almost always being asked by people who want to get to know me might be more succinctly put as: Who Do I Have to Fuck to Get Your Husband to Publish Me?

And I'm using the term *fuck* here nonliterally, that is, not to connote actually having sex, as my daughter might say, or actual physical

contact of any kind, since Washington is one of the least libidinous places I've ever been—reference the *nnnnnnnnnnn* thing that goes on all the
time. And this is *not just me*, as I came here as an okay-looking woman
and the getting of boyfriends, some of whom overlapped and even had
duplicate names, has never been my particular problem.

And I am also from *California*, where we have, as cultural inheri-
tance, a certain *je ne sais quoi*, yet in Washington, D.C., I'll go for days!
weeks! months! and have no one, absolutely no one at all, emit any kind
of buzz on any sort of frequency that isn't *nnnnnnnnnnnnnnn*, and believe me, I am really adept at scanning all these really odd and particular
interpersonal frequencies, even those that have nothing to do with me,
which is one of the few things you get from being *literally* psychoana-
lyzed by a *literal* psychoanalyst, *analysis* meaning spending six and one-
half years lying on a couch four times a week, listening to oneself really
expensively saying all this ridiculous crap.

The sexlessness of Washington, D.C., feels positively eerie, as if it
thinks in its own mind it's the 1950s, as if anybody cares whom you go
to bed with! No one cares! No one cares whom you do or do not sleep
with unless *it's children* or maybe *chimps in the National Zoo*!

And one thing I really do think my generation can take credit for
is really successfully driving our tractor trailers over the CDs that contain all the random encoded data referencing the manners and mores
and popular culture that might grow back by sci-fi increments from the
1950s! which is why the right wing of the Republican Party, which wor-
ships the *1950s* as the Last Normal Time (for White People) and completely lacks a certain *je ne sais quoi*, really hates our collective guts.

෮෮෮

So I am trudging up and down seven flights of stairs at the phone company, having the perfect boyfriend with whom I am actually in love, and this is a huge relief since you really never know—when your father kills himself and your mother is sent away to a mental institution for almost a decade—whether you're going to turn out to be so ruined that you're incapable of loving anything more complicated than a goldfish.

And I have shoes that go with the dresses I wear to work and I am driving my very own brand-new VW Bug that my maternal grandfather, a banker and staunch contributor to the Republican Party named Virgil Elmo White, has helped me buy by paying the some-amount down payment, after which I pay my own monthly car payment of $54.93. And I am really well on my way to this certain secure middle-classness, and have even semi-convinced myself I resemble a girl some guy who resembles my boyfriend might want to marry, and when he goes away to Mexico City to study Spanish over my phone company summer and writes me, he calls himself *tu novio*.

According to my smattering of Spanish, this translates as *your intended*, though I may never bother to actually look it up.

There are a couple of tiny little glitches in the perfectness of my paper doll–like life, such as his being, well, gay (though this is *pre* or in advance of our actually calling it that), or his having at least this sort of twilit sexuality, as the only lover he's had—and I actually did and do deeply despise the word *lov-ur* and wish no one would ever use it for any kind of reason, but what other word do we really have in American English?—is a man.

Because he and I also aren't actually *sleeping together*, as is said back then, as this is way back in the Twentieth Century, which is a more modest and decorous time.

∞

So if Time is a river into which you cannot step twice, I've arrived at a bend in the river where there's a jam-up because the river has frozen and the ice floes have simply backed up upon themselves and glacial formations are being thrust skyward, in that the Time that exists at the phone company is still pre–Civil Rights.

It is the Civil Rights movement that has begun to move us all toward the future. This is happening everywhere, not only in the South, and it has begun to liberate not just blacks, but all of us, to go and do all kinds of things that will be completely disapproved of by Virgil Elmo White and my CIA great-uncle, because they are the kind of tall white men who are *used* to being in power, and no one gives that up willingly.

So the Colored Gentleman who mans the elevator and wears the white gloves to open and close the grille and mind everyone's comings and goings does so with a little subservient, hunched maneuver of his head and shoulders that I know stands for his deep and abiding hatred of All Y'all White Folk, also the Very Horse We Rode In On, which was actually a railroad train that was called the Industrial Revolution.

This man's despising me is another reason I don't want to ride in his fucking elevator.

Point being, *my intended* is conflicted, but so what? *Everyone* in my family has *always* been conflicted—we are all these twilit, questing souls, which makes us interesting and seems natural to me, and I, unlike my father, may actually get to live long enough to discover who I am and what my true nature is made of.

Point being, being conflicted is *our tradition*; my own father's being conflicted was why he *kept* getting arrested, in that some of us are simply constitutionally incapable of *not* doing the thing we're not supposed to do, which is—when the spirit seizes us—climbing out a window.

◌◌◌

So *mi novio* is conflicted—so what? I'm totally down with this. He and I don't even have to discuss it, and have evidently formed this wordless agreement that we will conduct this mutual fakeish-romantic, completely sexy but sexless–type 1950s thing that looks good on paper.

And it is not that we are not mutually and even ardently attracted to each other, which we are, but this exists in the complicated part of Twilight, in that there are all these shades and gradations that no one wants to hear about, so we name ourselves into these boxes that say Gay or Straight, in order to gain control of what—in the Twentieth Century—used to be thought of as this *great big deal.*

Which isn't actually even true to human development, which I know from having simply flipped through the pages of my Zoology textbook, which is only to say, the tadpole you start out as isn't necessarily the frog you become, given shades and gradations.

But *Other*, of course, is not what anyone high up is actually going by in those old-fashioned days when I am working at the phone company while *mi novio* is off learning Spanish in Mexico City, only to come home in late August to say he has fallen in love with his Spanish teacher, and I have no real way of asking if this is a man or a woman or to really know which would be the more devastating answer, and my heart is legitimately broken.

But he wonders if he and I can stay *tangential friends* because he really likes my mother and my brothers, with whom I am now suddenly living in this kind of hippie-ish house a few blocks from the beach, decorated with furniture from all our rich and well-traveled relatives' basements and garages, so we have really beautiful if dilapidated old things: careworn old Persian carpets and a coffee table made from a teak door shipped home from Indonesia after a diplomatic posting.

My brothers and I all sleep on mattresses on the floor in our own rooms, and we've hung the windows with Indian-print bedspreads we get at Cost Plus Imports and that emit this certain dusty and exotic reek of Elsewhere, which shows us to be well raised and to have turned out to be what our parents intended, which is Bohemian.

And because we are now Bohemian, I learn to make ragout and Quiche Lorraine.

We're Bohemian except for our mom, who—and we must struggle to remember this—was raised as a somewhat spoiled only child and now requires her privacy and so is off in the back of the house, which is her own private quarters, where she has her own bedroom with a private bathroom, and a screened porch that is like her sitting room, and this area is sacrosanct. Our mother, who is the lady of the house, presents only when she cares to present and comes forth from her realm almost regally, like the Empress Dowager.

She has regular, honest-to-Jesus furniture that actually matches, including a bureau, a proper bed, a chest of drawers, and even a decorative runner made from the mud cloth of a certain tribe in Africa to cover the top of the bureau and disguise its nicks and scratches.

She is extraordinarily modest in terms of her person in a way I have never before noticed, and she never emerges from her rooms unless she is completely and neatly dressed in hose and heels, a skirt and a sweater, like she might have worn in college. She also carries her purse around with her, in which she keeps her cigarettes, and this may be one of the few vestiges or signs of her having been a mental patient for such a long time, and the times, they are a-changin' and the ice floes have given way and our mother has been delivered back to us intact. She is just very astonishingly *here*, completely lucid, and startlingly together.

And in this house, whose common rooms are really crazy and chaotic, an enormous amount of alcohol is being consumed by everyone but me, and drugs are being taken by my brothers, but privately, because my mother does not approve of drugs, and the only drug I use is this truly unbelievable amount of caffeine—I drink dozens of cups of black coffee every day—and the truly astonishing number of cigarettes I smoke, because I can see no daylight between myself and cigarettes, cannot imagine that I ever didn't smoke or that I might ever not smoke again.

I also take the diet pills they give you at the health center if you go there saying you're feeling, you know, low—saying the regular shit, like how your father killed himself and now your *novio* has run off with his Spanish teacher, so you're feeling a little . . . ?

And I am not kidding that they give you amphetamines, saying, *Of course* they're a crutch, but if your leg were broken you'd use a crutch, wouldn't you? and I think, *Well, that makes entire sense,* and I go home and pour the entire bottle of pills into a pile onto the teak coffee table that was once an Indonesian door, and my brothers and I pop them like Pez and we talk and talk and talk. We talk all night and all day until the drugs run out, and then we crash and sleep for days in a row, and it is in this circumstance alone that the three of us together can actually out-talk our mother, who suspects substances and stays largely off in her rooms, listening distantly, disapproving mildly.

She tells us later it's the most astonishing babbling sound, not unbeautiful but indecipherable as human language, that it's as if her three children have somehow been transmogrified into two dozen chanting Gregorian monks.

〇〇〇

The night *mi novio* breaks up with me, we drive around while I am supposedly deciding whether he can still hang out at my house with my amazingly cool mom and my totally bitchen brothers, who are both so interesting and hip that all these fantastic people want to just drop by and sit on pillows on the floor of our living room at any time of the night or day.

And this is in fact a magical time, and Will has only just come home from Europe, via Greenwich Village, and is now enrolled in college. He was in Germany in the Army and has an amazing gift for languages and has read Marx in German and has been totally radicalized according to the Frankfurt School and has been given back to us as this preternaturally worldly and really attractive person. He is so well read and he sets about educating the rest of us in what is actually important and so gives me and Geo a reading list and conducts study sessions, and I read these books, or mostly do, and Geo doesn't because he probably can't, as he's already off picking up sailors on the pier and is sort of a rent boy doing who knows what with them in the $1.50 triple features.

And because Will's a few years older and seems to know what he's doing, he becomes this charismatic leader of student protests who is part of the governing body deciding whether we will occupy the college president's offices, and Geo tags along, just like in the Olden Days, and he is like a brilliant innocent who has this mysterious aura of humor and knowingness, which makes him impossibly cool. And Geo has also already been Inside, as my big brother and my mother and I have had to spring him from what is an Actual Institution, and this, in these days, is a badge of honor.

It's like an open house all the time. You stop by. You stay. You crash on the floor of the living room on laid-out pillows and no one ever wants to leave. Our house is just four blocks from the ocean, and with the windows open, you can hear the wave action on the shore, and all these friends of ours begin to arrive from all these different places in the country and widespread parts of our lives and everyone is intermingled and everyone gets along and there is no class or caste or snobbery and no one is ranking on anyone; no one is asking, *But did you graduate?* Everyone is just together for once and listening to music. Everyone drinks coffee and wine and beer and smokes cigarettes and goes into another room to smoke pot or hash, in deference to our mom, who prefers that both drugs and sex be performed discreetly and—*if you don't mind*—out of her earshot.

When Will and I are both enrolled in college, classes hardly matter, as we are closing the schools as soon as the government tries to open them and opening the schools when the government tries to shut them down. They are *our schools*, we deeply feel, so we believe we get to use them to launch ourselves as this massive assault on the Establishment. The kinds of political actions my older brother leads involve the United Farm Workers, and he's in organizations that are marginally communistic, and we put our bodies on the line for all kinds of actions and go to a peace march with the name of a sympathetic lawyer inked in ballpoint on our arm, then raise our hand if we're willing to be arrested.

Because it's always been important, in fact, to be willing to be arrested if it's for the right reasons, which is something my parents taught me and something I, in turn, have taught my son and daughter. It's important to remember that it was the children who were arrested during the Civil Rights movement, because if their parents had been arrested, they would have lost their jobs, and we need to be arrested because it wears The Powers That Be down and uses their manpower and their resources, because this is the way we break them. We are willing to be arrested over and over again, and when you are arrested, you call the ones who love you, who then drop everything and rush to the station house to bail you out.

So when my mother and brother are arrested together at one action or another, they call me and their voices are entwined and they are singing "La Marseillaise."

〇〇〇

What has happened to Time over this single summer is that it seems to have suddenly cracked open, and from this place where the frozenness has broken, a whole bright and beautiful future has spilled, everything surging, roiling, alive with possibility.

The Powers That Be are tacitly finished. We have identified them as being positively evil, in that all they can ever think to do is cause another ceaseless war in which they always manage to economically benefit, and theirs is the terrible reality that we refuse to honor. This is something we are now collectively deciding and we are the 77 Million, so what we say goes.

We are interested not in power, but in the realm of skin on skin, the realm of the intimate, the place where one actually living human opens his or her mouth and says one true thing to another living person and even saying the word *fuck* feels defiant of the Old Ways, which are destructive and calcified and Republican and oh-so-bank-president and oh-so-CIA.

And we are simply such a huge demographic group that we know we now get to change a couple of important things.

By now I've had the antiwar argument with my Grandfather Virgil, the banker and staunch Nixon-ite and contributor to his political campaign, and another similar one with my Great-uncle Bobby, and I've begun to notice that I am now not being invited to family functions that traditionally have excluded my mother. It was when my father died that my mother began to be excluded; then she went to the mental hospital and—according to many in my family—was never seen or heard from again.

What that Time Period is suddenly producing is what you come to in art: People seem even more real than real, in that everything is suddenly heightened and alive and every moment matters and everyone begins to suddenly understand that it's allowed and even required that you write what you really believe and not what is merely expected of you and draw what you believe and say it and show it and *behave* vividly, as if you imagine yourself alive. And it's now that you suddenly understand that it all actually really *applies to you*, that you really will get to one day ride in a taxi down a snowy street on your way to the Met in New York City, having accidentally ended up on the other coast in the same patch of time as Your Intended (even if this is somewhere off in the brackets of your mutual future). This is when your own life suddenly snaps to and can be seen as containing the great themes that literature contains and you suddenly understand that history *pertains* to you, that history is what is happening every single day and that what is written in books is put there only to point this out to you.

People are suddenly brave enough to be saying or at least trying to say *true things* and do *true things*, and to get arrested for the right and not specious reasons, and this feels like you can suddenly breathe, which feels almost dangerous because it means you have to actually trust yourself, and suddenly in America we are no longer these fakeish, shallow, paper doll–like people, but have become the brave ones who will risk something, and it is exactly then that I begin to love my country.

ᨀ

I make my former *novio* take me to the liquor store to buy me a bottle of wine, since I'm not yet old enough and in my house they drink mostly beer, and I'm figuring it's right about now that I'm going to start to behave alcoholically, which is, after all, my destiny, but me being me, and basically a fuckup even in *fucking up*, I forget the bottle on the floor of his car.

I have a couple of things on my mind, the first of which I tell him before I get out and slam the door.

No, I say.

The answer is actually that no, my family and I have come through all this hardship as this one tight little unit, and *some guy* isn't going to stop by every now and again in order to enjoy how unusual we are just because I now live in a house full of these cool-to-the-point-of-bitchen characters who are as entertaining as anyone in someone's stupid play.

And he likes my family because we are, you know, so twilit and original. Because he's been raised in the upper-middle-class humdrum stupid repressed conventionality we exist in defiance of, and because he particularly likes my effortlessly hip mom, as *she's exactly* who this kind of guy will always go for, in that she's so vivid and extreme.

No, I say, he cannot continue to hang out with my family after disdaining me.

Because I can suddenly see him for exactly what he is and what it is he has meant to me, and I suddenly hear in him *the condescension* in his deciding he has found it in himself to admire my family for their, what? Unusualness?

Nope, I say, he has to go on now and figure out on his own what he's about and what he is and isn't actually into, and about this I actually have no idea.

And anyway while he was away in Mexico I have undergone a transformation, and under Will's spell and guidance I am now this hippie child whose hair is impossibly long and almost infinitely curly, and I am going around barefoot, dreamy, and often stoned. And I am wearing my high school prom dress that was, no shit, sewn at home by hand instead of being bought at Macy's or Bullock's. My dress is this long flowy thing made from dark-green-with-pink-flowers-all-over-it *hopsacking*, a fabric that got me talked about and that I chose in ironic protest against, you know, all that is Prom Night and all that boysie-girlsie conformist crap that killed my father.

And I have anyway also been fired from the phone company after being brought before the Safety Committee for my practice of climbing up and down seven flights of stairs.

This being the safety committee's reasoning: *No One Else, Jane, is doing this, and what if you trip and fall down and we never find you?*

I am fired not for climbing up and down seven flights of stairs, per se, but for sitting in that meeting frozen with rage, knowing these are exactly the kinds of *bitches*—the committee is all women, and I know that the word is like a physical slap to the face of My People, which is why I use it rarely and only advisedly—who would have actively scorned my mother, so I refuse to sign the thing they've drawn up, which is A Written Safety Committee Conclusion, together with its Order to Comply.

So when I slam *mi novio*'s car door on that chapter of my life, forgetting the bottle of wine, what I actually think—because my heart is legitimately broken—is that I don't hate him, in that this isn't really *his fault* any more than it was my father's fault to have been born in a society that wasn't mature enough to accept a person like him. But because I have been such a complete and dismal failure in my last really ardent attempt at what is called in my family *conventionality*, as I step into the street, what I think is: What now, for fuck's sake? I have to go be a *writer*?

12
Research Methods

IT'S JUST THAT I AM intrinsically so *like* my mother, in that we are just so *bad* at being feminine, so I come of age imagining that I am not a real girl at all, but am rather a transvestite version of a girl, more of a Holly Woodlawn or Myra Breckinridge, this beautiful (to me) creature who is only a semiworking replica of what a girl would approximate, like I am this girl disguised deep within the soul of a man who is somehow only *in costume* as an adequate girl.

Given my okay, even All-American good looks and my somewhat upbeat and well-adjusted demeanor, it is even *more* confusing that I harbor the secret that I am a cross-dressing man or—even more im-probably—a heroin-addicted lesbian hooker who stands in the smear of neon-wet street corners in Hollywood with mascara weeping down her face. You just wouldn't *get this* from looking at me, in that I am what is called *high achieving* despite all my various, *you know . . . ?* my *blah blah blahs . . . ?* as my mother would say, then draw in the air with her cigarette. In my mother's somewhat musical-comedic take on things, we might refer to these as the Tra-la-la-ge-dies.

I am simply so *An-tee* Girl, Lina would say. Lina is my dusty, Daughter of the Golden West great-granddaughter of the Prairie Schooner pioneers grandmother, as opposed to Delia, who's more proper, one, who was more Daughters of the American Revolution. But from both sides everything is saturated with this sense of dripping oppressive history and altar guild and Girls' Friendly Society and the Heroic Nature of Suffering, and it just makes me sick, in that it has all these expectations about Our People packed down into the subclauses of the membership requirements, and I do not want to have to even *know about* these clauses and subclauses, let alone try to qualify, so I immediately bring up the Tra-la-la-ge-dies, the Suicide for a Dad and the Mental Patient for a Mom and so forth, almost immediately on any interview or college application.

I am very closely identified with all kinds of transgressive behaviors, and I never have much of a damper on my mind and barely have one on my mouth, so I tend to say things as they come to me. This shows me to be my mother's daughter, though my respect for her defiance of conventional society is offset by an equal and opposite force that works in the reverse direction, which is that I honestly often cannot stand her. And one of the reasons I can't stand her is that she's so terrible at doing feminine things, which must be the way boys feel when they notice their fathers have no guy skills, like they've been essentially robbed.

And it's not that my mom isn't maternal—oddly, she is. For instance, she worked in the first integrated cooperative nursery school in the country and was, as she always claimed, very good at it. This was in Berkeley, when Will was in preschool and I was a toddler. People were being told, she said, by the medical establishment that the educated woman, the modern woman, wouldn't want to be *bothered* to breast-feed her baby, as bottle feeding was so much more scientific. My mom didn't *go by that*, as she liked to say, so she nursed all of us defiantly, saying all that was part of the Larger Plot intent upon intruding into all aspects of our private life.

And, of course, telling American women not to nurse *did* turn out to be a marketing scheme designed to sell infant formula to middle-class women, by promulgating the notion that only *the lower classes* fed their babies in that primitive way, as if they were animals on the feedlot.

But it is clear to me that I, like my mother, am coming of age conflicted over what I think of regular, missionary-position, Ozzie-and-Harriet sex—that is, nice-polite-little-white-girl sex, boring sex, which is the only kind of sex that a nice little white girl (which I am currently disguised as) is supposed to be interested in having.

I have boyfriends because—like my mother before me—the having of boyfriends doesn't turn out to be my own special problem, but I've been raised so counter to having respect for Ordinary Sex that while my body participates, my mind seems to dwell in the hiatus in between the twin beds. I'll be doing one thing, which is having okay sex with some okay-at-least-on-paper boy, but I'll be thinking about, for instance, having sex with an entire cadre of Indians as some kind of ritual sacrifice, or having sex with cowboys in the hay barn, and I know this isn't the kind of sex Real Girls are supposed to be having over there in the sector of what I tend to think of as Conventional Society.

Instead of Being Here Now, as the Buddhists say, I'll be the skinny, drugged-up blonde the LAPD will pick up and require to suck one of them off as the other one fucks her in the ass. I'll also be oddly aloof from *all that*, thinking of it as Screenplay or Poem, on which I'll be essentially—even as I am having good-little-white-girl sex—mentally doing an *explication de texte*.

I'll be this girl within a man dressed as a girl, imagining being the woman who's been stopped by the cops in a routine traffic thing and fucked two or three ways from Sunday in a city park in the evening, and these cops would be being really elaborately courteous to me, calling me Mrs. Van de Veer or whatever, and this story, a version of which I read in *Playboy* magazine, is *supposed* to be condemning police brutality— I noticed—but it so very obviously has a completely different intent, which is as pornographic as the movies Mindy's stepfather showed us.

Will says *Playboy* is designed to be read by Episcopal priests so they can get off and still feel good about themselves. This is how this works: You read a story about what assholes the cops secretly are, but what the story is *really* about is the same old thing, which is how to get the guy to come. It is also telling us that the woman, who is helpless because she is handcuffed, is secretly excited, too, so the story that is *supposedly* about being against rape is actually saying something also in favor of it, though anyone who's ever been raped knows that this isn't what rape really is.

I am just starting to suspect, but don't fully know, that this is a plain fact regarding our *imagined* pornographic experience: Most of us do not want the actual *visceral* experience of the things our minds can dream, in that it serves us well enough to allow our minds to make the imaginative leap, which allows our bodies to follow, as if we were, instead of listening to music, in fact singing along.

But I *feel* like my father, feel that this is my own more true experience, that that is *me* getting arrested in the bathroom of the Lighthouse, that I *am* the heroin-addicted lesbian hooker standing on the rainy street corner in Hollywood, that it's *as if* it really happened.

As if? There's nothing about that life that is the slightest bit *as if*.

But I've come of age just being so closely *identified* with sexual misfits, with homos and hookers and fags and mental patients and drug addicts and drunks and poets, of course, and painters, if they are the real things, and just any kind of social misfit, anyone with a sense of Otherness that will keep them out of the D.A.R. or the Holland Society that when I read the words of Allen Ginsberg's *Howl* aloud and he says, I am *with you* in Rockland, I am so totally *identified* with my mother, who is—even as I read those words—very literally locked away on Ward G-1 in Camarillo. Except that I have this essentially middle-class piece of me that worries about essentially middle-class things: that I don't really *want* to have to fuck a bunch of guys who smell bad and don't actually appeal to me, that I don't *want* to go to Ward G-1, where you actually don't get to sit in your private room that's painted in soft pastels and crack up in this genteel manner and sip tea with milk in it and compose broken lines of poetry, and I can't actually paint—as I happen to notice—and my poetry, when I deign to write it, is just so frankly bad.

∞

I have no tolerance for alcohol, and there should be no surprise in this, since my family is so completely and diligently alcoholic that we're like certain tribes of American Indians, in that we probably have a genetic pedigree. I get drunk at a carnival and am so instantly messed up and disinhibited that I almost let some boy I've just met fuck me, and from that safe, drunk, porn-star place I often inhabit when it comes to sex, I'm thinking, *Good, at least this'll get rid of my by-now-bothersome virginity*, and the only reason he doesn't fuck me in some bushes is that my body—at fifteen, sixteen—*itself* rejects him; it begins vomiting convulsively, proving that it takes a certain strong constitution to stand on a street corner in Hollywood and get in the car with whomever it is who stops, who is not, as a class of person, going to be Richard Gere and you aren't going to turn out to be Julia Roberts and the entire experience is, very honestly? really brutal and unattractive. It's brutal and I'm a person who is simply too sensitive, many days, to be able to leave the house even to go shopping for fruits and vegetables.

One day a girl I know from my part-time job asks me if I want to double-date with her and go out with these two guys who're a little bit older, who want to take us to this fancy restaurant. I say okay, though I immediately begin mentally equivocating: What does it mean if they take to this fancy restaurant? That there's a Monetary Transaction involved reminds me of pornography and Reseda, and how we're all in one way or another always going to Reseda to fuck someone whose real name we do not know, and how Mindy continued to get *residuals,* and exactly how messed up *all that* turns out to almost always be.

But I go out with these guys, who're excited because I'm young, and this woman, who's a little bit older and who's named Teri and who comes to work, I've noticed, smelling of sex, doesn't like the way I look when I meet her at the restaurant. I'm in one of my Persons in Black Period, one of those times when I shop only at thrift stores and I buy couture—but from the Olden Days: Chanel, Valentino—and I wear little rosy-tinted sunglasses everywhere I go, inside and out, and strange quasireligious symbols that are charms, in actuality, from a very personal religion. I think I look bitchen, but Teri gives me the once-over, as if to say, *Is* that *the best you could do?*

And these guys, too, who *are* honestly older and who travel for business and are in town as Visiting Firemen, look at me and then at Teri and raise their eyebrows, as if to say, *Where the hell did you get this one, Central Casting?*

And we're drinking our drinks at this Fancy Place, to which I'm supposed to be excited about having been brought *on a date,* but which impresses me about as much as the floor. A date means these guys are paying. It's also what you call your trick when you're a drugged-up lesbian hooker, which—in this particular moment—I feel it'd be way more honest to go and be.

And I'm thinking, *Yeah, they're paying, but* for what, *exactly?* And I happen to know, because I am not stupid, that this fancy meal at this fancy Italian restaurant is going on their expense account, when it suddenly hits me: *Oh, I get it! These guys are married!* Teri goes out with these *married guys* when they come to town, and that's what they are paying for, and it's exactly like my uncle and exactly like whoring, except it goes on their expense account so it costs them personally nothing and so, as women, we are spared the standing-on-the-street-corner-in-the-neon-rain part of this transaction, which is—in fact—the part that appeals to me most, even as their wives, glancing at the credit card bill, are spared the outrage.

We're drinking our drinks and eating the appetizer, which is calamari, when I say, So, you guys are married, huh?

And the three of them look at me like I've issued the kind of string of profanities that used to get my mother slapped back onto Ward G-1 in the state mental hospital: shitfuckfuckingcocksuckingmotherfuckingmotherfucker. And Teri coolly asks, Now, Jane, why would you want to bring that up? And I suddenly remember, too late, that she's technically my boss.

Why? she's wondering. And I honestly would have launched into the whole long story of how my aunt, after all these years of what actually constitutes abuse, has recently told my uncle she wants a divorce, and he doesn't want to divorce her because he wants the Both/And part of being an upper-middle-class White Male—*both* the wife and family and the gag-reflex White Picket Fence, *and* the glamorous mistress on the side. My uncle's is one he's promoted from Las Vegas showgirl, who is what the women in my family disdainfully call "the little blonde cute one," and I'd say all this at this dinner, except I've noticed that my throat has begun to close.

Because I've started being allergic, not just to the more exotic things, like calamari, but, as my allergist has recently told me, to almost everything.

So I say, Sorry, throat's closing, gotta go, and I get up from the table, taking my little jet-beaded bag, which is like something my mother would have carried when she was still going out with my dad to fancy Beverly Hills parties in the 1950s, and I go outside and hail a cab.

Which shows that if I ever do have to start earning my living as a prostitute, I'll starve.

000

From the boy at the carnival, I learned that I should never get drunk with anyone unless I'm completely willing to let him fuck me, and eventually I do let boys fuck me. I have lots of friends from school who are guys, and I'm good at being friends with guys—it's from growing up with brothers and boy cousins—but these boys just don't particularly interest me.

So I go to Ozzie-and-Harriet bed with them and they fuck me and I think of other things, which isn't exactly their fault, in that they seem to lose a piece of their bestial edge by being friends of mine.

I only like boys who are kind and intelligent and sensitive, because I myself am kind and intelligent and sensitive, but I meet a boy like this, and he just isn't *interesting* to me in *that way*.

It's that he isn't enough like an animal, I'm guessing, or enough like some porno guy who is cock only, or enough like a faceless-seeming brute of an LAPD Vice–type person who'd brutalize a girl in a breeding crate. I have this memory that may not even be a memory, but it's something I believe I've seen, of going to a party where there were all these hay barns and pig barns, and being at this thing called a kegger, where beer is served in big cups and someone's car radio is playing Jim Morrison's "Light My Fire" and the guys have rigged this barrel on four ropes thrown over the rafters that's got a saddle on it and is positioned in the center of the barn so a girl can ride it. I guess guys are riding it, too, but this doesn't seem to be its point.

The point is that a girl's encouraged to get on this saddle in the center of the room, and to try to hold on while the guys at the corners pull it so the barrel tips and bucks as if it's a horse, and it's to get these girls, who are wearing tight T-shirts, to become more and more helpless and to eventually scream, while there are all these guys in the room who more and more want to fuck them.

The guys I know are nice and would never do this. The boy I'm with in my memory or dream or whatever it is is nice and is uncomfortable with the way the cruelty in the barn is becoming tightened down and concentrated as everyone gets drunker, and he says, Let's get out of here, so we do, but that porn-star, whorish part of me that's completely impervious to risk stays back at the barn and watches as ten or twenty guys fuck the girl they've locked in the breeding crate.

000

So, noting that I am having this usually-not-hot sex with guys, and missing the piece of childhood that says you aren't supposed to *do* certain things, I guess what my problem is is that I am Other, in that I'm not cut out to be a Practicing Heterosexual.

I have gone to bed with all kinds of boys, but not yet one I'm in love with. I'll traditionally fuck my boyfriend, then his best friend, which often seems the friendly thing to do. I usually do this in a serial fashion; the one time I do it concurrently, I find out the true secret of the threesome, which is that someone is eventually going to feel left out. And these are two young men who aren't yet particularly experienced, so they don't at first get that they're using my body to get at what they're really all about, which is fucking each other, which is what does finally occur to them, which is such a jolt to my vanity that I stay in bed for three days, watching the Miss America pageant and having a nervous breakdown.

So I decide I'm probably gay, which makes sense since I've always had lots of friends who are gay, though this is the 1970s and being out, though not unheard of, isn't altogether common. My mother's theory these days is that everyone's simply acting out what she's always already known: that we're all Other, which she's lately calling Bi-Homo-Momo to let everyone know she has no intention of taking all this seriously at this late date.

I figure being Bi-Homo-Momo probably runs in families at least as much as being a drunk and sort of in-and-out-of-crazy seems to in our family. My mother almost famously says that it's fairly easy to *go* crazy but it's actually difficult to stay that way, and in the twelve years since my father's death, she more or less has cycled through the worst of her craziness and now goes around sounding more sane than *sane*.

Not that she actually approves of much of my behavior, which strikes her—I'm guessing—as not really settled down. She doesn't like me, for instance, going to bed for three days and watching the Miss America pageant after having suffered some boy-related heartbreak, and she doesn't approve of my not washing my hair and my habit of not getting dressed all weekend, lying around reading and writing poetry, which she says is, frankly, not particularly good. She doesn't approve of my taking whites with my brothers and staying up all night talking, or reading *all of* Walt Whitman's *Leaves of Grass* or *all of* Emily Dickinson aloud, or anything I'm doing that has started to seem extreme and probably makes her worry about my turning out to be both creative and chemically sensitive, which my mother, quite frankly, just really wishes

I would not be. My father was like this, suffering as he did from what they call Pathological Enthusiasms.

It's as if she and my father have already suffered enough for those sins, and can't one of the three of us just go to *law school* and earn an honest living? And she'll whip around and stare at me, as if I'm the most likely candidate.

The house my mother and brothers and I are living in is starting to crowd me anyway. We have a dog named Angus, a wire-haired retriever that my mother says reminds her of something covered with pubic hair. And when the guy I'm sort of dating comes to pick me up, Will asks, Hey, Richard! Whatcha got in the bag there, Richard? Will and my mother have a way of making people feel all overawed, usually by the spectacular nature of their verbal pyrotechnics, so Richard stumbles and stutters and says, I went to the fish market and got some prawns so I can make Jane a risotto (and we do have this plan to go to his perfectly respectable apartment, where he's hung Renoir prints, to eat dinner and listen to classical music), and Will says, Well, sheeeee-it, Richard, I was hoping you'd brought us drugs or that that is—at least— a bag full of condoms.

But I don't actually like Richard in that way, nor does he like me, and he basically just wants to talk about his girlfriend, who's gone away to school in Moscow, Idaho, but my brothers and mother have begun to seem like this huge weight around my neck in my process of trying to be the person I'm in the process of becoming, whoever that is, in that I have absolutely no privacy.

So I move out and get this perfect hippie girl's apartment, and I start grad school in literature and continue to have these unsatisfactory relationships with boys and am thinking I'm probably Bi-Homo-Momo, in that I have all these English major–type friends who are gay, in that being gay seems to come so naturally, and all I have to do is tell the story of LAPD Vice and what they did to my dad to have the whole gay world, such as it is, open to me.

And this is a better, happier world in oh so many ways, so alive with humor and solidarity, and people on the outside of the gag-reflex White Picket Fence are simply so much funnier than the normal ones, who view things from that dead center where they try to get in order to be safe, only to then find out they're dying anyway.

I've just started grad school, and of course it isn't in law or medicine or anything useful where I might pay a mortgage or earn a decent living or even meet someone who'd marry me who'd be in law or medicine and earn a decent living. I've turned into the consummate English major, of course, even though this is already an almost perfectly useless degree and I hate poetry that rhymes and the kind of poets—I think of them as *faggoty*—named Byron and Keats and Shelley. I like almost *nothing* English, in fact, past the age of Shakespeare, except Dickens, whom I'm a little ashamed of liking since I can't remember ever reading him and only know the stories from my grandfather's practice of reading Dickens aloud. I like one poet, Gerard Manley Hopkins; four writers who are British, W. Somerset Maugham and Evelyn Waugh (Waugh because he's both witty and nasty); George Orwell, because he's such a good writer; and E. M. Forster, because he's nice.

But I'm enrolled in a preliminary class called Research Methods, which will test us to see if we have what it takes to get a PhD in English, and I'm already deciding I will not ever be able to do this. Research Methods necessitates your learning how to look up shit in the library and take notes on three-by-five-inch cards, which seems to me to have nothing to do with literature. You also have to do this almost impossible research project that has this Catch-22 element, in that you first have to find someone who has enough citations pertaining to him to do a hundred-citation bibliography, but this also has to be someone simultaneously so obscure that no one has yet published this bibliography, which seems to me to have nothing to do with reading.

I hate this class and am about to drop it, but then I find the mad poet John Clare, who teaches me all about what the Enclosure of Public Lands did to ordinary people of Great Britain and confirms what I've always known about the English lords and ladies: that they're a bunch of snobbish shitheels, like my Grandmother Delia, to whom I'm currently not talking for political reasons. I've stopped talking to everyone in my family who's Republican and who supports the Vietnam War, which is trying to take my poor, psychologically maimed brother Geo and make him go fight in it. At first, Geo was addicted only to the small bottles of Coca-Cola, but in no time it became all manner of drugs, also alcohol, also picking up sailors at the pier who paid him money for unspeakable random things.

When they institute the lottery, Geo draws the number three, so my mother, Will, and I hire a lawyer and go to testify before the draft board and file appeal after appeal, saying our dad's dead and our mother's been in a mental institution and he's our little brother and can't they tell just by looking at him that The Military isn't the place this particular boy *really needs to be*?

Meanwhile, I am needing to find all these citations and then write a hundred-page paper not *about* John Clare, exactly, but more about what it's like to *research* John Clare, which is—I'm deciding—exactly what's wrong with sex, in that it's never sex, exactly, that I'm experiencing; it's something that exists more in the vicinity of sex, that somehow *has to do* with intimate relations, but that is weirdly drained of all but the Ozzie-and-Harriet aspects.

And this is in the summer in the evening in an un-air-conditioned classroom at Cal State Long Beach, which I deeply feel is a mediocre public institution that is somehow quite beneath my exalted, though shaky, sense of self-importance, and I'm taking this class only because this boy has fallen in love with me—and *why*, you might ask, since this very obviously is not going to turn out very well, as he is working nights, and part of the reason that he loves me is because he loves my mother and my brothers and is brotherly to me, which I so totally get. So I'm in this class but am not good at it—I've already worked at the phone company in Downtown Los Angeles, which is where I *so got over* being good at alphabetical order—because I see one letter and almost immediately begin to fixate on how to move the *h* so it comes *before* the g.

This place is mediocre and our professor sucks so much that his seminar on writing this scholarly bibliography has only seven people in it. The class is so small that I can't even hide in the back and write my wretched poems about being a miserable person who wants, three-fifths of the time, to kill herself.

A friend of mine is also in the class—Roseanne Larissa is someone I know from undergraduate creative-writing classes. She's Italian and is from North Carolina, where I never realized smart and sophisticated people live, as that is not what the Anonymous They would have us believe about the South. Roseanne is very pretty and has long, thick, beautiful brown hair that is naturally straight and big blue eyes and a smile that crooks off to one side. And her parents are both educated, as is said in my oh-so-snobbish family, so she speaks not Oakie or Arkie but in a soft Southern drawl that comes and goes as she wants and that you can sometimes hear only imperceptibly, which makes it all the funnier when she says things that are so right on, which is when you start to get how really, really smart she is.

She said things in the poetry-writing class we took together, in which, almost every day, we had to discuss whether or not Bob Dylan and John Lennon are as great as Shakespeare.

Nah, she said, but Bob Dylan's probably as great as John Lennon, who's probably as great as Dylan, but we are just gonna have to wait and see.

The way Al Jolson didn't turn out to be *actually* as great as Jesus, I said, and Roseanne turned to look at me, and she and I knew *exactly* what the other one was talking about.

She once said, Trying to make a poem with abstract words like *Love* or *Truth* or *Beauty* is like trying to build a sand castle using only water, which *exactly* pointed out what I could never stand about the Romantics.

I dislike these poets so much, I don't even like the term *romantic*, which reminds me of Ozzie-and-Harriet sex and the gag-reflex White Picket Fence aspect of living in what I've lately begun to think of as Amerika.

Roseanne is really, really pretty and she's as loud as I am and her language is as profane, and she confides easily and naturally and talks about exactly the things white girls usually will not speak of, saying, for instance, that honestly, the reason she's just not into having sex with a man isn't that she doesn't like men, but that she doesn't really want to have anything stuck into her vagina, which seems to me to be a pretty good reason to be a lesbian.

Her girlfriend is a type I've heard about but never knew before. Josey's dad was in the Army, and Josey herself stands as straight as if she's always at attention. Josey's obviously like the guy in this relationship and Roseanne's like the girl and, very naturally, Roseanne gets to have nongay girlfriends.

And I am technically so nongay right then that the boy I'm living with is thinking we should get married. I don't want to but don't want to tell him this, as I'm afraid it will hurt his feelings.

But Josey doesn't like me as much as Roseanne does, no doubt, because she's a really serious person and is in graduate school herself, at UCLA, which is no doubt more rigorous than what Roseanne and I are up to, which seems stupid, as if we could do it with our eyes closed if we decided it was worth doing, which it so clearly isn't.

We're always being hilarious and loud, much of which comes from the pressure of trying to behave in Dr. Crawford's seminar, to listen to his completely idiotic droning about what you write on the three-by-five-inch cards. I've already had him for Shakespeare, and he's such a terrible teacher that he almost ruined Shakespeare for me, except I realized I could go sit in a study carrel in the library and play the Nonesuch recordings done by Laurence Olivier and the Redfords, listening on headphones as I read the words on the page, and I could suddenly *hear* the language, as it began to make sense to me.

Speaking of who should and shouldn't be brought up on charges for obscenity: a person like *Dr. Crawford* being allowed to teach *Shakespeare?*

The class is so terrible, it makes me think I will die from it. It is simultaneously hard and boring, which is what I've heard about law school, to which I've actually applied and been accepted, though I don't really want to go.

Because the class is so hard and boring, people drop it continually, so now it's down to only the four of us.

But Roseanne and I still show up. We're both good students, even if people don't instantly recognize this, since we're usually having too much fun. Josey doesn't really approve of fun, in the way certain men don't, the way they'll come along and ask girls to settle down and grow up and get a sour look on our face and unpack the groceries and put them neatly away and have another baby and, by the way, bleed to death—if not literally, then at least psychologically.

Roseanne and I just really like each other. The only things wrong with this are that I'm not gay, and that she and I are both involved with other people.

We like each other so much, which is—I realize—not what I often feel about my girlfriends; honestly, you can't often even get to know someone, so hampered are we by what we are and are not actually allowed to say.

The boy I'm not in love with who works nights is really kind to my mother and brothers, so he seems like the person I probably ought to marry. But I'm smarter than he is, for one thing, or at least I have this protective thing going on with him whereby I don't want to get out and really gallop around in my intellect while I'm with him, so that I don't, as my mother says, make him feel diminished. This is one of the reasons I probably won't go to law school, another being that I don't want to, so here I am, concentrating on Dr. Crawford's Research Methods, but this is also something I have no real interest in doing.

This boy has recently intimated to several friends of ours that he and I are engaged, but I am so uninterested in the relationship that I'm not sure I've heard him correctly.

I'm hanging out with Roseanne so much both before and after class, including when I'm stopping off at my mom's to see Will or her or Geo, because theirs is a really fun place to be as long as you don't have to live there, that my mother distinctly does not approve of Roseanne, or more precisely, of the me-and-Roseanne part of my relationship with Roseanne.

My mom and I have always had these struggles over what I think of as the soul of me: She both does and doesn't want me to live the entirely conventional, settled-down, middle-class life that has always eluded her; she believes that the middle class, being married to what's called a *professional* in my family, is a safe place to stuff your daughter.

But she and I now have enough of a normal mother-daughter relationship that when she wants me to do something (like go to law school), I'm unlikely to do it, and if she doesn't want me to do something (like hang out with Roseanne constantly), I'm likely to do it more.

And I don't actually get it, since Roseanne is like one of the friends I know my mom had in college when she was at Cal and was the editor of *Pelican*, and she went around like she was part of the three musketeers, Becky and Jo and Maggie. Becky and Jo were—in everybody's estimation—Top Girls, so why wouldn't she want the same for me?

But then, I've started to notice my mom being jealous of any woman or girl who's ever shown any interest in me—my aunt, certain teachers, various faculty members—as if my loving another woman can in some way come between the two of us, which strikes me as ridiculous, since I all but channel my mom, since the good and bad of her are all but woven into the warp and woof of me. This channeling is my strength. It is also the reason I cannot stand myself.

It happens because no girls in my family ever have any sisters, so we never learn how to be friends with other girls, or to talk to them or share or be honest, and having no sisters is the reason I'm actually afraid of women and not afraid of men.

Men, as my mom has pointed out, are pretty simple. Usually they just basically want to fuck you, or they both do and don't if they're conflicted, or they totally don't, which is why it's such a relief to be with a guy who's gay.

〰

One night in Dr. Crawford's class, Roseanne and I are trying so hard not to laugh at a fly that's droning above his head, a fly that every once in a while lights on the brown saran doll hair of his toupee, that we have to avert our eyes. We start to write notes.

BORED! NEED A DRINK!

NEED TO DRINK HEAVILY RIGHT NOW! MUST BE DRUNK RIGHT NOW OR I WILL KILL MYSELF! WILL KILL SELF IF I DON'T LEAVE AT BREAK AND GO SCORE DRUGS!

ME TOO! I NEED DRUGS TOO!

YOU HOLDING?

NO, YOU?

NO, BUT AM GOING HOME TO GET *IMMEDIATELY* DRUNK. WANNA COME?

And this is a night with a fat full moon that hangs out heavily over the water of the interior channel where I often swim the half mile or so across and back in the moonlight, methodical strokes that are not fast but get me where I'm going, so I swim across in my not-fast-but-serviceable backstroke, then home swimming freestyle, and while I'm in the water I am so completely calm and at peace that I feel I could swim forever because these sturdy, patient strokes of mine are taking me away from here via the river that is never the same river twice.

Roseanne and I come home to where my boyfriend, who wants to marry me and has recently moved in, isn't home and change into our suits—she borrows one from me—and we're shy as we take our jeans off and take our shirts off over our heads. She has a tiny waist and slim, boyish hips, which are a turn-on, but her breasts are large, even pendulous, which isn't actually my thing. She's athletic and I'd expected that she'd not be so big on top, which is stupid—I realize—because I'm comparing her to a boy, which is actually what she is not.

We open a bottle of wine and take it and our wineglasses and our towels down the street to the beach, where we don't actually get in the water, but instead sit on the end of the pier.

I haven't kissed a girl since back in the days of the Dunnigans', when Max was showing us movies and the four or five or us would sit there, owl-eyed and suspended in that twilight before we were what is called at the Health Center *sexually active,* and we were simultaneously turned on, overwhelmed, and disgusted, our bellies roiling with the edge of nausea that feels like desire. It confused us that we'd seen these scenes, acts we did not necessarily approve of—like getting semen shot in your face and pretending to lap it up like you like nothing better than that—but we hadn't looked away. We reacted, but only by making out with one another in the most mild way, unwilling to let the other see any true emotion, as what we were feeling then, and for whom, was just entirely too confusing. Our pants were wet, but we called our kissing and feeling each other up only *practicing.*

And now Roseanne and I are kissing, but she—I realize almost immediately—is much more animatedly into this than I am, which is, frankly, very often my problem. So we kiss, and she and I take the tops of our bathing suits off and sit on the pier in the moonlight, and I feel the weight of her breast but it doesn't excite me, which I'm afraid she's going to be able to tell, but she is talking, saying things I'm worried about her saying, since I am—as Josey imagines—frivolous. She's saying she's thought about the two of us and how we can maybe end up together, and she's saying these words in hot breaths as she's kissing my face and neck and breasts, which I'm thinking about and much too carefully noticing, which is what's always wrong with me: I'm like this observer of my own life, not a legitimate participant.

And now she's telling me heated and confessional stuff about Josey's being jealous of me, and how we can work around that because they aren't necessarily all that exclusive, or maybe I can get to know Josey, too, which I don't actually want to do, in that as much as I admire Josey—who's a little older than we are, also fluent in both French and Spanish—she's too much like all the other scary women I've ever known who'll let you babble on and on but be secretly judging you without their ever telling you what they themselves are thinking, except you do know this: This is one of Our People who is not actually On Our *Side.*

And Josey and Roseanne have these terrible fights over, for instance, who used whose hairbrush, which simply confuses me, because wouldn't one of the reasons you'd want to be with a girl be that you'd share your stuff back and forth? This is exactly the kind of thing I get in trouble for doing in my own relationships, in that I'm always making this kind of mistake, like borrowing something I'm not supposed it, because I can never tell which of the old-fashioned rules to follow and which we're not expected to go by anymore—for instance, fidelity, which I basically don't go by—and with a person like Josey, who is really sort of a bitch, I'd already be in deep, deep trouble.

What I want in a relationship is to not be afraid of this person, which is what Roseanne and I have, but also what I have with the guys I go to bed with. I want to not be afraid, but I also want the thrill of transportation, to be taken somewhere new by a person who feels and thinks and is at least as wild in his or her mind as I am.

And so it's revealed to me that I'm not going to turn out to be a lesbian, at least not right this very instant, and after a while Roseanne knows it too and knows she has to go home to bossy old Josey, who's no fun and who fights with her over who used whose hairbrush and the mundane Ozzy-and-Harriet part of life invades everybody's life, as I'm only now beginning to realize. All of us, no matter how out-there our lives might seem on the outside, have to get up in the morning and make our beds and go about living our day, which was always my aunt's basic point, that sex is just this part of things, not the entirety.

And Roseanne gets it, and it's sad that my being a lesbian or not has so little to do with the love I feel for this girl, my admiration for her beauty and the lilt of her accent and her astonishing intelligence.

As my aunt would say, Life isn't fair.

And Roseanne and I agree we'd have made an amazing couple, better than I do with this boy, whom I do not want to offend, and we're walking home from the beach, still in our suits with our arms wrapped around each other, imagining how great it might have been, when she asks, Am I not worried? And I say, Huh? And she says, About what people will think?

This is still the 1970s—as I seem to have forgotten—so there's still this societal overlay that hasn't been removed, and gay men and lesbians do not yet kiss or hold hands in public, as Vice is still around and Long Beach is a really conservative place, so you're taking certain risks.

That this is your neighborhood, Roseanne says. That they might see us?

I am startled to have been asked the question. This is the deep-down secret of my life: that I don't *live* here any more than I've lived anywhere since the day my father flew off the back of a building and I then, almost immediately, went to live in Other People's houses. Four people—my mother and father, my big brother, my little brother—are the only place I have ever come from and the only real home I have so far known, so caring about what people think in Long Beach, California, in some year in the mid-1970s in the middle of the Vietnam War wouldn't actually *occur* to me.

No, I say, I don't care. I look at the blank rows of houses in which blinds are drawn and the bluish light of TVs enunciates the body count, as the war goes on and on and on. I *can't* care, I tell her.

You know what my father always said? I ask her. The public is an ass.

In truth, he once told me, no one usually even notices what you're doing. And I feel myself, right then, to be almost entirely his daughter, in that I feel impervious to what my mother calls Public Opinion, and if it happens that people fall in love with me, this is their fault and not actually my own special problem.

13
A Pocket History of Sex in the 20th Century

A CHILDHOOD GRIM as Dickens—odd to have lived it in such a naturally beautiful place, those few blocks from the ocean. Years of strife, one tragedy, then another one, then a grief that just settled in, becoming so profound and sedimentary it'd put you in mind of Geologic Time and the epic way in which everyone will ultimately lose everything.

Which reminds me of history, of the boyhood story of a friend of mine, a chieftain's son, and his having to walk out of Namibia as a fifteen-year-old because he had worn either the red tail or the white. And these designations—I could never recall which was which—were no more meaningful than the colors of football teams and were a difference without distinction invented wholesale by the European colonists, all these boys being Bantu and all members of one nation. Yet *the color of his loincloth* was used to determine whether this boy would stay home with his baby brother's beautiful mother—also married to his father— or be force-marched into exile.

Another story of tribalism: how those who own everything encourage us to fight amongst ourselves so we won't notice them perpetually robbing us.

My friend, Bahimwa Kapute, ended up in a Quaker boarding school in Philadelphia, where he learned to dress in a suit and tie and have the most impeccable manners. Thence to San Francisco, where he went to college and lived in a rooming house on Divisadero Street. And he was almost exactly my own age, each of us born at midpoint in the American twentieth century, and I liked him in the way I would always actually prefer the boys I'd never go to bed with.

Nor would Bahimwa have wanted to sleep with me, since he was a shy and stately African and I basically did not attract him. I was just this poor kid with a rich girl's name, living in a cold city yet unable to afford a coat, so I went about buried under layers of boys' cast-off sweaters, a look someone later called "drodgy." I was in grad school, working as a ticket taker, popcorn maker, one-sheet hanger in an art-movie house a couple of blocks off Polk Street where Bahimwa was projectionist.

And I was typically in a relationship with one man yet having an affair with another, going upstairs as the last reel ran to fuck this other projectionist on the stereotypically dirty couch in the owner's office, hurrying to get this pathetic, sordid lovelessness over by the time the dinger began to ding—we'd then dress and lock up, and he'd drive home to his wife and nine-year-old daughter.

The nine-year-old daughter seemed an important detail, since I was beginning to watch the way history did not so much *repeat itself* as *rhyme*, and nine was the exact age I was when my father killed himself: *Ding!*

And Bahimwa—who was an honest innocent—would have been shocked by this behavior. Because he liked me and thought I was a really sweet, smart girl, which I actually deep down was, and a *good person*, as he liked to say. Bahimwa still believed in decorum, in verbal modesty, as did I.

And do.

And anyway, he was much in love with Aretha Franklin, also still very ardently involved in his imagination with the very young mother of one of his littlest brothers back home. He would always become somewhat stiff and formal at this point in the telling of his story, saying, But all this transpires in a very orderly way, as is accustomed by our kinship system.

Unlike the mess you all have here being what Bahimwa was no doubt thinking.

This woman was beautiful and not much older than he. She'd picked Bahimwa as her favorite and cuddled him and once removed a cinder from his stinging eye by opening the lids with her fingertips and swiping his entire eyeball with the softest motion of her tongue.

My God, he said, eyes closed now against the thrill of that particular ecstasy.

There were also two Pakistani men who rotated through as projectionist, and neither of them was interested in me, either, though the younger, smaller one was a flirt and tease who believed I harbored all kinds of wild imaginings about what and who Muslims were and what they would and wouldn't eat—when I actually had never thought much about Muslims one way or another, except to misguidedly imagine it might be Muslims who thought having your picture taken with a camera could steal your soul (or did that actually have more to do with depicting a deity?). The short one told me that both men had written on their resumes (which were virtually identical; honestly, their names may both have been Muhammad, if I'm not merely elaborating) that it was possible for a Pakistani man to work for up to a twenty-eight-hour period without sleep. Though I now wonder if this was yet another of his jokes at my expense, since I did still believe just about anything that was told to me. He may have been saying that the idea of *Muslims* to a person like me was analogous to what Flannery O'Connor in *Wise Blood* called *a trick on niggers*. She actually had one of her characters say this, of course, a character who was describing the historical personage we know as Jesus Christ.

That this devout Roman Catholic would have a redneck, white, protestant lowlife proclaim the Historic Jesus as something invented as *a trick on niggers* was about the most shocking thing I'd ever seen a woman—or anyone—write. But it also seemed so poetically *true* as to sound like something my mother would say, something that would make people snap their heads around to stare at her, wondering if she was going *in* or coming *out* of the door marked PSYCHOSIS, and I've always wanted to have an occasion to quote it without the travail of having to write an entire doctorial dissertation in which to plunk it down, as the phrase does encompass so many intricate levels of blasphemy.

Which is the kind of thing I was always wondering while lying upstairs with the formerly fat, white, married, Midwestern projectionist, whom I never particularly liked. I would wonder how the Pakistanis came up with that particular number, would be guessing that it was never scientifically measured, that it was meant metaphorically to state that a Muslim wasn't a total loser fuckup, like the now only-pudgy white guy. I knew his wife. She and I were both just so much *better* than this man, so much smarter and more attractive.

She had a good job at Blue Cross and was supporting him while he imagined himself a novelist, which wouldn't have been that bad had he been any good. But he read books by Henry James and wrote these labored stories whose one main point was to make nuanced, nasty observations about how acute and far-seeing this narrator, who read Henry James, was—at least in contrast with everyone else who hadn't read Henry James. That this work did manage to sound like some strangled version of Henry James only made it worse.

This ass thinks you need to write like Henry James from way out here? I thought. From the wrong side of the country and the *wrong end* of the twentieth century? It was such honestly awful writing that, after reading only the first few pages, I knew I needed to break up with him. I'd anyway only fucked him because he imagined himself a writer and held himself in high esteem.

But he was a pig, I saw, a commoner, while I felt myself to be more the princess of a displaced people, like Bahimwa's. My childhood felt analogous to Bahimwa's, huge in dislocation and events. In these cinematic tales of tragedy and heroism, it's always up to the children to go forth, to somehow walk out through the scorched earth that is a childhood without a childhood.

⚇

Because I was a girl, I knew I needed to carry my body carefully. I felt precariously balanced, walking lightly across a strange landscape that might be like *a minefield*, but I don't much like putting it that way, since I am not Princess Di and have no actually living experience of *a minefield*, so I call Will. He was a soldier in South Korea, where the whores of Seoul would abuse him by spitting on him if he passed them by, not persuaded enough by their allure. He'd walk by, not interested, so they'd call him Number Ten G.I., a Ten being the worst thing a person could possibly be.

I'm wondering if my brother might have walked point in the U.S. Army.

Was our childhood, I ask him, pocked with misery as a minefield, or more dark and cartoonish? More the graphic novel with that wide-eyed wop, remember him? That little Italian orphan kid they called Dondi?

Nah, my brother says. Maybe it's just my mania, but I remember large parts being delightful.

That's because you're more like Mom and the two of you were delightful, I say. For one thing, you could talk. For another, you weren't suicidal.

Right, Will says, if that works for you. This is what Will always says when he's on the phone with me while simultaneously IMing or participating in some online chat-room situation.

So I back up, restate, because I'm honestly interested.

Were you suicidal? I ask.

I was suicidal once, my brother says, popping back into focus. It was the second or third time I'd started my PhD, he says, and I was still married to Michelle. Lilah had just been born when I started sleeping with always just *the least likely* person in my program. Once, it was this hundred-pound former gymnast named Bonnie, who was really chalk to my cheese, and she dumped me. And I immediately started drinking again, as I always would when I was washing out of this or that PhD program by sleeping with another of these really unlikely women. This was at Irvine. I figured I'd show her by going to the bell tower and throwing myself off. I was drunk, of course, but not so drunk that it didn't occur to me that killing myself over some hundred-pound former gymnast, who was, by the way, inane, was a really stupid thing to do.

I, too, have almost never been suicidal; it feels like an indulgence. I believe myself instead to be this precariously balanced mobile, a gizmo of Alexander Calder–like self-invention. Bright metal, wires, and springs that don't really go together, and huge pieces, of course, that are very literally missing, but I have walked out carefully, as Bahimwa walked out of Namibia, because walking out is the only thing—aside from lying on the trail to die—you are allowed to do.

Wherever I go, I still feel hounded and pestered by the clattering footsteps of all the sundry members of my dead and still living family, this entire *population* that is always popping up inappropriately out of a Stephen King–esque graveyard of creepy, cartoonish ghoulishness. They are *loud* and extreme, and seem to exist in caricature, being expelled from an overstuffed VW or crawling out of a Sgt. Pepper–like hole in the floor or dropping from the attic, like Gregor Samsa cockroaches in clown shoes.

And they are often brilliant mimics, these Westerners, these round-the-campfire storytellers, so I feel taunted and mocked if I ever think I *might* get away from them—also for my slight belief in my own small sad joy, a tiny faith in my own delightedness, about the notion that even one of us could imagine one day getting on a plane and flying off to land someplace that isn't just still more and more *California*. I keep it hidden in one hand that I shove deep into a pocket, a hope as bright as the light of Tinkerbell.

Because we've been here so long, our family has become ingrained and turned into really bizarre creatures of this place, wizened by the bright aridity that doesn't go with our skin tone. Our skin is quite wrong for this place of light and space, and hope is no longer the doctrine to which our family subscribes. And we are so totally representative of the dominant ethnic grouping, so typical, too, of our kinship system, these tall, fair-skinned northern European types, deeply depressive, defeated, all completely alcoholic.

So I don't drink and I do not take drugs, though everyone I know is suddenly washing down handfuls of all manner of substances and shooting shit into their arms and sticking it up their noses with what seems like reckless abandon.

Hey, I think, *you behave like that, and something really bad might happen to you . . .*

Anyway, I am already completely addicted to heroin and cocaine without ever having to try them. I've been emancipated from all family support and own only a single pair of shoes that are shaped like hamburgers, shoes that the man who called me *drodgy* refers to as my Little Man Shoes, and am anyway already so addicted particularly to cocaine that I feel entirely *at one* with it, as if there is no difference at all between my own substance and my abuse of this substance.

I am nothing aside from my addiction, except that I can't afford it.

And while I've slept with plenty of boys, a few men, and a couple of girls—but never a grown-up woman—and am actually not all that prudish, I don't want my addiction to some drug to be the sole determinant of whom I let fuck me.

Alcohol is at least legal, but I just can't drink. One of my more recent doctors, who's actually the nephew of John O'Hara (yet another hopelessly alcoholic American novelist) and is named for him, calls this condition being *clinically sensitive.*

I just can't do what these other people are all doing—if I did, I would lose my mind.

If I drink, I lose all sense of the world's verticality, my brain goes reptilian, and I am instantly lost from linear time. I once drank wine while trying to follow a recipe on the lasagna box. I was having an English professor over, a woman my mother jealously called Mrs. Poetry. Her name was actually Professor Dora Polk, PhD, and she was from England and was a Fabian socialist—she gave me Waterford crystal one of the several times I was either briefly married or engaged, or on some analogous occasion. Dr. Polk, oddly, believed in me—I had some kind of hokey-though-paid TA-ship under her, whereby I had no responsibilities aside from my own writing, then going by one department of Our Institution of Higher Learning every month to pick up a check from a certain window.

I'd invited Dr. Polk to dinner at my neat hippie girl's apartment as a thank-you, and it is completely typical of the abject nature of my really quite riddled self-esteem—I think of it as the part of the Calder that is the formerly beautiful copperish sheath that's now shaggy with bullet holes—that it truly astonishes me that I can still reach back through the dark halls of time and hear this woman, whom I admired, whispering her few curt British words of encouragement.

I saw how drinking immediately ripped through the metal of the Calder I'd been balancing so carefully, how it sapped me of strength and even the most basic kind of reason, made me now *completely nihilistic,* and how this happened *absolutely instantly,* so one moment I'd be this sweet, smart, well-compensated girl cooking in her neat hippie-ish kitchen, and the next I'd be noticing how little the order in which adding the fucking ingredients actually mattered to the Act of Committing Lasagna, lasagna being another of the huge raft of items that simply do not in any way existentially matter, as my mother would say, not even the *tiniest fucking bit.*

So I am both from here and from elsewhere, both the red tail and the white, and always oddly new to my most recent place of exile. My brothers and I arrived on a refugee ship filled with such real and cartoon orphans as Bahimwa and Dondi, which is strange because this is actually the same place we've always been, except that now the rules are changing. This is California, where the rules are always changing, the manners and mores morphing, so you never know what is right or wrong—just that it's different from what it was just yesterday. It is *crazy!* which might be bad or good. Someone is hung up, uptight, straight; one day that's a compliment, the next it's an accusation.

For a while it is all New Games, in which aggressive energy is pushed down and subverted, when someone will put a huge, heavy rock in front of the bathroom door, holding this door open. The bathroom is right off the main room where the party is going on, so the New Gamers can watch you run the humiliating video behind your eyes as you're trying to figure out how much you really need to pee, and whether moving the rock is even possible, or if maybe it isn't time to leave this party, to go home and find some new friends, some friends you actually like?

And the words for things are changing, so you never know what the more accurate thing to say is. What something is called is always different from what it formerly was. Sex isn't *making love*, but is it really *fucking*? Isn't it more *having intimate relations*? Were these relations even *intimate*? Here, as in other important arenas, I always feel like someone struggling to learn the language.

And we are suddenly nonviolent and we are vegetarian and we are reading Gandhi and thinking hard about not wearing leather shoes, though we go ahead and do it, and our not being meat eaters has to do with the bloodlessness of sex, which, while friendly enough, is also actually passionless and perfunctory.

So I am trying to learn to live by the laws and rules of the new Western world, and these have everything to do with Time Consciousness and successfully completed goals and monetary success and high status and achievement.

I know only that it is important to try to follow instructions, and that two of our most basic instructions are You Share Rides and You Do Not Take Intoxicants, though sex is one intoxicant still being pretty freely shared. It simply seems to suit me to work in close tutorial in the new guidelines, so I seek out tutors and often sleep with them, and I fall in love easily and well with all of my friends, and these friends are often boys, even as I am also sleeping with a man like the projectionist, whom I do not much like, though sleeping is, of course, not what is ever going on.

I once notice a body like his in the San Francisco MOMA, when the museum is still on the second floor of the Herbst Theatre, down the street from city hall. It is a small bronze, a squat, thick-thighed sculpture Matisse did in 1900, called *Le Serf*. The figure is armless and seems almost animal—penis and ball sack full, belly sticking out, bottom lip drooping. The man seems as elemental as one of the hundred Russian words for dirt, a heavy-bodied thing that looks like it was dug from and is returning to the earth.

I am young, so I tell myself, *This is what a man must be.*

And I understand our *kinship*: that he is alcoholic, *of course*, and therefore afflicted by gravity, as is everyone in my family. And since he's read books I haven't read, I believe he has something to teach me.

It's so easy to notice, in the Inevitability of Retrospect, how like the casino girl Susan Sarandon played in *Atlantic City* I am, the one who washes her hands and arms with lemons to take away the smell of the oysters she's shucked, how yearningly she asks the elegant old man she's just about to go to bed with if he will teach her things.

And I am someone so completely and even naturally alcoholic that a single beer or a glass of wine lights me up internally like a jar of shook moonshine, a substance I tasted once in the moonlit night of a Tennessee parking lot out behind a printing plant. *This is the Deep South*, I was busy telling myself, *and this is the wine of their communion.* The pure grain alcohol shimmers in that eerie light—hence its name—and drips viscously from within the lid as something so colorless and lethal, it might remind you of gasoline.

I ended up making out with some other traveler in the backseat of someone's car, no doubt utterly humiliating myself. But I didn't go to bed with this person that time, didn't get pregnant, didn't get venereal disease, as I was being careful with this vessel that was my girl's physical body, knowing it had a particular destiny. And we, the Big City guests, were such completely foolish assholes as to be in Tennessee touring this printing plant with locals who were *so clearly entertaining themselves* by winding each of us up and turning us loose upon ourselves. They knew we thought they were hicks, so they were acting exactly like the stage rednecks we needed to speak slowly and carefully to.

Tribalism. And just one more case of Us Versus Them, and of the Dominant Culture's (of which I was still obliquely representative) hanging onto the belief that it was *winning*, that it would *always win* when up against Our Inferiors, which meant anyone marginalized, anyone poor or dispossessed or rural, Bantu or Pakistani.

Or female.

ᴆᴆᴆ

I'll make out with some publishing boy but am meanwhile honestly only into Mrs. Poetry and her ilk, my wont being to fall almost instantly in love with any of the better-looking senior faculty, any man or woman who might be able to teach me even a single thing: that, for instance, the comma goes inside the quotation marks. And this person, who might or might not be married, is always completely inappropriate, given the terrible discrepancies in power and proximity-to-power between the two of us and the very obvious vibe of my status as a waif, my Little Man Shoes, my no coat, my no parents.

I love the kind of English professor who is, of course, married, but this is the part of the seventies in which the sixties are still alive and we aren't yet all hung back up and we still share rides, still occasionally hitchhike or live communally, as these activities make us feel young, free, and European. So we might still fraternize across the class/caste discrepancies, and some great-looking professor will come sit on the grass of the quad with what Will always refers to as A Group of Us.

And it is always A Group of Us, as these are deeply communal times, which are actually wrong for me, since I hate being in any group for longer than a minute or two, as I have the most intense need to pay way too much attention to every detail of every single individual.

So I'm able to fake Group Think for only a little while, whispering to ask which page we are on in the Big Book, only to have some tiny sparkling prism thing in my Calder start communicating with me by wireless from high in the armature, issuing an SOS of warning.

Fuck the lasagna, it says. We need to get out of here and go drink Antisocially.

I am porous, clinically sensitive, and the stress of anyone's special needs makes me marginally psychotic. I am balanced pieces that move in the wind and have no proper spatial boundaries. I am a chameleon and the elements are reflective; they mirror the surroundings, enabling me to disappear so completely that *any* group becomes yet another place where I can lose my mind.

And what other people are doing during This Time Period is being really sure of themselves. They admire psychosis, which does seem a fairly rational reaction to the United States of America's current government, which seems to have traduced us into an endless war and are yet again unwilling to enforce anyone's civil rights, aside from the tall white men of northern European extraction that my own family is so good at producing.

The Dutch are some of the tallest people on the earth, on average, reasons for this being usually ascribed to a combination of national wealth, nutritional habits, quality of healthcare, and genetics. The Dutch are admirable in all ways. The Dutch can also, as was always said in my family, drink *like fishes*.

I could never fall in as one of these fellow travelers of psychosis, as there is almost nothing about actual insanity—with which I have more than a slight familial acquaintance—that I find in any way attractive.

So I am always carefully rationing my impulses, which are a girl's and therefore ardent, but which feel shameful to the degree that I am led around by them, even though, in retrospect, they are completely innocent and age appropriate. One day A Group of Us are lying on the sun in the grass while discussing Saul Bellow's *Mr. Sammler's Planet* and I'm noticing the sunbaked look of the side of this particular professor's very tanned and sturdy neck. He is lying on his side, chin in hand, head propped on his elbow, and I understand how easy it would be to scoot just a little ways this way so my girl's body lay parallel to his, and for me to pull his weight, which I knew to be willing, down onto me.

He is married, of course, but he has paid particularly kind attention to me and let me know I am somehow curious to him: He has noticed, perhaps, my spinnaker at full sail or the glints off the polished, high-up, clanging riggings, or has seen or sensed all those particular gaps and lacks and emptinesses that always make a well-meaning, slightly parental person such as my professor want to offer me sympathy and solace, which are of almost no possible use to me.

He asks which character I identify with in Bellow's novel, meaning am I reading along with the story of the old man behind his eyes—the old man is intelligent and crabby and in every way a perfect crustily misogynistic, Chicago Jewish, Bellow-ish character—or am I more in league with the slightly distasteful hippie girl to whom Sammler (or, more likely, Bellow) finds himself uncomfortably attracted?

Mr. Sammler, of course, I say, but am shocked by the question. I add, He's the protagonist—it's so totally *his planet.*

Did my professor ask me this because he took me for some vacant hippie chick who doesn't wash her underpants? My current version of myself is that I am more like a girl Will Shakespeare. I think Shakespeare would have totally *got me* and my drodgy getup, which is why it seems that he speaks directly *to me* across the ages, it being Shakespeare who teaches us you don't have to *be* a blackamoor to *be* Othello.

My great-looking professor invites us to his house and we meet his wife, named Nona, and they are very happily married, so I don't lie back on the grass and ask him to put his weight on me, which I sometimes do, often with some usually pretty random and unlikely man whom I actually have not even the slightest intention of honestly fucking.

I want to feel the weight of an actual man, though I am probably not yet old enough to deal with the gravity of what that might mean. It's a conceit of girls and women that we can somehow *handle* a man by keeping our most true self hidden from him. We speak from this hidden place in order to control him, thinking we can either reason with him or beguile him. They are not the same as we are, my mother said. We think our being attractive to these men makes them stupider than we are, which makes us feel omnipotent. It's this dangerous arrogance that can get us into trouble.

What a less Calder-like and better-integrated girl might have done is more likely fall in love with the slender boy who'd then thicken alongside of her, so she'd end up at an older age lying with the person who goes with her.

And I am anyway outgrowing boys, and I am so honestly sick of the cult of California. I want someone East of Here—someone less sunny, more doomed? I want someone who went to a decent college or university, as everyone in my family has all down the line, until we got to my own particularly, urchinish generation.

I am being very patchily educated, since I am doing it myself and am barely competent. I wasn't an early reader—more an early watcher, an eavesdropper, the habitual overhearer. I wasn't even a reader of books;

I was more the reader of the titles of things, the spines on my parents' bookshelves, for instance, where I'd spell out *The Gathering Storm* and *Look Homeward, Angel*.

And I am beginning to understand that these words are only dust, pinpricks of ancient light on the most all-encompassing star chart; that the title of every book is only a single atomic particle in the whole huge and cosmic swirl that is all written human history, and that is as universal and ongoing as one vastly expanding pearl.

〰

When I leave college, my professor with the beautiful neck says to me, You won't just get married, Jane, and vanish down the rabbit hole? You'll let us hear from you?

Hear from me? I think. *I am still just this hidden girl who has nothing original to say, and he is asking me to become the hero of my own story?*

He is asking me to go and *do something*, but in order to do this I'd have to stop letting my life be all about my parents, which is anyway an impossible assignment.

I'd have to stop being a girl, which is all I've ever been; I'd have to set out alone on a galactic journey that would separate me from everyone. Become that singular event that results when a bit of dust caroms across the night sky, he is saying to this person who feels as weightless as an electron. He is asking me to become the grain of sand inside the shell of the oyster that will allow experience to adhere to me.

Which is a terrible assignment for me, as I feel I've *already* been sentenced to a lifetime of loneliness. I'd need to become the subject of the sentence, rather than its direct object, and I'd need to abandon the only identity I've ever known: In the case of orphans, as it is with girls, it is our lack that most easily defines us.

In order to become the hero of my own story, I feel, I need to find a better-muscled and more self-confident vocabulary, need to dress like a different person, buy some shoes, a couple of good outfits. I need to break up with the projectionist, who is bad not only for my soul but for every other part of me as well.

Who, when I tell him, thinks it is for all the societal reasons: that I want to now go off and find some suitable person who is actually better than he is, someone who has a good job, a nice car, some view of a reasonable future.

From high up in the armature, I watch and I decide I'll let him think this. I believe it is a kindness not to say what I really think, which is that I simply can't continue to have sex with a man whose writing sucks as bad as his.

He is so furious that he throws his big bunch of keys down onto the hood of his own car. They scratch the paint, bounce over the front of the car, then clatter down a storm drain.

Fuck! he yells. Now see what you made me do!

This is in the alley across from the theater's entry. That night it is crowded with moviegoers and bar patrons who catch my eye in passing, all of us thinking, What an *alcoholic* way to act.

◌◌◌

Will and I are each working our own way through school, and it is still possible for a girl as poor as I am to live alone in an amazing apartment. A studio in my building in Hayes Valley rents for $75 a month. Mine is one huge unfurnished room with a great view and a walk-in closet so large I even consider—since I have so few clothes—putting my bed in there.

This is on Market at Hermann, a couple of blocks from the San Francisco Zen Center. My seventh-floor windows sit in a bay that looks

out over the streetcar tracks. A couple of miles away, beer is being perpetually poured into a frothing glass on top of a building at the foot of Potrero
Hill. Ribbons of pale yellow and gold and white are formed into streams
of liquid and bubbles by thousands of small, blinking incandescent bulbs.
It is the sign on the roof of the Hamm's Building at Second and Howard.

My building has an elevator and is well maintained: 1930s art
nouveau, all black-and-white tiles and polished brass detailing. It has a
grand foyer with a locked front door and someone always at the desk.
It's full of gay guys, some very newly, very raucously OUT. AIDS is
already happening, but no one knows this yet, so boys and young men
and older men are all still frolicking in the bathhouses. This is pre–
Harvey Milk, a really sweet guy with a bitchy boyfriend, who's not yet
been elected to anything and still just has the camera shop.

There is militancy about the gay men in the Castro and in my building, a new tribalism, I think, that has them dressing amazingly alike—it
is the peacoat time, the era of the Greek fisherman's cap.

For the first time I hear someone refer to heterosexuals—or it may
be all women—as *breeders*. I am a breeder, I think, have always been a
breeder, which is why, as I was surviving my own childhood, I needed
to guard my body.

Breeder. The word is repulsive.

I get a new job, a day job, so I don't have to get to and from work at
night using public transportation. I needed to leave the theater because
I was robbed in the ticket booth. One night after the first show started,
a guy who'd hidden in the bathroom followed me into my little cubicle.
He said he had a gun, but I didn't for a second believe him.

He didn't really much scare me. He was a tiny white dude, actually
diminutive, and his head was shaved in the manner of Synanon.

Sorry, man, he told me, even as the robbery was going on, but I'm a
junkie, you know? To which I said, Sure, sure, I completely get it. I was

busy emptying the till into the paper bag he was holding out to me. This robber was so small he looked like a little boy on Halloween, trick-or-treating for candy.

My new day job is right down the street at Ninth and Market—it is even at a company that sort of pertains to me. I am answering phones at Scrimshaw Press, which has a best-selling picture book called *Handmade Houses*.

This feels like the end of my hippie days, the first moments of my attaining purchase in the Middle Classes. I am so busy leaving poverty and risk behind, moving my body on toward its next adventure in—I hope—much more prosperous surroundings and a better wardrobe, that I am honestly surprised to let myself into my locked apartment after work one evening and find the dumped projectionist.

Oh, fuck, I think. My heart contracts. The door, which is heavy because this is an old-fashioned building, just then closes behind me.

He is sitting on my couch. On the little table in front of him are a bottle and a glass. He's been drinking in the dark, as this sort of self-pitying person always likes to do—my glass, my ice, his whiskey.

Hey, I say. Fancy finding you here . . . ?

My voice is fake, flat, nonchalant. I need to hide from both of us the enormity of what he's done: This man has *broken into my apartment.* Sane people don't act like this. I need to pretend he is a different kind of person, a more well-balanced one. I need him not to know I am physically afraid of him.

You didn't return my phone calls, he said.

Sorry, I say. Meant to. Don't really know how to work that thing.

I gesture at the big answering machine next to my phone on my desk in the bay window. These home telephone-recording devices are new, but I've used one before, when I made the message that told the start times of the movies at the theater. I would then call myself from home to find out when I needed to go to work, would hear my own soft voice so earnestly saying the times, saying the titles of films—*lays ON-fawn d' pair-a-dee*—as a phrase of music, as sounds learned, to disguise the fact that I don't know languages.

I honestly meant to, I tell him; then I say his name, say it carefully, as if I am talking to an animal.

How did you get in? I ask him.

Some faggot in a Greek fisherman's cap, he says.

Oh, that would *vastly* narrow the field, I think but don't say.

What I say is: No, not in the building; I meant—and I only mouth the words—how did you get *in here*? and I point at the floor.

Used this, he says, and he shows me a credit card, which can be stuck into a doorjamb beside the lock and slid along to work the sloping edge of the bolt back into its chamber. This works only in older buildings like mine, whose doorknobs and locks were manufactured in other, more innocent times.

And you're here because . . . ?

Because I need to confront you about some of the things you said, he tells me. Some things said, others left unsaid.

Right, I say. *Confront me?* I think. *Said and unsaid?* I am just some grad student who sold tickets where he works with whom he had a dalliance.

Still sitting on the couch, he hunches forward to tip the bottle, which is empty, over the glass, which—except for the ice—is also empty.

I advance a few steps into the room, my bag still slung over my shoulder, still holding my mail in my hand. I am terrified of him but need for him not to know this. I need him to think this could still be resolved without consequence, that no one has to be angry, that no part of this is hopeless.

I, as usual, play both parts: I am myself being robbed, even as I am simultaneously the Synanon junkie who is robbing me—a form of mind meld known as *painful empathy*. I became good at it by growing up in a crazy family.

Because I've just moved in and have been fixing things—painting and hanging pictures—my tools are out, lying along the top of a bookcase above which I've hung a print of Mark Rothko's *Black Over Red*, which I had framed. The three-shelf bookcase is waist-high and still empty—I have painted it the exact red that's in the Rothko.

I arranged these two objects—the framed print and the red bookcase—to look like two spatial pieces that match or rhyme. I like that kind of thing, a visual joke or resonance, with the one object being mundane and the other transcendent, the one standing out, planted in a physical room, the other falling back and away into timelessness.

My tools—including a hammer and nails and the fasteners for picture hanging—lie atop the bookshelf. These are close enough to the projectionist that if he turns only slightly, his eyes will fall on the hammer and screwdriver. I worry that if he sees the tools lying like weapons in a story, it might occur to him to use them.

I am still naïve, a vegetarian, and I thought we'd evolved to a moment in our species' history that says war is pointless, that violence between a man and a woman isn't necessary. We can have sex *as equals*, a girl can think, can talk to one another *as equals*, so I am in shock that someone could break into my apartment and sit here exuding a threat to me.

As bad as anyone in my own family ever acted, we didn't do *this* kind of thing. I keep thinking it isn't even possible for me to know a man like this. He's educated, even if he—okay—only went to the same kinds of shitty public universities I myself attended. I can't believe that a man would become so desperate that he'd resort to violence.

Really? I keep thinking. *People actually behave like this?*

My childhood hasn't actually prepared me for further disasters and has not taught me you are in fact powerless over people, places, the current of the river, the large events of history. Rather, I imagine I can, by way of my total understanding, control not only that robber but also this projectionist. I still imagine myself as someone so far-seeing that I am like a character in James, controlling everyone with my acuity.

But he is drunk, labile, seething, and his anger is far past rationality. The light from the streetlamps plays upon his facial planes, hardened, masklike, the skin around his mouth pale, the pupils of his eyes so hugely dilated they look concave. It is rage that blinds someone, makes his eyes go as dead as that.

And I know this look. It means this person who has loved me in the past can no longer see me when he looks at me, and has now locked on to something in the shadows behind me, so he's looking past me to his own more base and elemental lack.

Lack, cast large, is projection.

You're a nothing, he tells me.

I shrug, bite my lip. He can go ahead and think that if he needs to.

She kicked me out, he says. We're in a trial separation.

Jeeez, I say. Well, that's too bad.

She knows, he says. I told her.

Told her?

About us.

And I think, But there *is* no us! It is his inability to use the proper pronoun and the proper tense that makes me really begin to worry about his sanity.

Hey! I say, suddenly energetic. Not to change the subject, and we will talk about all this, but would you like something to eat? I'm starving, and you look like you could maybe eat something. We for sure need to talk about all this, but let's eat something first. And my brother's in town—you remember I mentioned him? The older one who's in the PhD program in sociology at the University of Texas? He just flew in from Austin and he's coming over in a little while; let's just give him a call at his hotel . . . ?

My brother isn't really in town, of course, but I suddenly need to hold the heavy black earpiece of the Bakelite phone in my hand, to enjoy the weight of it. I take a step toward my desk, where the phone sits, and my hand reaches out, but before it makes contact the projectionist comes at me.

He doesn't actually hit me, more wrestles me across the room, and there is, as there always is, a discrepancy between people whose body masses are not balanced and whose levels of rage and desperation are not matched, one also lacking the other's upper body strength.

Girls and women can't be expected to fight these fights, because we so rarely can win them. Being a sister among brothers and boy cousins taught me this. Female athletes respect this: We can swim our fastest and not ever beat the faster man.

He shoves me back onto my bed, holds my upper arms so tightly they'll be visibly bruised. I am astonished. No one has ever treated me like this.

He knocks me back, falls on top of me, holds me there with the power of his insistence. Pushes our clothes out of the way. It happens. It continues happening.

When he is done, he collapses and weeps on top of me. Like the junkie, he is instantly sorry for what he's done.

Men? my mother used to say in her fake French accent. They are such *BAY-bees*.

We are each only partly undressed. He is still lying atop my body, weeping for himself, weeping over his disappointment in himself, over his maybe ruined marriage, but mostly for the generally shitty way his life is turning out.

I am thinking about his nine-year-old, what a father would feel knowing someone has treated his daughter like this, if his girl or I ever had one.

Light falls through the three tall windows beyond my desk that look out over Market Street, where far below the streetcars are still running. The only light in the apartment remains the one I flipped on in the entryway. I am breathing carefully, am staring at the Rothko, in which the image of one swath of color floats above another. I use it to calm myself. I've already joined the only church I'll ever belong to, which is art, which has the power to redeem us from the complete chaos of our confused and sordid lives. I'd heard that red was called a fugitive pigment for the way light tends to fade it. I want to not turn out to be fugitive pigment.

The surface of the framed print catches the light from the window. In the reflection, the sign on the Hamm's Building keeps pouring beer endlessly.

My head is turned. I keep my eyes fixed on the Rothko. I don't look at the hammer that is lying right beneath it. It is my hammer, so I know exactly what its weight feels like in my hand.

I am perfectly prepared to kill him.

The projectionist falls into a deep sleep, breathing noisily. He is still lying half on top of me. He is a big man, tall and overweight, and I am afraid to move because I think it might awaken him. On the nightstand there stands the kind of illuminated clock that isn't actually digital but works mechanically. Time is spelled out on thin, yellow plastic flaps that flip over in columns that hang on a horizontal axis, the numbers printed in black Helvetica. A card flips every minute, then every ten, then—on the other side of the dot-dot that makes the colon—every hour. Time is the river into which you cannot step twice. The flaps flipping over and hitting the ones they are replacing make a small, satisfying smack.

Time passes as it always passes, a lesson I learned in childhood.

It is ten, then eleven, then twelve. The streetcars stop. He wakes. He's sobered up enough to look around anxiously for the authority who'd confirm he is in trouble.

He lied earlier, he confesses. He didn't actually tell his wife about us, because he didn't want to hurt her.

Anger sizzles along the surface of my skin like it is giving off electricity.

That's nice, I say.

When he leaves, I call Will in Texas and tell him what happened.

Jesus, shit! he says. Where do they even *get* these people? What's his name?

Henry James, I say. Number Ten G.I.

Name and phone number, Will says. I need to call Mr. Henry James and read him the riot act. Someone *will be speaking* with Mr. James. This *will be happening* first thing in the morning, when Number Ten G.I. is still suffering from the whiskey flu.

This manner of speaking in the future progressive is a technique my brother has perfected working his way through college as a psych tech—you calm a mental patient by convincing him you have complete control of the narrative. A crazy person has no use for options and can be settled down by hearing what's what and what is going to be definitively happening. The future is not the process for the crazy person, as it remains for the rest of us. Rather, it's this tableau that is already fixed.

Either you'll be doing this for me *now*, as my brother would instruct the mental patient, or you will be doing it for me in a little while.

I tell my brother his name, say we can't call the police, that I've already done enough to mess up the lives of the projectionist's wife and daughter, who now have to continue to put up with him.

Later that day, Will phones me back. Jesus, what an asshole. You gotta promise you're gonna do better next time.

Couldn't probably do much worse.

You didn't see that coming?

No idea. I just didn't believe anyone would actually act like that, at least not someone so pretentious and Jamesian and *antique*. What'd you say to him?

Told him who I was, that I knew what he'd done and where he lives, works, where his wife works, where his kid goes to school. Told him I have a shotgun. Said I have a shotgun, described my shotgun, said I'd trained in the Army as a marksman, that I'd already killed someone, which isn't actually true, but he doesn't need to know that.

Said it'd disturb me *not at all* to have to kill again, my brother says.

So Mr. Henry James puffs up and says I can't threaten him. I said, *Wellllll*, actually, I obviously *caaaannnn* threaten you because I *aaaammm* threatening you. Said I'd kill him if he ever so much as spoke to my sister again, said I am, and I quote, *A very angry person*, that this derives from our shitty childhood, so forth. Said killing him would actually give me a great deal of pleasure. Told him I participate in a voucher program with a certain airline, that I have tons of these $25 vouchers that I've saved for free flights, that I'd be more than happy to redeem all of them to come out there and shoot him, that it'd cost me nothing more than the cost of a cab from the airport. I told him his address—I talked the operator into giving it to me; she used the reverse directory. Told him I could read a map, that I was looking at his cross street, right there a couple blocks off the park in the Richmond district. Told him it would take me seven hours to get there.

♾

Before was when a girl might still hitchhike, might stand on a street corner with her friends, wearing miniskirts or hiphuggers, faces hidden behind long cascades of hair, eyes shy but hips tipped forward into the future, where, they sense, they will be using their bodies to bring them toward infinite possibility.

Before was when we were still young and hadn't coalesced, were still simply pieces of who we'd turn out to be. We believed we were weightless, had almost no idea of the power our bodies had, and so would still have sex for the most slight and silly reasons, not in the name of love but out of these *ideas* we came up with, from a certain political stance that said a girl got to do what a boy might do. Or we'd screw, say, out of friendliness or a philosophical commitment to international brotherhood or some hyperarticulated bullshit for the sake, say, of gender equality.

Manners and mores still exist in the *before* as cultural artifacts of a girlhood like mine, a time when my brother could still go to the airport and board a plane to fly west from Texas while carrying a loaded shotgun, when a girl didn't have the experience to know that *sex* and *violence* might mean SEX AND VIOLENCE!

That was *before*, which was a more innocent time.

14

Take Me With You

CAROLE AND I ARE sitting in front of a fire in the wood-burning stove in the main room of her house, wrapping gifts for Our People, which is what my mother called girls and women. These are the beautiful things Carole has owned that she now needs to give away. Before we wrap each gift we discuss who it ought to belong to, as if there's an element of spiritual ownership that pre-exists in these items, things she's made and artifacts of her travels and friendships.

She is giving my daughter a dried rose, for instance, brought by a friend of Carole's from Paris, this flower preserved by some miraculous French process. Something Americans will never master, she says, and I agree, Americans don't care enough about beauty to have made a cult of it, like the French have, with all their *produits chemiques*. There's probably something wrong with it, she says. Probably nuclear, I agree, they're so *into* nuclear. The Japanese, too, she adds, they're nothing if not part of the cult of beauty.

Have you heard, she adds, that there's this swirling island of crap—plastic bags and Q-tips—that's half as big as Texas and is just out there floating about in the Pacific Ocean, just outside various shipping lanes? Carole looks up at me, gamine, shock of black hair, grinning broadly, amused by the way the human animal acts like such a global toddler, dropping its junk here and there.

The flower she's wrapping looks fragile but isn't and all its colors seem to have been preserved though it's been pushed to the side of what it was, like it's a three-dimensional photograph.

This friend, the one who gave her the flower, divorced her husband, Carole tells me. Then instead of hunkering down in some house on a piece of land and holding on for dear life, she went to Paris to spend her money on ephemera. This rose, she says. Great food, learning to speak the language.

All of which will die with her, Carole adds, her face animated with humor.

Carole is one of the few people I know who can manage to physically smile even as she is speaking—nothing she's endured has caused her to lose her sunny countenance. Like my husband, Carole is one of those lucky people who are simply gifted at happiness.

We nod in our small conspiracy, acknowledging the horror that actually *spending money* would strike in our two very similar California families, all these staunch, upright Republicans, these oh so determinedly *middle class* individuals, so tidy and thrifty and modest.

The sameness of our two families makes us like sisters. It also preserves a certain class/caste fiction that has Carole and me more *well-born* in our husbands' minds, these manly guys who like to claim more hardscrabble, less elegant early existences. Each has, according to their somewhat elaborated fictions, created himself—before they *married up* when they married us.

Gary once came home from the dentist in Nevada City, smiling to show Carole that he'd had one of his eyeteeth capped in gold, and Jack, who'd gone to town with him, had evidently done nothing to dissuade him and had probably even aided and abetted, which is why Carole turned to me and said, It's what we get for marrying crackers.[+]

What we get for marrying these two particular crackers is to be sitting together wrapping presents in the warmth of our now long and loving friendship, which began in our husbands' lives and work—they've now been together as poet-and-publisher for more than forty years—and has grown as we have come to know one another deeply.

Oh, well, Jane, she tells me now. I supposed we've led *original* lives?

Our original lives have the two of us spending this dark day in the shelter of the beautiful house that was built by hand with Japanese woodworking tools on a huge piece of undeveloped land. The land is in the watershed of the south fork of the Yuba River in the foothills of Sierra Nevada mountains. We're in Gold Country, high in the range whose backbone lies along the California-Nevada border.

It's tax day, and it's pouring a cold and drenching April rain. Jack and Gary have taken our dogs and gone into town to make what Jack will later tell me is two and a half hours out of twenty minutes' errands.

[+] *Gary Snyder writes:* When I was a poor graduate student at Berkeley studying Chinese, I was admitted as a patient into the UC Dental College. I needed to get my teeth fixed before I went to Japan to study Buddhism, so I'd bicycle to the Oakland ferry, take my bike across to Market Street, and ride up to the Med School, over the course of many months. When they asked me what sort of work I wanted done, I asked, What's best? They said gold because it flexes. So I said let's do gold. They were delighted because all the students had to do a certain amount of gold work to graduate and there were fewer and fewer people who wanted it. So I got a lot of gold work done at a great bargain. This was the 1950s, and many of the dental students who worked on me were Japanese American, who had spent some of their youthful years in the camps.

My new dentist agreed that since I already had so much gold, we might as well match it up. Contemporary dentists will always ask me, Where and why did you get all that gold work? and I tell them, and they nod. Nobody today, they say, could afford all that.

Though these are Carole's last days on earth, the house looks the same and has not been transformed into a hospital, little reference to her illness is even made in the common rooms aside from the notes she's first calligraphed and then posted as reminders to herself in the places your eyes automatically fall, opposite the toilet, for instance.

On five-by-seven note cards, Carole has written: TIRED? IN EXCRU-CIATING PAIN? I HAVE A GREAT IDEA, CAROLE! WHY NOT *PUSH YOUR BUTTON?*

The button is on the pump that's been permanently affixed to her belly under her shirt and will, when pressed, deliver the most powerful of opiates straight to her gut. The sound it makes is a click, a mechanical gulp, then a pronounced *whoosh*. This soft rhythmic sucking, followed by an expelling sound, along with the pounding of the rain and the crackle of the fire, in which a log rolls down every once in a while with a thump, make the only music we are listening to, as this house is off the grid.

I'm here to stay with her while Gary and Jack are gone. It's been weeks since Gary's been to town—he no longer leaves her alone, as attending to Carole's dying has become the one main thing each of them is doing.

◌◌◌

Carole has been sick for so long it's become her vocation. Like any job that comes along and appears to pick you and at which you feel yourself to be a natural, Carole does this with what seems like grace and ease. What's hidden in the notion of vocation is the sense of true unmitigated agony, that each of us must so often wish to have anything but *this* job, which is too inhumanly hard.

Carole objects when she's heard her relationship with this cancer characterized as being *a battle*. It has none of the drama of warfare, she says, it's more an isometric exercise of mutual resistance, as if she and this cancer each have the rather simple need to occupy the same space, which happens to be Carole's own physical person. Less a battle, she says, more like sitting next to some huge bullying life form in the bleachers at a sold-out football game where you need to be constantly vigilant that Its Largeness doesn't take more space than it's already claimed.

It's forced her to concentrate, Jack feels, has purified her, has made her so much what she already essentially was, that is, direct and honest, generous and fun.

Let's face it, Jane, she said recently to me, dying is one of those okay now, let's-just-cut-the-crap experiences.

Carole's other vocation is what she might describe as *homemaker*. She's *made her home* here on this land as a subsequent wife to this big-deal man, entering fully formed into his large and famous life already well-populated by various literary and political celebrities. To do this she needed to take her place, one that had been very thoroughly occupied by the wife who came before. Carole accomplished this in the way she does everything: with style and wit and patience.

The place is called Kitkitdizze. It's in part of what was once a land cooperative founded in 1968 after Gary came back from living in a Buddhist monastery in Japan. This was during the back-to-the-land movement of the era of the Vietnam War that saw groups of people trying to implement change as part of a social matrix by moving together into the back country. They were artists or writers, teachers, crafts persons of various kinds, builders and designers, marijuana growers, those on a spiritual quest, those seeking to implement a new political paradigm. Unlike many of these intentional communities, this one became viable and has lasted for what is now three generations. These people think of themselves as those living On the Ridge. Grown children will go away, marry, have children, and then miraculously return.

Community is what these back country types turned out to be all about. This wasn't some sentimental notion that folks ought to be neighborly. Rather the rigors of life out here demanded that people work together toward common goals. This deep interconnectedness has nothing do with that strange American solipsism that produces an isolate like Ted Kaczynski, who was trying to live off the grid even as he perfected the mail bombs he was launching back into the society he was at war with.

When Gary and his family and friends moved to the San Juan Ridge, they invented a different kind of grid that was constantly being expanded and altered. These people vote and are elected to boards and committees, essentially redefining the society to which they've become an active part, just as the 77 million have become the power we once thought we needed to overthrow.

Nevada City, when they came, was another played-out gold mining town—a poor, mostly forgotten place, with its couple of stoplights. It was not only not a city, it was a barely economically viable village that was then peopled largely by under- and marginally employed rednecks, laboring in the dying industries of mining and forestry. Who were hardly welcoming to these longhairs, Beat poets and visionaries with their Buddhist chanting and their swimming naked in the river.

Nevada City lies about four hours northeast of San Francisco and has been made recently prosperous by tourism and by the wealthy tech-ish Bay Area types who're able to telecommute from a place like this, which works for their get-away houses. But Kitkitdizze is even more remote, lying another forty minutes out of town north and east along a gravel road you meet by taking the turnoff at the mailboxes into one of the more barren landscapes you're likely to see. These are the Malakoff Diggings that resulted from the high-tech hydraulic strip mining that was begun in the 1850s and used high-pressure hoses to wash alluvial gold from the ground.

The gravel road in through the Diggings to Kitkitdizze is kept open in winter snows and in floods and guarded from fire during the summer cooperatively by those who live along it in widespread outposts that include the Ring of Bone zendo and the Ananda sitting group. You bump along this road scraping the undercarriage of the ridiculous minivan you have recently come to own, this because you've returned to California to find yourself having acquired multiple grandchildren, including infant twins, all these children requiring car seats that must be rigorously tethered and affixed. You drive this silly low-slung soccer-mom-ish car through yet another muddy clearing to find an expanse of the great broad blue Georgia O'Keeffe once described as the color the sky will once again be when all mankind's destruction is done.

That was yesterday afternoon, before this monumental storm rolled in.

But it is possible in a place like Kitkitdizze with its great wealth of silence and modest, human-scaled industry to believe people can live what we once called *intentionally*, that folks can dig a pond and clear it naturally over time, can get their electrical power from solar panels, can exist like this for decades in a kind of active, working equilibrium, with periodic upgrades to running water and propane, to electrical illumination, to email, to an indoor flushing toilet. Writing. Living within the seasons, growing fruits and vegetables. Painting. Playing piano. Making things by hand.

The most important thing they've made is this *homestead,* whose lesson is that it still might be possible for humankind to mend its ways. The solidity of this home is instructive, as Jack and I have spent the past decade living first in Berkeley, then in the East, then home to Berkeley again.

Jack and I usually come up once or twice a year. Until this last winter, during which Carole's been too sick for guests, we would usually sleep on tatami mats in the main house or out in the barn that they've converted to a workroom and study. We like to haul our bedding out to the deck there in the summertime to sleep under the stars. At 3,700 feet it's high and arid, and there are remarkably few bugs here on a summer's night. The night skies, here without the haze of moisture, are crystalline. No humidity, no bugs, these woods lack the hum and whirr of cicadas, also the great flocks of songbirds we were used to in the hardwood forests of the East.

The dryness of California's summers have always startled the new immigrants, often refugees from the hotter, wetter places. The dry weather has a certain effect on the Western imagination and children growing up— such kids as Gary and Carole, Jack and I—who were taught to believe in the healthful purity of our air and our water. Nature has seemed the most basic Western god, all else being such citified obvious human elaboration.

To sleep outside at Kitkitdizze under a night sky so thickly blanketed with tiny brittle pinpoints that seem to flicker and bounce, is to regain a childlike perspective. These are the same stars you knew in childhood and they exist in the same numbers, are stable and unchanged, and you realize we've done nothing that can diminish that, something we tend to forget back in the city where you're sealed under the glaze of the light-smeared dome of human time.

෩

Sometimes Jack and I will stay at Bedrock, the little cabin that's a five-minute walk through the woods from Gary and Carole's. Bedrock was built by Allen Ginsberg, but Gary and Carole have owned it since Allen's death in 1997.

Jack tells the tale of one of the last times he saw Allen. He and Allen and Gary were all staying at the same upscale hotel in SoHo—all were in New York for a meeting of the American Academy of Arts and Letters, where someone else in their circle was being inducted.

The Academy sent a car to their hotel to call for them. These two old beats hopped into the stretch limo in their black tie, accompanied by Jack, who after moving east had become strangely expert in formal wear, the tux? the morning suit? My husband is the same man born, according to Jack himself, in culturally impoverished circumstances in a home where no books were read or paintings hung or music played that wasn't his dad and his uncles on a peddle steel guitar, and who, in his longhair days, was regularly banned from certain brass plaque restaurants in Washington and New York where he'd go to eat with his committee of the National Endowment of the Arts, and it *was* specifically Jack, according to Jack, who was being refused service.

The *maître d'* just *didn't care* who Jack was or who he knew, and he was refused service because he dressed in boots and jeans and wore a buckknife on his belt and had the hair and beard of a wild man and it mattered not one whit to this restaurant's management that it was Jack, in fact, who'd been the one to bring the meeting to this fabulous place of exceptional dining, in that it was Jack who was the chairman of the literature panel, a committee he'd come to head before he turned thirty-two.

But time moves on and in one direction only and people grow and age and change and this night in New York found all three former iconoclasts being embraced by the Eastern establishment of literary society that once soundly rejected them, so here they came, all dressed alike in their penguin suits. Once seated in the limo, Jack told me, Allen slipped off his shoes so he could run his stocking feet over the plush of the car's thick rug, then sat back with his arms outstretched along the top of the back seat and sang out:

O it's *fine* to be a poet in America!

◉

KJ, Carole's daughter, who she brought to the Ridge when she married Gary, is a year older than my daughter, Eva. When they were still in elementary school we would ship Eva off to Carole and Gary's when our kids were still small enough that we could just simply tell them where they would spend their vacation time and with whom. Carole and I thought of this as an importation of interesting playmates, an activity especially vital to KJ since she lived so far outside town.

When Jack and I were living in Berkeley, before we moved East, Carole and I would arrange to meet halfway between our houses to pick a girl up or drop one off. It was in the aisles of the Tower Records in Sacramento that Carole once remarked, Well, this one is so entirely your kid, Jane, in that she can totally keep her part of the narrative going.

The Ridge has always been a place KJ loved and her big sister, Mika, didn't. Mika hated the dust, the dry look of the place, hated having to do her laundry in the wash house, the isolation from her friends in town. It was all hard. I imagined she saw every piece of life as physically arduous as it might have seemed to the original pioneers.

Mika resisted even the hues and tints of where the Ridge sat on the color wheel, she told me, its sparrow browns and nuthatch rusts, the drab brush that was sage and oak and manzanita. She went away to boarding school, then to Colby College, and found Maine to be so visually alive as to seem like somewhere put together after the invention of Technicolor, with birds whose names were bluebird, cardinal, the scarlet tanager. A *green* place, she said, and she didn't mind that winters were so cold her eyelashes froze as she left her dorm on a bright blue day with her face wet from the shower. She was born in California, she didn't know any better than to go out into the cloudless day not understanding that it could be freezing, and she didn't mind the Nor'easters or the ice storms that knocked down trees.

It just breaks my mom's heart, she told me, but the weather here speaks to me and what it says is I was *meant* to live in New England.

KJ and Eva are our younger ones, the daughters Gary and Jack never had. Our younger ones have always seemed to share an affinity with these two men, and why not, Carole and I would ask, when it is these men who've made their mothers happy?

◯◯◯

We're in Carole's house on this rainy day, one of the last she will spend on earth, and she's busy being resistant as ever to anyone's waiting on her. She's not letting me be the caretaker, a job at which I happen to excel. When our fire needs another log, it's Carole who gets up on her spindly legs and hobbles over to the woodpile.

Let me, I say.

Why should I? she asks. I *like* doing it, Jane. I *like* the feeling of actually being able to perform this one small simple task. Work is a *benefit* in the cost/benefit ratio, remember? she says, to quote our friend Wendell Berry.

We're drinking tea, eating chocolate thumbprint cookies. Sugar and chocolate have been hard for Carole to metabolize in the past, but what she can and cannot metabolize seems to no longer be the issue.

We've been talking about our parents and our siblings, our children and our husbands. I'm reporting amusingly about the horrific new car

Jack and I just bought, the frog green minivan with the seven seatbelts that's come equipped with something ominously titled The Crumple Zone, as if this car is wearing the kind of crinoline slip Carole and I might have once worn to Cotillion in the Bad Old Days of our more upmarket Republican youth.

This car shrieks so piteously, I'm telling her, that it gives you the piercing little ice-pick headache just above your eye. And it cries out for *no discernable reason* whenever you're backing up, screaming like it's in total sympathy for whatever you are just about to hit, even though it hallucinates and shrieks when there's *nothing there*, so you go ahead and begin to ignore the warning and begin to idly wonder how to disable it, this being its own distraction.

I hate that car, I say, plus which when Eva saw me in it, she laughed at me. Mom, she said, do you realize you're driving a *minivan*? My daughter is now living in Vermont, where she's a senior in college.

Carole's knitting, I'm sewing. We've been talking about the pure mindless meditative pleasure that derives from making crafts and how this is so completely different from the agony that goes into art.

My theory of the earth, I say, is that I was probably born a little too well adjusted to become a writer. She grins at this. No really, I say, Stuff Happens, and this is what I have. I didn't want to be a writer any more than you wanted to be sick.

Face it, I say. Art's its own particular agony and derives from whatever horrible depths and if I were given the choice I'd *so much* rather have my dead dad back and my dead mom back and I want Geo too, who's lost to the street, and to not have all this interesting material.

You know Gary's a snob about art?

Me too, I say.

Me too, she agrees.

Few do it well. I say, *No one knows why.*

I'm misquoting Lew Welch, as Carole well knows. Lew Welch, Beat poet, Gary and Philip Whalen's roommate at Reed, friend of Jack Kerouac's, who walked away from this house one day in 1971 and completely vanished from the earth. He was drunk, was in despair, was carrying a loaded gun. Friends looked for him for weeks but in woods like these a person's bones will be carried away by animals.

What Lew Welch meant was how hard it is to write a single good and original line, let alone the whole poem that line will need to stand in. You write one good poem, then you always need to go back, settle in, put your queer shoulder to the wheel to try to write *another* one.

And now I'm telling Carole about the time Jack and I were at a poetry reading given by _____ (and here you may insert the name of whichever crappy, second-rate poet who just now especially irks you and were it not for my CIA great-uncle who one day showed up with an interventionist plan this could very easily be mine) when Jack took out one of the note cards he keeps in his breast pocket and wrote something that he then passed to me.

His note read: *It was knowing I was destined to be a poet almost exactly this good that made me lay down my pen forever.*

Good for him, Carole says. Most people just frankly aren't any good at art—I'm not. Isn't the same in crafts, where you can learn to DO something, given a little dexterity and being willing to work at it. Knitting's been enough for me or playing the piano or painting canvasses no one else then needs to bother looking at.

Jack says the world needs more people like him, I say, more contented members of the audience.

I'm an expert opera-goer, she says. I am *really* good at listening to opera. I *love* disappearing into something as huge and beautiful as that, she adds.

I wish I could hear that well, I say, but I can't. Big music makes me feel stuff I just don't necessarily *want* to feel.

Not me, she says. The huge stuff is exactly what I want to be feeling.

The huge stuff, I admit, often makes me want to go take a pill to take the edge off. You know, the least little push of joy . . . ?

Carole smiles. She is surely the most intellectually confident woman friend I've ever had but I realize I've never heard her play piano, never seen a single canvass. I begin to say something lame and conciliatory about her never having been intellectually overshadowed by Gary, though he is one of the honestly original thinkers of the twentieth century, then remember I have no need to reassure her.

Crafts matter, she's saying, in the day-to-day. Work matters, anything that you make that's tangible, even if it's only this fire or maybe dinner. She grins at me. Or these chocolate thumbprint cookies. She picks one up and waves it in the air, like she's singing OutKast's *Hey yaaa, hey yaaa, shake it like a Polaroid pic-chur* . . .

God, how I love this woman.

And it's because she's so self-confident that she's never needed to spend a lot of time and energy being jealous about Gary being out there in his Big Life.

I'm reminded of the conversation she and Gary had before they were married, them both agreeing that theirs would be a monogamous relationship, his then coming back into the house from the barn a couple of hours later to ask her, But how are we defining monogamy again?

And how, as she was telling me this, tears were raining down she was laughing so helplessly.

۝

What she and I got for marrying the men we did was to sometimes need to wade through throngs of wife-dismissing girls at this or that writers' conference. One day, Carole and I arrived simultaneously at one of these—she'd had Eva on the Ridge with KJ and our two families were going to meet here, at Squaw Valley, to share a huge bizarre off-season ski chalet. It was equipped with a home theater system with hundreds of cable channels and a bank of swiveling captain's chairs, with drink holders, all this as shelter for a conference that maybe ironically was titled: "The Art of the Wild." We'd usually agree to do these things because they offered what seemed like a paid vacation where our kids could bring extra friends and tag along with us to this blissful outdoor place to swim and bike and ride horseback.

Carole was already dying of the rare and very specific cancer that she'd share the bench with over the course of the next fifteen years. Her sister, Mary Ann Koda Kimble, who was the first woman to head the department of pharmaceutical medicine at UCSF, had managed to get all kinds of expert opinion. Carole herself had a graduate degree in medicine from UC Davis, where she trained as a physician's assistant. Everyone knew the stats, which provided a clear picture of the rather grim prognosis, one that only further clarified Carole's wish to spend her time in a meaningful way.

On this one bright summer's day in the parking lot at Squaw, we had arrived just in time to see our husbands emerging from a building across the way—both completely surrounded by would-be poets and writers, all of whom needed whatever they guessed our husbands might have to offer them: time, attention, access.

These were young, long-limbed girls wearing shorts and halter tops. In my day as a would-be novelist during grad school, I would have positioned in my superior watchful way in the wings and merely *observed* a scene such as this. It simply would never have crossed my mind to yap up and be all eagerly participant. I was what one of my cousins calls the PIBs, or People In Black, a costume that let me imagine myself to be too cool for enthusiasm, a sophisticate. The PIBs wore clothes from the thrift store. We drank wine, smoked cigarettes. We spelled it Amerika. We hung out in coffeehouses named things like The Esoteric.

These girls, by contrast, were tanned, kempt, and enthusiastically engaged in the soul-sucking activity known as *networking,* something one friend of ours who works in Hollywood refers to as "sleeping one's way to the middle." This was the new variety girl—she looked clean, vegetarian, as lightweight as her lingerie. And here were Carole and I, arriving encumbered with all this shit: our kids, our complicated lives, her health, our middle age.

She and I watched the scene for a moment before she turned to me. Know what, Jane? she asked. I have an idea, if you're up for it. How about this? I leave KJ with you and Eva so they can have the week we planned and I go home? She asked this grinning brightly, as if this was truly an inspiration.

And she didn't mean home to the ridiculous 5,000 square foot off-season ski lodge that we'd walk around in asking, where do they even GET these people and how do they imagine they're going to HEAT this thing? Carole meant she'd take her dog, get in her car, and drive the two hours back to Kitkitdizze.

Tell Gary, okay? she said before she closed the door. She motioned toward the throng preventing our two husbands from even noticing.

Tell him I'm sorry but I just can't come up with *that kind* of energy.

〇〇〇

Carole and I had in common our being part of the subsequent marriages to the men who were full stride in their important careers, also the complications of the kids and dogs and travel, all the travail of the coming-and-going lives we led, the sidekick nature of our existences, also our being *Californian* in such a deep and thorough way that only happens over the span of generations that it was somehow in our souls.

Carole's and my families were also remarkably similar: educated, successful, Republican. The main differences between her family and mine were occupational and geographic, hers being rice and almond growers in the San Joaquin Valley while mine were merchants, landowners, in Los Angeles, church-going Episcopalians, WASPs, the class of people who had easy-to-pronounce white people's names who went to breakfast meetings and were elected president of Rotary.

Carole's parents were Japanese American of the Nisei generation— those that were born and educated here. My family was traditionally educated at Cal, where both my parents and grandparents had met. Her father went to Davis and both her parents spoke completely unaccented and idiomatic English.

In California racism was almost always subtle and genteel, everything accomplished by inflection or what was just never said. But then people came along who would say flat out what they were thinking and so we learn that it is only by listening to those who aren't in the dominant culture that we can learn how to talk about race.

Carole once told me the story of her making a new friend in elementary school, Jon'esquia. The word to describe Jon'esquia at that time would have been *Negro* or *colored girl*. Jon'esquia, who was named, she said, after her father—or maybe the word for a certain star in Swahili— had invited Carole to play at her house after school, and they walked home together. When her mother opened the door to them, she was frankly astonished. You friends with *her*? she asked Jon'esquia. *That skinny little yellow thang?*

〇〇〇

It was 1997 and Jack and I were living in the East when Carole found Dr. Paul Sugarbaker at Washington Hospital Center through research done by her sister Mary Ann and her colleagues at UCSF. It was then that Carole began her calm and insistent campaign to get accepted as his patient.

Carole's cancer had been variously diagnosed as that of the several organs its masses had first enshrouded then engulfed so by the time Dr. Sugarbaker agreed to take a look at her films, she had already had five different major surgeries.

Jack and I were back in Washington, D.C., where we'd moved when he was asked to come there to found a literary press. We still saw Gary often but Carole wasn't traveling much and I hadn't seen her in so long I was nervous as I drove out to Dulles to get her.

I was *scared* and I am someone who—while haunted by nebulous fears—is hardly ever frightened by anything that appears here in the physical world.

She and I had agreed to meet at baggage claim.

Here we are, she said. She had begun to refer to the disease as her traveling companion—in time she would start calling it Vesuvius. Carole looked smaller and thinner but in no way diminished.

Wanna see? she asked, then pulled up her shirt. She pointed at the bulges that showed through the skin of her belly. There, she said, and there. Carole, who was watching my face, saw that I was neither horrified nor shocked. Instead I was *interested,* as she would have been had our positions been reversed.

Each of us simply prefers the precise language of science and accurate diagnosis to the eliding words that allow the thing-ness of something to remain both unuttered and ever mysterious.

It actually feels soft, she said as she placed my hand on the skin where one mass bulged. Which is why they call it *jelly belly*, she said. Cute name, no? For something so basically gross? She was smiling, also being professional, the physician's assistant—for which she'd trained, acting to calm my apprehensions.

And it was that the tumors were made of cells that produced mucus in the way of healthy perineal cells but in such obvious overabundance, as a natural process that's somehow gone wildly wrong, and that they behaved like *this* and could be expected to do just *this* and not some other thing, that they were caused by *this particular cancer*, whose name is pseudomyxoma peritonei, or PMP, that gave both Carole and me, if not hope, then at least an intellectual understanding of exactly what there was that needed to be reckoned with. Carole and I are simply like this: we prefer hard knowledge in the cold light of day to being left to our own wild and dark imaginings.

⌀⌀⌀

Carole knew she needed to qualify for the Sugarbaker procedure, and knew that because of the more than several surgeries, she did not look like the best of candidates, at least on paper. She'd started out weighing only a hundred pounds and each of the operations further compromised her digestive system. She now needed to struggle to keep her weight up.

The cancer is a peritoneal carcinoma, one of the skin of the abdomen—it goes anywhere and everywhere in the gut. Its repeated incursions had taken, so far, her appendix and her reproductive organs, as well as some length of her large intestine. Still she needed to show up at this meeting looking like someone who was going to not only survive the radical procedure—it is truly terrible to describe—but come down on the right side of the hospital's ledger, showing that no one had wasted his time and effort.

What is now known as the Sugarbaker Procedure demands an excision of every affected organ that a person can live without, then radically debulking the masses, then bathing the entire gut in a heated chemical bath meant to kill all the skin cells this chemotherapy can find. It sounded like medieval torture that took, if all went well, at least fourteen hours.

She had a late morning consultation with Dr. Sugarbaker scheduled for the day after I got her at Dulles. We left the house early to go to my gym where she intended to run on the treadmill. Carole, who was thin but not frail, wanted to arrive at that meeting looking pumped up and vital. She asked me to come along to meet him, to sit in with them and take notes.

We got on side-by-side treadmills. She began to run while I—as was my habit—put my book in its holder and tilted the treadmill to a very steep incline that produced the slow trudge uphill. I was, just then, some ways into a new translation of *The Inferno* that had internal rhyme and sprung rhyme and off-rhyme which were supposed to somewhat approximate in English the sound of Dante's terzarima. I like to walk and to read aloud. The gym, with the noise of its machines and everyone else wearing earbuds, is a great place to not be heard. I like to read a poem out loud under my breath in order to help myself hear it better. Moving while you are reading allows the language to enter your brain in a deeper way, or at least differently, lodging it in a more physical three-dimensional place.

I don't understand the brain science of how this happens and only know that it was a personal discovery of mine when I was in high school and was trying to memorize verb declensions in Spanish and found out I simply learned better when I walked in circles in my room while saying the words aloud.

So I was reading out loud to myself on the treadmill at my gym when I noticed that the skinny little yellow thing—who was also, by the way, dying—running along on the treadmill next to me had started laughing.

What? I said.

Nice pace, Jane, Carole told me. She was winded, gasping, which seemed to be getting in the way of her laughing.

Mind your own business, I said. I'm reading. I'm hearing the ter-zarima, if you need to know, which—in Italian—is rumored to *sound like rain.*

She was laughing so hard by then she'd stopped her treadmill and was having trouble speaking. *Like rain!* she asked.

Anyway, I never run, I told her. I'm saving my knees.

Saving your knees? Carole, now doubled over, whooping helplessly with laughter.

Saving them? she asked when she could speak again. May I ask for exactly *what?*

⁂

There was a map of the U.S. on the wall of Dr. Sugarbaker's office that had roundheaded glass pins in different colors stuck in it. There were fifteen or twenty pins sitting close to one another in California's still largely agricultural San Joaquin Valley. Many of the pins were right around Modesto, the closest large town to where Carole grew up in her family's rice farm in Dos Palos.

That's a cluster? I asked Dr. Sugarbaker.

A cluster, he agreed.

He turned to Carole. And many of my patients are your age and the majority are women though we don't yet have any good idea why that would be. PMP is perhaps most often positively diagnosed early when a mass is detected on the ovaries so it may be that it's still being more often missed in men.

Carole grew up twenty miles from the Kesterson National Wildlife Refuge, where over a period of time in the mid-1980s birds were being born horribly deformed. I remember the shock and dismay on the faces of the wildlife managers in the refuge during that time who came on television to talk about the ecological disaster that was transpiring before their eyes. The wetlands of the Pacific flyway had become a place where species, instead of finding rest and food, were being poisoned with heavy metals, including selenium—some were threatened with extinction. And it wasn't simple—toxins from the agricultural runoff from the flooding of the rice fields was involved.

Our future is all about water, I remember one of the wildlife managers saying. He was holding a chick in his hand that had hatched with two heads. There were holes where the beaks should be.

This kind of death will not stop in a single generation, he said. This is global, he was telling the television camera. This is the sort of death that will go *on and on.*

I was a new mother and had only then begun to live in what I'd started to think of as ecological dread.

This is about the watershed? I asked Dr. Sugarbaker.

Watershed is what Gary calls one's own geographical address, it's the ridge of high land dividing areas drained by different river systems, a drainage basin, a parting of the waters. A watershed is all the land onto which rain and snow falls that feeds a certain river system or any other body of water.

Watershed is also the poem with which Gary often signs an email:

Kitkitdizze
>north of the South Yuba River
>>near the headwaters of Blind Shady Creek
>>in the trees at the high end of a bunchgrass meadow

Watershed, Dr. Sugarbaker said, might be one really good way to put it.

⚹

Carole had brought her most recent films in a big manila envelope. Sugarbaker got them out and snapped them up on the light box on the wall behind his desk.

In Carole's films the tumors read bright white. I had no experience in reading x-rays but was having no trouble noticing that the masses were both numerous and huge.

Well, these aren't the *worst* films I've ever seen, Dr. Sugarbaker told her.

But pretty bad, huh? Carole asked.

Pretty bad, he agreed.

Carole already knew this—Mary Anne had helped her read the films before she came so even the worst news was never really news to her and Mary Ann was such a tough minded medical professional Carole once said to me about her: You know, Jane, my sister would make a really good *man.*

Carole sat forward, soberly. She was focused and completely serious.

I have a thirteen-year-old daughter, she told him. My older girl's eighteen and is going off to college—Mika will be okay. But KJ's adopted, so I have this small moral problem, you see? in that I need to finish my commitment to raising her?

Dr. Sugarbaker nodded.

I need five years, she told him.

Five years? he asked, and after the merest pause he nodded: Okay, Carole, you're on.

○○○

We are sitting on cushions on the tatami at the low table in front of the fire. Their electricity comes off solar panels and a generator so the lighting is always low, but this is one of the darkest afternoons I can remember, an ambiance that feels like an almost throttled daylight.

The sensation, Carole is telling me on the last afternoon we will ever spend together on this earth, is that she's completely entrapped by a nausea so grave she's unable to escape it even in her deepest sleep.

There's the constant nausea, also the extreme cramping in her gut, cramps that are as excruciating as contractions in transition during natural childbirth. Transition is the place in labor where the baby's head comes charging down the birth canal and the pain from one contraction begins to blend into the pain from the next so you finally suffer the one long unrelieved agony that doesn't end until the baby's out, which is what makes you really want to push.

Transition is up there at nine or ten in an ER room's Descriptive Pain Scale—it's the kind of pain that you honestly feel you may die of, though she and I are Western and we tend to be stoic about physical pain. The morphine in Carole's power pack doesn't make the pain go away, instead it *abstracts* her from the sense that she is the one who is feeling it.

I remind Carole of the phone conversation we were having even as we were all witnessing Bush stealing the 2000 election. I was upset, was acting exercised, was cradling the phone as we spoke, talking coast-to-coast and was all the while anxiously cracking hazelnuts with the grip of a pair of kitchen scissors held upside down when one nut slipped.

Oops, I said.

What's wrong?

I seemed to have cut off the tip of my finger.

Hang up, Jane, she said. You're going to have to go to the hospital.

Did you go? she asks me now.

Oh you know, not being sensible, I wrapped it in about a thousand band-aids and when it began to throb I took a Motrin and a sleeping pill and Eva came home after school and was furious, just furious—she's a First Responder, you know, trained in first aid since she's a lifeguard. But I did once drive myself to the ER.

Yeah? Carole asks.

I was stung by a hornet on my finger, which actually hurt like hell. Slow news day at Sibley Hospital, evidently, so I got the undivided attention of just about everyone around, and a bed and a nap and an IV of morphine and Benadryl.

This feels completely *ridiculous*, comparing our levels of pain—my wasp sting, her terminal cancer?

Good for you, Carole says cheerfully.

Jack wouldn't take me. Said I was overreacting.

That's because of Kathleen, she says.

Kathleen was Jack's mother. She was Southern. She was said to *enjoy poor health*.

Gary used to be like that, Carole says, but man, did he get over it.

Because of Lois, I say.

Gary's mother Lois lived to be ninety-eight. Lois attributed her long life to her habit of drinking a pint of half & half every morning. Lois, with her half & half, was proof to Carole and me of the fact of God's

Justice, in that there really is no rhyme or reason to any of this, so all any of us can ever do is to do the best we can.

Gary bought Lois a house in Grass Valley, even hired help, but Lois accused every one of them of stealing from her and fired them. Gary arranged for her to have Meals on Wheels, and for a social worker to come by to look in on her.

Once when Gary was in Washington staying with us—this was yet another time Carole was in the hospital—the social services called him to say Lois had been arrested.

Why? he asked.

Mrs. Hennessey seems to have a hole in her bedroom floor, they said. It's about four feet in diameter that you can see through to the basement, so her house is no longer safe, was the reply.

How'd that get there? Gary asked.

We have no idea. And your mother will not say.

So she's been arrested? Gary asked.

She has been arrested, the social worker said, because the house was red tagged and your mother refused to leave. We asked the police to come out in the hope that they might impress upon her our deep concern about the situation's seriousness, which is when your mother became abusive.

What she actually said to the sheriff, Gary told us later, was: Oh, you think you're so smart with your uniform and your testicles.

I miss Lois, Carole says now, though that's completely perverse.

Me too, I miss her, I say, and I've never even met her.

And now the firelight's flickering across one side of her face, making her cheekbones look pronounced, Carole now weighs less than seventy pounds. The wasting has now taken all the collagen from her face and it's collagen that does the padding. I keep being almost overwhelmed by an odd need, that feels very primitive and atavistic, to get my hands on her, to somehow minister to her physical person, though Carole won't let me DO anything more for her than get up and go boil more tea water.

Would you like me to wash your hair? I ask.

KJ just did it, she says. Why, does it look really terrible? KJ comes over every Monday and we have dinner and she gives me a shampoo. We eat in bed and watch a movie and I always fall asleep.

KJ, who was thirteen when Carole first met Paul Sugarbaker, is now twenty-two and is living on her own in Grass Valley.

I say: And that is the *exact* reason a woman needs a daughter or a sister or at least one special friend. One of Our People who knows something about hair *products*. Jack's good to great at most of it but he doesn't get *products*, what they are, which ones you need for shine or curl or volume.

I probably need more product, Carole says. Maybe a little mousse?

And she jumps up and we both go together into the bathroom where she whooshes foam into the palm of her hand, then combs through her hair with her fingers. Her hair has hardly grayed, is still thick and is still almost that entirely Asian black that looks almost blue aside from a few bright strands of silver.

She's sticking her hair up punkishly, when she catches me watching her in the mirror. There, she says, so now I look *even more* like Jiminy Cricket.

⊗

She is finishing knitting a little doggy cap for the two-and-a-half-year-old who lives with his parents in the Japanese house Dick Baker, then abbot of San Francisco Zen Center, had brought by freighter from Japan and reassembled on his land on the Ridge.

I'm sewing silky binding on a crib blanket. I try to make one of these for each of the new babies who comes along these days, adding a rich gloss to the new fleece ones parents these days like. The soft edge like this encourages thumb sucking, I say, but who honestly gives a shit? I believe in bottles and pacifiers and thumb sucking, anything that lets you grow up at the proper pace so you don't have to go out and practice chemical warfare.

Besides, it's pretty, Carole says, and everybody needs a little beauty.

I was a thumb sucker, I tell her, and I believe in having nigh-nighs and baby dolls and your own oinky blanket, anything that helps get you from this place to wherever.

We all need something, she agrees, to get us to the next place along this *long and difficult* migratory road.

She shrugs. The pain of this, for me, is now becoming almost unbearable.

We're both quiet for a moment.

I brought my mother home from the hospital to take care of when she was dying of cancer. She was supposed to die any minute but when she got to my house ensconced in her hospital bed in a back room that had a great view of the redwoods and the rose garden, she perked up and lived for another seven weeks. Taking care of her was the hardest thing I have ever done, it was also the most important thing, since it taught me how brave I am and how natural and normal bravery is, that it's something we're actually born to.

I suddenly want to tell Carole that watching my mother die was just like watching someone grow up, and it was delicate and even beautiful. It was like she was growing up except that my mother was growing down and she was being born but she was going in the other direction, born into that poem of Wendell Berry's where he describes the world as being "birthwet and shining, as even/the sun at noon had never made it shine."

None of which I can gracefully say, under the circumstances, without sounding mawkish and sentimental.

〽

It's always been her idea that we need to fill our kids with lore. We need, she says, to equip particularly our daughters with the items of housekeeping that they will one day need, and these are the realistic stories of what men and women are and how our people came to be here and these need to be things like whatever items might have once gone into a girl's hope chest: her own sewing kit, a teapot.

And I've brought my own daughter's special teapot up to the Ridge for us to use so Eva will have this material object into which I can somehow place the story of this day, so her teapot will, I think, somehow contain a part of the memory of Carole, this implement, its usage. She and I are drinking the Chinese Silver Needle tea I bought at Teance on Fourth Street in Berkeley, a tea so heavenly and light it tastes like extremely expensive nothing.

Our conversation, never linear, now roams more than usual in the way of poems or dreams and it is this that Gary says is the proof that the mind is a wild system, in that we can never know what the next thing is that we are going to think, as the mind, like art, will always follows its own unpredictable logic.

Carole is losing her memory, she's told me, also her remarkable assuredness in language. This halting, stumbling, hunting around looking for a term is simply more than she's signed on for, and throughout the afternoon her pump heaves and clicks and wheezes and she is, as always, uncomplaining. The Japanese call this kind of physical bravery *gaman*—it's associated with the values of the Samurai or war-rior class, from which her family is descended, or at least—and she almost twinkled when she told me this—according to some people's *version* of things.

∭

Carole has given our granddaughter a packet of beautifully painted rice candy from Japan.

I don't want Hazel to eat it, I tell Carole.

Why? Carole asks.

She needs to save it, I say, I want her to have it for the future when she gets to some big event, when I can explain what it means.

Save it? Carole asks and I hear myself, out there beyond the break-line, waiting, always saving it, *like my knees or this story.*

This is all there is, Jane, Carole says, and each of us nods. We need to buck up now, she says, and go out and spend the principle.

And *buck up* is, I realize, exactly the kind of thing my mother might have said.

We're wrapping the last of the gifts and Carole's huge and inspiring love is now being concentrated down into each of the notes she's writing with her Mont Blanc meisterstuck, this note-writing being a process that started out hard and has now become arduous.

Every part of it is difficult, she says. All the people coming over or else studiously *not* coming over, since they've already said their goodbyes.

Because Carole was supposed to have died last summer and she quit eating entirely and was sent home from the doctor with palliative care, which is when the cancer was finally starved into remission. Vesuvius jumped ship, but it was then way too late.

Everyone on the Ridge knew she was dying. Then one day she appeared among them, there in town with Gary, standing in line for the penguin movie.

What are *you* doing here? they asked.

Bored, Carole said. I got bored. Dying's *boring,* okay? same old *boring* thing day after day.

That was hard, she says now, and it's hard that I won't become a grandmother, that I'll miss knowing Mika's children and KJ's and that I'm going to miss growing old with Gary, who is honestly one of the most remarkable men. And I'm going to miss training Emmy to sit and stay with this clicker method I've been learning.

Miss my friends, she adds. She glances up, smiles at me cheerfully.

And I ask if there isn't one little teeny sentimental part of her that thinks there could be some dark bar somewhere in the cosmos paneled in mahogany where her dad, who died when she was twelve, and my dad and Jack's mom and mine, Gary's too, are all drinking colorful Boat Drinks and congratulating one another on their clever and amusing children? Bragging on us, as the crackers would say.

Nope, she says. I mean it isn't actually very *likely,* when you think of it. I mean, how old is everybody, and whose *version* of heaven is this, anyway, and why would *Lois* have to be there? *Lois?* who might conceivably amuse your mom but she would simply *horrify* my father, who was above all *decorous* man.

My dad too, I tell her. Really dedicated to preserving his dignity.

Something Lois, Carole says, never actually heard of.

〰️

Carole is one of the best readers I've ever known. She is keenly and justly critical and has always seemed to know exactly what I'm hoping for in my writing so I gave her the manuscript to my second novel during one of her long stays in the hospital when the book was still a work in progress.

Have you ever had anal sex? Carole asked. Since she was in recovery from her Sugarbaker I was slightly shocked that she'd ask, under the circumstances.

Well, um, sure, I said.

I know why Alec and Anna do it, Carole said—she was talking about the characters in my second book, whose sexuality I'd set out to write about graphically from both a man's and a woman's point of view, because this seemed like work that hadn't been done well by most of the writers I admire.

It's because they're so crazy about each other they want to do *everything*.

I nodded.

And Carole says, Gary and I were like that.

〽

The dogs romp in, with Emmy leading, wagging her pompom dog tail—our men are home from town. Emmy's a standard poodle in the variety known as *apricot,* this being one tick off the color more commonly known as *pink* and seems, in her styling and coloring, the most unlikely dog for this old and weathered Beat to have, whose dress is more woodsman-homesteader. But KJ has allergies so this family has always needed to own dogs with hair instead of fur.

Carole's given all these gifts for me to carry away, but nothing for me to keep. I am wrapping Eva's teapot and each of the four cups the four of us have used to drink from and the needy atavistic feeling that's washed over me in waves all afternoon begins to come surging back.

Because our fathers died when we were children, Carole and I are each well acquainted with death—neither of us has ever been afraid to call it that but this in no way spares me the shock of this here and now actually being true.

I look at her and think: *She's dying* and this makes me want something. I want to eat Hazel's candy or to belong to some old religion where they give you a sacred wafer or a sip of ecclesiastical wine, or I want a whole great lot of crappy liquor to swill or anything I can ingest and carry away in my own stomach and therefore take away, in my physical person, a grasping, desperate feeling that's both base and primitive.

And it's this neediness, I know, that makes even the most loving relatives act so insane when someone dies and money and property are involved. It's as if we are all overtaken by this same archaic hunger, like we need to *take things in,* like eaters of carrion. The three dimensional objects are translated into a different more age-old language and the things stop being whatever they were and are transubstantiated into the currency of memory by which the mysterious transaction is being performed.

And art figures in here too.

But the agreement is even more complex than our loved one simply being present in the object, as Carole will forever reside in the teacups we've been using to drink from today. It isn't only that we, the living, will go on remembering them—it's that our dead, through what they've given us, seem to promise to continue to cluster around us and hold us to this place that we have shared.

My hands are aching with grief and need and, as always, it's the same loss, my father or my mother or a house or place I loved, and I suddenly want my own mother back and I want my father to have lived to be proud of me and I want Carole to have given me something, even as I understand that if she had it would only have made us cry.

Kitkitdizze is one of the truly beautiful houses, Japanese in style, both elegant and simple. Its main rooms are built around star-shaped tree limbs, Carole and I are standing under the skylight in the center of this house where the light is very quickly leeching upward and away from us, escaping through the roof toward the more ancient light that lies outside our own atmosphere.

As I hold her to me, I whisper, My mother died the day after her birthday in the back bedroom of my house. The last words she said were *Take me with you.*

You do, she says, you will, and as she and I hold one another she adds, Know what, Jane? You *will* see me again, I know it now.

◌◌◌

And in truth I've gone for years saying goodbye to her, over and over again, each time believing I was seeing Carole for the very last time. She's been so frail a cold might have killed her, and she and I lived for a decade not only a continent apart from one another but then far off at the end of a long dirt road.

So we would say goodbye and I'd privately weep and cry out and I'd drive out to our barn in the country and wail aloud to the heavens, the sound I was making drowned out by my vacuum. The barn sat a hundred yards from a horse barn and in the dead of winter, as this was, the floor was dark with the bodies of freeze dried flies.

I'd cry and vac and go with my current dog to a place on that land where I discovered that it was possible to see and hear not one single thing that had been made by the hand of man, even in looking upward for the space of time that stood between this moment and the next plane flying over.

I'd listen to the animated dark, in which I have always been at home, and get myself in hand and know my friend Carole to be a better, braver person than I could ever be, more heroic and more peaceful and that this display of psychic agony was somehow beneath her dignity, as this loss wasn't my loss, this grief, my own particular grief, and that remonstration of this kind really helps me not at all.

And I'd need to then accommodate to the knowledge that she would no longer be here as my friend on this our shared plane of time and that, more than likely, I'd never lay eyes on her again, then she'll just oddly turn up, alive, right there standing in the movie line.

000

The last year Jack and I were living in the East, we came home to Berkeley for the holidays and—as usual—were staying at the Golden Bear Motel at Cedar on San Pablo Avenue. The Golden Bear's everyone's favorite fleabag motel—everyone who was ever young in Berkeley has a Golden Bear story, some interlude that's either colorfully sordid or almost tragic, having to do with low-rent romance and the way we're all so adept at ruining blissful marital happiness, so no one actually really *minds* staying at the Golden Bear where the whores will sometimes fight loudly with their pimps in the room right upstairs from where your little family is conducting its out-of-town holiday rituals, then these same whores will stomp outside to smoke and sit in their cars in the parking lot, scheduling dates on their cell phones even as they re-do their elaborate makeup in their car's rearview mirror.

Prostitution isn't actually legal in Berkeley but our cops no longer arrest even the streetwalkers, who are considered to be participating in what everyone around here imagines is a victimless crime and if you don't like it, *you can always go live someplace else.*

We always stayed at the Golden Bear because it's cheap and clean and takes dogs and has a great Japanese restaurant called Genki in its parking lot and is right across San Pablo from Café Fanny, where you can get the most amazing poached egg on toast on, maybe, earth.

Isn't that Emmy? I asked, pointing at the large poodle that had just come rocking around the corner of a building. She was prancing lightly on her pink puffs like she's a circus dog and this is a dog so honestly *pink* she might put you in mind of an alcoholic's nightmare.

Synder's dog? Jack asked, just as Gary came rounding the corner, looking as he does these days, his half-Japanese to three-parts-wizened-elf, wide-brimmed felt Australian outback hat and gold tooth gleaming. *Synder* is what Jack often calls him after a long-ago typo.

Hi ho, Jack and Jane, he said. *Thought* we might be running into you here.

He and Carole, who'd been at Mary Ann's for Christmas, had just put Mika and Tom on their plane for Maine in Oakland, but Carole was too torn down from the all the busy-ness of the holidays to drive the four hours from Berkeley back up to the Ridge.

Carole was also, as it turned out, too tired to sit in a restaurant, so Jack and Gary went to eat at Genki while she and I hung out in the bathroom of their room. She was soaking in the tub, reading *The New Yorker* magazine, adding hot water constantly, as a hot soak was one of the few things that calmed the cramping in her gut.

Bye, I told her that time. I'll call you soon.

And if I'm not answering, she said, just leave me one of your long *to longish* messages, all right, and don't worry that it's long, I'll listen to it a little bit at a time, so just feel free to go on and on.

∞

Carole's here, I feel her here with me. I can hear her and see her, particularly her face, which is, as always, lit up by the intensity with which she smiles. She's right here, standing in front of me as she did on that last day as she shows me the painting she's recently done.

And I am completely amazed, as it's completely unlike anything I imagined Carole would ever do. I thought she was spending her time doing impressionistic watercolors, seascapes, doing what Eva used to call *painting her mind.*

But this isn't that at all. What it is is exactly like a Wayne Thiebaud, who worked for Disney in his youth, so this is like one of his jokes within a joke. Her oil is like his gumball machines or the dialed out lipsticks, but Carole's is a series of five of the various brightly painted fire hydrants of Nevada City, each different, each carefully and very jauntily, rendered as if from life.

I didn't know you could paint, Carole, I say. I mean really *paint* paint—this is completely wonderful.

Nah, she says, it's so derivative. I'm not a painter, Jane. I'm not original.

But, Carole, this is all *any* of us is ever doing. All any of us is ever doing is looking hard and trying to listen really carefully, then seeing if we can get it down?

I'm just so embarrassed, she says, which is why I hang them in the bedroom.

But it's *good*, it's funny, it's wonderful. Wayne Thiebaud would *love* this painting, by the way. His paintings are meant to be cheerful, you know. It has to do with animation.

Our kids are original, she says. We did that, didn't we?

And they aren't even ours any more, have you noticed? In that now we get out of their way and let them go become the heroes in their own stories.

And we've had interesting times? she says. And now you get to go and write something and tell this one little piece of it.

And of course this was exactly what she meant, that she was giving me this part to tell, that she thought I was up to the work of writing what has often just felt much too hard, so I stay there waiting, out there beyond the breakline, imagining I still have all the time in the world.

She's given this to me to tell: how we need to remember how physically she smiled and how physically she laughed and how on the day she and Gary met—this was at the zendo at the Ring of Bone—they rocked forward at the same instant laughing so hard they literally bumped heads.

15
Random Incident

THE FIRST TIME Jack and I were hit by a car in a crosswalk, we'd just left the community theater after hearing Thich Nhat Hanh. It was nine-thirty or ten at night, we were surrounded by hundreds of Buddhists moving along according to some no doubt widely known law of physics that governs disbursal of crowds, the arc of carsplash or outfly of particles from the explosion marking the inception of the universe.

This was in Berkeley where our Buddhists are diverse and maybe more representative of what I think of as My America, so the shaven-headed ones were men and women, young and old, white and black and Asian. Robed Buddhists don't really walk, rather seem to float almost imperceptibly along, wearing saffron or crimson or their dark brown everydays, their bald heads gleaming dully.

And it was a foggy night so our town's dim yellowish anti-crime lights cast this preternatural glow as droves of Buddhists crossed the park and floated down the streets along this grid of organized randomness. They moved quietly in and out of shadows in sets of twos and threes.

And though Jack is a Buddhist he doesn't walk around dressed like one. He was wearing clothes from the office, a crisp white dress shirt with a Robert Palmer collar, slacks, sport coat. His tie was Italian, one I'd recently bought for him.

As we were walking back to our car Jack was explaining the difference between the Greater and the Lesser Vehicles, this being doctrine intrinsic to the larger understanding of Buddhism. I was not intently listening to what Jack was saying, rather I was aware of the voice with which he was saying it. His voice is deep and bass and comforting, a voice for the radio, as a French friend of mine once said, a voice you enter as you do music, as you'd enter a peaceful room.

I wasn't listening to whatever he was saying about the tenets of Buddhism because I really don't care about Buddhism. I know American Buddhism likes to pretend it isn't *really* a religion involving anything as distasteful as Some Embarrassing Deity, but it actually is a rigorous system of well-organized historical belief that requires actual study, practice, discipline. And I've never been adequately gulled by all the Buddhistic stuff that surrounds us, what's for sale in the yoga aisle of Whole Foods, for instance, made of 100 percent unbleached cotton and no animal cruelty. It's marketed to make you feel slightly better about your same old rampant consumerism but I know even as I'm purchasing it that this is just more physical stuff, that it's just me standing at the check-out paying for things I'll have only until I lose track of them, that my buying things in no way constitutes a holy act.

Spiritual devotion is simply one of those aspects of human endeavor—like Late Capitalism or the single-minded accumulation of huge amounts of anything—that's simply lost on me. I just can't *get* and *stay* interested enough long enough to pay attention to why you do whatever y'all folks all've agreed to do—bow, ring bells, genuflect—not even when a person I know to be a good man, and thorough, is saying something no doubt brilliant that is also interesting.

I therefore scuttle along at the side of listening, having to settle for sights, sounds, and smells—color of robes, incense, sound of plainsong, of chants or matins. I have to settle for my admiration for the variety of head shapes in the species *homo sapiens.*

And I'm polite about Buddhism, trying not to mock its stupider aspects to our countless Buddhist friends just as I try to be respectful of the devout High Church Episcopalians in my own family and the largely secular Judaism of the family into which I was once married, as I'm most recently respectful of Muslims, who are surely our most persecuted religious minority. I don't want my own looking askance at religious practice to fellow travel with persecution so I try to make my face look benign and above all *accepting* whenever I catch the eye of some woman who's veiled her face from me for complicated and archaic reasons I can't hope to understand.

Buddhists may just have a better attitude toward whole grain breads, toward locally grown organic fruits and vegetables, but it's only in Berkeley that *shopping* would begin to take on this pent-up aspect that makes people act like they're experiencing a sacrament.

And honestly? I am someone who compulsively chews great wads of Trident sugarless bubble gum when I'm writing—this in lieu of the mafia-truckload of cigarettes I'd prefer to be inhaling or the seven gallons of wine or the as-much-hashish-as-the-world-contains I'd actually like to be consuming and so remain this gum-chewing wiseacre who can't keep this tiny voice from mentally piping up to mimic, mock, and scorn whenever I get stuck in some pious situation.

Listening to Thich Nhat Hanh, for instance?

Thich Nhat Hanh, quite honestly, reminds me of just another one of these soul-saving televangelists spouting platitudes in barely comprehensible baby talk and I don't care that he's short and round and cheerful or that he's Vietnamese and what all we did to the Vietnamese. Thich Nhat Hanh has always struck me as a type of Chauncey Gardner, another of those really clever simpletons.

∭

The car that hit us that night actually didn't hit me, since Jack saw it turning the corner in the fog and was able to push me out of the way. It was a big light-colored American car, heavy, solid bodied, grand, an Impala or whathaveyou, the kind of car that sailed forth as if out of our extravagant youth, given to this girl, no doubt, by her more-our-age uncle. A car that might have achieved Classic Status, might have earned the Grandfather Exemption that kept it from having to be smogged each year by the State of California.

An Impala driven by an angel of perfect Berkeley girl with gorgeous middle class dreads and some interesting ethnic mix—Jewish/African-American/Korean and/or Haitian? A junior at Cal majoring in I can't remember, working nights at the Y where she'd just ended her shift as a trainer in the women's gym. She'd just started her car and was pulling away from the curb, just turning the corner onto Oxford and was reaching forward to rub a clear place in her fogged-up windshield with her bare fingers so she saw us at the *exact* moment we saw her.

So the entire event had this almost known-beforehand quality, slow motion and underwater that partook of *recognition.* It's what's so comforting about fairytales, that all the charmed pieces are magically numbered, all the parts fit together and are already somehow known to us, that her car was one we understood from our California youth, that it was going slowly, that Jack was knocked down slowly, that she immediately stopped and got out to render aid, that we were instantly surrounded by all these really comforting Buddhists.

The cops and ambulance immediately appeared and were articulate and highly educated. In Berkeley you can almost always trust people to know how to act in these situations, as this is part of our deeply shared social compact, an agreement as to how we must courteously occupy our town's Neutral Middle Distance, at least in moments of grave emergency.

Jack had done something instinctive, I'd noticed, which was to reach out when he hit the ground in order to pick his wallet up from where it flew. That what he believed to be his wallet was not actually his wallet, but one of those flatish but still fully three-dimensional reflectors used to mark the crosswalk, seemed immaterial. It's the kind of mistake you'd make if you were Jack and had just been hit by a car. He tried to lift his wallet, and couldn't understand why he couldn't until I explained that it wasn't *really* his wallet but was actually this wallet-shaped object, this piece of glowing goldish orange reflective plastic securely affixed to the street.

Jack is the kind of a person who simply gets proactive in a crisis and tries to immediately set things right by packing and organizing while I—in extremity—begin to cast off, to care even less than I ordinarily do about all these *objects* we're required to lug around. I wished I cared more about physical things but my relationship to even the necessary items has always been both transitory and tentative.

Sure, I'll like something even overmuch for a little while, I'll become *really* attached to it. People may find it strange that I wear the same clothes day after day for weeks, or at least some version of the exact same clothes, then abruptly change to another outfit, but remember this is what a toddler will do if left to his or her own devices. Both the toddler and I feel simply most *ourselves* in our bathing suit or this certain pair of shorts for a time, as we're moving along toward the next developmental milestone, which will come with its own sandals or shirt that becomes the object of our next passionate attachment.

That it's Jack—the Buddhist in our household—who must maintain our material possessions probably approximates someone's definition of irony. What I seem to care about deeply are the tools: that my pen allows the right milli-micronic amount of the right color of archival pigment to flow onto the right weight of really expensive paper.

◊◊◊

When Jack got hit that night, he steadied himself, got his real wallet out, offered his real ID and insurance information to whomsoever, checked the time on his pocket watch, then informed the ambulance guys he wasn't going with them. Not only that, he wasn't going to the hospital, period, that I wasn't taking him, either—he announced this in his deep authoritative voice-for-the-theater voice.

And the folks involved began to get right away that they were not going to change this man's mind. Jack's supremely confident, also a brilliant negotiator who's both calm and patient. He waits, I've seen him waiting. He waits as a carp might wait, half hidden beneath the lily pads down in the murk. He waits knowing he can and will outwait you. Jack's calm. He knows he's going to get his way, if not now, then in a little while.

Folks forget he's waiting then there's this quick deft flash of brilliance that has expended no angry energy.

It was pointless trying to make him go to the hospital, so the ambulance guys gave up, as did the cops—what were they going to do, *arrest him?* Hold him for seventy-two hours under the California Statute called the 5150, this being the period of observation in a hospital designed to determine whether you're a threat to yourself or others? His judgment might not have been *all* that sound, as he did formulate the argument that it was he, of the two of us, who was obviously best equipped to drive our own car home.

And I can no longer remember who won that one but when we got home I called John, Jack's doctor, who is a friend of ours. John said to take his temperature, which was scarily low. Jack was in shock, John said, as well as probably all methed up, as John put it, on an extra dose of Emergency Adrenalin. John told me to tell Jack he had to take pills or else go to the hospital—John knows Jack hates taking pills. John said Jack was to take a horsetab of Ibuprofen, also a sleeping pill. If he did *exactly* as John said, Jack could stay home, sleep in his own bed, and John would see him in the morning. John's the kind of doctor we used to have, this sweet, smart, practical man who one day ran screaming from private practice, which is when Jack and I were consigned to Soviet Medicine.

Jack was—John assured me—going to be fine.

And Jack was fine, aside from the headlamp-shaped bruise on the side of his upper leg that turned a lurid and melodramatic purple, then shades of brown and sickly yellow that eventually melted greenishly down his leg from thigh to knee to calf to foot where it somehow evaporated back into the dust-unto-dust, demonstrating that even the injured tissue in a bruise is a *physical object* and thus susceptible to gravity.

The girl's insurance paid for several months' worth of excellent massages billed as physical therapy and everyone acted exactly as they're supposed to act, in that Green Green Grass of Home that marks the circular kind of storytelling you find in fairytales: the girl was charmed and her car was charmed and we were charmed and no one took anyone to court or needed to hire a lawyer and no one was ever even angry at anybody. Our Berkeley, This Peaceable Kingdom, where everything can be amicably resolved.

And soon enough the accident faded and changed and became a dinner party story in which Jack was hit by a beautiful girl in a white Impala as we walked in a floating world where robed Buddhists moved through the fog like koi.

∞

Jack's reaching out to calmly retrieve the reflector is what immediately occurs to him. Jack wants to pack things up, catalog, alphabetize, set things right, hence his need to quickly knock back a shot or two of Emergency Adrenaline.

My own psyche's different: in any kind of traumatic situation I get really quiet and very, very logical. I abandon any interest in any object that can be replaced, I begin to immediately fictionalize. The story I start writing is often this rhapsodic Third Person Rural thing I began as a young girl reading about places I'd never been.

This necessity of mine to fix on *what might be* reminds me of the global positioning system of our dog, Wayne Thiebaud, who cannot relax on a car ride because he has the profound physical need to remain alert and attentive as he watches out the back window in order to memorize the exact route by which we've come.

I've never met a dog like this before, one who enjoys a car ride but only so he can observe the journey in *vigilant retrospect*. I think it has to do with Wayne Thiebaud's relationship to yearning or The Past—but that's just me again writing my own version of the Green Green Grass of Wales or Wyoming, my thinking he's studying our path so—if we ever do get lost—he can lead Jack and me home.

I read *The Incredible Journey*, I know his species operates by way of extrasensory breadcrumbs but I so sometimes wish the dog could just *relax*. He doesn't sit, will not lie down. When we drove 3,000 miles along

Route 80 moving home from the East two years ago, our dog acted like an interstate trucker on whites: he didn't eat, didn't drink, didn't nap, but stood the entire time, positioned for balance on his long thin well-muscled legs. He's quite a feminine dog, almost delicate, and while balletic, hasn't the heft and meat you'd expect from the dog version of Mikhail Baryshnikov.

Thiebaud is part greyhound—and we don't call him Wayne, very obviously, because of the serial killer connotations—and resembles a ballerina on point, all black except for his dipped-in-white-satin-finish toe-shoes. Ours is an almost too-tall dog to stand in an ordinary car so he has to lower his head to look back like a sight hound. He'd probably prefer better animal transport, horse or cattle trailer with a half door so he could commune with folks in the car traveling behind us.

The How Green Was My Valley thing harkens back to a converted barn we kept in West Virginia—this is where Jack and I rescued Wayne Thiebaud from the Morgan County Animal Shelter where our dog was poised standing on the chicken wire fence, waiting for us as if he was sure we'd come. Thiebaud and I are just *really* attentive in this way, we just have to memorize every particle contained within every mica-like bit embedded in the surface of the roadbed.

It's our job.

〇〇〇

So when Jack and I were hit by a car in a crosswalk a second time and I began to immediately write my Green Green Grass of Wherever even as I flew, it's because no one in his or her right mind would want to experience the actual reality to which I—who did not lose consciousness—was suddenly really carefully attending.

The car presented as a quiet moving wall of metal, it hadn't braked, slowed, honked, swerved, hadn't acknowledged Jack and me in this incident, which is known in legal/medical circles as the Vehicle vs. Pedestrian.

We were about ten paces into the crosswalk at seven o'clock on a clear, cloudless summer's evening when the car plowed directly into us. The car was going between 25 and 30 MPH, it weighed—these are statistics gathered later—2,373 pounds.

It came quietly, out of nowhere, which did feel sinister. What remains most odd about the incident is that it hit both Jack and me completely silently. They say hearing is the last sense to go. It occurred to me that this might be what it was like to die.

⦙⦙⦙

Jack and I were not actually mowed down by this car as we were mowed upward, were actually scooped up and launched by the force of impact, his body flying away one direction, mine another. We flew—and here comes my Green Green thing—like the myriad winged insects that fly out in every shimmering direction before my older brother's riding mower as he trundles up and down the wide lawn of his river-viewing hillside.

My older brother is the last surviving non-psychotic member of my natal family and so is the person I've known longest on this earth who still might recognize me if we met on the street, and it was Will who recently reminded me that our mother deemed me *conventional,* which I've always found to be her most crushing and effective put-down.

Anyone knowing the first thing about the childhood my brothers and I endured might appreciate the work it's been for me to achieve anything like *conventionality.* To be able to get up in the morning and make one's bed? To own an outfit or two whose parts go together intentionally even if it may look to others like something tattered and cast off, like something that someone with an interventionist spirit—my husband, say, or daughter—will sometimes confiscate from the floor of my closet which serves as my costume shop and walk this bedraggled item down the hall toward the trash saying, That'll be about enough of *that*?

That I own silverware? my own full complement of nesting measuring cups?

That I *got* to eat dinner at the House of Curry on Solano Avenue with my husband on the night of July 30, that I *got* to be mildly annoyed with him as he was in one of his pasha moods, in which he'll order Indian food expansively from all the several columns and categories as if participant in some banquet though there is no possible way two people can eat all this? Nor will we be carrying these fragrant parcels home because Jack will not eat leftovers, which he calls *dead* or *penicillin*.

That I had the luxury of being vexed by his needing always to have New Food? And because he imagines he needs to always eat some kind of organized legitimate *dinner*?

That we got to walk out into that perfect evening in which the sky was an arc of azure, that we got to step into the crosswalk at Curtis and Solano being completely untroubled by any thought more complex than our need to get Wayne Thiebaud out of our car so he could pee against a tree, and did our dog need another walk and would I like to go for a coffee and a gelato?

Shall we try Scoops on Fourth Street? he'd asked to which I was about to say, We'd be fools not to.

That Will and I get to be conventional? That my older brother *gets* to have a wife and daughter, *gets* to live in a renovated farmhouse on a hillside overlooking the Mohawk River, that he *gets* to have a PhD and a wide sloping lawn to mow?

〇〇〇

As I flew one way and Jack another, I remember thinking *And now they've hit us with a car?* then wondering who this *they* is, since I don't actually believe I have any organized enemies. I don't even believe in the construct known as Enemies or The Terrorists or even A Terrorist or why this Terrorist would take any interest in me.

What I know to be the real enemy of any and all of us is plain cold indifference.

So I then became *affronted* by being hit by this car, believing whoever driving it to be insensitive, thoughtless, rude.

The car had come down Solano following a gradual slope from the hills westward toward the bay. Jack had been walking on the uphill side and had turned to face me as we tackled the gelato question, so he was struck first and harder. I heard nothing, but saw him fly off backwards as if he'd been summarily plucked away. He simply disappeared from my field of vision. So had the car that kept going without ever slowing and I knew immediately, given my hyper-vigillence, that no matter how terrible whatever was happening to me was, what was happening to Jack was likely worse.

I hit the street on one shoulder and upper arm and back, then my head hit immediately, then hit again as I bounced to the other side. The compression of my chest knocked the wind from my lungs. I heard the pained sound as my breath was expelled. I hadn't lost consciousness but I could neither take a breath nor speak.

I'd been struck in my left leg, both above and below the knee, but that leg didn't particularly hurt and was even oddly numb. My toes stung. What hurt most was my chest, my head.

My sunglasses had vanished as had my shoes and I remembered happening to *want* those shoes. My clothes—a skirt and shirt and my year-round all-purpose undergarment which does happen to be a certain lap-swimmer's bathing suit—were in disarray. But that my shoes were gone really hurt my feelings, as they'd been part of my everyday summer uniform for as long as I can remember.

These were wooden thong sandals, fabricated in India, I believe, and I liked their height and weight and the precise clip of footsteps taken in these sandals, which made me sound self-confident. Their leather straps were embossed with a very faint pattern in beige and rust and rose, a subtle pattern of flowers and you'd actually have to look closely to decide these were flowers, which is important as I'm not the kind of person who'd ordinarily go about with an obvious floral pattern on the leather straps of her wooden thongs.

And I, who can barely be bothered to manage my own possessions, only had these sandals because Jack had once brought them home to me, and this is the kind of man I was married to on that summer's evening: someone who would buy shoes for a woman while away on a business trip, shoes that not only fit her but in every way *suited* her.

Nor am I the only woman for whom Jack had a history of successfully buying shoes. He once bought a pair of shoes for every woman in his office, and I can imagine exactly how this came to be: he first noticed a pair of shoes too perfectly Trish for Trish to not own them and as he was making his way toward the register holding the box, he noticed the display that held the perfect Heather ones and right over there were Keltie's.

In, no doubt, one of his pasha moods.

And when our daughter was younger and more unsure he'd take her shopping for clothes, and when she couldn't decide between the two colors of a certain dress, he'd make a little gathering motion with his fingers to tell the clerk to go ahead and wrap one of each.

Doesn't it ever bother you that he orders for you in a restaurant? a friend once asked.

No, I said. Saves me from having to read the menu.

But this *is* the twenty-first century, she said. Have you honestly never heard of the concept called *feminism?* Or is there some *clinical* reason you can't read the menu?

I can read the menu, I told her, witheringly. I just don't particularly *want* to. There're just too many words on a menu and all these B heads and A heads and lists and asides and parenthetical comments and oh my god the illustrations? I get way too involved in the grammar and punctuation. And the hyphens! I added. Home-made? Fresh-squeezed?

She glared at me.

Okay, I said, I admit it, it's actually the adjectives, you have to have noticed how food adjectives go all lurid and purple—juicy? creamy? succulent? I mean, Jesus Christ! It verges on *pornography*.

But she was not amused as she was one of those friends you have who basically don't really *like* you. She disapproved of me. She considered my whole existence a form of gender treason.

Look at it this way, I said. There are so many good things to read that are not a menu.

Have you honestly never ordered something of your *own free will?* she all but yelled.

I can, I said. I totally can if I absolutely have to.

But she knew I was being less than honest, as this was a way-too-elaborate excuse and the truth is usually a simple thing. The truth is plain. It is also something I just didn't happen to want to tell her: Jack didn't order for *me*. Rather he liked to thoughtfully compose the meal he was ordering for *the two of us*.

000

This man—who in a pasha mood might buy a young girl the same dress in alternate colors—lay some ways down the street from me across the entire intersection. I knew where he was because I could see where the other crowd was gathering.

As soon as my body came to rest and my head hit once and then again and I was still alert and counting, I understood that I would live. I was conscious, even supersonically conscious, so I quickly realized certain distressing things.

I knew, for instance, that Jack had flown way too far away for this to have its usual storybook ending. I also felt he'd used up some of his Green Grass of Whatever in the incident with the girl in the white Impala, that that in and of itself had required an expenditure of luck.

Jack's always said he is a lucky man. He credits this to chance, he doesn't believe he's earned it. He never, ever, calls it karma, though he is one of those few people who might actually have a glimmering of what the term *karma* might actually mean.

I do not know what karma is, and I will never know, and I therefore never say the word, never allude to my positive or negative parking karma and also try not to make those gacky pseudo-metaphysical statements that always sound self-congratulatory, at base, about how stuff goes around then comes around to substantially reward you, or how you pay something forward, or my least favorite of all, which is Everything Happens for a Reason.

No, I'd say aloud if I were less spiritually tolerant, it actually does not. Encountered any twelve-year-old sex workers in the Philippines? Met an AIDS orphan lately? Been to the circus recently, seen what they've done to the Zulus?

And the term *mantra*? That one's mantra is not whatever trite, cliché-ridden crap one's always habitually saying, as in Amy Winehouse's

"No-No-No" had become my mantra that summer! when no, actually, it isn't, and no, actually, it hadn't.

I recently heard the term *mantra* bizarrely pronounced like the first syllable in the phrase *manhole cover.*

And I get agitated by having these perfectly good terms admitted to the American language only to have them immediately wasted. They're tamed and the first thing we know is they come looping back at us, *baa*-ing and hysterical, as shorn of meaning as sheep on their way to slaughter.

If I had a "mantra," which I do not, it might be *Remember the circus Zulus*, which isn't a mantra but a motto. It might be saying to anyone who insists all of this is well planned out for one's own personal American benefit, Oh, won't you please shut up?

∞

I'd flown X number of yards, been deposited by an arc of so-and-so many feet from the point of impact that's marked on the Factual Diagram as A. Jack and I are given to describe any unknown numeric quantity as Carry the Nine, after the name of a rock band that doesn't exist but might.

The distance flown by each of the bodies of the trauma couple became an issue later for legal reasons, since the car hit us while we were in an occupied crosswalk but had knocked us way the hell out of this crosswalk, which was then no longer occupied. Among the jobs and duties of the Responding Officer was to pace off distances, chalk the accident, and then map it, all measurements simplified these days in that they're marked with that laser measuring device invented by real estate brokers and called the Lidar.

Had I walked, rolled, inched, or crawled any distance, or was the place I lay in the middle of the intersection at Curtis and Solano more or less the true and accurate placement of where my body had come to rest? This was being asked over my head. In the diagram, my body is named B.

Oh she totally landed right there, Witness One said. I work over there. I had the outside tables so I completely saw it.

In the small town world that is My Berkeley, Witness One turns out to be the friend of a friend of our daughter's, working at Fonda that night, which is the tapas place on that corner.

And there were other confident witnesses, stepping up as competent First Responders, delegating responsibility, identifying themselves aloud by their individual skills, an M.D. in Internal Medicine who quickly checked my vitals. Because I was having trouble breathing, he put his head down on my chest.

Winded, I whispered as his head lay there. He checked my pulse, my pupils, gave my hand a squeeze, then ran down the street toward Jack.

And a social worker—Witness Number Three in the Factual Statement, who announced herself an MSW with clinical experience—said she'd stay by me as others moved the crowd back. Witness Number Three had the kind of gray hair I want, really straight and shiny and silverish. As she reached over me, some strands brushed my arm. She'd just washed her hair and it was still slightly damp.

What hurts? she asked.

Head, I said. Chest, I added. I happen to know the names of the 206 bones in the human body, or I did until I *got hit by a car!*

Sternum, I whispered.

Chest injury, she reported to the cop who came over to us. Leg, shoulder, head.

Toes, I whispered helpfully.

Heart condition? he asked. He was talking over his squawking shoulder to my First Responder. It was immediately apparent that she'd act as my advocate.

Do you have a heart condition? she asked me.

Winded, I said.

She's just winded, she told the cop.

He asked the State of Consciousness questions, but in the pro forma way that meant he wasn't interested in the answers, only that I continued to put the effort into answering. Name? Age? Date? Time of day? He seemed clipped, rushed.

My husband? I asked.

Witness Number Three leaned closer to hear what I was mouthing, then sat up.

She's asking about her husband, she said to the officer. But he'd turned to other items of business, talking to witnesses who were volunteering information on road conditions, lack of skid marks, angle of the sun, how fast the car was going. He had a clipboard.

He turned back to me to ask more questions. Can you hear me? Date? Never mind. Day of week? Can you hear the siren?

My husband, I breathed. Is he conscious?

The cop didn't answer and the social worker couldn't know, but still she said to me, He's fine, he's like you, he's sitting up and talking, and since I was neither fine nor sitting up and talking, I knew she meant well but was lying. Had I been able to speak I'd have told her that in order to be believed you just need to lie less enthusiastically, less grandly.

You're doing a really good job of staying calm, said Witness Three.

Same ambulance, I told her.

I was talking to Witness Three because the cop was multitasking, doing traffic stuff, crowd control, and intermittently asking the same

State of Consciousness questions to stay in touch with me: Name, Date (which I never know anyway), Time of Day (which I can usually make a pretty good stab at), Name of the Asshole President.

She's asking for them to go in the same ambulance, said the woman with the silver hair.

Day of week? the cop evaded.

∞

We needed to ride in the same ambulance because I knew Jack would be more gravely hurt than I and I was worried that if we were triaged separately, I'd never see him again.

I began then to notice other things, that Witness Three had never let go of my hand and that there was another woman now at my feet dangling my own car keys, that she was showing me an opened cell phone, that she was talking past the cops and the just-arriving EMTs.

She was speaking right to me:

I'm going to go get your dog from your car and take him home with me. I've called your daughter. You're going to Highland Hospital. She's on her way already. She'll meet you there.

Wait a minute, I thought. *Do I somehow know you? And then, Highland? Why not Alta Bates? I understand Alta Bates. Alta Bates is where I was born. My children were born there too, and Alta Bates is closer.*

Same ambulance, I whispered.

Same ambulance? the woman above me asked the cop again.

Berkeley's here, he was telling someone. Does Berkeley want this? Where's Albany? We're a block from the line. Does Albany want it?

I hear Albany, someone said, they're on the way.

It's Albany's, but Berkeley can easily take it.

Either way—we're one block in.

Can they go in the same ambulance? the social worker said again.

Albany's here, someone said. Albany's got it if they want it.

Same ambulance? the cop above us yelled to someone.

Need to ask down there.

There were four ambulances by then, I'd heard them converge, two each from either town.

Albany's got it. They can do it in one, someone came back to say. We have to load her first so he's first out when we get there.

Got it.

Okay, one ambulance, he said to me. Then the EMTs were there in numbers.

Now we're going to move you, do you understand? You're not to move. We're going to do it for you. This is a neck brace, and this is a backboard, and we're going to roll you onto it, all right? Okay, now on my one-two-*three*.

The social worker was pulling my clothes down, smoothing them. There, she said, you look presentable. She still held one hand. I tried to smile at her.

First out when we get there meant Jack was still alive.

000

Jack's theory of the universe doesn't revolve around karma. Rather he believes all this to be an interesting Time/Space occurrence, this three-ring circus, and that it's my own particular circle where the more fun participants tend to congregate, the clowns and kids and animals.

He believes that if there's anyone vaguely madcap or slightly psychologically tipped or marginal they'll gravitate my way, this according to some kind of Family-Share Plan or Affinity Grouping or Team Building

Exercise. Maybe it's that I'm used to these types from my childhood and therefore tolerant of them?

My version is that I've just always been pretty good at telling exactly where the story stops being the How Green Was My Valley and begins to turn grim. It's when you get that sinking feeling.

Take the time my friend Diane and I took our kids to the Ringling Bros. and Barnum & Bailey Circus. We'd just paid some astonishing amount of money for this event, way upwards of one or maybe two hundred dollars and had then begun to automatically buy all the kinds of crap kids at circuses need to have, the thirty dollar light saber, for instance, that was done as a bush warrior sword thing because the theme that year was "Africa," but even as we climbed the steps to our seats, these wands had begun to flicker and go dim.

This sucks, Mom, Noah said. What am I supposed to *do* with this?

Got me, Noah, I said. Trade it for the Day-Glo num-chucks?

And as we found our seats each of our children had been equipped with a $7.50 pre-made multicolored sno-cone whose ice was already hard, dry, and stale, and Leah had begun to fuss because she didn't *want* her flavors mixed but mixed was the only way a circus sno-cone came.

I don't want this, Leah said. What I want is a cherry Slurpee from 7-11.

The circus parade was starting—it was all on a Zulu theme. Zebras, elephants, showgirls dressed as Zulus atop elephants, followed by more parading animals, giraffes, giant cats in cages.

And then came scores of Zulu warriors. These were actual *Zulus* in regalia, dusty, barefoot, defeated, all of them up-and-downing listlessly in time to the *om-pa-pa*-ing music, raising and lowering their own bush warrior swords that resembled actual artifacts.

Diane, I said under my breath, those are *Zulus*.

Yup, she said.

Real Zulus, I whispered urgently.

I know, Diane said.

Leah was fussing, Noah'd thrown his light saber thing away. Diane and I were staring straight ahead trying to ignore the two of them.

Is it just me, I said, or do the Zulus seem suicidal?

We waited a minute, then another minute. Leah was still discussing sno-cone vs. Slurpee, Aaron telling her to be quiet because no one was actually listening.

Diane, I asked. Do you think we're going to be able to *do* this?

We waited. A moment or two ticked by.

It was Diane who broke it to the kids: Okay, that's it. Well, *that* was another fun childhood experience. Okay, let's pack it up. Check under your seats. We can get a fifty-dollar cotton candy on our way out and maybe a hundred-dollar hot dog.

BUT WE JUST GOT HERE! our kids started screaming. AND THE CIRCUS HASN'T EVEN STARTED!

Right, Diane said. We're leaving and not one minute too soon.

෩

The circus atmosphere of the storytelling inevitably begins to give way, for me, to the realm of the Harsher Brighter Realities, whereby light begins to leak in under the edge of the tent and the tragic faces of the suicidal Zulus are seen etched in dust and the showgirls dressed as Zulus look like sex workers kidnapped young and sold into slavery and they all seem to be afflicted with leper sores and this wasn't probably *exactly* the theme circus management was looking for.

Real life simply does intrude and when it does I simply notice it: I was being rolled onto the backboard where they strap your arms to your sides and your forehead and thighs to the board, and then your knees and ankles, but the board itself is slender so these extra parts of you seem to fall off on either side unbecomingly, like they accidentally issued you the child's size.

I was on the backboard, my head and neck in braces being hoisted *on-my-three* by several burly firemen, when I saw this woman standing at my feet, looking down at me with a certain intensity. What began immediately to worry me was that she was wringing her hands in a Lady Macbethish way and that her hands were covered in what looked like blood.

I also knew immediately that it was she who'd hit us, and as the driver of the car, it made no sense that she'd be way bloodier than I was, but there you go. She seemed to be what you'd call Older, also a little out of register, in that she wasn't immediately explicable in the way of the sturdy solid EMTs or the take-charge cop and the MD in Internal Medicine or my own personal MSW with the freshly washed silver hair.

This woman was older, for one thing, but she was wearing disturbing hair items, these being these really infantile barrettes, way too spangled and pink to go with her age or race or caste or class or even *species*. These were poodle barrettes, the ones you'd buy for your twelve-year-old at Claire's as a consolation after explaining why today was *not* the day she'd be getting her ears pierced.

And I immediately did not like her, as I was getting possibly karmically involved vibes from her, that she and I were there because Everything Happened for a Reason. According to this version, this would need to *mean* something. According to my usual version of life, there is coincidence, and she and I had simply arrived at this one place and time in this large and often sullen universe and it was there that the paths of our Lines of Action had intersected, which did not mean we were symbolically linked.

But the way she was looking at me made me feel like I was being asked to participate in a Ray Carver story in which she and I were going to furnish one another with some cheap and crappy redemption. She seemed right on the verge of wanting to keen, moan, cry out, loudly remonstrate, and while you do get to largely do whatever you want in this life and say whatever idiotic thing, no one has to listen to it and life actually is *not* a stage. Right that moment was not the time for her to discharge her anxieties, in that Jack and I had problems of our own.

And no one else, I noticed, was being very nice to her, either, not the EMTs nor my personal MSW, who was tidying me up, as if she were an emissary from my Grandmother Vandenburgh who was always telling me to Stand Up Straight, for Gawdssake, and to please, Jane, get your clothes on right!

And the Mental State cop was now speaking to her in his talking-to-a-mental-patient voice, saying, I'm going to need for you to step away, Ma'am. I need for you to go back to where we've asked you to sit. You cannot be here. Do you understand me? Do you need someone to help you get back over there?

But she ignored him so her yearning blue-eyed look was the last thing I saw as I was loaded into the back of the ambulance.

They ratcheted my gurney up and rolled it over to the ambulance, where they slid it in in that really well-engineered, very thought-out way so its legs collapse automatically, folding up like an insect's. Then they moved me way far over to the left facing the back door and began securing the gurney to the frame with belts and loops and flanges, like the LATCH system on kids' car seats. I was shoved right up against the wall, which made it tight, so the EMT who was attending me was hunched and crowded. It was obviously awkward for him as he got oxygen going through a feed and then tried to find my best vein for the IV.

We were crowding against the side to make room for Jack—this space that would remind you of an elevator—and there his gurney was in the open doorway, then it was slid in head first, then ratcheted up to stand at the same height as mine, and here lay my husband, with one arm and shoulder wrong, his glasses gone, forehead open and blood all over his face.

There you are, he said.

Our heads and necks were strapped down and braced, making it hard to turn, but he reached out with one hand as I reached out with mine.

000

Does everybody else already know they cut your clothes off in the ambulance? They cut off all your clothes, and you can't negotiate, you can't save your two hundred fifty dollar Christmas shirt by arguing that Jack bought it for you at By Hand on Shattuck right by Chez Panisse, that you've hardly worn it because you still have these few pounds to lose, you can't save your Eileen Fisher skirt that, okay, wasn't all that expensive since you bought it at the outlet store. Or your best everyday bathing suit or your Brown Jesus T-shirt from the Chicano art show at the de Young, sponsored by Cheech Marin.

Jack later said he found the experience of having his clothes cut off *invigorating,* but I have no idea why. It may be because he managed to save his boots.

The EMT was struggling with my IV, a complicated process involving precise needle-piercing-vein in an ambulance that's rocking back and forth, cornering, and starting and stopping because it's on the freeway.

The EMT said the worst was when they had to work on motorcycle riders who have the most gory accidents, gaping wounds, compound fractures, friction burns, loss of vast amounts of blood, and these guys may be way more than half dead but still rouse themselves to beg the ambulance guys to please not cut off their leathers. This is not only because the jackets and pants are so expensive but because a biker doesn't really feel like a true biker unless he's in his colors.

It was that kind of institutional resistance that my husband was up against as he undertook his Save-the-Boots campaign.

His legs and feet were fine, Jack said. If the EMT could just slip these boots off—they were soft, easy to get off—Jack would wiggle his toes to show him. He'd just got these boots, Jack said, which had been handmade for him by a bootmaker named Armando in So-and-So Forth, Texas, for which Jack's feet needed to be measured in something like seventeen places, including width of individual heel and height of right and left instep, all this accomplished by mail order and by intricate phone messages and you don't even pay for the boots until they're done and fitting perfectly. This is the same bootmaker used by Sean Penn and Peter Coyote and Willie Nelson, Jack said, and he'd begun mentioning other famous people, I noticed, that Jack either did or didn't know—Robin Williams, Boz Scaggs—who either did or didn't own boots handmade by Armando.

Jack wanted just two things, well, three: his boots, his cashmere socks, and the medal around his neck. If his EMT could just slip the boots off—great!—and the socks, then unhook the chain and drop the metal down into one boot and put the socks in after it, everything would be safe and Jack would know where to find it later.

The medal Jack wears is a St. Anthony, patron saint of lost things.

⦿

The EMTs explain Shock Trauma to you as the ambulance is arriving, that it may seem chaotic but that's because there will be a lot of people working frantically on you at once to do one simple thing, which is save your life. There are teams who have specific jobs, each in one area of expertise, and they'll be talking over you and won't waste a lot of time explaining things to you.

Jack was going in first. I'd be right behind him. We'd be in the same place. As soon as we got in there, we'd be given something for the pain.

Right, I remember thinking. *Oh, I well imagine, probably a Tic-Tac sized Tylenol with codeine.* What you want in a situation like this is something Heavy Duty. I've had babies naturally and that's right up there at the top of the pain scale. This is misery of a different order. It's simply hard to explain how it feels to hurt so much in so many places.

Shock Trauma seemed to me to be a jolly place, reminded me actually of the cocktail party atmosphere that attended the birth of my first child where all these relaxed people are going about their business calmly, their business being helping you, meanwhile they are talking over your body because you're this project of theirs that they're cheerfully working together on. It feels like it's the afternoon before the prom, they're decorating the gym, and *you're* the gym.

The person in our family who was no doubt suffering the most was our daughter, Eva, who'd arrived at the hospital before we had and had been shown, with her boyfriend, Tyler, to a grim silent private family waiting room, where she was handed a box of Kleenex.

Someone recently receiving terrible news in that waiting room, Eva told us later, had kicked a hole in the wall so fresh the plaster was still lying there.

The only information she had was from the woman on the cell phone, the passerby who'd inexplicably dangled my car keys at me. She called Eva to say we'd been hurt and to tell her where we were going, that she had our dog at her house. She had dogs too and Thiebaud was fine.

Your mother's fully conscious, she said to Eva.

What about Jack? Eva asked.

Well, the woman hedged, maybe not so much. Maybe not fully?

But it was Jack—while semi-conscious or maybe slightly *un*—who had put together the plan. He'd rolled over and asked this woman, one of the first on the scene, to get his cell phone from the pocket of his jeans, saying our daughter would be the first number on Recently Dialed. Then, if she could find his wife's car keys from the big blue bag that read Moon Books—it'd be around there somewhere—and use the transponder on the key ring to unlock our car? Our car was right across the street, Jack said, pointing with his good hand, showing her where Thiebaud was standing watching the entire thing. If she called our daughter, she would come and get him.

Jack had performed these management skills while lapsing in and out of consciousness. I've seen this capacity before. Once, when we were living in the East and he'd just had oral surgery, the nurse followed him out into the waiting room to reiterate the instructions. She also handed me a sheet titled "Aftercare."

He's not to smoke, she said to me. He's on a powerful pain med, no driving, no heavy machinery. He needs to get into bed. The most important decision he gets to make today is which movie he'd like to watch. We've discussed this.

She turned to him. No deal making today, remember? No signing contracts.

This was on K Street in Washington, D.C., where the most politically powerful folks in the world might stagger out of the oral surgeon's and head off, all drugged and omnipotent and woozy, to go make policy.

Jack and I rode down on the elevator, went out to stand on the sidewalk while we waited for the parking valet to bring our car. We were standing in the sun. Jack immediately lit a cigarette.

I can drive, he told me.

Of course you *can* drive, I said, but you sure as hell *aren't going to*.

But you could swing me by the office?

Why would you want to swing by the office?

He paused, considered. He smoked. I can make executive decisions, he told me.

∞

Our own Trauma crew chief was a spirited young woman named Dr. Kwan, who had a four-inch ponytail sticking horizontally out the back of her scrub cap. It was her really jaunty attitude that completely cheered me up.

You guys, she said, as she was working over me, shaking her head as if to say *tsk, tsk, tsk*. You pedestrians. You just never win these things.

It was like we were discussing Cal vs. Stanford.

We kinda won, I said. Her car's totaled, for instance.

What was it?

I didn't see it. Someone said some off-brand VW—a Golf or Rabbit? Someone said it looked like she'd hit a deer, then someone else said, Or *two* deer.

You guys did not win this one, Dr. Kwan said. Your husband's elbow and shoulder and face took out her windshield.

But we're not totaled, I said. At least not totally totaled, and her car's not going anyplace anytime very soon.

I really liked her. Her attitude was completely reassuring. I was also cheered that Jack and I were each being given massive amounts of IV Fentanol, a powerful narcotic painkiller and muscle relaxant that doesn't knock you out. You're not supposed to be knocked out if you have a head injury—you need to be as alert as possible in order to tell

Shock Trauma what's currently hurting to help them find whatever secret thing might be quietly killing you.

In Shock Trauma they do that one thing really well: save your life. They don't nurse, don't bandage, don't do wound care, don't cast or stitch, but none of this mattered to me because both Jack and I were alive and fully conscious and on Fentanol.

I had something bad going on in my sternum and on the right side of my abdomen but was jolly because Jack—with his face and head and shoulder and arm all obviously messed up—was just on the other side of some machines and monitors.

After a while they let Eva and Tyler come right into Trauma, a true kindness because Eva really needed to lay eyes on us and see that it was still just me with my hair all which way and hear Jack talking about holding a dead pencil in the dead hand of his dead arm, which turned into Bob Dole's commercial on erectile disfunction.

It just doesn't do any good for people to reassure you that so and so's okay. You don't know what *okay* is, don't even know what the definition of "still alive" might be, or what it means when someone's lapsing in and out of consciousness.

And Eva is our youngest child, the youngest of the four we brought to our marriage, and our only girl, and it was she who needed then to call our three older boys, leaving the terrifying message on all their various voice mails so it was she they were calling back.

The great thing about Fentanol is that it's amazingly effective, and it really needs to be because when you're hit by a car, you manage to hurt almost everywhere. They know this, they're really sympathetic, but they still have to do all these things to you involving manipulating parts of you that may be broken.

Pain of this kind almost immediately becomes abstraction. I'd also already begun my fictionalizing wherein we'd each miraculously bounced and *against all odds* had landed with no broken bones! No internal injuries! A version which, while comforting, didn't happen to be true.

◯◯◯

It was CT scans and X-rays and more Fentanol, and no water or anything to drink, and we'd been moved and were waiting in a large bright room commanded by a huge nurse named Hazel, who drank a Mountain Dew right in front of Jack while humming "Getting to Know You" from *The King and I.* When Jack said he too was thirsty, Hazel told him that was how it was and how it was gonna be.

What is this? he asked her. Some kind of Big Nurse type torture?

There's one main difference between us, she said. I happen to work here, and you? You're in the hospital because *you got hit by a car.*

Jack was NPO because they didn't know yet whether he'd need surgery.

I wasn't going to need surgery, I knew. I was completely confident of this and I told Sean, our oldest, when he and his wife, Heida, arrived, that I intended to go home.

Why? he asked. If you stay in here, there's someone to take care of you. There's also that. Sean nodded at the IV pole that held the drip that held the Fentanol.

Yeah, but they don't really take care of you, I said. We're in Observation, where they're observing us. We're not really being treated. *Treated* isn't really what Shock Trauma does. Then you're in Observation, where you're observed. First there's Shock Trauma, I said, where you're not really treated . . .

Right, Sean said. Then comes Observation?

Where you're observed, I agreed.

He and Heida were eyeing one another like, You're getting this?

And where you also are not treated, I went on.

There was one nurse-ish person who might have been cleaning Jack's face and washing the blood out of his hair except that she had her book open and was sitting in the exact center of the room monitoring the monitors. She was also obviously studying for an exam. She once brought me a bedpan. I hated to ask her, hating to interrupt her studies.

Everyone was waiting to get the results of tests, waiting to take MRIs or CT scans or X-rays and then waiting for these to be read. Meanwhile we were observed by Hazel, who called Jack "31" and me "34."

Where's 31? someone would ask.

Out in radiology, Hazel would say. He'll be back in a little while.

Or, Where's 31? We need to get some sutures in.

Then 31 would be back parked across the room diagonally from me, negotiating with Hazel for ice chips. Hazel wasn't gonna budge. He'd settle for a wet washcloth. He wanted to wipe his face, which she guessed was okay as long as he didn't suck on it.

There was the usual workplace banter about who stole someone's *People* magazine. I know, I said. This actually is the kind of triviality I am extremely good at.

You do?

Female, I said. I'm almost certain it was definitely female.

Blonde? she asked. About this tall?

Can't remember, I said. I seem to have lost the detail.

Why should you remember? she asked. You just got *hit by a car!*

And there was some strange form of twenty-four-hour clock that might have been running backwards and then a woman was rolled in on a gurney who was simply drunk and homeless and she was put in a corner with blankets over her and a curtain pulled around her to sleep and nothing was ever said about her again so you thought she might not have even been an official patient.

And 31 was over there trying to get someone to help him clean himself up, and Hazel, who didn't seem to like either of us at first and wouldn't let our kids stay with us because there were too many of them and we talked too much and what did we think this was some kind of fun-type family reunion? eventually warmed to us, especially Jack who gets his way, if not now then in a little while.

When iced tea appeared in the form of a whole plastic pitcher from the cafeteria, it meant 31 was not having surgery, at least not that evening, night, or whatever day this now might be. Jack told Hazel that we were naming our first grandchild after her.

And at two or three in the morning, the cops began arriving with the 5150s, folks in restraints being admitted against their will. First came Beverly, who was white and blonde and had an expensive haircut, whose husband had variously beaten her or thrown her down the stairs and practiced such mental cruelty as to call the cops over some slight disagreement so, as of that moment, she was having nothing more to do with him.

She had what my mother-in-law would call *airs*.

Are you a *Registered* Nurse? she asked Hazel. What's your full name? Write it down for me. I want your badge number. I demand to see my own *physician*. No? Well, when will I be seen by a *medical doctor?*

Could happen, Hazel said, looking at the backwards clock, maybe five-six hours from now?

But I need my *medications*, Beverly said.

And what *medications* might these be? Hazel asked.

The ones my husband flushed down the toilet, Beverly said, then began to enumerate what all she'd been taking, and Hazel listened for a while then drifted off to do something else. She sent an aid to write the list. Beverly knew the PDR by heart, which drug, what shape, which strength, how often, which tint or color, cap or tab, brand or generic. The aid was still writing fifteen minutes later.

She said she takes belladonna, Jack told me later. Do they still even *have* belladonna? What's belladonna good for?

Then, almost immediately on the heels of Beverly came Dante, who'd been 5150ed by his mother. Dante was a twenty-one-year-old African American youth brought in by cops in restraints and whose mother was not his mother but, in fact, a demon, and Dante had been called forth pre-birth from the better place at the right hand of Jesus and was only here to testify in order to save his brother.

Dante didn't want meds. Dante wanted a cigarette.

Hazel wanted him to *take this*, which was an antipsychotic medication that would dissolve upon his tongue.

Don't want it, eh? Dante asked. Don't wanna be all tired out, eh?

That one won't make you sleepy, Beverly called out. That's actually a pretty good one.

Don't want it, Dante said. Need to be my own man, eh? Need to keep my wits about me, think own thoughts, eh? With my own mind?

Your mind's a shithole, Beverly called from my side of the room, and if I were you I'd take as much as you can of *everything* they offer.

Beverly, Hazel said. You are not being *helpful.*

Hazel then leaned over and spoke to Jack, who was washing his face with his washcloth and enjoying his iced tea, also observing the Observation Room like it was about to become our favorite program on HBO.

It's gonna get jiggy in here now, Hazel told him. Then she went to get an orderly so she could move Jack's bed from next to Dante to the space next to mine. Hazel pulled the curtains around the two of us, saying, Okay, we're gonna designate this area The Honeymoon Suite.

Or we could go home? I said.

No you actually can't, she said. You're not ambulatory.

But we *could* be, Jack said.

You can't go home, she said. You have to have your ADLs.

I knew that one. The ADLs, I told Jack, are the Activities of Daily Living.

Dr. Kwan came in some while later.

Guys, I know you want to go home, and here's what I think, she said. Here's what I don't like. Usually when someone's hit by a car and they just wanna go home and crawl into their own bed, it's okay because there's this *other person* to take care of them. In your case your other person was *also* hit by a car.

But we have all these kids, I said, who're grown and who totally *owe* us.

Your call, Dr. Kwan said. She was looking at 31. It was 31 who was more gravely injured. We all knew 31 could *make* an executive decision, but we really needed for this to be the right one.

⁣⁣⁣⁣000

We had no clothes that hadn't been cut off then stuffed down into white plastic hospital sacks so they gave us paper surgical booties, scrub pants, green paper modesty drapes, hospital gowns, which we wore tied back to front and front to back. We had to dress ourselves to demonstrate that we could perform the ADLs—getting dressed, getting ourselves to the toilet, using the toilet, getting back from the toilet. We were unhooked from the Fentanol so each little movement became an increasing agony.

Hazel approved of none of this. We were not assisted. We needed to prove we could walk out of there so there were no helpful wheelchairs. Hazel had her arms folded across her chest, still skeptically observing.

Eva and Tyler had gone out to bring the car around to the ER entrance.

Jack and I were set to do this. We started out. We got to the doorway, turned right, began to make our way down the crowded hallway by people lying on gurneys waiting for whatever was their next step. A man with his shirt open and blood spurting came dashing past us toward the Trauma Center, as if whoever shot him was still chasing him.

These gowns are really *green,* Jack observed. We look *wrapped,* we look like *Christmas presents.*

Our paper clothes were making this *shush-shush* sound.

Hazel watched us walk, and then she came quickly along to bring us another white plastic bag of our cut-up clothes. She also needed to add her own two cents—I thought it'd be another little scolding, but what she said was this:

You two really are about the cutest trauma couple we've had here in a good long while.

We still needed to make our way along this very well-lit hall and out through an over-populated waiting room to the door where the kids and Eva's car were waiting.

Highland is in East Oakland and its ER was packed that night with people displaying every kind and degree of human misery, but as we walked, folks stopped, looked up, openly gaped at us: the battered, still-bloodied trauma couple still improbably dressed in their hospital clothes, holding hands and, inch-by-inch, escaping.

16
The Gates

THE BEGINNING, as Aristotle tells us, falls *exactly* where its ending starts, so you'd think we'd all somehow be better prepared for it, or at least understand which elements we might expect an ending to contain.

In fact, an ending often comes upon you so unexpectedly as to hold almost nothing but the shock: to realize we really *are* mortal, that the last days are *always* upon us, and to be, therefore, joyful because, bam! there you go, being suddenly mowed down by a ridiculous car being driven by a woman wearing poodle barrettes whose husband has died—as we later discover—and who has either no kids or none who have been by recently to notice she's become a Rescuer, and to deal with it by at least taking away her car keys. The ignominy? To be hit by *a Golf!* about which the reporting office will write, This car was *full* of dogs! But that isn't the ending of this story, because it hasn't happened yet. The ending of the story I am currently engaged with falls somewhat earlier along its narrative arc and is—as things often are—out of chronological order.

It is February of 2005. Jack and I are living in Washington. Our boys are all in the West. Eva's away at college but is coming down by train from Vermont to meet us in New York. This for a four-day weekend in Manhattan that has been very meticulously planned.

The planning for the event, in the larger sense, has been intricate and has transpired over a quarter century. The project artists, Jeanne-Claude and Christo, began working on *The Gates* in 1979, the year before my son, Noah, was born. They always knew *The Gates* had to go up in February, as Jeanne-Claude said, as this is when the foliage in the park appears most dead, its trees most lifeless.

They needed the wet-black to buff to the gray leafless trees so nothing would interfere with their palette, none of that hazy greenish blur of promising early spring. It's always Jeanne-Claude talking, Jeanne-Claude who is explaining these things in that clipped, really annoyed French-seeming way of hers, while Christo is bent over his drawing table, hair in his face, continuing to sketch or paint or draw.

〰

The Ending starts, you realize, when the story you've envisioned suddenly *contains* you, and you and Jack see yourselves as part of the processional that is old and moving and universal, only you're walking along behind the rest of the group. We are walking behind them when I notice that the colors of their clothes—and, by extension, ours—are being used as part of the pattern of brushstroke and smear. Because it's the dead of winter and we are all in dark colors, bundled up on our first cold morning here, and the trunks of trees—as Jeanne-Claude has decreed—are naked bark, pale or darkish browns, with only a thin gray etch of branch or twig.

The Ending has started. It is always surprising to realize it contains what you have not necessarily put into it, which is to say, these matters of chance and coincidence, these meetings in Time and Space that seem to speak of Larger Factors being at work and play.

The date is February 24, two days before the one I've dreaded since I was ten years old, for what is now, so far, five-sixths of my life.

And it has snowed the night before, so the fields and meadows around us are immaculate, an absolutely brilliant white. The two women a few paces in front of us are of almost identical height, the younger one so young she's probably only recently begun to call herself a woman, the other elderly but erect. Their heads are leaning into each other, talking as they walk together beneath one of the gates. One points upward with her black gloved hand and the other sees and nods, and they both turn to make sure we're seeing what they're seeing.

Because these women belong to me: They are my aunt and my daughter, and it's been my aunt's idea to make this trip, to spend four days in New York staying at an excellent hotel that's close enough to the park to get to without a cab ride, which is why we chose the Warwick. She set this trip in motion months before, saying she'd fly into Washington from Salt Lake City, where she lives, one of the staunch Episcopalians who live like an almost hidden sect within the dominant culture, which might remind you of a cult. Salt Lake is where she finished raising her children, divorced my uncle, and embarked on her own career.

She flew into Washington so she could take the train to New York with Jack and me. She loves trains. It was the sound of trains, she told me, that made her feel connected to the world when she was growing up in California, in that you could at least get on a train and end up somewhere.

She's left it to Jack to make the arrangements, as she understands him to be someone at home in the world. Her only requirements are that we have a suite with a common area, that her room have its own bath, and that we get tickets to a couple of Broadway shows. She left the dates to him, as he's the one with the busy schedule.

And this: She wished to walk in Central Park *twice*.

My aunt's arm is resting in the bend of my daughter's elbow, so Jack and I, behind them, take turns pushing the hotel wheelchair. My aunt walks perfectly well, if slowly, but she's had trouble with her balance recently, so, though she doesn't *need* this wheelchair, we bring it along in case. Using it would humiliate her, but *that* humiliation would be preferable to her worrying over slowing down the rest of us.

My aunt, my daughter, all of us are moving against the shimmering blur of orange of the gates in watery reflection. Snowmelt sends wet sheets satining across the path. There are 7503 gates along twenty-three miles of walkways. The sun is so bright now that the new snow is audibly melting, which is why it's flowing from underneath.

They walk carefully, my aunt, who is in her mid-eighties, aided by the springform cane she uses not for support—as she's careful to say—but for stability, and my daughter, who's patient, attentive and kind, though she had no grandmother to teach her this.

The trees are etched like pen scratches. The gates, which are made of a heavy woven fabric, flap in their rigging like flags. People walking by—and the paths are crowded—are respectful, but there is nothing somber about any of it. We are simply all part of the same processional: the light, the dark, the bright or somber, whatever's needed for this sense of pageantry.

My aunt and my daughter are passing beneath one of the gates, which catches a gust of wind, catches, seems to heavily undulate. Three robed monks pass them coming toward us, their robes a somewhat darker but more washed and duller saffron. My aunt turns to make sure we too are missing no part of the spectacle.

Jack? my aunt says as she turns to him. Look, she mouths, I think those are *actual Buddhists.*

∭

Late afternoon, back in our suite, I reading aloud from a pamphlet called "Factual Errors" to anyone who will listen. Actually, no one is listening, as Jack's in our bedroom on a business call and my aunt's in her own room, resting before dinner.

My only audience is Eva and Lou. Lou is my aunt's oldest grandson, so these two are the children of first cousins, which makes them either second cousins or maybe thirds, or maybe they're once removed, or maybe Lou's my own second cousin? My aunt can do this, what I think of as deep and institutional memory that used to serve some sort of function but that's now completely outmoded. It has to do with *one's lineage*, about which no one, anymore *cares.*

I'm reading aloud, but Lou and Eva, who know each other only slightly, are having their own conversation. They're about the same age and in the same year in school. She's in theater at Castleton, which is a small state college near Rutland, and she's telling him why she loves it. Lou's at Bard and he's telling her why he hates it.

No really, this is interesting. Listen to this, I instruct them, it's almost even *philosophically* important. Listen, I tell them, and begin to read out, This statement contains six factual errors.

And you might want to take notes I say—a quiz may be given, look. You'll want to receive full credit.

No, Eva says.

No, what?

I won't participate, Eva says. She says to Lou, We don't have to participate; my mom just gets like this, you know? And you don't have to play along. It's just more of her fun and games.

You do so have to participate, I say.

Can't make us, Eva says.

I can too, I say. Do you want to, for instance, eat? And Jack's hired a car to take us to the theater. Do you want to ride with us? Or maybe you'd like to try your luck getting a cab.

I rock getting a cab in Manhattan, Eva says to Lou. I so totally can get a cab, any time of night or day—she snaps her fingers—like that.

I know how to take the subway, Lou says.

We can totally rock the subway, she says.

No, I say, I'm the grown-up and I say you're going to participate. Okay, here's the statement that has six factual errors. I read: Christo wrapped some islands in Florida off the coast of Miami in Key Biscayne in pink plastic.

I don't think we had a unit on this yet, my daughter says. Sorry, Ma, she adds; then she yawns, stretches, opens O magazine, puts it in front of her face, and starts elaborately turning the pages. My daughter belongs, as she likes to say, to the Church of Oprah.

But I still have *Lou's* attention, I notice. Six factual errors, I say, which are . . . ?

Just ignore her, Eva says from behind her magazine.

That Jeanne-Claude isn't mentioned? Lou asks.

That's one.

That they didn't use pink plastic?

Bingo, I say.

That none of this ever happened? he asks. I mean, what's the empirical evidence? Could have been Photoshopped.

Exactly, I say. It's all right here. That's what this whole little book-
let is—*what never happened*—and it's really excruciatingly detailed.
Jeanne-Claude lists them. Factual Error Number One is that, and I
quote: Jeanne-Claude and Christo never wrapped *any* islands, they *surrounded* the islands. Most journalists do not understand the difference
between *wrapping* and *surrounding*, even though they *do* know that
England, for instance, while *surrounded* by water it is not *wrapped* in
water . . .

Eva is looking over the top of her magazine.

Did you hear it? I ask them. How, in trying *to correct* the factual
errors, someone will *always* go ahead and introduce some new ones?

Lou asks, Is it that *England*, strictly speaking, isn't actually *an island*, that it's a geopolitical unit?

Totally!

And that *actually*, he goes on, it's part of the British Isles, which
would also include Ireland and Northern Ireland and Wales and
Scotland, and that one's called Great Britain and the other is called
Ireland?

But *Jeanne-Claude* couldn't be expected to know that, Eva says,
since *Jeanne-Claude* is French and the only thing the French know about
the English is how much the French detest them.

If no one likes the English, my aunt says, as she emerges from her
room, it's their own damn fault. Why, hello, Lou, happy to see you've
made it.

No one likes the English, Jack says, as he enters from our room,
which feels—because this is a perfect weekend and everyone knows
their comedic lines—like stage right. Because, like us, he goes on, they
wouldn't stay home and tend to their own business, and so they became
imperialists.

My aunt is holding a plastic see-through bladder with a red-tipped spout that seems to be filled with about a quart of urine. Is it time for drinks? she asks, and she walks over and plops whatever this sack is down on the sideboard where I've put the barware.

She and I share a horror at the cost of room service, which may be congenital. While each of us is perfectly happy staying at a nice hotel, we aren't going to be paying a hundred dollars for a couple of cheeseburgers. She won't order from room service at all, while I do it the first night only, ordering all kinds of things, tea and desserts and cheese platters, in order to get the setups, the cups and saucers, creamer and utensils, which I then wash myself and hide from the housekeepers.

Drinks? my aunt says again. Lou, you go get ice. Jack, will you do the honors? Jack is staring at the bladder that my aunt seems to be holding out to him.

Don't tell me you're a wine snob, she says to him. This is a perfectly adequate pinot grigio. You take it out of the box, you see? It costs $14.99 at Target and packs quite wonderfully.

⚭

We have tickets to *Twelve Angry Men*, which the five of us see and is excellent. We come and go in a white stretch limo with colored disco lights and a hip-hop soundtrack that my aunt finds hilarious. We also have tickets for *Rent*, which Jack doesn't want to go to because he has business to do and this is a matinee and, while he's an opera lover, he simply cannot stand musical comedy.

It isn't a comedy, I say. It's actually a musical tragedy. It's actually *La Bohème* set downtown and done in modern garb.

Don't *want to*, Jack says, making his mouth very small. *Please* don't make me.

Why? I say.

Because it has music, story, lyrics. I *hate* that kind of thing. I always hate the *La Bohème* kind of thing set downtown and redone in modern garb by someone not as good as Puccini.

His mouth is very tiny: Please, please don't make me. So he doesn't go and so misses the spectacle of the final act, during which I sit between my aunt and my daughter and we three hold hands, our faces awash, as we weep uncontrollable tears.

〇〇〇

Do you think he was actually gay? I ask my aunt. She and I are alone in the room. I mean, *gay* gay.

The kids are out. It's our last evening in New York.

She sips her wine, which she drinks from a stemless wine glass.

Your mother thought not, she finally says.

But what do *you* think? I ask.

My aunt, even in old age, is very beautiful, and her not actually realizing this about herself is a piece of what seems now like her almost exaggerated dignity. My mother's dignity looked somewhat wounded, while my aunt's is oddly triumphant. And her looks, her coloring, the structure of her face, so closely echo those of the face of the man I can almost not remember and whose death date is today, a fact that neither of us, for whatever reason, now mentions.

And my aunt—to whom I've become close over the past decade or so—has previously confessed her theory that if she's been silent at times, it is because she is naturally left-handed but—as was the custom then—her teachers made her write with her right. Her late career was in working with developmentally handicapped children, some of whom lay along the autism scale, all of whom were delayed. She believes—as

I do—in the verities of brain science, believes that we now might have known more about what went wrong with Geo and might have been able to do more to help him. She believes that her sense of physical clumsiness lies along the same neural pathways that make her feel verbally maladroit. She simply becomes tongue-tied, she has told me, when feeling what she calls *emotional*.

My mother used the term *emotional* in exactly this same way, as in, Let's not become *all emotional*, as if this were beneath us.

Your father, my aunt says. She stops, she sips. She drinks her wine with ice in it.

People were drawn to him, she says. Oh, I never really understood how these things worked. I wasn't like that, in that people, you know, always wanted to . . . Her voice trails off.

He was charismatic? I ask.

She nods immediately. Like you.

Like me? I think. I am *dumbfounded*. In this part of my family, *no one* ever, for any kind of reason, would offer anyone else a *compliment*.

But she goes on: And it was all kinds of people who loved Johnny, who wanted to be with him, or maybe just wanted to listen to his stories. He was a marvelous storyteller. She stops. I don't know about *gay* gay, she says.

Maybe *gay* gay, I ask, but not *gay* gay gay?

My aunt smiles. Or maybe, she says, he was what we called an *opportunist*.

∞

Her God, her church, has been—as she's explained to me—her absolute salvation. After Lizzie left for college and my aunt divorced my uncle, she volunteered to work with handicapped children, eventually becoming the assistant director of the center. Then she had another late career that involved going with the church into impoverished Africa; these were the first of the tiny enterprise ventures that gave women of certain villages microloans to start their own home-based industries, a model that has proved so astonishingly successful that its inventor has won the Nobel Prize in economics.

I love my aunt—the dry style of her humor and the sound of her voice, whose cadences rise and fall with the rhythms of the Book of Common Prayer that she forced into my hands when I didn't want it there, that she made me read aloud while I stood next to her in church, and whose language I didn't understand until I was old enough to read Shakespeare.

We do not, of course, know each other very well. I more or less vanished from her life when I left for college, when she was still astonishingly young, a fact that was completely obscured not just from me, but from all of us: She was barely older than a girl—only in her thirties—and suddenly raising seven children.

So now we are almost like new people to each other, and I know she reads my work and admires it, even if she doesn't altogether approve of it.

I'll publish something, and no matter how far off and obscure the journal, someone will find it and—unhelpfully—send it off to her, and I'll get the call from Graham, my oldest cousin, who lives in Hawaii and who is appointed in these instances to deal with me.

Mother read your piece, he says.

So I guess I need to call her? I ask, and it's *exactly* like hearing your name being said over the PA, ordering you to the principal's office because you are in trouble.

I phone her, hem and haw, stumble around about how I'm sorry for angering her, and she cuts me off.

I was not *angry*, she says. I was depressed for *three days!*

〇〇〇

The second time we walk in the park, the two are passing beneath a gate. Beyond them are the leafless trees, the unimaginable white of the snowfields. The gates above them shimmer and flap; they are the color of saffron that lies directly opposite, on the color wheel, the pure blue of the bluest sky you can imagine. This is *azure* and the whole thing feels like a dream or a scene from a movie or a symphony, when you know the thing is almost over and you're going to finally, finally, get to *get out* of here, which shows in the perfectly restful yet upbeat way the parts have begun to come together and this whole vexing experience that is Art is finally ending and we're about to be released from its spell.

When I walk with my aunt, I have to remember to relax and let her hold on to me, rather than to cling to her.

The Ending has already started in that *The Gates* are coming down tomorrow, so they will no longer exist. They are something made to be unmade. We are here together on this day, in celebration of what the Buddhists call impermanence.

The night before, looking at the catalog, I'd asked Jack, Gateless Gates? That's *mu*, isn't it? *Way will open.* That's Buddhist, right? *Way will open*, right? The Gateless Gates?

Mu's a koan, he said, not looking up. *Mu* means *no.*

Mu means *no*? I ask.

It's really complicated, he said.

I thought it meant *Way will open*, I said. I'm always telling people that that's what *mu* means.

Way will open? he asks. *Way will open* isn't something Buddhists say.

〇〇〇

My aunt, if she spoke of these things, which she does not, would call it grace, and it is by grace that we are given this last day in which we will walk in Central Park under a dome of heaven that is this pulsing burning blue.

The color of the sky this day is why we have need of the word *cerulean*.

And this color stands—with the light of my aunt's High Church God behind it—exactly opposite the color saffron, which seems to belong on the metaphysical color wheel where we go to find all the many tints and hues and variations that are in no way satisfied by our saying *orange*, and that seem to belong to my Buddhist husband. These people are something I can never be, which is actual practitioners of faith.

And there is new snow on the ground and the snowmelt leaks across the walkways so they are gleaming, turning silver and mirrorlike, and all this casts the sunlight upward, and there is suddenly light so loud that it seems to drown out shadows, and it is light that lies everywhere and we are alive in it, and almost breathless in our awe of it, and this is what is meant, I know, by the hymn that sings, Light, Oh Light Abounding.

I have been so afraid. I have been so afraid, but I am older now and I am not alone, and it's not that I'm no longer afraid, but that the fear now comes intermittently.

The Gates, which took twenty-four years to erect, are here now for only this moment. It is February 27. The ending is happening, The End is now, and it is final, so we can't even say to one another, by way of solace, Next year in Jerusalem.

I am walking with my aunt. Lou has gone back to school. Jack is behind us, pushing the wheelchair, which, because the day's turned warm, is now heaped with our bags and jackets and then with Eva, who has plopped herself down in it, yelling for Jack to push her. Jack pushes her for a while, then dumps her into a snow bank on purpose, and now she's screaming and throwing snow chunks at him, and her cheeks are aflame with cold and her burnished curly hair is flying, and she picks up to heave what looks like lightweight snow brick, but this flies apart as she hurls it, and we are all dusted with infinite particles of what feels like both beauty and timelessness.

Then she gets up, forms a hard real snowball, and lobs a good one that connects. She screams with laughter and comes around us to crouch down, laughing as she's yelling, Save me! save me! save me! using the bodies of her mother and her really quite aged great-aunt as cover from a snowball counterattack.

Like this, dear, my aunt says to me, as she slips her hand from mine and rearranges our arms, changing hers so it lies lightly on top of mine.

Her skin is delicate, her bones are frail—I keep forgetting it. Dear, she says, you tend to hold my hand too tightly.

She always does that, Eva says. My mom has a grip like a vice.

I do? I ask.

You do, she says, and my aunt nods. Eva adds, You act like everyone's made of helium.

God, I'm sorry! I say. I am *so sorry*. I honestly had *no idea*.

And that is what I'm saying, but what I'm thinking is: *Dear? My aunt called me dear, that she said the word so fondly.*

Acknowledgments

WITH SO MUCH LOVE for my big brother, Hank Vandenburgh, and for my cousins, Douglas Godfrey, Peter Godfrey, Gordon Godfrey, and Carolyn Godfrey Roll.

And profound thanks to those other family members, friends and colleagues who've helped me over the many years it took to write this book: Susan Bobst, Trish Hoard, Alice Powers, Brian Powers, Heida Shoemaker, Jan Wurm, and Eva Zimmerman.

And with particular gratitude to Laura Mazer, whose editing has been an inspired gift to this project.

And to Jack Shoemaker, who does actually know what the word "penultimate" means and means it when he says it.

"Take Me With You" is dedicated to the memory of Carole Lynn Koda, 1947–2006.

For George:
Where there is injury, pardon,
Where there is doubt, faith.

About the Author

JANE VANDENBURGH is the author of two novels, *Failure to Zigzag* and *The Physics of Sunset*. Her fiction and essays have been published in the *New York Times, Boston Globe, Los Angeles Times, Wall Street Journal, Threepenny Review,* and other publications. She lives in Point Richmond, California. Visit her at www.janevandenburgh.com.

Printed in the United States
by Baker & Taylor Publisher Services